The Culture Series
of Iain M. Banks

ALSO BY SIMONE CAROTI

*The Generation Starship in Science Fiction:
A Critical History, 1934–2001*
(McFarland, 2011)

The Culture Series of Iain M. Banks
A Critical Introduction

SIMONE CAROTI

McFarland & Company, Inc., Publishers
Jefferson, North Carolina

LIBRARY OF CONGRESS CATALOGUING-IN-PUBLICATION DATA

Caroti, Simone, 1972–
　　The culture series of Iain M. Banks : a critical introduction / Simone Caroti.
　　　　p.　　cm.
　　Includes bibliographical references and index.

　　ISBN 978-0-7864-9447-7 (softcover : acid free paper) ∞
　　ISBN 978-1-4766-2040-4 (ebook)

　　1. Banks, Iain, 1954–2013—Criticism and interpretation.　2. Science fiction, English—History and criticism.　I. Title.
　　PR6052.A485Z56　2015
　　823'.914—dc23　　　　　　　　　　　　　　　　2015003450

BRITISH LIBRARY CATALOGUING DATA ARE AVAILABLE

© 2015 Simone Caroti. All rights reserved

No part of this book may be reproduced or transmitted in any form or by any means, electronic or mechanical, including photocopying or recording, or by any information storage and retrieval system, without permission in writing from the publisher.

Front cover images of planets © 2015 iStock/Thinkstock

Printed in the United States of America

McFarland & Company, Inc., Publishers
　Box 611, Jefferson, North Carolina 28640
　　www.mcfarlandpub.com

To the memory of
Iain Menzies Banks
(1954–2013).
Thank you for everything, Sir.

Table of Contents

Preface: The Early Days of a Better Nation — 1
Introduction: The Many Faces of Iain (M.) Banks — 5

1. Beginnings — 21
2. The Culture Militant: *Consider Phlebas* — 42
3. The Morality of the Rule Set: *The Player of Games* — 63
4. Diziet Sma's Dilemmas of Intervention: *The State of the Art* and *Use of Weapons* — 82
5. The Years of Taking Stock: The Culture as a Critical Utopia — 110
6. The View from Above, the View from Below: *Excession* and *Inversions* — 126
7. The Encroachment of Reality: *Look to Windward* — 155
8. The Last Trilogy: *Matter*, *Surface Detail*, and *The Hydrogen Sonata* — 182

Conclusion: The Future of the Culture — 211
Chapter Notes — 215
Bibliography — 234
Index — 239

PREFACE
The Early Days of a Better Nation

As every utopia contains, if only as a nightmare to haunt the sleep of its happy citizens, the shadow of dystopia, so does every dystopia harbor, if only as a yearning in the waking minds of those trapped within the workings of its world-machine, the promise of a better place in a future brighter than the present. The early months of 1997, the year I discovered Iain Menzies Banks' Culture series, were also the time in which I realized that utopia and dystopia belong to the heart of the individual as much as they do to the collective soul of a society. My mother was gone, taken by cancer, and my internal horizon had shrunk to the range of the day; when the sun pulled the curtain on the afternoon, I quietly reset my internal clock to zero, waiting for the next iteration. I didn't think beyond tomorrow—my future felt uncertain right then—nor did I go back in my memory to a time before the day just gone—my past was full of a life spent with her, and that did not quite bear dwelling on.

In the normal course of events, I came to understand that I was going through the same process of grieving everyone else goes through when such things happen to them, but at that time, mired in the immediacy of the moment, all I knew was that I needed to find evidence that a future existed at some point along the line in which I could reboot and restart. So I started seeking this evidence, and because I'm a bookworm, both by temperament and by training, I sought it in the voices others had committed to print. I read a lot, anything from *Macbeth* to *Calvin and Hobbes* (this pairing feels, to me, strangely appropriate), and because I was at least taking some form of action against my prevailing internal weather, things started improving.

Then came the summer of 1997. I went to Cambridge, England, for three weeks, and among the many books I brought back home to Trieste, Italy, was

Excession (1996), whose paperback edition had just come out. To this day, my memories of reading that novel come back to me as an undifferentiated timespan, a succession of mornings and evenings disconnected from any sense that a calendar had anything to do with anything I was thinking or feeling. There it was, a future, drawn out in trajectories across hyperspace, told through the serene clear agency of godlike AI, and spelled out in a voice modulated so that the pain of one's existence became a small section of a far larger context. And there was a past, also contextualized so that I could now see it as part of a four-dimensional flow of which I, with all my angst, was only a microscopic subset. *Excession* contributed to ease the burden on my shoulders; it helped return my yesterdays and my tomorrows to me, all of them, so that The Commonwealth Of Simone Caroti could now begin to seek a life in, as Alasdair Gray once put it, the early days of a better nation. *Excession* also opened up the path to the other Culture novels: I backtracked to read *the State of the Art*, *Consider Phlebas*, *The Player of Games*, and *Use of Weapons* (in that order), and when I was done I waited patiently, along with everybody else, for the next installments. Absurdly, part of me still waits today.

By the end of 1997, budding and wildly under-read literary critic that I was, I'd decided I would write a book about the Culture when the appropriate time came, and now, seventeen years and a bit more reading later, the moment has come. I made the original proposal to my publisher in December of 2012, when Banks was still with us, and I was fully determined to interview him. I was also going to go to WorldCon 2014 in London, where he was going to be Guest of Honor, and tell him everything I wrote above. I wanted him to know he'd made a difference.

Instead, I found myself looking at the history of the Culture not as an ongoing project, but as a closed body of work, and I didn't go to London. I stayed home and wrote, which given the circumstances was for the best—my love of Banks' writing had started out as a personal affair, and it felt appropriate that I should write the book in the same spirit. That I really didn't have any other choice helped the decision along in no small measure.

This book is meant as an introduction to the Culture series, not as any sort of presumptive final word on it. Researching Banks and his work, even confining myself to the ten books comprising the Culture universe, I found so much to discuss that a book twice the length of this one still wouldn't have exhausted the topic. This gives me as much joy now as it frustrated me when the time came to decide what to put in and what to leave out. I bear full responsibility for the choices I made, although I do hope to have at least partly succeeded in illuminating my subject.

Many people helped make this book what it is and worked to let me know what I needed to do to improve it. As usual, if you find merit in the arguments that follow, thank them as well; if you don't, blame me for being fully forewarned and still botching the job.

Thanks to John Clute, who took time to speak with me in the very early stages of the book's composition and make me understand exactly what I'd set out to write and for whom I was writing. John's voice also pervades this book through his reviews of the Culture novels and his writings on fantastika, all of which happily accompanied me on my way. I am deeply grateful for his help.

Thanks to the many participants to ICFA 35 in Orlando (March 2014) who graciously dedicated part of their time to discussing with me Banks' impact on SF and his legacy. Ian McDonald, Russell Letson, Mary A. Turzillo, Geoffrey A. Landis, Suzy McKee Charnas, and James Morrow in particular were of significant help.

Thanks to Douglas Texter for proofreading everything I wrote and pointing out what I was doing well, but especially what I was doing wrong. He made this book far better than it would otherwise have been.

Thanks to my colleagues and my students in the Creative Writing for Entertainment BFA at Full Sail University, Winter Park, Florida. Throughout the many months of this work's gestation, they enfolded me inside a community of discourse wherein my thoughts returned to me clarified, cleaned, and sharpened. Their voices echo through this work, again making it better than it would otherwise have been.

Thanks to Noelani Cornell and Christopher Ramsey, my program coordinators, who helped me get through the more intense months of this book's composition.

Thanks to my colleagues in the Astrosociology Research Institute, and especially Jim Pass and Christopher Hearsey. My work with them helped clarify many of the lines of reasoning I deployed here.

Thanks to all the people at Auddino's Bakery in Cape Canaveral and at Juice 'n Java Café in Cocoa Beach, Florida. They brought me cappuccino (medium decaf espresso, soy milk, in a ceramic mug), tolerated my rants with grace, and generally made me part of the kind of coffeeshop community I cherish. Most of the book was written in those two establishments.

Thanks to Vincent Ostertag and Patricia Burns for their friendship and support. I owe them a considerable debt of gratitude. Thanks also to Marco Lerra, Sumiko Kuboi, Raymond and Dakota Wheeler, Tom and Cindy Graham, and Joe Dowdy for pretty much the same reasons.

Thanks to Donald Stewart, PsyD, who, despite coming relatively late into the picture, provided a calming, grounding voice whose effectiveness far exceeded the physical amount of time we actually spent talking.

Thanks to my father, Mauro, and my brother, Niccolò, because they're there. Thanks also to all my friends, everywhere.

And finally, all my gratitude and all my love to my wife, Gioia Donna

Massa, who makes everything make sense. She does at Kennedy Space Center what I write about on the page, and besides acting as a sounding board for my ideas, she tolerated me when I had my face constantly stuck to the screen, encouraged me when I doubted myself, and yelled at me to get back to work when she saw that I was spending too much time on Facebook. This book literally wouldn't have happened without her.

Introduction
The Many Faces of Iain (M.) Banks

A few weeks before his passing, while discussing *The Quarry*, the novel that would ultimately see the light of day posthumously despite Little, Brown's efforts to rush its publication, Iain Banks expressed a certain regret: "If I'd known it was going to be my last book, I'd have been quite disappointed that I'm going out with a relatively minor piece; whereas something like *Transition*, a wild splurge of fantasy, sci-fi and mad reality frothed up together … now that would have been the kind of book to go out on. I'm still very proud of *The Quarry* but … let's face it; in the end the real best way to sign off would have been with a great big rollicking Culture novel" (Kelly 2013, n.p.). Without romanticizing, and without pretending to know what was going on in Banks' mind at the time, it seems reasonable that, of all the multifariously hued stories he wrote during his life, he would have preferred his last to belong to the Culture's multi-volume statement of optimism for the future.

This book is about the history of the Culture; it's about the birth of the idea and its growth from a hopeful conceit into a publishing reality that transferred such hopefulness from its writer to its readers, making it one of the very few literary utopias most of us actually agree would be nice to live in. My argument will explore the gradual process by which Banks developed his space-opera setting over the course of forty years of personal exploration and twenty-six years of published history, and the discourse he built around it on such tropes as utopia and dystopia, including the definitional gap that separates one from the other. Who decides what a utopia is, and who gets to call their own society that? Who gets to point their finger at other societies—or even at their own—and decide that they are dystopias instead? Most importantly, when does one decide that one's self-described utopia has not just the means, but also the right to intervene in the affairs of dystopias? The Culture stories exist within the gray area established when the boundaries of those definitions touch and interact, and the characters in them are citizens of a liminal country, a place where The Right Thing to Do, whatever that is, becomes the result of a one-time situational calculation. And yet, at the end of every story, the Culture does remain a utopia, still viable as a concept and inviting as a place to live in. Banks created a lay heaven whose heart and soul reside in constant self-questioning, because such questioning enables the Culture to endure. The first civilization it puts to the question is its own.

But here, at the beginning of the book, we have to start at the end, as is only proper. It would be nearly impossible, and arguably disrespectful, to write it as if the death of the man whose imagination provided it with its subject matter were a simple chronological occurrence to be dealt with when appropriate—for any given value of the word "appropriate" in this context. It's still near enough to hurt a lot, that moment in time when Iain Banks' announcement of his terminal illness and his passing a mere two months thereafter devastated fans across the world and suddenly turned his Culture series, until that moment a work in progress, into a closed opus. To all of us remain, here and now on the other side, nine novels, a novella, and two short stories. This is no small stash, and it gives us reason to be happy. Banks was a prolific writer, and in the twenty-six years of the Culture's existence as a published entity he wrote well; at his worst he was entertaining, thought-provoking, and worth reading no matter what. At his best, he was superb.

But the feeling that we have been cheated out of at least twenty more years' worth of stories, and that Banks deserved to live those years to the fullest, is hard to dispel, and maybe it is necessary to keep it in the back of the mind, like a small, prim voice reminding us that yelling at the universe is occasionally good and proper. That is, after all, what Banks' last interviewer, *The Guardian*'s Stuart Kelly,[1] does in the article's introductory paragraph:

> "You know, this might be my last public statement," Iain Banks said to me on the phone when I was setting up this interview, and at the time that simply didn't seem likely: he was too full of ideas and opinions and schemes. He emailed me a fortnight ago, saying that he was hoping to be out walking around the village again by the end of the week. In fact, he died on 9 June. Nevertheless, the plans and hopes he had capture his quicksilver, optimistic personality, regardless of what transpired. To be robbed of 30 years he thought he might have had is one thing: to lose the few months he was cautiously anticipating seems especially cruel [2013].

The circumstances surrounding Banks' April 3, 2013, announcement that he was "officially Very Poorly" have since become famous, not least because of an entirely accidental correspondence between art and life: *The Quarry*, nine-tenths of which were already finished when he found out about his condition, featured a character—Guy, the protagonist's father—who is dying of cancer.[2] But it was mostly the voice we heard in our heads that made the difference, and the poised, peaceful tone with which that voice delivered the news. "It looks like my latest novel, *The Quarry*, will be my last," Banks wrote. "As a result, I've withdrawn from all planned public engagements and I've asked my partner Adele if she will do me the honour of becoming my widow (sorry—but we find ghoulish humour helps)" (2013a, n.p.). In the event, Adele Hartley, his partner since 2006 and founder of the *Dead by Dawn* horror film festival, transitioned from wife to widow even more rapidly than expected; the doctors had originally given Banks a prognosis of several months' worth of life, and it is a safe bet to say that, had he been granted those extra months, he and his new bride would have lived them as richly as the circumstances would have permitted.

As was typical of him, and fundamentally for the purposes of this work, Banks approached the sudden news with the same humorous detachment that infused the basic philosophy underpinning the Culture's worldview. In the Culture, the basic attitude toward Life's Great Questions (Why are we here? Where are we going? Why do we have to die?) is that asking such things of an essentially mechanistic universe is meaningless, which in turn leads to the most basic and most important tenet informing the Culture's morals—in Banks' own words, that "we make our own meanings, whether we like it or not":

> To live in the Culture is to live in a fundamentally rational civilisation.... The Culture is quite self-consciously rational, sceptical, and materialist. Everything matters, and nothing does. Vast though the Culture may be ... it is thinly spread, exists for now solely in this one galaxy, and has only been around for an eye-blink, compared to the life of the universe. There is life, and enjoyment, but what of it? Most matter is not animate, most that is animate is not sentient, and the ferocity of evolution pre-sentience (and, too often, post-sentience) has filled uncountable lives with pain and suffering.... In the midst of this, the average Culture person—human or machine—knows that they are lucky to be where they are when they are [2004b, 172–173].

Banks wrote these words in 1994, ten years after bursting onto the British literary scene with *The Wasp Factory* and seven years after the publication of the first Culture novel, *Consider Phlebas*. Back then, in the immediate aftermath of the end of the Cold War, the millennium was around the corner, the towers still presided over the New York skyline, and the terrors of the 21st century seemed improbable; the world may have felt newer than it does today. Within the ranks of SF's sub-genres, space opera had only recently begun its resurgence from distant-granduncle-hanged-for-horse-theft status to that of meaningful artistic form, and that largely thanks to a relatively small group of writers among whom Banks featured prominently. Only four of the major Culture stories had been published at that time.

Nearly twenty years later, when Stuart Kelly asked him to comment on his state of mind in the wake of the diagnosis, this is what Banks said:

> I can understand that people want to feel special and important and so on, but that self-obsession seems a bit pathetic somehow. Not being able to accept that you're just this collection of cells, intelligent to whatever degree, capable of feeling emotion to whatever degree, for a limited amount of time and so on, on this tiny little rock orbiting this not particularly important sun in one of just 400m galaxies ... really, it's not about you. It's what religion does with this drive for acknowledgement of self-importance that really gets up my nose. "Yeah, yeah, your individual consciousness is so important to the universe that it must be preserved at all costs"—oh, please [2013, n.p.].[3]

So we make our own meaning as we go, until we don't go anymore because we all have to die, and our fury at the waning of the light ends in silence like everything else; everything matters, and nothing does. There is a consistency of transference to Banks' worldview, and a coherency of vision that moves effortlessly and sincerely from the pages of his fiction to his statements as a human being. He spoke and wrote what he thought, irrespective of whether what he thought represented an opinion given during an interview, an analysis in a nonfiction piece, a direct mimetic observation in his mainstream writing, or a statement issued out the corner of the mouth, obliquely, through the harlequin mask of space opera. And Iain Banks thought a lot of things and shared those thoughts with us in his works; soon enough, we were thinking them too, which was good. It still is.

Read any one essay on Banks' overall body of work, any one attempt at summing it up as a whole, and you may find a restlessness in the author's voice, a sense of occasionally awed frustration at the resistance it offers to categorization. In a recent collection of essays, Martyn Colebrook, Katharine Cox, and David Haddock make this resistance the central notion of their assessment of Banks' achievement. "Banks' fiction," they write, "represents a continued fascination with the transgression of borders and limits, whether technical, cultural, corporeal, national or otherwise," and this penchant for transgression, in their opinion, is chiefly responsible for keeping away from it the critical attention it deserves:

> Over the course of his career, Banks' work has been traditionally marginalized for a variety of reasons: these include the prominence of his early fiction (especially his debut novel), which has tended to overshadow his later work; his decision to write and maintain himself as a science fiction writer, which has drawn an uncertain response from literary critics; his geographical and political focus on "niche" Scottish concerns or, ironically, that his writing is too removed from such concerns [2013, 1].

Banks' dual publishing personas—Iain Banks for his mainstream fiction and Iain M. Banks for his science fiction—have also conspired to further complicate the picture, especially considering that this distinction was not always observed to the letter (pun intended): one of his novels, *Transition*

(2009), was published in the UK by Livingstone under Iain Banks, whereas in the United states it was classified as a SF novel by Iain M. Banks and came out under Little, Brown's science fiction and fantasy imprint, Orbit. And when we actually take the trouble to read the books, many of them display a pervasive cross-pollination of themes, political views, narrative styles, and genres; in particular, Banks' first three novels, which remain grouped under the "mainstream" label, contain heavy doses of horror, fantasy, and SF. *The Wasp Factory* (1984) reads very much like a blend of supernatural horror and Gothic, especially in the parts that focus on Frank Cauldhame's grisly rituals of totemization and immolation. The three intertwined narrative paths of *Walking on Glass* (1985), on the other hand, weave generous helpings of science fiction into the plotline and refuse to completely dispel them at the end of the story, thus leaving readers in the grip of a dilemma. And finally, *The Bridge* (1986), one of Banks' best and most famous novels, splits its attention between its protagonist's recollections of a life spent in mimetic Scotland/England and his existence in a fantastical shadow-world into which he entered in the aftermath of a car accident that left him comatose. Once again, the narrative refuses to fully account for its estranged elements, so that, by the time the protagonist awakens in his hospital bed, the question of whether He'd Dreamed It All remains ultimately unanswerable.

It was only in the wake of *Consider Phlebas*' publication in 1987, and the opening up of the second main strand in Banks' writing, that his mimetic and non-mimetic work began to diverge. Iain Banks' novels started hugging reality a little more closely, whereas his science fiction seemed to become more estranged and complex with every installment. When *Against a Dark Background*, the first M-Banks novel not set in the Culture universe, appeared in 1993, yet another facet presented itself to further complicate the process of categorizing his works. Now there were three strands in Banks' literary production: mainstream/mimetic, Culture SF, and non–Culture SF.[4] And every now and again—for example, in *The Crow Road*, *Whit* (1995), and *A Song of Stone* (1997)—Banks would infuse some of his mainstream work with non-mimetic elements, just to remind us that we shouldn't relax no matter which of his books we were reading. We were always in for a strange ride on a Möbius-strip circuit.

If Banks' fiction is protean in nature, resistant to easy negotiation between boundaries, so was his personality. He was witty, silly, and deadly serious, deeply engaged with politics and ethics at the same time as he enjoyed living a life of guilt-free hedonism. He was a lifelong atheist, and therefore dedicated to living a moral life outside the eternal-reward framework of organized religion,[5] but he held no contempt for those who did have faith, as long as they didn't set about fixing non-believers. He was passionate about Scottish independence, but suspicious of any attempt to describe him as a writer preoccupied with the Matter of Scotland.⁶ He loved the classic plotting of romance genres like science fiction and thriller (Alistair MacLean was an early influence), but also the inner-space complexities and narrative tricks of writers like John Brunner, Alasdair Gray, and Günter Grass. He would spend most of his year "driving his convertible black Porsche 911 top down along winding Scottish roads, zipping across country to meet up with his large circle of pals ... to drink gut-stretching quantities of beer, eat curries and gas about politics, sci-fi, old times" (Hughes 1999, n.p.), and then, over the last three or four months preceding Christmas, he'd sit down to write non-stop. The end result would be a novel—either mainstream or SF—that immediately hit the UK's bestseller lists. Banks grew to enjoy writing his "Hampstead novels," as he once called the mainstream side of his work, but he loved science fiction with a vengeance, and always indicated it as his favorite genre. "I do have a problem with [mainstream writing] being held up as the most important or most respectable genre," he told Colin Hughes in 1999. "It's just a particular way of writing, it's not necessarily the highest, it's just that: a way of writing. Elevating it almost becomes bigotry, saying that science fiction must be worse, less important. That really rankles, gets up my nose, both barrels" (n.p.).

The view from outside, that of Banks' friends, family, and fellow writers, reinforced this sense of dealing with a multi-faceted personality. There was the mad Iain Banks who, as a child, enjoyed hanging out with friends and displayed an unhealthy propensity for blowing stuff up with bombs made of sugar and weedkiller (Hughes 1999, n.p.; Garnett 1989, 52). Les MacFarlane, a childhood friend, once recalled an occasion when he, Banks, and a few other kids decided to build a six-foot model boat, filled it with explosives, and put a rudimentary pipe bomb in it. Of course, Banks was the one who stayed next to the boat to light the fuse with a match: "He lit it, started to walk back, and then you could see the mounting panic on his face thinking he wouldn't get away in time, and then he broke into a run.... The damn thing never went off" (Hughes 1999, n.p.). All those childhood years spent trying to inadvertently detonate himself didn't lessen Banks' passion for real-life pyrotechnics, though: in his university application form, when asked about his interests, he simply wrote "Explosives" (Hoggard 2007, n.p.).⁷

Nor were those the only instances in which Mad Iain popped out of the box. Once, at the age of seven, he came fairly close to falling to his death after a boulder he was climbing with his friends came loose and fell fifty feet to the ground; luckily for him, a bush a few feet below caught him, after which his friends made a human chain and brought him to safety. He went home shaken and slightly bruised, didn't tell his parents word one about the accident, and returned to doing the exact same thing the next day, and the next, and the one after that (Cabell 2014, Kindle locations 308–316). This pattern of life-threatening stunts continued well into his adult years: for example, once he got to London Banks started the practice Craig Cabell calls "Drunken Urban Climbing":

> First he found the route home along Grand Union Canal east of the Angel a more interesting route home than the surrounding roads, especially if he had to relieve himself of the remnants of recently consumed alcohol; but the real birth of the climbing escapades occurred when he found that a favourite towpath had been closed off because some work was being done on a bridge. Wooden boards had been erected across the pathway, making a wooden wall, which Banks decided he would climb and skirt along the bridge, hand over hand, legs dangling over the canal until he reached the other side [2014, Kindle locations 381–390].

Eventually, Banks' then-girlfriend Annie Blackburn[8] made him promise to stop his Drunken Urban Climbing practice, which he did until, in 1987, he found himself at Brighton's WorldCon. Neil Gaiman, who was present at the scene, recalled: "I was at a small party at the Brighton WorldCon in the wee hours, at which it was discovered that some jewelry belonging to the sleeping owner of the suite had been stolen. The police were called. A few minutes after the police arrived, so did Iain, on the balcony of the Metropole hotel: he'd been climbing the building from the outside. The police had to be persuaded that this was a respectable author who liked climbing things from the outside and not an inept cat burglar returning to the scene of his crime" (2013, n.p.).

Then there was the driving. By general agreement, Banks was something of a speed demon behind the wheel, which went well in hand with his longtime passion for cars, and there were consequences: he had his license suspended for twenty months in the late 1980s for hurtling into a brick wall with his Volvo. "I'd been drinking rather heavily for the past fourteen hours," Banks told *Journal Wired*'s David Garnett in 1989. "I put it down to the fact that it was only six days after the last general election, so I was a bit pissed off. Not much of an excuse, but it seemed like a good idea at the time" (59). About ten years later, in 1998, Banks ran his car off the road again—sober, this time—and upon emerging cut, bruised, and seemingly happy from the wreckage, said, "Thank God for airbags!" to a couple of tourists who had stopped to see if they could help. We should say, at this point, that one of Banks' lifelong nicknames was El Bonko—"nothing to do with bonking, sadly; it comes from bonkers, though I can't imagine why" (Hughes 1999, n.p.).[9]

There are many funny, astonishing, or ex-post-facto terrifying stories of Iain Banks, and many of those he happily told himself. His friends—among them Les MacFarlane, Jim Brown, Craig Cabell, and fellow SF writer Ken MacLeod—provided others. The picture emerges of a man untroubled by fear of public shame or of other people's opinions, slightly Frankensteinian and utterly gleeful in his penchant for left-field experimentation, and undaunted by the future, even when the planet didn't seem to be spinning in the direction he'd have liked (over the years, as the political landscape in the UK and the rest of the world darkened from his point of view, Banks would find this quality useful in keeping him rooted to a sense that things could, in fact, get better). This picture is entirely true.

It's not the only true picture, though. Next to Mad Iain, there's the man Hughes called "the affable Banksie." Aside from never being boring, Banks was a devoted friend; his childhood friendships lasted throughout his entire life, as did many of his high school and college acquaintances (as we shall see, the one with Ken MacLeod would prove to be particularly important for Banks' development as a writer and thinker). He was generous with his time, and money never warped him:

> I buy more than my numerically fair share of curries, but I don't buy as many as I should. It's difficult, very hard to get right. You don't want to insult your old friends by going, "I'm rich, I'm going to buy all the drinks." They know, and I know, that the fact that I'm rich is mostly luck, and the fact that the society in which we live values what I do absurdly higher than it deserves. Two of my friends are teachers, and they do a much more valuable job for society than I do. But we live in capitalism, and there's a huge market for escapism, art, entertainment, so I get paid more than I deserve [Hughes 1999, n.p.].

This way of caring for—and about—those people who comprised the flesh-and-blood connection to his roots was also part of another facet of Banks' personality: his sense of place. In the wake of graduation from the University of Stirling in 1979, he had moved to London, where he'd worked a number of jobs while he was writing. Soon after *The Wasp Factory* made him famous, however, he and Annie moved first to Kent and then, in 1988, back to North Queensferry, where Banks would spend the remainder of his life (Cobley 1990, 28). There, at the heart of his beloved Scotland, Banks kept hanging out with friends and family, driving his fast cars, drinking, eating spicy food, having fun, and writing one or two novels every year that would immediately top the charts. His very presence as a writing and publishing phenomenon contributed to the increased relevance of Scotland's literary scene, which Banks saw as a necessary counterbalance to London's dominance of the market. Immediately after returning, in fact, he began leveraging his influence into getting his publisher, Macmillan, to organize local book-launch parties (Garnett 1989, 57).

While Banks was able to relevantly influence Scotland's cultural affairs, the political landscape proved less easily negotiable and far more toxic for his tastes—and here, yet another aspect of his character comes to light. A lifelong friend of left-wing political causes and supporter of Scotland's full independence from the UK, he found England in the Thatcher years a hard place to like, an impossible place to live in, and a dark place to observe from next door, having to witness its influence on Scottish life. In his youth, two years before Thatcher took power, Banks was already personally involved in the political struggles of the time. Ken MacLeod recalls:

> He was quite willing to stick his neck out when necessary: he came down to London in 1977 to join the mobilization against the fascist National Front's attempt to march through Lewisham, took his place in a small squad of comrades none of whom he knew but me, and thoroughly enjoyed the fight that ensued. On a later visit he joined me when it was my turn to guard our group's bookshop and offices, which had recently been targeted in an amateurish arson attempt by the fascists. As Iain and I checked the locks on the building's back door, two policemen loomed behind us and tapped our shoulders. It took us some minutes to convince the coppers that we really were there to protect rather than attack the shop. Iain ribbed me about it afterwards: "I bet that's the first time you've ever had to say, 'Honestly, officer, I really am a left-wing extremist...'" [2013b, n.p.].

Over the years, Banks became less physically involved in political action just as his intellectual engagement with it ramped up considerably. He always made it a point to be well informed on the issues of the day—he read *The Guardian* every day, first to last page (2013b, n.p.)—and continued developing his political views (Noam Chomsky was a lifelong influence on his thinking, and on the formation of the Culture as well). In a 1990 interview for *Science Fiction Eye*, Michael Cobley asked Banks whether "although there's no overtly political stance in your novels ... you had an overtly political opinion." In reply, Banks didn't mince words: "Fucking right, I hate Thatcher and detest the Tories. The Tories are in fact the hyena party, if you've ever noticed the behavior of hyenas; they tend to go for the young and the weak, the sick and the old, which the Tories seem to do as well" (Cobley 1990, 28). Banks' opinion of both Margaret Thatcher and her party didn't change with time. In that last interview in 2013, Banks and Kelly, reflecting on the circumstances surrounding Banks' announcement of his illness, discussed Thatcher's own death, which had trailed the news by just five days:

> [Banks'] political zeal burns ... ardently. He confesses that "for half a second," as he and Adele travelled across the Alps from Venice to Paris on honeymoon, he was "elated" when he heard that Thatcher had died. "Then I realised I was celebrating the death of a human being, no matter how vile she was. And there was nothing symbolic about her death, because her baleful influence on British politics remains undiminished. Squeeze practically any Tory, any Blairite and any Lib Dem of the Orange Book persuasion, and it's the same poisonous Thatcherite pus that comes oozing out of all of them" [n.p.].

As the quote above intimates, the post–Thatcher years were not always positive from Banks' viewpoint, and they got worse in the aftermath of September 11. Famously, he cut up his passport in 2003 and sent it to 10 Downing

Street as a form of protest against Britain's intervention in Iraq, and the following year he signed a petition urging Tony Blair's impeachment. "I know it was self-harming, but what else could I do?" Banks told *The Guardian*'s Stuart Jeffries in 2007. "I was so angry about the illegality and immorality of the war. And this was me—a comfortably off, white Caucasian atheist from a vaguely Protestant background. If I thought it was disgusting, what would Muslims think about how their co-religionists were being treated?" (n.p.). Then, in the aftermath of the 2010 Gaza flotilla raid incident, he came out in support of the Boycott, Divestment, and Sanctions Campaign against Israel, and announced that he had "instructed my agent not to sell the rights to my novels to Israeli publishers" (2013b, n.p.).

It seems contradictory to think that the man who, in his more mature years, would not step beyond the remit of civil political protest should also be the writer who had his protagonist blow up rabbits and set dogs on fire in *The Wasp Factory*, began *The Crow Road* (1992) with the sentence "It was the day my grandmother exploded," and narrated the grisly, sadistically funny deaths of several corrupt politicians in *Complicity* (1993). Banks himself, however, saw the violence in his writing as an extension of his civic concerns, not as their contradiction or as an imaginative escape hatch from the restrictions they imposed:

> People usually just ask me "What are you *on*?" You can't be too prescriptive about what a writer does, but it's important to me to get these ideas into the books, just for my own peace of mind, so that I feel I'm not just doing this to make money, I'm not just writing pageturners for people to skim through, put aside and forget. Like anybody else, I want to make the world a little more like the world I'd like to live in, sad though that is. So I put forward these ideas however subtly or cack-handedly to the extent that I can get away with it. The good thing about writing is that you can do this in a non-invasive, non-penetrative way, you're not *telling* people this is what they should do, you're just presenting ideas [Mitchell 1996, n.p.].

This way of casting the writing of fiction more as a thought experiment than as a platform for advocacy informed Banks' defense of the violence pervading novels like *The Wasp Factory* and *Complicity*. This, for example, is how he responded to the outrage attending the latter's publication: "In principle, anything's OK, as long as I've got an excuse to put it in—which is a more honest way of saying, 'Is it artistically justified?' You shouldn't self-censor yourself just because you have a gut reaction that an idea is too horrible. If there's a reason for it, it has to be done. There's a moral point to that ghastliness, pain and anguish. Which is why I would absolutely defend *Complicity*'s extreme violence, because it was supposed to be a metaphor for what the Tories have done to this country" (Mitchell 1996, n.p.).[10] Over the course of his career, Banks was the recipient of plenty of outrage for this kind of choice, although it is important to note that the majority of this outrage came from readers of the mainstream side of his work. SF audiences,[11] when confronted with similarly brutal passages in his non-mimetic writing, were consistently more capable of contextualizing it within that larger moral point Banks was providing, as he always did.

Thus far, we have discussed the facets of Banks' character as a series of items on a list, and while that is a useful strategy for illustrating the range of a person's character, the fact remains that this listing obscures precisely the element that made him the writer he was: that those multifarious, supposedly contradictory aspects coexisted inside him all at once, in the same moment and in the same thought. Often in his work, they appeared in the same paragraph, or even in the same line. He was Mad Iain, The Affable Banksie, the philosophical and political thinker, the student protester, the driven practitioner of literature, the SF writer, the mainstream writer, the moral atheist, the lover of whisky and curry and driving fast and sensationalist plots and intricate literary techniques and horrible people doing horrible things and good people doing good things—all of it. He was also, in Neil Gaiman's estimate, "a brilliant and an honest writer, and much more importantly, because I've known lots of brilliant writers who were absolute arses ... a really good bloke" (2013, n.p.). That was Iain (M.) Banks. Like Janus in a room of mirrors, his many faces appeared together for us to receive and consider. Often, and especially after some of his grislier passages, we might have been doing the considering with green gills, but thoughts lingered no matter what. If part of his literary aims consisted in shocking us so we'd think about the implications that shock carried, then he succeeded, and outraged or not, we should consider ourselves fortunate that we were exposed to it.

And finally, he was Iain M-Culture Banks, the face with which this work is most concerned. He was the writer who, in Tom Chivers' words, "takes the same simple but vital skills—well-drawn characters, clever writing, believable dialogue—from his non-genre novels and applies them to his sci-fi, allied to dizzying imagination and serious knowledge" to conjure in the mind's eye of his readers "[his] finest creation, the universe of the Culture" (2013a, n.p.). As Ken MacLeod pointed out in a recent interview, this transfer of skills from the mainstream to the non-mimetic resulted in a movement from the act of narrating the dynamics of contemporary life to the act of imagining a social context within which those dynamics would not turn harmful or deadly, either for those living inside that social context or for those living outside of it:

> Iain's most direct engagement with the present was in his so-called mainstream novels.... They became I think more conjunctural as he developed as a writer: you can imagine the stories happening around about the time they were written.... With the Culture books he was trying to do something very different: to

imagine a utopia that people would actually like to live in, his starting point very sensibly being to imagine one he'd like to live in himself. The external threats were his answer to the problem that no matter how exciting a utopia might be to live in, it would be very dull to write about [Winter 2014, n.p.].

The galaxy-spanning utopia of the Culture is at once a secret garden and an engine—a secret garden within whose safe embrace one can contemplate the thought-experiment of a society gone right, and an engine for the proactive advocacy of decency, non-violence, equal rights for all, and the chance to live a meaningful life irrespective of the circumstances of one's birth. Ironically spurred into action by the fruits of its own prosperity, and mindful of the reality that, in a universe without gods, one makes one's own meaning as one goes along, the Culture finds that meaning in its ecumenism; it meddles. It intervenes in the life of other, less advanced societies in order to improve their living conditions, both materially and spiritually. Its advocacy is outspoken, its collective good works pervasive, and its people cautiously proud of their goodwill toward others. The Culture meddles because, first of all, it can—it has reached a post-human, post-scarcity level of technological advancement, scientific knowledge, and industrial productivity that essentially puts it beyond reach of anything this side of Subliming (more on which in chapters 2, 7, and 8). Second, and most importantly, it meddles because it thinks it should: its ethical, moral, and social training has moved in step with its technological, scientific, and industrial supremacy, to the point that it is impossible to separate one from the other. Therefore, the people of the Culture believe themselves capable of engineering social change without damage to other societies—or at least, with less damage than the amount those societies would incur if the Culture left them to fend for themselves. And so, in story after story, the game of intervention plays out against the backdrop of the galaxy, which in the series is a rich and variegated meta-biosphere for millions of civilizations of varying degrees of cultural and technological advancement. The Culture travels, searches, analyzes, and generally sticks its nose into every interesting situation it encounters, especially those involving societies in need of assistance. Negotiations ensue.

Which, of course, causes trouble. Mary Worth types are usually resented for their penchant to tell others how to improve their own lot, and the Culture knows this. The difficult dialectics of bossing others around in order to make sure they either stop bossing *others* around or don't fall prey to those who'd like to boss *them* around are not lost on the Minds—capital "M" here; they are transcendentally powerful AIs—that comprise the Culture's event-planning committees. Every course of action is carefully weighed in terms of first-principle advisability, logistical practicality, and ethical desirability—otherwise, as the Mind of the General Contact Unit *Arbitrary* puts it in *The State of the Art*, "how can we be sure we're doing the right thing?" (83). But in the process of doing the right thing, the Culture often meets fractious, underdeveloped, violent, chauvinistic societies that either refuse to be altered or, if they are powerful enough to stand a chance, decide that the only solution for dealing with the nosy neighbor is a scrap. Either way, it's at this point that the ethics of meddling risk becoming fuzzy, problematic, and stained with blood. Does the civilized entity back away from intervention then, leaving the uncivilized to their usual ways, or does it stoop to using at least some of those same underhanded tricks whose employment it had come in to halt in the first place?

Again, the Culture is fully aware of this problem, because Banks was as well. As we will see, a number of critics throughout the years have suggested that the fundamental conundrum at the heart of every Culture story—who or what issues the definition of "civilized," and how long after getting its hands dirty can this entity claim that definition for itself?—is a sign that Banks' attitude toward its creation was fundamentally deconstructionist. In other words, the argument goes, the whole notion of the Culture as a utopia is a smokescreen deployed to hide the reality that this utopia is, in fact, every bit as imperialistic as every other society. One of the key contentions this book makes is that such an argument crucially misses the point; Banks was, in fact, dead serious about imagining a society one could genuinely call utopian. That he decided to problematize the existence of this ideal collective, and that every character in the Culture novels therefore is, among other things, a carrier-wave for one of the many viewpoints in this dialectic of problematization, does not indicate lack of faith on his part. Rather, it reveals the attention Banks brought to the creative process of world building, and the degree of awareness he displayed of the moral and ethical dynamics he was handling. Since he believed that, "as the one literature primarily concerned with change and its effects on people and society, SF is—at least potentially—the most important literary form in the world" (SFFWorld 1997, n.p.), Banks treated it as such. He was not a mainstream writer who dabbled in SF; he was a writer who could modulate his voice to tackle both narrative modes, and when his voice operated on SF wavelengths there was no sarcasm in it, no attempt at postmodernizing the basic template of non-mimetic storytelling. Banks took the genre seriously, and argued his position within it honestly. He did his homework, and it showed.

The path to understanding the genesis and development of the Culture series encompasses Banks' whole life and times, from the moment when, at the age of eleven, he decided that he would become a writer, to the day he died, and all his faces feed into it. Chapter 1 takes us from the beginning of Banks' writing days to 1987, the year he published *Consider Phlebas*. Those were Banks' formative years, an at times difficult but also enthusiastic period of discovery, self-imposed training, false starts, and rejections until, in 1984, he published *The Wasp Factory*. The following three years saw him cement his breakthrough reputation with *Walking on Glass* and *The Bridge*. Together with *Factory*, these two novels gave Banks the chance to practice the kind of slipstream skating between the boundaries separating genre from non-genre writing that he had learned from Alasdair Gray's *Lanark* (1981). They also helped him work out some of the ethical and political underpinnings of the Culture stories within a different context, and develop ways of adapting the narrative style he had developed for them to the Culture books.

Chapter 2 begins the close readings of the Culture stories in chronological order, thus providing us with a view of the gradual process of accretion that eventually gave us Banks' space-opera canon. In it, we will look at *Consider Phlebas*, which introduced the Culture not as the protagonist of the story, but as the putative antagonist. Banks plays a game of double blind in this novel, leaning on the reader's assumptions concerning the plot thread of the typical space-opera yarn to first establish the semblance of such a yarn and then gradually removing this semblance to display the real story being told.

Chapter 3 will look at *The Player of Games* (1988) as the Culture novel that is most representative of Banks' tendency to wed gameplaying processes to his assessment of moral, ethical, and political trends within a given society. Gaming and playing pervade the story, literalized and made into life by the Empire of Azad's creation of a game that is the society—that is to say, a set of rules whose complexity purportedly mirrors the complexity and moral order of social relations in the Empire itself.

Chapter 4 is divided into two main sections. The first will analyze the next two installments in the series, *The State of the Art* (1989) and *Use of Weapons* (1990), as a two-part narrative of sorts, each part entangled with the other through a sharing of characters (Diziet Sma and the drone Skaffen-Amtiskaw), of timelines, and of the central moral dilemma: how can one know one is doing the right thing? The second section will begin examining the slow accretion of scholarship on the Culture, beginning with Lawrence Person's article on the Culture in issue 6 of *Science Fiction Eye* (1990) and Colin Greenland's critical review of *Use of Weapons* in issue 50 of *Foundation* (1990).

Chapter 5 is dedicated to "A Few Notes on the Culture," the 1994 article in which Banks, after completing the publication of all the previously rejected Culture novels, discusses the shape and origin of the Culture as a society, as an idea for a better world, and as a programmatic set of instructions one might care to follow on the way to building such a better world. From there, the discussion moves to identifying the Culture as a "critical utopia" in the mold Tom Moylan established in 1986's *Demand the Impossible* and reinforced in the updated 2014 edition of the same book, which came out under the Ralahine Classics line of studies in utopian writing.

Chapter 6 will take a close look at *Excession* (1996) and *Inversions* (1998) as another pair: *Excession*, the first Culture novel in about fifteen years that Banks wrote from scratch, presents us with a view of the Culture from above. The moving forces of its plot are the Minds that control the Culture's ships and habitats, and the scope of the novel is at once wide and deep; *Excession* is peripatetic, galaxy-wide, and full of energy, without forgetting to observe, discuss, and practice the brinksmanship of well-intentioned intervention. *Inversions*, on the other hand, is the exact opposite: it's the view from below, a look at the Culture's meddling from the standpoint of those who suffer it without understanding what's happening—the narrators of the story are two inhabitants of a planet at the medieval/renaissance technological stage, and it's only through knowledge of previous Culture stories on the part of the reader that we realize the Culture is involved.

Chapter 7 is, like chapter 4, divided into two sections. The first will read *Look to Windward* in the light of 9/11, presenting the novel as a strangely prophetic work on the looming terrors of the 21st century's first decade. The second will continue gathering the critical voices on Banks' work that chapter 4 began, with special attention given to the discourse surrounding the status of the Culture stories as New Space Opera.

Chapter 8 looks at *Matter* (2008), *Surface Detail* (2010), and *The Hydrogen Sonata* as three stories linked by a shared trait—the enrichment of the galactic commonwealth with a host of developed spacefaring races that, for the first time, present the Culture with an environment of equals.

A brief concluding chapter will end the book, presenting a final assessment of Banks' relevance in today's SF landscape and attempting to take a look at the Culture's future in and beyond the field of literary criticism.

1

BEGINNINGS

The writing career of Iain Menzies Banks—"Ming-iss, you'd pronounce it south of the border"[1]—did not exactly begin with the Culture, but it was a close thing. Having decided he wanted to be a writer at 11,[2] Banks proceeded to compose his first novel in 1970 and his second in 1972 before alighting in 1974–75 on an idea for a third. Entitled *The Use of Weapons*, it was going to be a space opera, a sub-genre of science fiction Banks liked despite the right-wing ethos most of it propagated. In his 1989 interview with David Garnett, Banks recounted the circumstances of the novel's inception:

> I had this character, a mercenary ... a very ultra tough guy. Very successful, very good at waging war and all that. But I thought this was a bit militaristic. Back then, even fifteen years ago, I wasn't really too happy with the idea. I wanted some reason, some good moral reason, for him to be employed in this way. So I came up with the idea of these galactic good guys who occasionally had to stoop to using this sort of person, usually from outside.... The idea being that people have such a good time in the Culture that it just doesn't produce maniacal *Rambo* types. And the Culture, also being very moral, wouldn't stoop to treating people badly—you know, dirty manipulation or forcing people into some horrible militaristic Spartan type of training or whatever. So, I though, in that case, I'll have to find this sort of person on some *other* nasty little planet, take them away from some situation where they're going to get *killed*. So [the Culture] can say *all right, do you want to work for* us? Not that they'd put him back in the same situation, but they do say, "You're alive, and you *can* work for us if you like." And it all sort of mushroomed from that, since way back in '72 or '3 or '4. In fact, I've just been working on the ideas behind the Culture ever since [64].

That's when it began, Banks' complex, argumentative, funny, constantly self-interrogating, intensely self-aware model for a socio-economic system that could be meaningfully classified as utopian by more than just the person advocating it. Now, in the wake of Banks' untimely death, we have no other choice but to look at this body of work as a complete set and draw our conclusions from that. And if it is true that the Culture is "obviously your political theory," as Garnett told him, we must then consider that this political theory also informed his life. Therefore, we must look at its development as an expression of Banks' own convictions first, and then as a product of the environments—geographic, social, cultural—that he inhabited throughout his life.

Which brings us to its early years. Banks' childhood was atypical for the kind of personality one usually associates with someone who published the kind of fiction he did. In the wake of *The Wasp Factory*'s publication in 1984, and for years afterward as Frank Cauldhame's obsessive, brutally ritualistic psyche seemed to replicate itself in later novels into a host of similarly damaged personalities, several interviewers asked him whether this show of metatextual violence might not have been the result of a difficult childhood. But Banks, ever his disarming self, disappointed those notions:

> I felt very loved, and special.... And it's very difficult to have an only child and love them like that, and not spoil them. I think back and remember I always used to be given the best cuts of meat and so on. I got used to being treated as the most important person in the household, which can be very dangerous.... I mean, luckily I turned out to be a wonderful human being, but a lesser person could have had their head turned by that [Hughes 1999 n.p.].

Indeed, Banks' childhood was by all accounts a happy one. Born in 1954 in Dunfermline, Fife, he was an only child,[3] the son of Tom, an officer in the Admiralty stationed at the naval yards in Rosyth, near the Firth of Forth, and Effie, a professional ice-skater; the two had met at Dunfermline ice rink, where Effie was working as an instructress. Banks consistently ascribed his passion for writing to his father's influence, while his mother's seems to have been responsible for the stubborn streak that allowed him to keep trusting himself in the early days of his career, when publishers did not appear to want what he had to offer (Hughes 1999, n.p.; Cabell 2014, Kindle locations 253–270).

Banks spent the pre-university years of his life between North Queensferry and Gourock, following his father's postings in the Admiralty. His childhood and adolescence were "the standard writer's cliché, and I had all the classic symptoms—not quite talking to myself but definitely having my own little world, making up my own stories. I always got on well with my parents ... and I wasn't bullied at school or anything" (Cobley 1990, 24). Banks also inherited from both parents large families full of uncles and aunts, cousins and second cousins, among whom he spent his childhood. Some of them also led more interesting lives than might be expected on average in 1950s Scotland—a few were naval pilots, for example (Hughes 1999 n.p.), and the stories they must have told the young Banks probably contributed to first triggering and then fueling a lifelong passion for technological artifacts and high-octane action sequences.[4] Early manifestations of this passion prompted Banks to "[lead] his friends in daredevil games from climbing trees to re-enacting battles in the Great War and Second World War pill boxes scattered across the banks of the Firth of Forth," and to develop an abiding affection for the Forth bridge, under whose titan frame he spent a good deal of his early life. The bridge would return in his fiction under many guises, chief among all the eponymous structure in *The Bridge* (Cabell 2014, Kindle locations 270–283).

Banks was nine when his family moved from North Queensferry to Gourock, about eighty miles away, and it was perhaps the initial isolation accompanying the move that, combined with his status as an only child and his reflective nature, brought him to "[make] up stories in my head. Rather than novels, they were basically fictitious TV series similar to The Man from UNCLE or Danger Man. For some reason, the secret service would have to employ a young, but very cunning and clever Scots boy, of whatever age I happened to be at the time" (Leith 2003, n.p.). He also discovered the local library, which he began visiting regularly. He read voraciously, and while he happily read in every genre, he did discover in himself a preference for non-mimetic literature and science fiction in particular:

> I remember I used to raid Gourock Library every week for three or four books and I always looked for the yellow Gollancz covers, and I'd read them whatever the hell they were. As long as it said SF on the cover I'd read them. Until it was pointed out to me that these books were all written by different authors, I didn't know I'd read virtually everything Robert Heinlein had done, up to a certain point [Cobley 1990, 23–24].

By the time he started writing his own stories, Banks had already amassed a wide range of literary influences, genre and non-genre, as well as non-literary ones.[5] The most lasting among them were the works of Jane Austen,[6] Leonard Cohen,[7] Alistair MacLean, John Sladek, M. John Harrison and Brian Aldiss, Joseph Heller's *Catch-22* (1961), Hunter S. Thompson's *Fear and Loathing in Las Vegas* (1972), John Brunner's *Stand on Zanzibar* (1968), and Günter Grass' *The Tin Drum* (1959). Also, Monty Python and the Marx Brothers' movies, plus *2001: A Space Odyssey* (1968) and *Star Wars* (1977),[8] should be added to this relatively brief list, which is relevant for two main reasons: firstly because it is representative of the eclectic nature of Banks' overall influences, and secondly because, with the exception of MacLean's novels, the Marx Brothers' movies, and *Star Wars*, the aggregate of the works comprising it features a mixture of byzantine narrative structures, unreliable narrators, a shifting sense of the reality of the situation presented in the story, a strong tendency to play games with the reader's assumptions, and that uneasy blend of humor and horror that would later characterize a great deal of Banks' own writing. "Just the wealth of humor in both," he said of *Catch-22* and *Fear and Loathing*, "and they had a serious point as well. It's hard enough to do comedy, it's hard also to do something that makes people laugh and is viciously realistic as well" (Rundle 2010, n.p.). In developing his craft, Banks would take that particular lesson to heart.

So: a happy childhood, devoid of strife or fundamental suffering; a large, loving family full of interesting people; a tendency to make up stories in his head; a seemingly bottomless intellectual curiosity with a distinct literary bent, at once slaked and fueled by the contents of the local library; and a host of influences, ranging from straight adventure/thriller to comedy to involved social commentary to postmodern experimentation. That Banks should conclude he wanted to be a writer by the age of 11 is not surprising; what is remarkable is the determination and self-confidence he displayed in pursuing this vocation far past the age at which most other people decide it was just a phase and they need to move on.⁹ By his own reckoning, Banks wrote about a million words' worth of unpublished material before the second draft of *The Wasp Factory* was accepted for publication (Hunt 1999, n.p.; Rundle 2010, n.p.), and while most of this material was later published as well, albeit in modified form, some of it has, to date, not seen the light of day.

Among those unpublished works are Banks' two early novels, the ones that preceded the 1974 draft of *The Use of Weapons*. The first, written in 1970 when Banks was 16, was a spy novel in the vein of one of his early influences, Alistair MacLean, and also based on "a lot of the spy programs that were on television at the time" (Rundle 2010, n.p.). It was entitled *The Hungarian Lift-Jet*, and it involved Banks' "very cunning and clever Scots boy" in a sort of Hunt-for-Red-October mission to steal secret technology: "Hungary has invented this radical lift jet and the secret service had nicked it. It was just an excuse for vast amounts of mayhem. It all ended badly. Everybody died" (Leith 2003, n.p.). Banks wrote the novel in longhand in an Admiralty logbook his father had given to him, and it ran to about 140,000 words—"about two average novels. Terrible, but it meant a lot to me at the time" (Cobley 1990, 25). Even at the time of writing Banks must have felt that the novel didn't measure up, because he never typed it. Instead, he moved on to his next work, *The Tashkent Rambler* (also known in its abbreviated form, *TTR*), and his next set of literary influences: *Catch-22* and *Stand on Zanzibar*. He wrote the novel in 1972, and for the first and only time in his career, he did not plan it out. The result was a sprawling, seemingly unending narrative that "lived up to its title by meandering to a length of 400,000 words ... he struggled to end the novel and has plotted his work ever since. Banks' first rejection slip was for this work" (Colebrook, Cox, and Haddock 2013, 4). Set in the near future, *The Tashkent Rambler* features a non-nuclear Sino-Soviet border war that the Chinese win with the help of the United States, which enters the war only because "they needed to battle-test their weapons and hadn't had a decent war for a while." However, China's war prize, Mongolia, proves unappetizing, so the U.S. takes it over; the narrative itself "takes place in the three weeks before the ceremony in which Mongolia is going to become the fifty-first state of the American Union, renamed Mongoliana, and celebrate their Dependence Day.... It's full of bad puns and characters with names like Dahommey Brezhnev and Dogghart Jammaharry. Gropius Luckfoot was another one, and his very unpleasant sidekick was called Toss Macabre" (Wilson 1994, n.p.).[10] Banks' passion for puns, a phase he was going through at the time,[11] would later resurface in the baroque, comically long, essentially unpronounceable names that became one of the more readily recognizable features of his Culture stories.

By the time Banks came up with the original idea for *The Use of Weapons*, he seemed to have largely gotten out of his system one of the necessary phases in a writer's career: the direct emulation of fundamental literary influences. Whatever the failures of that early draft—before he could publish it in 1990 as *Use of Weapons* (no article), the fourth Culture story, Banks had to rewrite most of it—*TUoW* was his idea, set within a fictional environment of his own original devising. This environment was the first incarnation of the Culture universe, which was the product of Banks' rapidly maturing political, artistic, and ethical views. He was twenty at the time, and a student of literature, psychology, and philosophy at the University of Stirling (Hoggard 2007, n.p.). Among his intellectual influences in the realm of non-fiction, the most important were those of Noam Chomsky, whose ideas of free access to information as a prerequisite to a more just society struck a powerful chord within him, and of John Kenneth Galbraith, the economist and diplomat who became one of the pioneers of American liberalism (MacLeod 2013, n.p.).[12] Michael Herr, the war correspondent and author of the Vietnam-war memoir *Dispatches* (1977), also became a prominent influence (SFFWorld 1997, n.p.). Those who came into contact with Banks in those years, faculty and fellow students alike, remember him very much as Colin Hughes' "affable Banksie"—lively, intense in a fun sort of way, friendly, without pretense, and slightly distracted in the manner of those who seem to be always looking at something not quite on the horizon yet. But they also remember him as a studious young man with a steely determination to become exactly what he'd decided he wanted to become—a writer. Rory Watson, a poet and professor of English at Stirling in Banks' days, remembered that "he was always very lively and genial; he liked to play the amiable loon. But he worked hard. A lot of people sit and talk about writing, but if you're really going to write you have to do it, not talk about it. Iain was writing all the time" (Hughes 1999 n.p.).

So it wasn't enough that he wanted to be a writer; he wanted to be a good one too. He also wanted to say meaningful things through the medium of science fiction, and in that respect he found plenty of inspiration when, sometime in the early '70s, he began reading *New Worlds*.[13] Since Michael Moorcock had taken over the magazine's editorial reins about ten years earlier, *New Worlds* had gradually become the New Wave's standard bearer and the venue for many of its signature voices—besides the aforementioned Sladek, Aldiss, Brunner, and Harrison, there were also Norman Spinrad, Barrington J. Bayley, Thomas Disch, Samuel Delany, Roger Zelazny, John Clute, and Moorcock himself. Self-consciously literary, open to the larger world of postmodern experimentation of the 1960s, scornful of the hackneyed starship-and-raygun formulas of 1940s and '50s American SF, and dedicated to using the tools of the genre for the exploration of "inner space" (as Ballard had famously put it in 1962), New Wave writers gave Banks a fairly precise sense of the possibilities of science fiction as a mature, artistically self-aware, politically and psychologically articulate literary mode. Banks also received from *New Worlds* a strong grounding in SF criticism, mostly through the reviews and the articles M. John Harrison and John Clute wrote for the magazine. According to Ken MacLeod, Banks' close friend since high school and now a fellow student at Stirling, those articles and reviews "were, for Iain and for me, always the highlight of every issue of the paperback series of *New Worlds*. We read them so assiduously and delightedly that we burned entire paragraphs into memory.... Clute and Harrison took a scalpel to the flaws of the science fiction we loved, and we loved them for it ... the field as Iain found it presented a dilemma: American SF was optimistic about the human future, but deeply conservative in its politics; British SF was more thoughtful and experimental, but too often depressive" (2013, n.p.).

For these reasons, the composition of *The Use of Weapons*' first draft represented something of a flashpoint moment, the nexus at which Banks' developing skills as a writer, his political and ethical views, and his ability to engage in world-building from within a non-mimetic environment, began to blend. Ken MacLeod became a fundamental part of that process. Banks reminisced to Garnett: "I've got a very good friend of mine called Ken MacLeod; we used to get together and set the universe to right, as one does. And out of those conversations a lot of Culture ideas have grown" (1989, 65). More recently, MacLeod himself specified the genesis of those ideas:

> When Iain Banks and I were students back in the early 1970s, I was one of the first readers of *Use of Weapons*.... Iain explained that the Culture was his idea of utopia, in which advanced technology, inexhaustible resources and friendly artificial intelligence made possible a society in which nobody had to work and there was no need for money or a separate state apparatus. At the time I was reading with some excitement ... a collection of extracts from Marx's notebooks,

in which he allowed himself some bolder speculations than he ever saw into print. I explained to Iain that the Culture was very similar to Marx's conception of communism: a stateless and classless society based on automation and abundance.... [But] Iain had little interest in relating the long-range possibility of utopia to radical politics in the here and now. As he saw it, what mattered was to keep the utopian possibility open by continuing technological progress, especially space development, and in the meantime to support whatever policies and politics in the real world were rational and humane [2013, n.p.].

For Banks, MacLeod explains, supporting rational and humane policies in the real world involved voting for the Labour Party. When, in later years, the Labour Party became New Labour, Banks turned to the Scottish National Party and the Scottish Socialists out of the gradually matured conviction that Scotland would remain shackled to toxic Tory governments it hadn't elected until the day it became independent. Banks was no supporter of any notion of Scottish exceptionalism, however. His championing of separation from England "didn't come from nationalism but from reformism, and from a lifelong, heart-felt hatred for the Conservative and Unionist Party" (2013, n.p.).[14]

Supporting rational and humane policies in a science fictional world of his own creation, on the other hand, presented Banks with few obstacles besides those he had set for himself. In its basic setup, *The Use of Weapons* already contained the germ of the dramatic tension that would one day fuel every Culture story: a government-free, labor-free, non-violent, moneyless, humane, technologically advanced, AI-administered utopia possessed of bottomless resources that, in those few instances when it has to "stoop to using this sort of person," finds it necessary to hire someone to handle the unpleasant aspects of having to deal with barbarians at the gates. And because "people have such a good time in the Culture that it just doesn't produce maniacal *Rambo* types," this someone would have to be from a scarcity-based, heavily hierarchical society from whose crushing embrace they would probably welcome removal. This seemingly unproblematic solution, however, carries inescapable ethical conundrums: the moral standing of outsourcing one's uncivilized behavior is dubious, as is the notion of violent intervention in the development of other, less powerful societies—purportedly for those societies' own good; also, such practices threaten to belie the self-ascribed status of utopia that is implicit in choosing to fix others in the first place.

Originally, this built-in dramatic tension may not have mattered much. The Culture, Banks told *Science Fiction Chronicle*'s Sally Ann Melia in 1994, was supposed to act as nothing more than a background and moral escape hatch for *TUoW*'s tough mercenary protagonist, Cheradenine Zakalwe—doing bad work for a good cause would speak better of him as a moral being than might otherwise have been the case. In the course of writing that first draft, however, things began changing: "I'd read so much SF which seemed just to assume that our current political-economic systems—and especially U.S.-model Capitalism—would just continue on almost unchanged into the stars and that just seemed blind, blinkered.... So, I came up with the idea of the Culture" (42). And indeed, between 1975 and 1981, the year he wrote the first draft of *The Wasp Factory*, Banks dedicated most of his energies to two stories set within the Culture universe,[15] each of which further developed the shape of his utopia and explored one or more facets of the ecumenical intervention conundrum. The first was *The State of the Art*, a novella written in 1979 that brought the Culture in direct contact with Earth, circa 1977. The second story, which Banks wrote in 1980, was a novel entitled *The Player of Games*; its protagonist is a man famous throughout the Culture for his skills at mastering all kinds of games and simulations, and the Culture's agents persuade him to travel to a distant corner of the galaxy, home to a brutally dictatorial empire, to play the most complex game ever seen.

The State of the Art and *The Player of Games* were not accepted for publication, however, and neither was the first draft of *Consider Phlebas*, which Banks composed in 1982. In part, the reason for this string of rejections consisted in Banks' habit of working exclusively on a first-draft basis. He'd write a story and, if he felt it was worth submitting for publication, do so without revising it (Garnett 1989, 68–69). Invariably, the work would be rejected. And so, confronted with a number of returned manuscripts, Banks decided to branch out into mimetic writing—or, as he put it to *Spike Magazine*'s Greg Lowe, "widen my circle of rejection" (2008, n.p.). In 1981, the year before composing *Phlebas*, he'd written the first draft of *The Wasp Factory*, but unlike his other stories, this one received a second draft. Even then, six publishers rejected it before MacMillan picked it up in 1983 and published it in 1984 (Colebrook, Cox, and Haddock 2013, 3–4; Hunt 1999, n.p.).

So Banks had made it. "I think I'm basically a science-fiction writer, and I always have been," he said at one point, "but I broke into the mainstream first" (Leith 2003, n.p.). The breakthrough, however, came at the price of a certain feeling of selling out, of trading his faithfulness to his favorite genre for the chance to get published (Rundle 2010, n.p.), and this may be one of the reasons why, over the course of the three years that separated the publication of *The Wasp Factory* from the appearance of *Consider Phlebas*, Banks seemed intent on loading into his work as much non-mimetic material as he could get away with and still call it mainstream. In this endeavor, he found inspiration in the last of his great literary influences: the 1981 novel *Lanark*, written by fellow Scot Alasdair Gray. Banks himself happily acknowledged the depth of influence that *Lanark* had in shaping *The Bridge* (see Colebrook 2013, 28), but it is also important to consider that the novel, which Banks read right around the time he decided to try switching to non-genre writing, also influenced *The Wasp Factory* and *Walking on Glass*. Among other things, Gray's work provided Banks with a blueprint for the creation of thinly disguised fantastic narratives, hallucinatory tales giddily poised between nightmare and reality, vision and waking sight. *Lanark* is an intense metafictional scherzo, a maddened process of constant transition between a reality that feels like a fever dream and a dreamscape that looks altogether too solid for comfort.

By the time Gray published *Lanark*, he'd been working on the novel for almost thirty years; in fact, he'd started writing it as a teenager in 1954, the year Banks was born (*Lanark*, 569). When it came out in England, it was an instantaneous success, both artistically and financially,[16] and its appearance signaled in Gray's native Scotland the first stirrings of what would later become known as the Scottish Literary Revival (see Pattie 2013, 9–12). When Banks read *Lanark*, his reaction to it could hardly be overstated:

> I was absolutely knocked out by *Lanark*. I think it's the best in Scottish literature this century. It opened my eyes. I had forgotten what you could do—you can be self-referential, you can muck about with different voices, characters, timestreams, whatever [Wilson 1994, n.p.].

This brief list contains all the characteristics in *Lanark* that so impressed Banks, and which he duly imported into his own work. Subtitled *A Life in Four Books*, Gray's novel is the story of two people who are actually the same person: Duncan Thaw, a deeply troubled young man living in contemporary Glasgow and heavily based on Gray himself (568), and the eponymous Lanark, who wakes up one night inside a train carriage in the city of Unthank, one among the many nightmare locations in the shadow-world in which he now finds himself and with which he must come to terms, somehow. Duncan and Lanark are connected to each other through the former's suicide: a rebellious, fractious artistic personality, Duncan is constantly confronted with rejection and misunderstanding on the part of others, which his mercurial nature does nothing to ameliorate, and when it all gets to be too much, when he concludes that the people in his life seem to be happier without him around, he walks into the ocean and drowns himself—at which point Lanark wakes up in Unthank with grit and seashells in his pockets (17).

This crude synopsis seems simple enough, but the novel's timeline, scrambled and fractured into an epistemologically opaque alignment, makes things considerably more difficult. The four Books that comprise *Lanark* begin not with Book One, but with Book Three (3–105), which features Lanark's awakening in Unthank and his early adventures there. The sequence continues with a Prologue (107–117), and then we have Book One (121–219) and Book Two (221–354), which tell Duncan Thaw's story from childhood to self-destruction; they are separated from each other by a one-page Interlude (219). Book Four (357–560), which returns us to Lanark and concludes the narrative, contains the Epilogue, but not at its conclusion—the piece is wedged between chapters 40 and 41 (480–499), four chapters away from the book's end. In it, Lanark meets the author of *Lanark*, who calls himself Nastler and tells him the story of his own life—and of Duncan's—in a transfixingly offhand tone. "You are Thaw with the neurotic imagination trimmed off and built into the furniture of the world you occupy," Nastler/Gray tells Lanark right after confessing that he killed Duncan because "though based on me he was tougher and more honest, so I hated him" (493). He also explains that he structured the novel in such a counterintuitive fashion because "I want *Lanark* to be read in one order but eventually thought of in another," and that the Epilogue is where it is because "it's too important to go [at the end] … it lets me utter some fine sentiments which I could hardly trust to a mere character. And it contains critical notes which will save research scholars years of toil" (483). Those critical notes, which are literally placed on the sides of the Epilogue's text, amount to a long "Index of Plagiarisms" that Nastler/Gray claims he committed toward a considerable number of disparate sources (485–499).

The Epilogue and the ordering of the Table of Contents are the most evident signs of *Lanark*'s metafictional playfulness, and of its refusal to remain within the scope of one genre for long enough to allow us to firmly place it there. They are not the only ones, however; everywhere in the novel's text, allusions and parallels appear not only between Duncan and Lanark's life, but also between the real-world setting of mid–20th-century Glasgow and the secondary world of Unthank. It gradually becomes evident that one is the shadow of the other, although which one and which other remains open to debate. Nastler/Gray himself tells Lanark that the most profound connection between the two plotlines lies in the representation of the incapacity to care for oneself and for others: "The Thaw narrative shows a man dying because he is bad at loving. It is enclosed by your narrative which shows civilization collapsing for the same reason" (484). Indeed, the fate of individuals trapped inside brutal world-machines constitutes one of the main themes in Gray's writing:

> Throughout his fiction, the truth at which Gray worries is the old one—of exploitation, class brutality, man's inhumanity to man.… This is the truth which seeks out Gray's protagonists, and shatters their complacency [qtd. in Pattie 2013, 12].

Banks hadn't needed Gray's influence to develop the same set of concerns. His intellectual and political development of the mid-to-late 1970s already showed their presence in his writing. What Gray gave Banks was a

1. Beginnings 31

template for injecting those concerns into his writing and for making this writing work, both financially and artistically, within an avowedly mainstream environment. So, when Banks began writing *The Wasp Factory*, the lessons of *Lanark* were very much present in his mind, and their application continued past that first novel—indeed, they ended up encompassing the rest of his body of work, including the Culture series.

Taken together, the three novels that preceded the first Culture story—*The Wasp Factory*, *Walking on Glass* (1985), and *The Bridge* (1986)—fairly thoroughly showcase the main characteristics of Iain "no–M" Banks' writing; these characteristics would all reappear in his M-Banks work, appropriately re-morphed to fit its genre-specific environments. In no particular order of importance, they are:

- A tendency to utilize fantastic tropes and narrative techniques to blur and confuse distinctions between mimetic and non-mimetic literature.
- The reliance on untrustworthy narrators, altered mind-states, and uncertain reality frames.
- A strong preference for metafiction and textual playfulness.
- Self-referentiality. Every one of Banks' first three novels carries, embedded within its structure, tropes, themes, and plot twists borrowed from famous works of fiction—often non-mimetic—that influenced him in one way or another.
- The penchant for foregrounding the storytelling process as a game played between the author, the reader, and the characters in the story.
- A predilection for complicated plot structures, often anticipated in the many moving parts of the novels' Table of Contents.

A detailed examination of *The Wasp Factory*, *Walking on Glass*, and *The Bridge* is beyond the scope of this work, but a few examples from each will be enough to illustrate Banks' usage of these techniques. *The Wasp Factory*, for instance, represents an excellent showcase of the first two items on the list—the blurring of boundaries and the presence of unreliable narrators. The novel features a first-person protagonist/narrator, Frank Cauldhame, who in the aftermath of an accident that left him castrated has erected around himself and the island he lives on a protective system of supernatural totems surmounted by the heads of various animals Frank has killed (7). Those grisly trophies are part of a larger network of Sacrifice Poles spread across the island's whole perimeter. They are Frank's "early warning system and deterrent rolled into one; infected, potent things which looked out from the island, warding off" (10). The Bunker, Frank's temple of dark magic where he prepares the animal carcasses and the heads for his protective spells, complements this sacrificial arrangement. In fact, all of Frank's actions obey an essentially ritualistic mentality that imbues events in the novel with symbolic meanings connected to practices of premonition and magical control over the territory he has claimed as his own.[17]

And then there's the Factory of the title. If the Sacrifice Poles and the Bunker are Frank's warning beacons of Gondor, the Wasp Factory is his dark version of Galadriel's mirror—an engine of prophecy powered by the deaths of the wasps he captures and puts into the Factory so they'll run the gauntlet he has made for them. Frank built the Factory around the face of an old clock he found in the town dump (120–121). Each of the twelve numerals on the clock face leads to a trap, and each trap kills the wasp in a specific way—burning, electrocution, crushing, chopping, drowning, and so on.[18] The means by which the workings of the Factory lead the wasp to any one end reveal something about the future, or so Frank believes. His descriptions of the Factory's meaning-making system and of the rituals he has to perform to activate it (119–125) come across, in their deranged intensity, as at once revelatory of a genuine supernatural agency and, because of Frank's ultimately unreliable nature, skeptical of that same agency. In this sense, *The Wasp Factory* reads very much like a psychological Gothic narrative. Trapped as we are inside his first-person narration, and without any form of external referent to contextualize or verify the truthfulness of his tale, we have no way of knowing for sure exactly what, if anything, happened. Not unlike his literary predecessors, Frank speaks in a voice that seems invested in persuading us that its owner's actions, insane as they may seem, are in fact perfectly natural responses to a set of unfortunate circumstances. "Women and the sea are my enemies" (43), he tells us at one point, and while his hostility toward the sea carries a sense, however gingerly, of being connected to some sort of factual basis (it washes away everything he builds), his hatred for women does not at first seem to have one. Also, insanity run deep in the Cauldhame family: Frank's father, who refused to have his son's birth registered, also refused to send him to school, and the education he gave his son was laced with a string of willful lies whose truth Frank found out only when he was old enough to hit the local library on his own. And then there's Frank's half-brother Eric. Once a caring, well-adjusted personality in a context where nobody else was, he went mad in the aftermath of a horrifying accident at the hospital where he was stationed as a medical student (139–142). As a result, after he'd become violent and obsessed with decay, he was put into a hospital from which, Frank tells us at the beginning of the novel, he has only just escaped.

This brief look at *The Wasp Factory* highlights the nature of the novel as a blend of supernatural horror and Poe-esque Gothic tale, a narrative whose suspension between fantasy and realism cannot ultimately be resolved because there's no exit strategy that can remove us from under Frank Cauldhame's glare. This is his story, true or not, and we're prisoners in it. *Walking on Glass*, for its part, works well as a sample of metafiction and gameplaying at work. The gameplaying aspect becomes apparent upon looking at the plot structure, which is divided into three seemingly separate but ultimately converging plotlines. The first plotline involves Graham Park, an art student in love with a mysterious, sultry woman called Sara ffitch. Graham has a friend and confidant in Richard Slater, who has a habit of launching himself in periodical synopses for science fiction novels he always plans on, but never quite gets around to, writing (9–10; 61–66). It eventually turns out that Slater and Sara are not only lovers, but brother and sister as well, and that they had all along been playing a complicated game of deception with Graham to deter attention from their own illicit relationship.

The second plotline features Steven Grout, a man who believes he is a fallen warrior from a higher plane of reality trapped inside a human body. During the course of his service in the "ultimate war, the final confrontation between good and evil," he had made a mistake, or been betrayed, or lost an engagement; Steven can't quite recall what happened, but he knows that his punishment involves exile to the lesser reality of late 20th-century Earth, and he therefore seeks the key to the way out so he can return to the glory of his former existence (26). The only place he acknowledges as safe from the forces of chaos is the rented room in which he lives, a sparsely furnished, small locale forever cluttered with stacks of science fiction and fantasy books. He reads fantasy and SF because "he had long ago realised that if he was going to find any clues to the whereabouts of the Way Out, the location or identity of the Key, there was a good chance he might get some ideas from that type of writing. He knew this from the way he felt attracted to it" (30–31).[19] Thus, Steven is playing a game of hunt-the-clue against foes that seem to be playing a game with him, trying to keep him immured in our drab reality.

And then there's the third plotline: Quiss and Ajayi are guests/prisoners in a castle, which Quiss knows by the name of Castle Doors and Ajayi by that of Castle of Bequest. The castle towers over a snow-covered plain that extends in every direction as far as the eye can see, its location seemingly unknowable, and time passes without any apparent change in landscape, climate, or season (42). Quiss and Ajayi used to be Promotionaries in the Therapeutic Wars, fighting on opposing sides, and like Steven believes of himself, "they had each done something silly, something which called into question their very suitability for exalted rank, and now they were here, in the castle, with a problem to solve and games to play, being given one last chance; a long shot, an unlikely appeal procedure" (43). The two have to play games with strange names and stranger rules—they begin with One-Dimensional Chess—and at the end of every game they will have one chance to answer the question whose correct solution will set them free to return to the Therapeutic Wars. The question is: "What happens when an unstoppable force meets an immovable object?" (52). Gameplaying again, then, and some of them are literally games to be played on a board; others are played with the lives of the characters involved, just like in the Park and Grout storylines, so that one of the unifying principles of the novel is that everyone is at once playing and being played upon, at once gamer and gamed.

In the process of finding out how these separate plotlines converge and explain—or fail to explain—one another, we encounter a number of metafictional referents, all connected to the utilization of the colors black and white as signifiers of the storytelling process. As David Leishman argues in a recent article, everything returns us to images of ink on paper:

> The games played by Quiss and Ajayii ... all feature pieces which are black and white. Their monochrome nature has an evident mimetic function, mirroring the black and white of the type-written page, a link which is made more explicit by Quiss' Borgesian discovery that the castle in which they are imprisoned is in fact composed of text [Leishman 2009, n.p.].

When Leishman mentions Quiss' discovery, he is speaking literally. Quiss tears apart a section of the castle walls to discover that "on every surface so exposed a series of cut or engraved figures was revealed, arranged in lines and columns, complete with word breaks and line breaks and what looked like punctuation ... the stones, every one of them, all the tens of thousands of cubic metres the castle must be composed of, all those kilotonnes of rock were really saturated, filled full of hidden, indecipherable lettering" (44). Black-and-white imagery replicates itself across the expanse of the castle, where dark shadows and washed-out light spots interpenetrate each other like spilled paint, and on the plain, which the snow has made completely white. It also recurs in the other two plotlines, where a tangle of references to black chalk on white canvas, black and white clothing, and public places with names like "The White Hart" tie each plotline to itself and to the other two (3–4, 63, 67, 147, 155–156).

As we have seen, *Walking on Glass*—which, like *The Wasp Factory*, ultimately refuses to resolve the question of whether or not the non-mimetic elements in its plot are the products of feverish imaginations—connects the aspects of gameplaying and metafiction together because, within the novel's plot structure, one is the other. Ultimately, the gamers/gamed of *Walking on Glass* are we readers, who have to negotiate the meaning-making engine of the story while Banks' narrative persona complicates its workings through a constant foregrounding of the ultimate reality of all fiction: that every story is a puzzle because every life is, and that the games we at once play and suffer are the same we play and suffer in our lives. And if things don't make perfect sense, if the characters' paths remain impervious to unambiguous resolution, it's worth considering that these difficulties reflect the reality of our existence more than a clean tie-up of carefully engineered plot-strands would.

The remaining two techniques—the resonance with other stories and the construction of byzantine plot structures—find a good embodiment in *The Bridge*. Both are connected to the influence that Gray's *Lanark* exerted on the novel, an influence immediately apparent when we look at the circumstances of the story's protagonists: John Orr is a foundling, fished out of the water under the eponymous bridge, a titanic construct spanning the expanse of a great river that separates an unnamed City and an equally nameless Kingdom. The bridge is extremely long, and Orr can't see where it ends on either side (32). Because he is a foundling, and because he remembers nothing of his life before the bridge, he has been given the name he has—"John" because it's a very common name, and "Orr" because, so we're told, it was the first name starting with an O that the nurses at the hospital could think of.[20] The letter O comes from "a large, livid, circular bruise on my chest, an almost perfect circle stamped on my chest" (25). Orr lives a comparatively good life on the bridge, although the absence of any recollection of the time before he was found troubles him. And something else haunts his existence: when he goes home to the apartment he has been given by the bridge's authorities, his television will frequently and without prompting display the black-and-white image of a man lying comatose in bed in a hospital room. At times, people visit this man, and at times nurses walk in to check on him. Otherwise, the man remains immobile, merely breathing through the days of his life (40–41). This man's name is Alex Lennox, and he is John Orr's original self in the real world, trapped in a coma in the wake of a terrible accident on the Firth of Forth Bridge (1–3).[21]

Like *Lanark*, *The Bridge* gives us the parallel stories of two lives that are really one, and again like *Lanark*, it presents them to us in a complicated plot structure—three main parts entitled Coma (1–121), Triassic (125–243), and Eocene (247–376), each further divided into three sets of four chapters, each set of chapters collected under a permutation of the word "metamorphosis."[22] A brief Coda (377–386), in which Alex wakes up from his coma and John Orr vanishes, closes the book. The narrative pits John's life on the bridge and Alex's coma-induced recollections of his life in England and Scotland in an alternating rhythm, back to back as the chapters roll by and the two alter-egos of the same man explicate themselves and each other. In 1990, prompted by Ken MacLeod's advice, Banks would return to this sequence of alternating chapters to trace the two parallel paths of the same person's life in the rewritten *Use of Weapons*.

There are a couple of important structural differences between *Lanark* and *The Bridge*. The first resides in the generalized sense of hopefulness that, displayed in Banks, was missing in Gray: while Duncan Thaw and Lanark are locked in a connection without hope (Duncan is irredeemably dead by the time Lanark wakes up in Unthank), Alex Lennox and John Orr are linked by an ultimately solvable thread of suspended existence whose connective tissue is the hallucination—or alternate reality—of a deeply estranged place. For Alex, this place is the netherworld of coma, which in turn leads him to the otherworld of the bridge and his doppelganger, John Orr. Both Alex and John work their way through their worlds following plotlines that function as pocket versions of a *bildungsroman*, and whose ultimate goal is the psychological growth and physical healing of the original personality template, accomplished when, in the novel's last page, Alex wakes up unified and in full possession of his faculties.

The second difference resides in the figure of the Barbarian, a comedic take on Robert E. Howard's Conan who speaks in a hilarious Scottish brogue and carries on his shoulder a familiar that simultaneously talks to him in perfectly cultivated English[23] and keeps defecating down his back. The Barbarian is one of John Orr's many dream-selves, the one that comes out at night when John isn't dreaming of the man on the bed, and his exchanges with the familiar take on a superego-versus-id quality that identifies them as a microcosm of a larger relationship—in other words, the Barbarian behaves very much like a personification of Alex/John's subconscious. In the coda, he collapses when John Orr disappears, immediately before Alex wakes up.

As we have seen from the brief analysis above, once we begin examining the plot structures, literary borrowings, character profiles, and thematic concerns of Banks' first three novels it becomes impossible to classify them exclusively as mimetic. Their constant refusal to identify themselves as belonging to any one single mode of writing, as well as the pervasive gameplaying taking place between writer, characters, and reader, rob us of a definitive resolution, and the explicit presence of non-mimetic tropes, both as integral elements of the plot and as metatextual references to other works of fantastic literature, further distance us from pure realism.

Perhaps the most important among Banks' fantastic infusions concerns his use of doubles, twins, and doppelgangers. Several critics have pointed out the presence of doubles and doubling practices, first in *The Wasp Factory* (Butler 1999) and then in Banks' opus as a whole (March 2002; Colebrook 2010; Macdonald 2013; Jones 2013). The double/twin/doppelganger aspect is particularly important because this theme is central to the birth of *fantastika*, a term coined by John Clute "to describe the armamentarium of the fantastic in literature as a whole, encompassing science fiction, Fantasy, fantastic horror and their various subgenres" (*SFE* 2014, n.p.). Fantastika, Clute argues, is the mode of writing that came into being when, sometime after 1750, "a new kind of anxiety began to haunt the Western World: a fear that the engines that we made to turn the world might shake us off, that we were both responsible for that engine, and usurped by it, that Progress was not only a Process we might predict, but a Dark Twin grinning at us out of tomorrow" (Clute 2011, 3–4). As literary figures in late 20th-century fantastika, the characters in Banks' first three novels have plenty of Dark Twins grinning at them from tomorrow—and from right now, and from yesterday, and from other places that may or may not exist exclusively inside their minds. Frank Cauldhame is haunted by his brother Eric (who, like Frank himself, is mentally warped and prone to violence) and by Frances, his true identity—it turns out at the end of *Factory* that Frank hadn't lost his manhood in an accident; he'd been born a girl, and his father had decided to improvise a sex-change operation out of sheer misogyny (171–178). Quiss and Ajay in *Walking on Glass*, on the other hand, find a doppelganger in Steven Grout, whose conviction that he is a fallen warrior from another plane of reality closely mirrors theirs, as does the gameplaying in which he has to engage in order to find the way out. And of course, Alex Lennox and John Orr in *The Bridge* are mirror versions of each other, their doubling further complicated by the presence of the Barbarian, who rises from the depths to haunt both with gleeful energy.

Another fundamental signifier of doubling is represented by Banks' ubiquitous metafictional playfulness, which resulted in the metatextual references to other works of fiction—many of which constitute a good cross-section of fantastika over the last one hundred and fifty years—embedded in all three novels. We have already witnessed the doppelganger influence that *Lanark* exerted on *The Bridge*. *The Wasp Factory*, for its part, channels four— *The Tin Drum* (one of Banks' early literary influences), Gore Vidal's 1968 novel *Myra Breckinridge*, Shelley's *Frankenstein*, and Stevenson's *The Strange Case of Dr. Jekyll and Mr. Hyde*. The first two are explicitly referenced in chapter 3, within which they function as warnings of Frank's true identity,[24] while the other two are buried deep inside the novel's structure, providing much of its rhythm, its focus, and its preoccupation with altered perceptions. As Andrew Butler points out (1999, 19–20), the homage to *Frankenstein* involves a doubling between characters: while Victor Frankenstein is at once father and mother to his unnamed creation, Angus has to be at once father and mother to a son *and* a daughter. Also, like Victor's child, Frank/Frances is the monstrous result of a procedure poised far on the brink of Gothicism. The connection to *The Strange Case*, on the other hand, focuses exclusively on Frank/Frances: like Henry Jekyll and Edward Hyde, Frank and Frances are the two facets of the same character, one of which has been given life through the use of a concoction—Jekyll's potion in Stevenson, Angus' male growth hormones in Banks. In *Factory*, however, the polarity is reversed and the hidden doppelganger is the saner and less violent of the two.

Walking on Glass, on the other hand, references texts that share a common concern with gaming as the Twin of a non-mimetic storytelling process. In the tortuous topography and maddened hierarchy of the Castle of Bequest—mirrored in the other two plotlines by the intricate deception of which Graham is a victim and by the endlessly winding paths of Steven's room—we find powerful echoes of castle Gormenghast in Mervyn Peake's *Titus Groan* (1946), as well as the analogous structure in Kafka's *The Castle* (1926). The three plotlines' often anguished unspooling and their eventual convergence seems to replicate the structure of Borges' *Labyrinths*, and especially of two stories in the collection—"The Garden of Forking Paths" and "The Library of Babel," the latter perhaps constituting the one symbol representing the novel entire as "a perfectly inescapable heterocosm of text" (Leishman 2009, n.p.). Lastly, the aspects of judgment and condemnation built into the fabric of the novel find a counterpart in Kafka's *The Trial* (1925). But it's not simply by virtue of their thematic and structural similarities to *Walking on Glass* that these works of fantastika are relevant to it. If Quiss had made a Borgesian discovery at the beginning when he demolished part of the walls and found them made of books, Ajayi experiences another similar epiphany at the end when, looking at the shattered legs of the small table on which she and Quiss had been playing their games, she finds that these are also made of books, and that these books are written in English. Their titles are "*Titus Groan ... The Castle, Labyrinths, The Trial....* And another book, which had the title page missing." Ajayi decides to read this nameless book, and the chapter ends with the first sentence: "He walked through the white corridors..." (332–333). This is the sentence that sets into motion *Walking on Glass* itself when, at the beginning of the first chapter, we are introduced to Graham Park (3). We have come full circle, back to the beginning of every plotline's quest for knowledge, escape, and meaning, and we have found that everything is story, and that story haunts us. The plotlines, "instead of achieving coalescence ... remain an impossible mismatch of parasitical and competing truths" (Leishman 2009 n.p.), but still we have to deal with them somehow. The interpenetration between words, symbols, stories, games, quests, and the judgment that comes with them is complete, constructing an engine of meaning whose every word seems to diffract into a cacophony of mutually exclusive messages. And we still have to deal, because the Twin won't leave us alone until we have faced it.

If we consider that the doppelganger and the darkened twin "begin to nurse their injuries throughout fantastika ... because the Twin is what we leave behind when life moves so fast we cannot remember where we come from" (Clute 2011, 24), then the mimetic content of his first three novels comprises a thin veneer of realism under which the cauldron of the non-mimetic seethes, threatening to overflow like the dams Frank Cauldhame builds on the beach on top of his doomed toy settlements. There are plenty of amnesias in these novel—Frank and Angus', Quiss and Ajay and Steven's, Alex Lennox and John Orr's—and amnesia is what gives birth to the awful secret that is also the buried Twin who glares at us through the mask of the mundane. This is important. Iain Banks did not write exclusively mimetic fiction with *The Wasp Factory*, *Walking on Glass*, and *The Bridge*—he wrote a blend of the mimetic and of fantastika, which is another way of saying that, stifled in his aspiration to bring his SF to the reading public, he went one level deeper, accessing the more inchoate repository of non-mimetic story that fuels the visions of the three main genres of fantastic fiction: fantasy, horror, and SF. Fantastika is what we get when we access non-mimetic writing without genre, before the time the entertainment industry provided the pageantry that obscured the fundamental scaffolding. Banks had wanted to publish science fiction and he'd been rejected, so he wrote a trilogy of brutal, livid, sleek Trojan horses that, like the many Twins that lurk hidden in their pages, wormed their way into Macmillan's mainstream catalogue and from there, still masked, into the hands of millions of readers.

Even in the thick of his foray into these subversive, fantastika-scarred embodiments of not-wholly-mainstream writing, Banks hadn't forgotten the Culture. There are moments in *The Wasp Factory*, *Walking on Glass*, and *The Bridge* when the invisible hand of the author plucks at a chord that, in retrospect, one recognizes as echoing something of Banks' default Culture voice. *The Wasp Factory* features Frank Cauldhame's occasional reflections on morality, racism, and personal freedom,[25] but while these reflections do carry some weight in general terms, the personality broadcasting them is so warped that it's all but impossible to take them at face value. More relevantly, the revelation that Frank is Frances and that she became he because of a homegrown science experiment connects us to the practice, widespread in the Culture, of voluntary sex change. The difference in circumstances—in the Culture, the change is always completely successful, entirely reversible, and bioengineered inside the individual from birth—lies at the heart of Banks' conviction that the ability to switch between genders at will is essential to the creation of a more just society—once one has lived as both man and woman, misogyny becomes substantially more difficult to embrace.

Walking on Glass features clearer borrowings from Banks' as-yet unpublished body of work, largely thanks to the prominence of its explicitly science fictional elements. Some of the more obvious examples are Slater's attempts at crafting plots for SF stories strongly echoing the playfulness of the Culture plotlines, while a subtler instance of quasi–Culture talk occurs during a party: at one point, when the discussion drifts in the direction of the upcoming election, Slater explodes in an energetically entertaining leftist rant that lays out some of the basic political ideas around which Banks had decided to shape the Culture's ethos (208–212). Perhaps the most vivid example, however, comes when Graham reflects on Slater's expanded views on politics, ethics, and justice:

> His philosophy of life, he said, was founded on Ethical Hedonism. This was the moral system virtually every decent, unblinkered, reasonably informed human able to scrape together a quorum of neurons lived by, but they didn't realise it. Ethical Hedonism recognized that one had to enjoy oneself when one got the chance to these days, but that rather than immerse oneself totally in such diversions, one ought always to behave in a reasonable and reasonably responsible manner, never losing sight of the more general moral issues and their manifestations in society. "Have fun, be nice, veer left, and never stop *thinking*, is what it boils down to," Slater had said [269].

Banks is serious here; in Slater's beliefs, we can recognize some of his own, which would soon appear in the Culture novels. But his tongue is in his cheek, too. While the philosophy of life Slater embraces dovetails fairly well with Banks', Slater himself is a signally poor embodiment of those beliefs—he's a dissembler and a liar, happy to play games with someone else's feelings, and despite his strong leftist arguments, the reason why he plays that game is to protect the reputation and the political career of his Tory father. By putting those views in the mouth of a fundamentally untrustworthy character, Banks problematizes them, placing them under scrutiny as yet another ideological position—worthier than others, maybe, but still imperfect and subject to error, betrayal, and myopia. And *Walking on Glass* would by no means be the only text in which Banks questioned his own worldview; in fact, such questioning would become one of the key elements in the Culture's ethos.

The Bridge, on the other hand, features the presence of the Culture's ethos by the paradoxical virtue of its absence—in other words, the worlds inside which John Orr and Alex Lennox are stuck (and there's no escape from either) represent instances of those dystopias whose poisonous workings the Culture intends to either alleviate or stop in their tracks. While John finds, in the first half of the novel, that life as a ward of the bridge's government can be pleasant,[26] he discovers soon enough how arbitrarily awarded—and easily revoked—those privileges are (166–185). Even before that time, he is repeatedly made fully aware of the restrictiveness of the bridge's social mores, most glaringly when he witnesses the reaction of his friend Brooke to the unannounced flyby of three aircraft that scares and outrages many of the bridge's affluent citizens (52–56). Later in the novel, and in the aftermath of his fall from social grace, John steals away inside one of the trains that repeatedly leave the bridge in either one of two directions—the City or the Kingdom—and embarks in a mock-fantasy quest without grail or destination (233–243). The landscape that reveals itself to him on his journeys is an utter contrast to the world of the bridge: it's rural and savage, green and lush but oddly depressing, and while the society of the bridge was structured around a totalitarian bureaucracy of Kafkaesque intricacy, this place is given over to chaos and civil war. A particularly chilling figure in this part of John Orr's world is the Field Marshal, a warlord who rides on a train from battle to battle and who is in the habit of throwing screaming POWs into pools of boiling mud (302–315).

While John negotiates his deadly fantasyland, Alex remains mired in nothing more exotic than Great Britain in the mid–1980s, which is the exact nature of his problem. Two years after *The Bridge*, upon publication of *The Player of Games*, Banks would present, with the Empire of Azad, a funhouse-mirror version of the "loadsamoney factory farm solitude that is modern Britain" (Clute 1995c, 99), carefully engineered to be at once too close to the original for comfort and too hateful to be allowed to remain standing (which it doesn't). But in 1986 he didn't have the luxury of a fully non-mimetic palette, so he had to make do with what was actually there. It was enough: in witnessing the unspooling of Alex's comatose remembrances we find out that he, who shares Banks' left-wing beliefs, is haunted by a nearly unholy ability to make money and prosper in the deadly Thatcherite dream his author so despised, while at the same time he struggles with the open relationship that the love of his life, a woman by the name of Andrea Cramond, insists on living. Alex's adversary, a Frenchman living in Paris whom he has never met, haunts his memories throughout the novel like the Dark Twin he actually is, a mirror of his own desire for Andrea that, for pretty much the same reasons, he can neither forgive nor blame (252–278). The shadow of the Culture looms large here, in terms of both its economic setup—a moneyless utopia without exploitation—and its social relations—people are free to connect and disconnect as they please without externally imposed guilt, resentment, or shame.

The imagery Banks utilizes in *The Bridge*, as well as the characters that populate its many environments, would return in the Culture stories. The heavily urbanized, industrial dystopias of the bridge and of contemporary Britain would morph into similarly structured societies in the aforementioned *Player of Games*, in *The State of the Art* (1989), in *Use of Weapons* (1990), *Matter* (2008), and *Surface Detail* (2010), while the war-torn chaos of the countryside John Orr visits in the second part of the novel would reappear in *Use of Weapons* and *Matter* again, as well as in *Look to Windward* (2000). Like his mentor Alasdair Gray, Banks was deeply concerned with the fate of people trapped in the workings of the multifarious world machines we have managed to erect here on Earth, which was why he'd created the Culture to begin with. But until 1987, the Culture wasn't available to him as a public outlet, so he recreated those world machines within a *faux*-mimetic literary environment for the consumption of readers who might have wrinkled their noses at books explicitly labeled "science fiction," "fantasy," or "horror." But when *Consider Phlebas* finally saw print, everything changed.

2

THE CULTURE MILITANT
Consider Phlebas

By 1987, when the rewritten *Consider Phlebas* saw publication, Iain Banks was an established literary figure in non-genre circles. He'd also become fairly well known as the kind of writer who was always Up To Something, always working to create intricate metatextual games running inside complex plot-devices. It's not surprising, therefore, that his first Culture novel should set the tone for those that followed by continuing this trend: in its first appearance, the Culture starts out as the adversary in a sprawling galactic conflict, classic space opera's "comsymp hive of baddies" antagonist to the novel's protagonist and to the civilization that employs him as a mercenary (Clute 1995b, 28). *Phlebas* was also the first novel to come out under the name Iain M. Banks—Macmillan had requested this addition as a way to distinguish his genre novels from the non-genre ones (Clute 1995a, 28). In the long run, this doubling in publishing identity would saddle Banks with a doppelganger figure of sorts and, worse, provide him with a fairly constant source of irritation for being a useful tool in the hands of those interested in keeping SF separate from mainstream fiction.[1]

Part of the problem also consisted of the mode of SF that Banks had chosen to write. When Wilson Tucker issued his now famous condemnation of space opera as "hacky, grinding, stinking, outworn, spaceship yarn" in 1941 (qtd. in Pringle 2000, 35), the subgenre wasn't even twenty years old, yet it already appeared exhausted. For all its insistence on grand vistas of space, mighty technological constructs, and universe-shaking events, space opera seemed juvenile, shackled to formulaic plots, and possessed of a simplistically anthropocentric ethos that saw the universe as fundamentally comprehensible by humans because it had been made *for* humans. And since the universe was really ours to play with, so space opera held, it would be welcoming of traditional human power structures—empires, oligarchies, patriarchies,

Victorian-capitalist machineries, satrapies of various superficial hues—and dichotomies—human and machine, human and (subordinate or doomed enemy) alien, male and (subordinate) female, good and evil.

The subgenre endured, however. For all its faults, audiences treated it as the guilty pleasure it was and kept reading. Also, it proved capable of growth: it followed the gradual maturation of science fiction at large from its early pulp-magazine days to the *Analog* golden age of the 1940s and '50s, all the way to the New Wave of the 1960s and early '70s. Throughout those years, it gave us gems like Arthur C. Clarke's *Childhood's End* (1953), Alfred Bester's *The Stars My Destination* (1956), and Cordwainer Smith's stories of the Instrumentality of Mankind, so that by the time Brian Aldiss, who had previously defined the subgenre's writing style as "Widescreen Baroque,"[2] wrote his introduction to the 1974 collection *Space Opera: An Anthology of Way-Back-When Futures*, he had a slightly more flattering, appropriately nostalgic description to provide:

> Science Fiction is a big muscular horny creature, with a mass of bristling antennae and proprioceptors on its skull. It has a small sister, a gentle creature with red lips and a dash of stardust in her hair. Her name is Space Opera.... Science fiction is for real. Space opera is for fun. Generally. What space opera does is take a few light years and a pinch of reality and inflate thoroughly with melodrama, dreams, and a seasoning of screwy ideas.... [It is] heady, escapist stuff, charging on without overmuch regard for logic or literacy, while often throwing off great images, excitements, and aspirations [xi].

Nineteen seventy-four was also the year the last of the great New Wave space operas, M. John Harrison's *The Centauri Device*, saw print. Beginning in the mid-'60s, writers like Samuel Delany, Aldiss, and Harrison had begun re-crafting space opera into renewed shapes. Novels like Aldiss' *The Dark Light Years* (1964), Delany's *Babel-17* (1966) and *Nova* (1968), and *The Centauri Device* treated the vastnesses of the subgenre as playgrounds for the artist's imagination, great star-spangled canvases against which a mature writer could craft aesthetically rich narratives. The space operas of the 1960s and '70s purposefully ramped up the melodrama and the screwy ideas in order to encourage readers to view them primarily as artistic enterprises and aesthetic constructs. They also injected previously unknown levels of complexity into their characters' interactions, casting the intricacies of the human psyche against the backgrounds of star-fields, nebulas, and hyperspatial planes of reality. More than once, those vast spacescapes became Rorschach tests against which the characters projected their desires and fears, thus allowing space opera to meaningfully import J. G. Ballard's inner space into its outer-space territories.

It was those renewed shapes Banks found when he began reading science fiction. The writers of the New Wave who dabbled in space opera showed him that it was possible to utilize classic adventure plot structures and explode them to problematize and ultimately reverse the simplistic ethos they underwrote, marrying large-scale action scenes to advanced forms of literary expression. Speaking to James Rundle in 2010, Banks remembered:

> I just loved the scope of it—again, to quote Mr. Aldiss, he came up with "widescreen baroque space opera," that was brilliant! And there were a lot of things that I was trying to do with it, to use a fairly epic format to demystify, to bring it down from heroes and princesses to the level of the grunts ... I love space opera and I love the opportunity it gave me to work a huge canvas. I also felt that there was a moral high ground in space opera, and I wanted to reclaim it for the Left! I was fed up with reading these otherwise enjoyable books that ultimately turned out to be ultra-capitalist, or almost proto-fascist at times. I wasn't having this [n.p.].

Banks did reclaim the moral high ground for the left, and he did demystify the garish glamour of space opera, but that wasn't all. He also rejuvenated the entire subgenre, which had spent the intervening years in limbo, sidelined by the emergence of more contemporary modes such as, for example, cyberpunk (Langford 2005, 170; Rundle 2010, n.p.). In the years after *Phlebas'* publication, as Banks kept adding novels to the Culture series, a number of writers followed him into the faraway territories, each providing new viewpoints, new stimuli, and a new appreciation for the craft of writing space opera in the information age. Vernor Vinge, Colin Greenland, Paul McAuley, Charles Stross, Ken MacLeod, Lois McMaster Bujold—they and many others either followed in the footsteps of *Consider Phlebas* or, if they had already published space opera before its appearance (Vinge and Bujold, for example), found that the post-*Phlebas* market had become more receptive to their material than it had been before. The novel ended up being, among other things, something of a trailblazer.[3]

It's a heavy title to lug around, *Consider Phlebas*. The injunction comes from section IV—"Death by Water"—of T. S. Eliot's *The Waste Land* (1922):

> Phlebas the Phoenician, a fortnight dead,
> Forgot the cry of gulls, and the deep sea swell
> And the profit and loss.
>   A current under sea
> Picked his bones in whispers. As he rose and fell
> He passed the stages of his age and youth
> Entering the whirlpool.
>   Gentile or Jew
> O you who turn the wheel and look to windward,
> Consider Phlebas, who was once handsome and tall as you [16].

2. The Culture Militant

"Phlebas," Banks commented in a 1994 interview with *Science Fiction Chronicle*, "is the drowned Phoenician sailor in T. S. Eliot's 'The Waste Land,' which is my favourite poem, if you exclude Shakespeare." While Eliot's politics appalled Banks, he still thought of the Modernist poet as a "genius" and of *The Waste Land* as his "masterpiece"; plus, he liked the sound of the title (Melia 1994, 7).

The resonances between Banks' novel and Eliot's poem are relevant to *Phlebas*' very structure. Both writers, in Banks' phrasing, "use a fairly epic format to demystify [it], to bring it down from heroes and princesses to the level of the grunts"; Eliot demystifies the epic format of the quest for the Holy Grail, Banks the epic format of space opera, which, like many other romance genres, models its plotlines after the quest-patterns in the great heroic cycles of Western culture. The Big Dumb Object, the Lens, the Kwisatz Haderach, the intelligent mega-weapon asleep at the heart of the galaxy, the planet that feels, the Ship Who Sang, and their myriad cousins are the Holy Grails of space opera. Finding and using—owning—them, or at least receiving the truth they bring, turns the universe in the same way finding the Grail turns the song: it's an instant of wholeness that heals the wounds of the world and allows us to glimpse the vista of greater places and mightier times. And maybe those mightier times are not ours to own, but it is enough to know that our descendants will possess them, in the aftermath of the unstoppable human hegira into the depths of creation that, as foretold, no alien hand can tame. This is the promise of space opera.

And Banks, as he himself said, wasn't having it. The title *Consider Phlebas* is indeed a prophecy, but it is a prophecy of failure. It is also a warning: Phlebas the Phoenician is irrevocably sundered from the Grail Quest in *The Waste Land*, and so is Bora Horza Gobuchul, the protagonist of Banks' novel upon whose shoulders the burden of Phlebas' destiny rests—"for there is no miracle of the Grail for Semites, according to Mr. Eliot. So with the protagonist of this novel. Though no hint of racism ever begins to touch *Consider Phlebas*, the title *does* inescapably evoke an exile that is unredeemable, a death without point. The hero of Banks' book—let us make this absolutely clear—is Phlebas. And he is as utterly doomed as Phlebas to a useless death, sans Grail" (Clute 1995b, 29). Banks himself commented on the necessity to have Horza die:

> For the first few weeks that I was planning the book Horza didn't die; in fact at first he won.... Then as I thought through the story I decided he couldn't win; it didn't feel right ... I thought, shit no; he's got to die; it'll feel like a children's story if he doesn't. The whole burrowing, obsessive movement of the story was pushing toward just that result [Melia 1994, 42].

But before we get to the doomed knight, we have to see the Grail. The novel's prologue introduces us to it—a nameless Culture warship, vacuum-ridden and without crew, desperately built out of the cannibalized parts of other craft and sent out into the galaxy to possibly escape the destruction of its parent dockyard and reach friendly space. Nestled at the heart of the vessel's motley collection of force-fields, armor plates, and sensor arrays is the treasure, "the vastly powerful—though still raw and untrained—Mind around which [the dockyard] had constructed the rest of the ship" (3). When hostiles intercept the warship a few days after it has departed the doomed dockyard, the Mind inside opts for the only course open to it other than capture—a risky hyperspace jump directed at a nearby planet. When its pursuers find out what it did, they find themselves at an impasse: the planet is called Schar's World, and they cannot land or even get near it because "it was one of the forbidden Planets of the Dead" (5). For the time being, the mind is safe.

The Grail is now in its niche, both hard to capture and difficult to rescue because guarded by God—God, that is, in the shape of the Dra'Azon, one of the galaxy's elder civilizations. Upon reaching civilizational peak hundreds of thousands of years before, the Dra'Azon had decided to Sublime:

> Subliming was an accepted if still somewhat mysterious part of galactic life; it meant leaving the normal matter-based life of the universe behind and ascending to a higher state of existence based on pure energy. In theory, any individual—biological or machine—could Sublime, given the right technology, but the pattern was for whole swathes of a society and species to disappear at the same time, and often the entirety of a civilization went in one go … to Sublime was to retire from the normal life of the galaxy. The few real rather than imagined exceptions to this rule had consisted of little more than eccentricities [*Look to Windward*, 164–165].

In the case of the Dra'Azon, these eccentricities consist in picking out and cordoning off planets whose dominant species committed civilizational suicide, either through war or environmental mismanagement. Schar's World attracted the Dra'Azon's attention when its inhabitants annihilated themselves with biological weapons eleven thousand years before the beginning of *Phlebas*. Now a Planet of the Dead, it is kept in pristine condition inside a so-called "Quiet Barrier"; the Dra'Azon won't allow anyone anywhere around it unless invited (90–91). The Mind, which the Dra'Azon allowed to pass because it was in distress (92), now resides inside the military Command System of one of Schar's World's long-gone nations. This Command system is a huge network of subterranean train stations and rail lines, including the trains themselves (90–91). When its pursuers try to send a recovery team to the surface of Schar's World, the Dra'Azon attack them immediately (25).

The knight on the quest for the Grail, inside whom the curse of Phlebas waits for release like a secret poison sac, appropriately makes his appearance immediately after the prologue. Bora Horza Gobuchul is a Changer,[4] member of a declining species of humanoids that can alter their appearance at will to mimic the form of any other humanoid race. He is fighting the Culture for two reasons: first, because the Changers as a whole are fighting against it. Some time before the beginning of the war, their asteroid homeworld had ended up drifting inside the sphere of influence of the Culture's adversaries, the Idirans—a militantly religious race of functionally immortal, tripodal giants vaguely resembling overgrown preying mantises. The Idirans do everything loudly; their voices hurt human ears, as do even simple shipboard alarms, and their steps boom against the metal plates of their ships' corridors like doom bells. They are zealots, owners of a vast empire of violently subjugated species to whom they bring their God's often-brutal enlightenment. Resistance or simple lack of compliance triggers extermination (20–28; 403), so the Changers had little choice but to let themselves be employed as mercenaries and spies in the war against the Culture.[5]

And yet Horza works for the Idirans without complaint—enthusiastically, even, which brings us to the second reason. "I don't care how self-righteous the Culture feels, or how many people the Idirans kill," he tells Balveda, a captured Culture agent. "They're on the side of life—boring, old-fashioned, biological life; smelly, fallible, and short-sighted, God knows, but *real* life. You're ruled by your machines.... The worst thing that could happen to the galaxy would be if the Culture wins this war" (29). The Culture's decision-making routines, administrative duties, and high-level planning are indeed the province of the Minds, fully post-human AIs whose thought processes are several orders of magnitude faster, more complex, and more cogent than anything flesh sentients can muster. Their ships have crews but no captains, their orbitals and planets have populations but no rulers—the Minds run everything (86–87). It is this yielding to the machine that Horza can't countenance, and it is loathing of everything the Culture stands for rather than appreciation of the Idirans' cause that drives him to risk his life for his employers.

For the first hundred pages or so of *Consider Phlebas*, Banks appears to play the game of space opera to the letter, enriching it with plenty of highly skilled pageantry but otherwise seeming to remain within the ethos of the classic template. The Culture presents itself to us through its machinery first and foremost, which in classic space opera terms means that it's evil—the rise of machine sentience almost invariably triggers homicidal wars against flesh sentients. The prologue contains no Culture biologicals, either human-shaped or otherwise; only the Minds and the massive space-dwelling artifacts they reside within are in evidence. And when chapter one gives us the first Culture human—Balveda—she is accompanied by yet another living machine: a knife missile (13).

The Idirans, on the other hand, appear mainly through the character of Xoralundra, the officer in charge of the mission that captures Balveda. Aside from ordering the annihilation from orbit of several cities on a planet whose ruling class had made the mistake of siding with the Culture, and apart from throwing some of his soldiers around like rag dolls, he seems like a nice guy. Uncommonly for an Idiran, he treats Horza with respect, possesses a good deal of tactical and strategic sense, and even displays a wry sense of humor—all good and proper space-opera mensch stuff, the raw matter out of which Those Who Have to Make Tough Decisions for the Common Good are built (20–26). He forces the Culture knife missile to self-destruct and captures the Culture agent, at which point we learn that it was the Culture that originally antagonized the Idirans. The latter were busy expanding their empire and converting heathens, to be sure, but they hadn't actually threatened any part of the Culture itself or initiated any hostile action against a Culture ship or Orbital. The Culture got in the way of the Idiran Empire because the former felt that the latter's expansionist drive needed checking (28).

So far so good, it seems, and everything as per instruction manual. The Culture is a machine-ruled, socialist collective of meddlesome bad guys, the Idirans are—cautiously speaking, and hedging one's bets a lot—the good guys, and Horza is their Dominic Flandry. Xoralundra has a mission for him: years before, Horza had been assigned to the Changer base on Schar's World,[6] whose establishment the Dra'Azon had allowed for their own unfathomable reasons. Xoralundra believes that they will let Horza back in on the strength of his previous dealings with them, so he tasks the Changer with capturing the refugee Mind (22). On condition that he and another Changer among the Schar's World complement, with whom he'd once had a relationship he wishes to rekindle, be allowed to opt out of the whole war in the wake of the mission's successful completion, Horza agrees.

True to form, complications ensue. A Culture General Contact Unit attacks the Idiran ship and captures it, but not before Xoralundra manages to put Horza inside a combat suit and eject him out of an airlock. Drifting in space, he is picked up by Captain Kraiklyn's Free Company, a bunch of mercenaries flying the starship *Clear Air Turbulence* (or *CAT*), which has a pedigree that would make the *Millennium Falcon* proud (56; 58–59). Forced to fight for his right to remain onboard, Horza kills his opponent and takes his place in the Company (44–50), all the while trying to figure out a way to return to his quest. Without little choice but to go along for the time being, he follows his new crew in a disastrous raid on a temple on a remote planet, during which several of the Free Company's members lose their lives (68–82). Determined to become the captain of the *CAT* by killing and impersonating Kraiklyn, Horza bides his time.

It is at this point that the first expressly dissonant note intrudes into the well-practiced melody that the novel is supposed to be playing for us. In a fashion similar to that of *The Bridge*, the plot of *Consider Phlebas* is parsed into a fairly complex chapter structure. This structure is arranged in such a way that, at irregular intervals, the narrative removes its focus from Horza's adventures to concentrate on characters belonging to the Culture. Three of these intervals, each called *State of play* and consecutively numbered one to three, feature a "Culture Referer" by the name of Fal 'Ngeestra. A fourth interval, *Interlude in darkness*, briefly zeroes in on the escaped Mind hiding in the tunnels of the Command System, while the fifth and final is not so much an interval as an epilogue, written in the form of three Appendices, a Dramatis Personae list of the surviving characters, and the epilogue itself.

We begin with *State of play: one* (85–95). A Culture Referer is a unique creature, "one of those thirty, maybe forty, out of … eighteen trillion who could give you an intuitive idea of what was going to happen, or tell you why she thought that something which had already happened had happened the way it did, and almost certainly turn out right every time. [Fal 'Ngeestra] was being handed problems and ideas constantly, being both used and assessed herself. Nothing she said or did went unrecorded; nothing she experienced went unnoticed" (87). Her role in the novel, foregrounded by the titles of the three sections where she appears, is that of master strategist. She is the great chess player, Ingmar Bergman's Death sitting in front of the board; she is the one flesh sentient in the novel who receives the most recent information on the chase for the Mind, and the one afforded the overall view not just of the action itself, but also of the strategic landscape surrounding it, short- and long-term. Because she truly is unique, she is unmatched. No such figure appears on the Idiran side, or in the Free Company. Every other character in the novel, with the exception of the Minds, is a pawn in the wargame Fal plays for the Culture.

In a standard space-opera context, Fal would be either a prisoner of the machine empire, forced under some sort of threat to betray her people, or the ultimate expression of that empire's inhuman reach—a machine herself, typically, frigid except for her hatred of flesh, working the mathematics of war like an immensely souped-up version of the W.O.P.R. from *Wargames* (1983). In *Consider Phlebas*, however, she is nothing like either. She is a happy, well adjusted, good-hearted flesh-sentient, and while her talent does warrant monitoring, those supposedly inhuman Minds have consented to let her indulge her favorite pastime—mountain-climbing—without any form of observation whatsoever. She lives in one of the thousands of Culture Orbitals in a beautiful house within easy reach of the mountains, and her machine companion, the drone Jase, cares for her with secret, avuncular love (89–90).[7] And Banks makes sure to immediately dispel any suspicion we might entertain that her status as the ultimate oddity among the flesh-and-blood component of the Culture's population is the reason for all the attention. With the exception of her talent, she is in fact pretty standard as far as Culture citizens go, both in terms of education and upbringing, and her essentially unlimited access to technologically highly advanced material goods and services is the rule in her society, not the exception (87).

As for the Minds, it becomes hard to see them as monsters after reading a passage like this one:

> The culture had placed its bets ... on the machine rather than the human brain. This was because the Culture saw itself as being a self-consciously rational society; and machines, even sentient ones, were more capable of achieving this desired state as well as more efficient at using it once they had.... Besides, it left the humans in the Culture free to take care of the things that really mattered in life, such as sport, games, romance, studying dead languages, barbarian societies and impossible problems [87].

The Minds, it turns out, don't hate flesh-sentients at all. They rather like us squishy bags of fluids, and the worst that can be said about their attitude is that every now and then it gets paternalistic. And when they find someone like Fal 'Ngeestra, someone "capable of matching and occasionally beating their record for accurately assessing a given set of facts," they react with amused fascination rather than contempt (87).[8]

So where's the dystopia? Where's the machine hive-mind that moves us folk like puppets, or the Perversion that, in Vernor Vinge's wonderful *A Fire Upon the Deep* (1992), makes otherwise independently-minded people speak like they're reading the minutes at a Central Committee meeting? Even Horza calls the Culture a capital–U Utopia, if a little sneeringly (28), and Kraiklyn speaks in awed tones of the amount of genetic tinkering that makes every flesh-sentient in it very long-lived, healthy, disease-free, resilient, beautiful by whatever standards are relevant to their body-type, and equipped with glands capable of, among many other things, prolonging orgasm to astonishing lengths and secreting into the bloodstream a wide variety of recreational drugs without any negative side effects (64). So maybe we get to yell at the Culture for being decadent, although admittedly we'd do it to mask the envy; that aside, by the time the first *State of play* interlude ends it has become impossible to stay on script and see it as an unalloyed evil society.

It has also become impossible to see Horza's mission as The One That Will Win Us the War, or Horza himself as anything other than Phlebas: as Jase tells Fal, if the Idirans were to lay their appendages on this Mind, their intelligence coup would extend the duration of the war by only a few months (93). This is the point in *Consider Phlebas* where the template of classic space opera collapses completely. Not only is the Culture surprisingly brutality-free for a machine-ruled civilization, and not only are the Idirans more than a little disappointing as good guys; the mission on which Xoralundra has sent Horza is nothing more than a sideshow. Instead of *Triplanetary* we have a topsy-turvy SF version of *Saving Private Ryan*, and instead of Kim Kinnison we have Captain Miller (or rather, we would if the Germans in Spielberg's movie had had an equivalent of Tom Hanks' character). Worst of all from Horza's point of view, he doesn't know any of this. Neither he nor his Idiran employers have realized that the Culture, which had hitherto been on the losing side, now stands a statistically overwhelming chance of winning—so much so, as we have seen above, that the Minds in the War Council have already established a likely timeline.

So, even before Horza gets to take control of the *Clear Air Turbulence* and bring the Free Company along to Schar's World, his Grail Quest is already void. We're not looking at the turning point of the war, nor are we witnessing the birth or rebirth of an individual consciousness with the power—and the implied manifest destiny that comes with it—to radically influence events. As Banks told James Rundle many years later, we're looking at a relatively minor engagement featuring mostly mercenary combatants and narrated mostly from the viewpoint of the grunts themselves. The *State of play* interpolations serve to, among other things, bring home to us readers how removed from the larger scheme of things all the characters except Fal and Jase are.

We might have guessed all of this earlier, though. Banks loved to sprinkle clues to his plans throughout his stories, and there are plenty in *Phlebas*. Balveda is a particularly honorable and independently thinking adversary, for one; she pleads for Horza's life when he gets captured at the beginning of the novel and does not relish having her allies reject her appeal (11–13). When Balveda in turn becomes a prisoner of the Idirans and Horza goes to visit her, the two trade justifications based on ideological positions, but it's clear that each respects the other (27–31). Horza himself empathizes with Balveda's plight as an agent of both Contact and Special Circumstances, and the insight he provides is revealing of the actual shape of the Culture's bias:

> Special Circumstances had always been the Contact section's moral espionage weapon, the very cutting edge of the Culture's interfering diplomatic policy, the élite of the élite, in a society which abhorred élitism.... It had about it too an atmosphere of secrecy (in a society that virtually worshipped openness) which hinted at unpleasant, shaming deeds, and an ambience of moral relativity (in a society which clung to its absolutes: life/good, death/bad; pleasure/good, pain/bad).... No other part of the Culture more exactly represented what the society as a whole really stood for, or was more militant in the application of the Culture's fundamental beliefs. Yet no other part embodied less of the society's day-to-day character [30].

Thus, Balveda is as much a pariah as anyone in the Culture is likely to get because, in her militant practice of her society's beliefs, she has become the paragon of everything it rejects. Like her fellow operatives, and like Special Circumstances itself, Balveda is now "the repository for the guilt the people in the Culture experienced because they had agreed to go to war in the first place" (30). She and Horza understand each other because they are both fundamentally alone, both inhabitants of that moral gray area in every war where two enemies look at each other and, willingly or not, recognize their own face in the one staring at them on the other side. Generally speaking, Balveda belongs to the Culture, but she is part of a subset that the main society looks at with fascinated horror. By the same token, Horza belongs into Idiran society only in the broadest terms; he is a Changer, and therefore part of a subset of the Idiran military that the rest looks at with suspicion and distrust.

So the culture does have a bias, and it does have an antipathy for certain behavioral and social categories, but the bias comes from guilt at its own inability to remain peaceful and interfere with Idiran expansion at the same time, and the antipathy is aimed at itself. It treats the embodiment of its own warlike tendencies like Henry Jekyll treats Mr. Hyde—a horrifying reflection in the mirror, a distorted Dionysian doppelganger it has to unleash but can't bring itself to fully embrace. And even then, even when the Culture does show up under the guise of Special Circumstances, the "unpleasant, shaming deeds" it supposedly commits conspicuously fail to produce piles of corpses, mass graves, razed cities, or brutalized civilians. No Culture machine or flesh sentient is seen committing, advocating, or even lending ideological support to any atrocity or war crime, and every bit of information we receive about the Culture does not reveal anything worse than what we witness the Idirans commit without so much as a second thought. In fact, as the novel progresses it's the Idirans that start looking progressively redder in tooth and claw. The way they treat their client species and allies in the war—the so-called Medjel—does nothing to endear them to us, and Horza's deeply ambivalent feelings toward them only reinforce the sense that some terrible misapprehension lays at the heart of his reasons for fighting by their side. He knows that most Idirans are fanatically hostile to all other species, and he knows that the vast majority of people in the Culture are precisely the opposite, yet he clings to his beliefs on the strength of his relationship with Xoralundra alone (307).

And then there is Phlebas; the curse of the moneylender shadows every step Horza makes from the very beginning. We are introduced to him as a prisoner of the Culture's allies, sentenced to death by drowning in a sewer cell, and the first thought that crosses his mind is the recollection of a passage in his Changer lover's favorite book back on Schar's World:

The Jinmoti of Bozlen Two kill the hereditary ritual assassins of the new Yearking's immediate family by drowning them in the tears of the Continental Emphataur in its Sadness Season [9].

Two deaths by water, then—one literal and the other meta-literary. The passage from this pseudo-book, which comes back to haunt Horza at regular intervals in the novel, is remarkable because it refers to his specific function (he kills those he impersonates), and also because it connects Phlebas and Horza's ultimate fate back to the Command System—which, because Schar's World is currently in an ice age, is essentially locked under continent-wide swathes of solidified water. The place where Horza is supposed to find his Grail is basically the same kind of drowning chamber inside which he began the story, and his memories of the time he spent on Schar's World with his Changer lover return to him only images of snow and death (299–301).

When, at the close of *State of play: one*, we return to Horza and the Free Company, the narrative devolves into a chaotic sequence of adventures with little seeming connection to the main objective. The *Clear Air Turbulence* ends up on a Culture Orbital called Vavatch, which the Culture itself is planning on destroying because it's about to fall within the still-expanding Idiran sphere of influence. There, Kraiklyn plans on robbing one of the tourist megaships that ply Vavatch's waters, and once again it all ends in disaster: yet more of the Free Company's members die for no gain at all (99–136), and Horza ends up on a small atoll where a sect of bizarrely primitivist islanders led by an obese, cannibalistic "Prophet" try to eat him. He escapes again (139–173) and reconnects with Kraiklyn in Evanauth, Vavatch's main city, where the captain of the *CAT* has come to play his favorite pastime, a game called Damage (185–206). When Kraiklyn is eventually kicked out of the game and leaves, Horza follows him and, after a brutal fight, murders him, taking on his appearance and returning to the *CAT* (206–225). There, he finds the remnants of the crew, including Yalson, a woman with whom he'd begun a relationship soon after becoming a member of the Company, and Balveda. The GCU had rescued Balveda from the Idiran cruiser, and Fal 'Ngeestra's invariably correct predictive faculties had sent her once again on a collision course with Horza's path. She is now posing as the Free Company's new recruit, inevitably unaware that the Kraiklyn in front of her is actually Horza. This gets her captured again, along with Unaha-Closp, a maintenance drone who remains trapped onboard the *Clear Air Turbulence* when Horza kicks the ship into high gear and exits the General Systems Vehicle (also GSV) *The Ends of Invention*, on-site to evacuate Vavatch's remaining population before the Orbital's scheduled destruction. The escape, a terrifying flight across and through most of the GSV's internal volume, culminates in a breach of the *Ends of Invention*'s outer hull, after which the *Clear Air Turbulence* finally heads for Schar's World and the tunnels of the Command System (229–266).

If the synopsis in the paragraph above of the roughly two hundred pages that *Phlebas* dedicates to Horza's spinning of wheels seems byzantine—which it is—it's because we're supposed to witness the gigantic post–Gothic machinery of space opera grind into action, and we're expected to find it thundering and boisterous. Space opera, as Stephen King once said of the Gothic itself, is "*PRETTY GODDAM LOUD!*" (274). If anything, it is even louder than the standard Gothic mode (whatever that is), because together with the intricate, clanking Rube Goldberg clockwork of the plot it gives us the spacescape of the whole universe to look out at while we listen to the noise. It may be going too far to say that the plots of space opera are mostly excuses to show us vistas of otherworlds, but that is definitely part of the job, and Banks, who disliked the politics but loved the view, knew that. *Phlebas* spends a lot of time spinning its wheels because that's part of the argument—if space opera is baroque and intricate without any particular reason other than to provide a few thrills, then a partly deconstructionist approach should in fact heap those aimless thrills upon one another and foreground the aimlessness. And since Banks is clearly having fun making stuff blow up, and because he likes to share the experience, we readers are having fun watching it all go. This is the good news.

The bad news, as John Clute points out, is that nearly two hundred pages' worth of freewheeling come close to losing us completely:

> The problems Iain "M" Banks had with *Consider Phlebas* ... lay not in any absence of space opera paraphernalia, which he was markedly un-chary of supplying in crates, or from a lack of stylistic muscle, because he is a writer jovial with energy, a jostler of material, a flexer. What flummoxed *Phlebas* had nothing to do with any failure of excess, but with the fact that his tale of self-destruction and futility constantly *argued* with the space-opera frame in which it took place, so that whenever Banks flexed his muscles he tended to break every bone in the book. It all made an unholy racket ... and *Consider Phlebas* ended up pounding the shit out of itself [1995c, 97].

Beginning with *The Player of Games*, the next novel in the series, Banks would learn to keep arguing with the format of traditional space opera without doing damage to the story. In *Consider Phlebas*, however, he indeed spends so much time making noise that we nearly get lost in it, and it's only his skills as a writer—his stylistic muscle, as Clute put it—that keep us coming back to the story and hanging on until we finally glimpse the plot again. We do get a few thematic pointers, though: throughout his lonely peregrinations in those two hundred pages, Horza is never far from water—literally. Between the mega-ship, the island of cannibals, and the fight with Kraiklyn, which takes place by the shore under the thundering jets of a hovercraft, water chases the Changer, lapping at his heels with the patience of a curse, which it is. Before long, the progression of events in the novel starts looking like the increasingly more frantic and inevitably doomed attempts of a drowning man to save himself. We also witness Horza's contempt for AIs when, while still on the island, he unnecessarily and without regret kills the mind of a shuttlecraft and flies the vehicle away on his own (168–173). In the middle of all the noise, we also get to briefly catch up with the Mind inside the Command system in *Interlude in darkness* (177–181), which serves the twin function of (1) reminding us that there still is a story to come back to and (2) of getting us to empathize with the prize everyone is looking for. Banks' description makes it clear that the Mind inside the tunnels isn't damaged—it's wounded. Its higher thought substrates are inoperable (i.e., it suffered a massive concussion), its field-manipulation faculties are partly compromised (i.e., its hands are mangled), and the tools it has to work with to set up a defense perimeter are, from the rarefied viewpoint of the Culture's technological state of the art, hopelessly crude. We get to look at its thought processes, which, even when forced to run at substandard speeds, still manage to convey the full dread and agony of having to hope in the face of overwhelmingly negative odds—otherwise how can one find the strength to survive? There's no Fred Saberhagen berserker here, and no Agent Smith right out of the *Matrix*'s most xenophobic routines; there is, on the other hand, a wounded soldier behind enemy lines, whistling in the dark while it tries to build a hiding place out of sticks and stones.

Immediately before *Phlebas* finally brings us back to the quest, *State of play: two* returns us to Fal 'Ngeestra. She worries about the Mind, about the mission, and about her role in shaping events—she even has time to briefly empathize with the Idirans before a child manages to upset her with a callous comment on the outcome of the conflict (he believes the Idirans will win; 274–275). Most of all, she worries about Balveda:

> She had stuck her neck out by insisting that Vavatch was the most likely place, and that the woman agent Balveda should be one of those to go there, and now it had all come true and she realised it wasn't really her neck she had stuck out at all. It was Balveda's [272].

Fal 'Ngeestra is as good-hearted and decent a human being as any of us are likely to meet either side of a work of fiction, but for all that, she *is* Death at the chessboard. Her decisions, whose consequences she never pays because, precious as she is, she's kept several thousand light-years away from the fighting, will spell doom for a lot of people, which eats away at her. Fal knows she's sending them to their death for the same reason she knew that Horza would be in Vavatch—she's a Referer. She can also see, much as she wishes things were otherwise, that she'll never get to meet Balveda, and that the Special circumstances agent won't survive the war. Fal also sees Horza's death, at least in the sense that, when she tries to zero in on an image of him, she can't do it—"The Changer did not seem real" (273). Horza, whose calling it is to take on the faces of others, doesn't seem to have a face of his own—that is to say, he doesn't have an identity. He is, after a fashion, already dead because there doesn't seem to be a set of core beliefs inside him to hold on to, or at least nothing more completely formed than his ideological hostility toward the Culture. This lack of foundation returns to haunt Horza more than once in the novel—most notably during Kraiklyn's game of Damage, when Horza literally loses his sense of self for a few moments (203–206), and in a dream while onboard the *CAT* on its way to Schar's World, when two ghostly, cloaked figures come for him and, after questioning his lack of beliefs, take his name from his head (296–297).

Finally, the *Clear Air Turbulence* gets to the edge of the Quiet Barrier, where it stops to ask the Dra'Azon permission to pass. "YOU MAY ENTER. THERE IS DEATH HERE. BE WARNED," a titan voice tells the Free Company, which now includes the drone Unaha-Closp and Balveda, whom Horza has spared (295). He does not heed the warning, however, and for the last time, everything turns to ash. Once on Schar's World and inside the tunnels of the Command System, Horza and his companions find the whole Changer complement murdered, including Horza's former lover. The remnants of the Idiran attempt to rush Schar's World in the wake of the Mind's escape—a few full-grown Idiran warriors and a number of Medjel—had crash-landed not very far from the Command System, and after a deadly march in the miserable cold, which had accounted for yet more among them, had reached the base. Once there, they'd killed all the Changers for no particular reason other than their contempt for anyone not Idiran, after which they'd begun hunting the Mind (371–374). When the Free Company comes within range, the Idirans attack them too (346–352), and once again the action devolves into a chaos of death and accident and capture and disaster, at the end of which Balveda recovers the Mind, now even more badly wounded than before, the equally badly damaged drone, and Horza's dying body. Everyone else, human and Idiran and Medjel, has died, including Yalson, who at the last moment sacrificed her life and that of the child in her womb—hers and Horza's—to save the Mind from Idiran fire.[9]

The novel proper ends with Horza's death under a starlit sky. After the one remaining Idiran soldier had used Unaha-Closp's body-case as a battering ram against his skull (438),[10] he'd never regained consciousness, and Balveda simply witnesses a letting go, a final release of his already slackened facial features indicating the departure of consciousness, forever. At the end, the Changer looks like a concoction of the bits of all those he'd impersonated during his life, and at the same time like nobody at all. His is a double death—a cessation of the biological processes of his life and an annihilation of the memory of it, because his life was either a blank or a shadow existence, subsumed and absorbed in those of the people he'd imitated (445–446).[11]

Phlebas is gone, and so is his quest. His allies, whom he'd been able to fool himself into seeing as honorable while he only had Xoralundra to deal with, are revealed to be nothing more than a gang of xenophobic bullies, cruel without reason and violent without point. There is no decency in

Xoxarle, the Free Company's temporary prisoner and main interlocutor in the hundred or so final pages of the novel. He killed the Changers on Schar's World because they weren't Idiran, and murdered everyone in the Free Company except Balveda and the drone despite being told—with proof—that Horza was his ally. "Fuck your animal soul," Xoxarle tells Horza at one point (359), in a sentence whose simplicity perfectly captures the Idiran attitude toward everyone who isn't them. The only mercy Horza receives comes from Yalson and Balveda, who are essentially Culture humans, and from Unaha-Closp, who helps him and tries to save his life despite Horza's contempt for its machine being (315).

For once, Fal 'Ngeestra can't help us see the details of what's coming. *State of play: three*, wedged between the chapters set on Schar's World, sees her back on top of a mountain, leg mostly healed and head clear of extraneous thoughts as she enters a meditative trance that she hopes will yield some insight into what might be happening. However, perhaps because she stands in the same freeze-dried water that buries Horza/Phlebas and everyone else inside the Command System, the insight the trance yields consists not of foresight concerning the Free Company's fate (although she does know that Horza will die), but rather of an appreciation of the Idirans' philosophical position with respect to the Culture's. Both societies were born out of trauma: the Culture is, in Fal's thoughts, a *"mongrel race,"* the end result of a *"rowdy upbringing full of greedy, short-sighted empires and cruel, wasteful diasporas,"* while the Idirans, originally a peaceful race of meditative creatures, had found themselves invaded thousands of years before the events in the novel, *"pawns in somebody else's squalid imperialism"* (333). But while the Idirans, pure and unique in their god's eyes even under their conquerors' repressive regime, favorite even in defeat, only learned the wisdom of preemptive brutality and neverending aggressiveness, the Culture, spatchcocked together out of myriad parts, drew from its beginnings the conclusion that the universe doesn't care, and that the meaning of one's life is ultimately shaped by one's own actions. We make our meanings as we go:

> *Everything about us, everything around us, everything we know and can know of is composed ultimately of patterns of nothing; that's the bottom line, the final truth. So where we find we have any control over those patterns, why not make the most elegant ones, the most enjoyable and good ones, in our own terms? Yes, we're hedonists.... We seek pleasure and have fashioned ourselves so that we can take more of it; admitted. We are what we are* [336].

In its fundamental underpinnings, this notion isn't at all far from Slater's philosophy of Ethical Hedonism in *Walking on Glass*; but while Slater is a liar who doesn't practice as an individual what he preaches in his public statements, Fal 'Ngeestra is citizen of a society expressly built on the pervasive observation of Ethical Hedonism. This is a galaxy without gods, and there's no doubt that, within *Consider Phlebas*' internal economy, the Idirans are worshipping at an empty altar; Banks makes this point before the novel's beginning through the use of an epigraphic passage from the Koran—"Idolatry is worse than carnage"—and continues to make it through his description of the island cannibals' inane, self-harming ritualistic practices. The only reason why the Idirans are what they are is that they decided, in the wake of their suffering, to become the same thing as their long-ago oppressors: religious zealots excused in their behavior by a self-concocted belief system. Their very expansionist drive is described as a jihad in *Phlebas* (455).

But it doesn't have to be this way. If space is cold and dead, technology can make it warm and alive. If the universe doesn't care, we can do so ourselves through an essentially altruistic system of ethics. If flesh-sentients are intrinsically less capable of developing this system of ethics than machine intelligence, then the distant descendants of the first self-aware AIs to which we gave birth will take over the running of our society and leave us free to enjoy ourselves without doing harm to others. If the only godlike beings are self-upgraded sentients originally born out of the same muck as everyone else, the implication is that it is indeed possible for us to be better than we once were. And if one among the thousands of races in the galaxy grows cancerous, swallowing other civilizations and digesting them to make them exactly like it (ironically, the Idirans are, in their Von-Neumann-machine brand of single-mindedness, more machine-like than the Culture), then we can choose to intervene.

The ethics of intervention and the final outcome of the war constitute the subject of *Consider Phlebas*' final part: the Appendices, the Dramatic Personae, and the Epilogue. Written from the point of view of the Culture's people, both its flesh and its machine citizens, and from a relatively distant future, these three sections telescope us readers away from the novel's ground zero and, going straight through Fal 'Ngeestra's more refined viewpoint as well, slingshot us up and out into galactic history (Fal herself is listed among the dramatis personae). For the first and only time in *Phlebas*, we get the space-opera view of the world, the action on D-Day from a plane flying high above the beaches. But it's a recording. The beaches are empty now, and there's nothing left to do but retrace the steps. It's all in the past. Also, as we should know by now, the territory looks nothing like the maps had led us to believe it would.

As Fal had correctly surmised, Balveda does not survive Schar's World—not really. She lives through the end of the novel and goes on to fight far and wide across the expanse of the war. At the end of the conflict more than forty years later (462), most of her friends have died, and her own mind is still on Schar's World, haunted by nightmares of dark tunnels. Eventually, unable to find peace, Balveda commits suicide (465). The other Culture survivors, both of the Command system and of the war, fare somewhat better, although everyone bears scars (466–467). Xoralundra, for his part, survives the GCU's attack and continues fighting in the war until his death in battle towards its end (465). The Command System on Schar's World, when the Culture finally goes back to it after the conflict, looks as if nothing ever happened there—with the exception of the debris and the bodies of the dead, which the Dra'Azon bury deep under the ice. At the bottom of the hyper-compressed pile of bodies and equipment lies a book, its first page open, and the story it tells begins with the line "*The Jinmoti of Bozlen Two…*" (467).

For Horza's people, on the other hand, there is only an epitaph: the Changers do not survive the conflict. They die to the last of their species, and the tides of war carry them away and into oblivion (467).

The final assessment of the origin, causes, and nature of the war rests in the hand of a group of Culture historians. The brief extracts from their pseudotextual *Short History of the Idiran War* gives the conflict an overview that, in its turn, opens up a fundamental window into the soul of the Culture as a collective. The Culture's post-scarcity industrial, technological, and scientific means, we read in the excerpts, put it "beyond considerations of wealth or empire … [it] had no need to colonise, exploit or enslave." The one need its people do have that cannot be satisfied from within the Culture itself is "the urge not to feel useless":

> The Culture's sole justification for the relatively unworried, hedonistic life its population enjoyed was its good works; the secular evangelism of the Contact section, not simply finding, cataloguing, investigating, and analysing other, less advanced civilisations but—where the circumstances appeared to Contact to justify so doing—actually interfering (overtly or covertly) in the historical processes of those other cultures…. Contact—and therefore the Culture—could prove statistically that such careful and benign use of [its resources] did work, in the sense that the techniques it had developed to influence a civilisation's progress did significantly improve the quality of life of its members, without harming that society as a whole by its very contact with a more advanced culture [451–452].

By virtue of its moral convictions, when the Idiran Empire's war-machine clanks into high gear, aimed at every civilization in its path, the Culture finds itself threatened not physically with destruction of territory and annihilation of life, but morally and ethically "with something more important: the loss of its purpose and that clarity of conscience; the destruction of its spirit; the surrender of its soul." Faced with such prospects, and however reluctant to employ military force, the Culture girdles itself for war, which in the fullness of time it wins decisively (452).

Thus the Culture scholars, who write the history of the Idiran War from the point of view of the winners, which is the only viewpoint we usually get.

But this pretend-historical overview comes at the end of a novel that showcases exactly what kind of values the other viewpoint held dear and exactly what they would have meant had it come out on top, and Banks' tricking us into initially supporting the bad side out of simple genre-based expectations, a ploy reminiscent of those Fredric Brown used to favor in such stories as "Sentry" (1954), deftly removes the ground from under our feet, leaving us in the uncomfortable position of having to face the questionable nature of assumptions we can no longer safely retract. By and large, space opera had always been forgiven its unexamined biases; it was fun and colorful, and provided it didn't try to think of itself as a serious literary mode, we left it alone to pretend that the hierarchies and the scarcity economies of the past could and should survive far along into the deep future and out among the vastnesses of space. But Banks wasn't having it; he'd learned too much from too many people, and he knew what he wanted. It's unlikely that *Consider Phlebas* will ever be regarded as among his best works, but warts and all, it remains a crucially valuable book, and for reasons that go beyond its simple status as the first Culture novel to see print. First of all, it's worth considering that, despite the vast amount of space the book dedicates to largely aimless freewheeling, the plot does come home to us in the end. The thread of story, frayed thought it is at the conclusion, still connects us to the basic message—to wit, that post-scarcity economies, machine-ruled collectives, and hedonistic techno-hippie commonwealths are not only not necessarily evil, but they can also be merged into a single society embodying all their traits and broadcasting them into an environment within which they can be made to work for the owners and the owned alike, until there's no difference between the two categories because owning loses its scarcity economy-derived meaning. To this day, the thought retains its revolutionary taste.

Secondly, and in connection to the first point, *Consider Phlebas* frees us from the obligation to obey the ubiquitous space-opera notion of the Great Human Hegira from Mother Earth of Long Ago, and that in the very same pages where the story seems to pay ultimate homage to it. Ken MacLeod explains:

> A galaxy filled with humans is another Golden-Age premise. What makes this book radically different from its ancestors is that the humans are not descended from us. It is completely given, within the story, that evolution has converged on the human form—close enough for sexual attraction, different enough to be mutually sterile—on countless worlds. No explanation is proffered, and no explanation could be remotely plausible. This is what is given, but consider what is taken. With one clean cut, all the tedious backstory of human expansion—generation ships, faster-than-light-travel, conquest and Empire—is gone. There is no need for an imagined future between her and there [2003a, 1].

Nor is there an actual future, per se. As always, the clues are there, but subtle enough that we may miss them altogether: the passages from *A Short History of the Idiran War*, we find out on their title page, are an "English language/ Christian calendar version, original text AD 2110, unaltered," and together with a number of other materials, they form "an independent, non-commissioned but Contact-approved Earth Extro-Information Pack" (447). Accordingly, the timeline of the Idiran War is given in Earth years throughout, at which point we discover how truly belated our apprehension of these events is. The first skirmishes between the Culture and the Idirans began in 1267 and continued in infrequent bursts until 1327, when the war proper started. This main phase lasted more than forty years, ending in space in 1367 and planetside in 1375—a total of slightly more than one hundred years of war across expanses that beggar the imagination while we on Earth were busy with the Crusades, the bubonic plague, the beginnings of our own laughably tiny century-long war, and God's plans for our self-evidently key role in shaping creation (461–462).

We've been contacted, in other words. Sometime in our future (the book was originally published in 2110, but when was it translated into English and distributed on Earth?), the Culture reveals itself to us and attempts, like they've done with countless techno-barbarian societies before, to teach us about the real state of things out there. Their hope is that we can be persuaded to be nicer to everyone else than we've thus far been to each other. Had Banks not inserted these tidbits of information, we bunch of unreconstructed anthropocentrists might have lulled ourselves into the comforting notion that the Culture exists in the distant future, and that, since it's largely a pan-human civilization, we plucky Earthlings might have had something to do with its formation—thus space opera again, in all its classic self-satisfaction.

But we didn't; the Culture exists right here, right now, and before as well. We've missed the party, and worse, we don't get to wrap ourselves in the flag of utopia. We had nothing to do with its birth, and if anything, we have a lot more in common with the Idirans. The punch to the gut is considerable, and more far-reaching in its implications than the space operas that had inspired Banks had been. The New Wave writers, as well as those that began publishing around the time Banks did, still retained the notion of Earth as the starting point (even when it's only a backwater, as is the case in *The Centauri Device*), and of our free-market economy as the engine that powers the expansion into the galaxy—a key example in this case would be C. J. Cherry's beautiful *Downbelow Station* (1982). As we have seen, those novels were already divorcing themselves from the Golden-Age template of space opera, and to put them on the same level as the stories of "Doc" Smith, Edmond Hamilton, and A. E. Van Vogt would be doing them something of a disservice. Some remnants of the Fable still remained, however, and Banks decided to get rid of them as well—and just in case we'd missed the point, he had an as-yet unpublished story ready in which the Culture comes to Earth to take a long, hard look at us.

Finally, after thirteen years of mulling over the Culture and its adventures, Banks had broken through. *Consider Phlebas* was out, and whatever its flaws, it had become a commercial success. Banks would spend the next few years redrafting, correcting, and updating the Culture stories he had already written but been unable to publish at the time of completion. It was time to expand the envelope.

3

THE MORALITY OF THE RULE SET
The Player of Games

The theory and practice of gaming inform Banks' fiction from beginning to end.¹ We have seen how many of his stories thus far feature games in which the characters are involved with varying degrees of interest, understanding, and success: Frank's live-action wargames in *The Wasp Factory*; Quiss and Ajay's one-dimensional chess, open-plan go, and spotless dominoes in *Walking on Glass*; and Kraiklyn's Damage in *Consider Phlebas*. Games figure prominently in Banks' later works as well—most evidently but by no means exclusively in *The Steep Approach to Garbadale* (2007) among his non-genre work, and in *Inversions* (1998) and *Surface Detail* (2010) among his genre work. His second Culture novel, *The Player of Games*, belongs to this group as well, and arguably represents it.²

But playing acquires multiple valences in Banks' fiction, and the actual games that appear in his novels are only the physically visible portion of a set of play-related processes that pervade the vast majority of the stories he wrote. This is not an exaggeration: as Will Slocombe argues, "Banks endeavors to show that reality (or at least our understanding of it) works through games; they do not just reflect reality but inherently color our perceptions of it. The choice is not *whether* we play the game or not, but *how* we play. Moreover, the way in which we play the game reveals more than just our understanding of its rules: it reveals who we are.... If games embody the idea of competition, of agonistics, then how we compete reveals our ethical stance towards others, the extent to which our strived-for victory is due to, or at the expense of, others" (2013, 136). The reason why Slocombe's assessment applies to the entirety of Banks' body of work is that Banks himself saw the process by which games at once reflect, express, and shape human life as integral to the writing of fiction. Besides arguing, as Slocombe does, that games are symbolic signifiers of our struggle to understand ourselves and our lives, Banks also connected the act of gaming to the tripartite relationship among the writer, the work of fiction, and the reader. If games are a structured system of rules designed to replicate certain conditions prevailing in real life, so are novels—each is "a self-contained universe, something that is set in front of you. A game is like a novel—it's a set of rules and symbols and patterns, and in certain novels you have to work it out…. To simply tell a story, tell everything, all shown, every card on the table, not left to chance in a sense, then it's a bit boring actually. You could do so much more, why not make it live beyond the last page? Make the characters live, the plot live, the ideas live. And games imply that as well, games imply a continuation of the play" (Cobley 1990, 27).

So we're all players, characters and writers and readers, and the games we play intertwine with each other to form systems of meaning that do indeed live beyond the book that physically contains them. The characters don't just play games with each other in the sense that, like Quiss and Ajay or Kraiklyn, they often sit at a table with a board in front of them. They also play with each other's lives (Sara and Slater with Graham, for example, or Horza with the Free Company, or Fal N'geestra with everyone else in *Consider Phlebas*—hence the three *State of play* titles),[3] or they play with the lives of creatures that they consider beneath them because those creatures are powerless to fight back (Frank with the wasps in the Factory, or the Idirans with every less advanced civilization they meet); they also play games with themselves (Steven Grout and his stacks of novels), or devise complex systems of signifiers that represent an aspect of life as they see it (Frank again).

And watching it all from our own vantage point, we readers play our own game of detection, which gamemaster Banks put in front of us the moment we bought the novel. The novel is the board, the words the map, and the intertwining paths of the characters' lives the traces we have to follow to make sense of the game, which is the game of story that is the game of life. Above it all stands Iain (M.) Banks, who has his own game to play because writing a novel is a game unto itself and, like every game, it reveals the player. There are several levels of agency in this heterocosm of play, and Banks' is clearly the highest, but that doesn't mean that influence only flows in one direction. The empathy of story creates a permeable membrane of emotional attachment that shapes the writing, the reading, and the thinking about the story once the reading is over, which is another way of saying that nothing is without consequence. Banks constantly fielded questions about his own morality because of the things he made many of his characters do (or made happen to them), and his responses repeatedly connected to a higher ethical point that justified playing with these characters' lives and with the feelings of the readers who'd become attached to them. His thinking on games and gaming was the same:

3. The Morality of the Rule Set

> Morality is involved in the games we play with one another. The morality of games is the rules. Games have a very definite and set morality, you play according to the rules or you don't play at all.... It's trying to make the connection between the games that societies play on each other and on the individuals within those societies and the games played on the basic interpersonal level ... in the books I try to use games as symbols of the way we react to one another and to society. There's a conscious effort to make sense of all that, but there's no conscious answer because it's too difficult for any one individual ... in fiction the trick is to give people a choice of potential answers so they can disagree with what you're saying, or what you think you're saying [Cobley 1990, 27].

Banks seems to be arguing here that the ultimate objective of a game is not to win and dominate, but to understand and grow, to map out the play-related dynamics that regulate our behavior toward each other and toward the world around us. In this respect, he is echoing a point that Peter Hutchinson had made a few years earlier. In his book *Games Authors Play* (1983), Hutchinson had argued that notions of a rule set "suggest competitive play, but Suits (as well as Huizinga and Caillois) refrains from using the concept of 'winning.' He sees the aim instead as 'an attempt to achieve a specific state of affairs.' In literature, too, the emphasis is rarely on triumphing at the expense of another: it is on the pleasure which is derived from analysis and recognition, on the pleasure of *mastery* over a text which has been presented as a specific form of challenge" (7). Thus, engaging with *The Player of Games* means accepting an offer to play and therefore to feel the pleasure implicit in the act of playing, a pleasure that is independent of material rewards. Decoding the novel and mastering the meaning of the text will not result in someone's loss of property, honor, or goodwill from others. It will result in a moment of epiphany and joy, in an instant of recognition. It will be good.

Banks' point about the individual's inability to fully encompass the meaning of a social context is also crucial here. In his non-genre work, where the reality of the setting was either a mimetic given or an otherworld teetering over the brink of dreamlike fantastika, the morals of the games the characters played were subject to an assessment on the part of the reader that was, by necessity, aimed at the individual agent before it was aimed at the system itself. We can say, for example, that Frank/Frances Cauldhame, Steven Grout, and Alex Lennox/John Orr lead lives controlled and bent out of shape by the systems within which they exist: Frank/Frances is the victim of a biological experiment and of a social construction of masculinity that turns him/her into an outcast; Steven is suffering from paranoid-schizophrenic delusions in a public context that rejects and avoids him without helping his condition; and Alex/John are prisoners of social machineries within whose workings their desires are either frustrated or dashed without warning. All this is true, and Banks' attention, like that of his inspiration Alasdair Gray, was always focused on society's play on the individual—of particular interest, in this sense, is a piece Banks wrote for *The Guardian* in 2008, in which he recounted the process that led him from out-and-out SF to the exploded mimesis of *The Wasp Factory*. The novel, Banks wrote, "was *supposed* [italics mine] to be a pro-feminist, antimilitarist work, satirising religion and commenting on the way we're shaped by our surroundings and upbringing and the usually skewed information we're presented with by those in power. Frank is supposed to stand for all of us, in some ways; deceived, misled, harking back to something that never existed, vengeful for no good reason and trying too hard to live up to some oversold ideal that is of no real relevance, anyway" (2008, n.p.).

The majority of readers, however, didn't receive *Factory*—or either of the other two novels—that way, mainly because, fairly or unfairly, they focused more on the characters' personal choices than on the social setup that shaped, influenced, and often constrained those choices. Frank/Frances, Steven, Quiss, Ajay, and Alex/John are people within (problematically) mimetic worlds, and their lives are of interest because of the things they do or fail to do, and of the consequences those things have on others.[4] Expressing the same thought in terms more germane to this chapter's subject matter, their lives are of interest because of the games they play with and on themselves and each other, and of the outcomes those games have on other people. There is an element of utopian/dystopian speculation in all three stories, but its agency is limited because the genre within whose operating principles those stories were published didn't allow for more than a certain amount of 'official' divergence from the norm. Within a mimetic paradigm, the world is the world and it can't be changed. In the long run, readers of fiction labeled mimetic (irrespective of whether the narrative itself actually deserves the label) focus on these characters' weight of personal responsibility for the same reason they focus on the same thing in their lives: wishing for a different world, while understandable and to an extent necessary, makes us all helpless against the moment. We live here, now, and things are what they are—that is to say, the rules of the game are known to us, so whatever strategy of play we decide to employ, that strategy will have at least as much to say about us as it will about the constraints the system places upon us. We readers are individuals; as Banks himself pointed out, making sense of it all is beyond our capabilities, so we work with what we have: ourselves and other individuals.

But say that mimetic literature, however problematized and estranged, is not all you have. Say that now, in 1988, you're also a published SF writer with an open brief to return to and revisit the works you wrote ten years before, those that contained the concept of a social order designed precisely to make wishing for another world a *fait accompli*. Say also that one of those

3. The Morality of the Rule Set

works foregrounds the concept of gaming not just as a reflection of or symbol for life, but rather as life itself, literally and directly. You couldn't have done that in mimetic literature; there's no place on Earth where a game is a society and vice-versa, and while you can get your hallucinatory dream-realities to do part of the job, as in *Walking on Glass*, the environment of mainstream fiction—i.e., one of the rule sets you have to work with in the game of publishing—constrains you to an epistemic position that is incapable of unambiguously announcing them as legitimate otherworlds in their own right. No, that's the job of the other rule set you have chosen to play with: SF.

So it's 1988, "you" is Iain M. Banks (Iain Banks' player character for SF, a gamemaster might decide to call him), the game-novel you have redrafted and happily published is *The Player of Games*, the game that is also the world is called Azad, and the player is, on the surface, the Culture and its agents. But the beginning of the novel immediately warns us of the actual number of layers of play involved:

> This is the story of a man who went far away for a long time, just to play a game. The man is a game-player called "Gurgeh." The story starts with a battle that is not a battle, and ends with a game that is not a game. Me? I'll tell you about me later [3].

There's a riddle for us readers here, and an equally enigmatic announcement on the part of the narrator that he[5] is present in the story. Also, he plays coy with us, withholding his identity, which inevitably triggers the question of how many other things will remain hidden from us and for how long, or whether we'll ever know them. We're in the hands of the gamemaster, in other words, and the fact that his direct-to-reader address immediately withdraws into third person after the opening above changes nothing. He'll be back.

Thus, the game is known, at least in its broadest outlines, and so are the players. There's Iain Banks, who plays as Iain M. Banks who, in turn, plays as the narrator—his/their objective is to say something, or make a point, or just have some fun; could be all three. Then there are the readers, who play without the necessity of adopting another persona (but who, given the chance, probably will); our objective is to decode the novel's meaning, or message, or moral lesson, and if we could also have fun in the process that'd be nice. Then there's the "official" player of games: Jernau Morat Gurgeh, the most renowned gaming generalist in the Culture—"Morat" means game-player in Marain, the Culture's language (21). He shows up as soon as our gamemaster's voice fades into the pretend third-person narration through which most of the novel unspools, and he is indeed participating in a battle that is not a battle—it's a live-action game, which the high levels of technology available to Culture citizens makes perfectly realistic without the deadly side-effects (3–7).

In the chummy, happily hedonistic social intercourse of the Culture,

Gurgeh is something of a spiky character: he's mostly a loner, surrounding himself only with a select few friends, and at public gatherings he tends to be a little brusque with others (10–13). His accomplishments as a game-player have made him a bit egotistic, so that he is not above patronizing fans who approach him with ideas or questions (41–42). From Gurgeh's own point of view, his problem, as he himself tells his two best friends, is that "this is not a heroic age…. The individual is obsolete. That's why life is so comfortable for us all. We don't matter, so we're safe. No one person can have any real effect any more" (22). This is one of the reasons why he has always nurtured a fascination with barbarian societies, even before becoming involved in the study of their games (30).

The blight in Gurgeh's existence, he feels, *is* that existence: as a Culture citizen, he lives in a society without want, disease, danger, or exploitation, readily granted everything he may conceivably want upon asking, just like everybody else. And because everyone can have everything and anything, nobody wants much anyway. The concept of ownership retains its value only in a scarcity-based economy; once a society hits the post-scarcity track, both the desire for and the concept of possession become unnecessary. And in Gurgeh's view, the safety and happiness of this state of things have removed interest from his life because they have removed interest from his games. As he explains to his friends, what would be the point of wagering anything on the outcome of a game? This is the Culture; if one wanted something, it'd just be manufactured for them, and without money as an indicator of status there is no exchangeable currency to lend gravitas to the proceedings (20–21). Because the Culture has made life safe and pleasurable on every possible level, the point of both gaming and living is lost; without tangible risk, one loses its flavor because the other does. Little wonder that one of his two friends, the drone Chamlis, tells Gurgeh that instead of Morat, he should have chosen the name "Shequi"—Marain for "Gambler" (21). That's what Gurgeh is, at a fundamental level. The gambler is a player who won't find pleasure in playing unless the outcome of the game carries consequences beyond the game's immediate context. But because living in the Culture means living in a context beyond the game where the possibility of taking such risks is nonexistent, Gurgeh feels that his life has now become consequence-less.

This view of the relationship between life and gaming, valid in a world like Earth between the 20th and 21st century, would appear obsolete to the point of immorality in a place like the Culture—as indeed it does. Gurgeh's other friend, a young woman called Yay Meristinoux[6] in whom Gurgeh displays a good deal of interest, repeatedly fends off his advances because "I feel you want to […] take me … like a piece, like an area. To be had. To be […] possessed…. There's something very […] I don't know; primitive, perhaps,

3. The Morality of the Rule Set   69

about you, Gurgeh. You've never changed sex, have you?" (24). And Gurgeh hasn't, in fact. In the Culture, changing one's gender is as easy as thinking about it and waiting for the changes to take effect, but Gurgeh has remained willfully wedded to the gender that, in most primitive collectives, is traditionally dominant. In his world, Jernau Morat Gurgeh is a throwback, a barbarian of sorts.

The embedded absurdity of Gurgeh's position, which gives *The Player of Games* an aspect of rite of passage, of a *bildungsroman* tracing the growth of a human being from arrested development to full adulthood, is that he is perfectly free to feel that way and safe in expressing those feelings. He lives in the Culture and is as much a product of it as everyone else—even more so, in fact, if we consider that it is the free use of the Culture's educational and logistical infrastructure that allowed him a level of access to information, knowledge, and training beyond anything anyone living anywhere else could imagine. Talent and personal qualities matter, to be sure, which is why Gurgeh is the Player of Games and not some other Culture citizen, but in bemoaning the Culture's ethos he is willfully ignoring the other key ingredient in his success. He is also unaware of how much he is romanticizing his yearning for primitivism: it's easy to wish being Conan the Barbarian from the safety of one's couch, and convenient to pine after the passing of a more heroic time when one doesn't have to suffer the consequences of actually living in it.

This is where the actual gameplayer in Gurgeh's near-future life comes in: Contact first and, immediately thereafter, Special Circumstances, which want to make Gurgeh's existence a lot more heroic than it has been thus far. The coy narrator of the novel's beginning, it turns out at the end (308–309), has two identities in the story: the first is that of Mawhrin-Skel, a decommissioned SC drone who failed the screening process and was offered either reprogramming or de-fanged exile, deprived of its vastly destructive array of offensive sensory and weapons systems (14–15). Mawhrin-Skel chose the latter and settled on Chiark Orbital, where Gurgeh and everyone else on the Culture's side live in *The Player of Games*. The drone's attitude, already callous, is helped in no way whatever by this form of gelding, so that its presence at public functions and parties is always punctuated by some form of horrible behavior in which it engages for the sake of shocking people (like dissecting a dead bird in front of a crowd of appalled onlookers; 13–14). Everybody accordingly dislikes Mawhrin-Skel, except for Gurgeh, who fancies the drone a sort of kindred spirit, refreshingly cynical and brutally direct in a social context where everyone is polite and happy with their circumstances.

But Mawhrin-Skel isn't decommissioned, and it's not in exile either. It's working for Special Circumstances, and it has come to Chiark to recruit Gurgeh, which it accomplishes by exploiting his game-player vanity.[7] Now unable to decline SC's offer, Gurgeh listens in astonishment as the ambassador drone sent to brief him tells the story of the Empire of Azad. Seventy-three years before the beginning of the novel, Contact stumbled upon a society in the Lesser Cloud[8] whose structure and reason for being stumped even the vast intelligence of the Minds. Azad is a unique case in the Culture's records, and therefore impossible to game out according to preexisting models (78–79). The reason for the Empire of Azad's uniqueness, which is also the reason why, in the drone's explanation, such an archaic social system was able to survive the move from a single-planet to a spacefaring-commonwealth existence in the first place (74), is a game so fundamental to its society's existence that the society took its name from it. The game is thus called Azad, and it literally holds the empire together:

> The idea ... is that Azad is so complex, so subtle, so flexible and so demanding that it is as precise and comprehensive a model of life as it is possible to construct. Whoever succeeds at the game succeeds in life; the same qualities are required in each to ensure dominance ... the set-up assumes that the game and life are the same thing, and such is the pervasive nature of the idea of the game within the society that just by believing that, they make it so. It becomes true; it is willed into actuality [74–75].

So, as far as the Azadians are concerned the game is life, life is game, and the game truly is fantastically complex and absorbing, which is the whole point as far as the Empire's ruling classes are concerned and the whole problem from Contact and Special Circumstances' perspective: life in the empire has reached such thresholds of social inequality, exploitation, injustice, and cruelty toward both its own people and the aliens it subjugates that, without the seduction of Azad, those ruling classes would already have collapsed.

Instead they remain standing, and so do the crimes they perpetrate. Banks hated the institutionalized brutality of imperialistic power structures, and we have seen the fate he assigned to one such structure in *Consider Phlebas*, but this is something else. Even by Idiran standards, the Empire of Azad is a show of horrors: eugenic intervention against the male and female sexes has lowered their intelligence in favor of the dominant third sex, appropriately called apex. Millions have died in the wake of a program of deportation, race-based taxation, birth-control fixing, and purposefully engineered starvation aimed at making everyone on the Empire's home planet the same basic color and body-type (80). The treatment of conquered races, as well as that of Azadian veterans returning victorious from those same wars of conquest, is appalling (207), and the punishments meted out by the courts for such crimes as murder are wildly skewed in favor of the dominant sex—an apex convicted of killing a female gets a year's worth of hard labor, but a female convicted of killing an apex dies over a period of days, tortured with a variety of chemicals (204).

3. The Morality of the Rule Set

The mentally ill, especially if they are male or female and can't pay for a place in a hospital, are "de-citisenised" and sold to apexes as property (206).

And on and on it goes, this list of the horrors of empire, which Banks distilled from our (at times immediate) past but didn't invent. And next to the more appalling examples of exploitation and unholy suffering are the comparatively little things, the beatings and the rapes and the displacements of the poor and the life of prostitutes on the streets and the fights and the racism, the sum total of which joins the grand crimes to paint a composite image of nearly unbearable ferocity. The Culture, well-intentioned meddler that it is, won't stand by and allow such things to keep happening, so its specialized sections, Contact and Special Circumstances, have finally resolved upon a course of action: send Gurgeh to the Empire of Azad to play the game without telling him precisely why that should make any difference at all. For his part Gurgeh, who is utterly engrossed with the game of which he has received a brief glimpse, doesn't ask questions. And so he goes, the reluctant curmudgeon who doesn't even like leaving his mountain retreat of Ikroh, on a journey that'll take five years to complete and will end with the death of empire, as we've known all along it would.

With Gurgeh goes Mawhrin-Skel's (and the narrator's) other identity, a supposedly meek and pointedly unarmed library/diplomacy drone by the name of Flere-Imsaho. In keeping with its job description, the Flere-Imsaho personality behaves very much like its conceptual parent, C-3PO from *Star Wars*: fussy, overly worried about minutiae, excessively mindful of social niceties, and nearly useless in a pinch—or so it leads Gurgeh to believe. In reality, Flere-Imsaho is no more an unarmed protocol drone than Mawhrin-Skel was a de-fanged exile, and like its now-discarded alter ego (which faked its own destruction), it is a fully-fledged SC agent that saves Gurgeh's life in two separate occasions (290, 297). Behind the curtains, it also speaks to the Emperor himself as the true ambassador of the Culture, managing Gurgeh's increasingly worrying successes on the boards of Azad in a meta-game of aggressive diplomacy whose ultimate goal is the capitulation of the empire—"Gamespersonship," Flere-Imsaho calls it when, at the end of the novel, it finally reveals *nearly* the whole truth to Gurgeh (295).

And the Player of Games truly does win it all, beating opponent after opponent until he faces Nicosar, the Emperor of Azad, and defeats him as well. At that point, in the aftershock of defeat on the board, the empire simply falls apart in real life as well, so completely and irrevocably that the Culture's direct large-scale intervention becomes unnecessary (305). According to our first-person narrator, Gurgeh never gets to find out that Mawhrin-Skel and Flere-Imsaho were the same person (309), nor does he ever discover what larger forces were at work in the game played within and without Azad, although Flere-Imsaho does hint at their presence above the board:

SC's been looking for someone like you for quite a while. The Empire's been ripe to fall for decades; it needed a big push, but it could always go ... Azad—the game itself—had to be discredited. It was what had held the Empire together all these years.... My respect for those great Minds which use the likes of you and me like game-pieces increases all the time. Those are *very* smart machines [296].

This is the second time Gurgeh receives an acknowledgement that he has indeed been a piece—albeit a fundamental one—on a playing board whose boundaries he couldn't see,[9] and it's not the first time for us readers either. The voice of the narrator comes to talk directly to us in four different occasions (3; 99–100; 231–232; 308–309), reiterating every time (1) that a game is being played, (2) that Gurgeh is a playing-piece in it, and (3) that we are playing-pieces as well. "I haven't told you who I am so far," it says at one point, "and I'm not going to tell you now, either. Maybe later. Maybe" (231). And even when the time comes to tell us that it is both Mawhrin-Skel and Flere-Imsaho and someone else entirely all at once, the narrator still has a game to play with us:

Let me recapitulate. This is a true story. I was there. When I wasn't, and when I didn't know exactly what was going on—inside Gurgeh's mind, for example—I admit that I have not hesitated to make it up. But it's still a true story. Would I lie to you? [309].

The answer is yes, absolutely, since the narrator belongs to Special Circumstances and we're playing the game. We're reading the novel.

Does utopia get away with calling itself so if some or all of its agents are fine with strong-arm tactics, deception, and withholding information? Before officially blackmailing Gurgeh into speaking on its behalf, and in order to make one hundred percent sure that he takes its warning seriously, Mawhrin-Skel physically restrains him—something previously unheard of on Chiark Orbital and, by implication, in the Culture at large (56–57). Also, the drone shows him video/audio footage of his bedroom at Ikroh while he is involved in intercourse with a young admirer (60). Is Special Circumstances the worm in the apple, the cancer eating away at the heart of the perfect society until the perfect society ends up resembling it? How many people is it all right to manipulate and coerce for the greater good? And whose "greater good" is it anyway? Who gets to issue the definition?

As before, we can express those questions in gaming terms. "Games have a very definite and set morality," Banks had told Michael Cobley; "you play according to the rules or you don't play at all." Thus, the morality of the rule set is the first of two crucial requirements for the existence of a good game, which also means a good society; in *Player*, the Culture represents the quintessential example of one such game, whose rules are fair because the philosophical, ethical, and moral variables that went into designing them were

3. The Morality of the Rule Set

fair. By contrast, the Empire of Azad is the quintessential example of a rigged rule set: Azadian society is designed for the advantage of one third of its population, with the other two suffering appalling deprivations and punishments. Strangely, however, Azad the game does not initially appear to reflect this form of privilege—the Azadian constitution grants all three sexes the right to play, thus seemingly allowing males and females the chance to improve their lot in life (137).

But in fact the game does reflect privilege. It's in the second crucial requirement for the existence of a good game/society, the unanimous acceptance of—and equal participation in—the rule set, that Azad starts echoing the culture within which it was born. First, the Azadian educational system stacks the odds heavily against males and females by having the best colleges accept only apices. Second, the draw is arranged so that males and females will be eliminated immediately.[10] Third, a recent "improvement" in the rules, introduced at the behest of the privileged classes, allows poor people to stay in the bidding with rich people by wagering what they call "physical licence"—i.e., the performance of tortures or mutilations on the game's loser. But because the rich apices already have a considerable advantage over everyone else, the physical license option does nothing to actually redress the balance—it's always the lower-class player that pays that awful price (79–80).

Azad is easy to gauge on any relevant moral scale. *Player* provides us with so many horrifying scenes of injustice, exploitation, and abuse of the helpless[11] that, within the novel's dramatic economy, to let either the empire or the game continue to exist is unthinkable. The philosophy of Azad, compressed into a single sentence by one of the government's highest-ranking members, amounts to a violation of what Banks had said about the morality of games: "one can be on either side in the Empire. One can be the player, or one can be [...] played upon" (222).[12] In Azadian society, there is no choice not to play, and because the odds have been rigged from the start, there is also no hope of an outcome different from the one already assigned. Winners and losers have already been decided, and the true game, the true fun as far as the Azadian elites are concerned, lies in the pleasure of watching others be subject to their every whim (220–221).

The Culture, on the other hand, is more difficult to assess. From the perspective of every character except possibly Gurgeh and Mawhrin-Skel/Flere-Imsaho, the Culture truly is the utopia Banks created it to be, and here we come to one of the more remarkable aspects of this novel: the plausible, credible, sustained description of day-to-day life in paradise. Usually, to describe utopia is to destroy it: from Thomas More's 1516 original to Edward Bellamy's *Looking Backward* (1888) to Ursula Le Guin's *The Dispossessed* (1974), the vast majority of attempts to describe the actual daily life in what the story construes as a utopia results in the reader wishing for something else. One's utopia is invariably someone else's dystopia, and our history is full of figures that tried to enforce their utopias on others. Martin Luther King had a dream, but so did, for example, Pol Pot; the difference between their respective dreams is that, while Pol Pot's began and ended at the muzzle of a gun or at the gate of a camp, King found a way to express his in terms that most others could agree with and wish for. He folded us all in his dream and promised we'd be safe in it, happier than we'd been thus far. And we did believe.

But even then, there were many who listened to King's voice and heard the Devil's, and one of them acted upon his fear. Conversely, many others listened to Pol Pot and saw the dream, which was easy to embrace because it had been custom-made for them. And in *The Player of Games*, we can certainly say that the apices in control of Azadian society, those in the country villa who listen to music played on the body parts of their victims, would unhesitatingly describe their circumstances as utopian. Once again, who gets to announce their dream and enforce its advent?

So Banks had one hell of a job to do, convincingly describing utopia and setting it against dystopia. He pulled it off, though, chiefly through the use of a variation on a classic trope in utopian fiction. In his seminal book on the utopian imagination, *Demand the Impossible* (1986), Tom Moylan observes that all literary utopias, from the earliest examples of the form to the latest, share two common traits: the alternative society and the visitor to that society (43). The visitor to the alternative, utopian society—Julian West in *Looking Backward*, for example, or Bron Helstrom in Samuel Delany's *Triton* (1976)—is someone who, because they come from a more dystopian reality (sometimes Earth at the time of the story's writing, sometimes a future society gone wrong), must be introduced to the kind of life they will lead in their new world. The dialectic of differentiation between the visitor's native values and the ones their guide to utopia espouses serves (1) as background information on the creation and nature of the utopian society under scrutiny, (2) as a critique of our society in the here and now, and (3) as the trigger for a discourse on the process of utopian creation itself, this last task accomplished through "[drawing] on both the traditional eutopian evocation of a new spatial reality ... and the temporal, dystopian, account of personal suffering, systemic discovery, and radical action" (Moylan 2014b, xviii). Banks' Culture stories are, in this respect, no different from other utopian writings, although he often varies the dynamics. In *Consider Phlebas*, for example, Horza acts as the visitor whose unsupported prejudice against the primacy of Minds (he's never actually visited the Culture) further accentuates his role of willfully ignorant, doomed viewpoint character at the same time as it helps us readers see utopia in its true light. Horza's would-be guides, Balveda and Fal N'geestra, speak on behalf of the Culture without hope of reaching him—

Balveda because she is *from* the Culture but not *in* the Culture, and Fal because she is; that is, she's never in the room with anyone involved in the search for the Mind. Ultimately, everyone is talking to us readers, who are the only beneficiaries of the lessons imparted at the end.

The Player of Games presents another variation on the visitation template, this time through the viewpoint of Jernau Gurgeh as a socio-chemical reagent of sorts—a discontented citizen of utopia who perversely managed to cast his own experience of Culture life as a nearly dystopian encounter. The first hundred or so pages of the novel are exclusively set on Chiark Orbital (3–95), among beautiful vistas of mountain ranges, fjords, lakes, green meadows, clear torrents, and clusters of human habitation carefully arranged for maximum aesthetic effect and perfect symbiosis with the natural world that interpenetrates them—Gurgeh's home of Ikroh is a particularly beautiful example of such architectonic care (72). The Culture people in the novel go to parties, attend public functions, study at the local university, visit each other, and generally engage in every kind of pastime or endeavor that catches their fancy without qualms or guilt. Resources are, for all intents and purposes, infinite, and the technology that makes use of them is so advanced that even the most extravagant whims are within range of the individual's grasp without damage or offense to others. People can still experience suffering—love still goes unrequited at times, for example, or like Fal N'geestra in *Phlebas*, one may occasionally fall and get hurt—but those instances of suffering are accidents of chance, not of design, and as such they fall into the realm of personal rather than systemic responsibility.

And in the midst of all this guiltless, blameless fun, nestling like a grub inside the heart of a nearly perfect social contract, its one discontent continues bemoaning the loss of dystopia. It's easy to become irritated at Gurgeh's attitude toward the Culture, especially because—and Banks knew this very well—*we* don't live in it. We have to make do with Earth between the end of the 20th century and the beginning of the 21st, and unfortunately that's closer to Azad than it is to the Culture. To watch a person express his desire to be rid of something we'd give anything to achieve, even if it's "just" a story, feels galling. The description of life on Chiark Orbital, which is shorthand for life in the Culture at large, receives an added air of plausibility and desirability precisely by virtue of the presence of this one famous contrarian who keeps insisting on making himself miserable when everything around him invites happiness.

Then the novel switches scenery from the Culture to Azad, and Gurgeh retains his role of socio-chemical reagent—now reversed—when he is confronted by the reality of life in the Empire. In the terms Moylan established in his study, Gurgeh can be described as a visitor to both dystopia and utopia, in the sense that he is finally learning what life in the Culture truly is like through the experience of life in "a more heroic society." For all his spikiness and pretend-savagery, Gurgeh is a Culture citizen and a decent human being. The very language he uses to craft meaning out of his surroundings betrays his belonging to the Culture: the words relating to concepts like "prison," "dominant sex," "ownership," and "illegal" continue to escape him, so that either the ambassador drone from Contact or Flere-Imsaho have to explain them to him (see page 118, for example). Also, when he is compelled to register his philosophical and ethical beliefs with the Imperial Game Bureau, the *Limiting Factor*—the demilitarized warship[13] that has taken him from Chiark to Azad—contrasts his opinion that he doesn't really have any structured beliefs with an argument that is also a warning:

> A guilty system recognizes no innocents. As with any power apparatus which thinks everybody's either for it or against it, we're against it. You would be too, if you thought about it. The very way you think places you amongst its enemies. This might not be your fault, because every society imposes some of its values on those raised within it, but the point is that some societies try to maximise that effect, and some try to minimise it. You come from one of the latter and you're being asked to explain yourself to one of the former [170-171].

For a while, however, barbarian-loving throwback that he is, Gurgeh feels the attraction of the Empire through the attraction of the game. Upon arriving in orbit around Azad's home planet and witnessing the martial discipline of the soldiers who come onboard to greet him and inspect the *Limiting Factor*, he unfavorably compares the Culture to Azad according to authoritarian thought patterns that a Culture citizen would find ludicrous (116), and at one point he falls prey precisely to the feelings of greed for conquest and victory that keep the Azadian élites in power—"He hadn't realized how seductive Azad was when played in its home environment," the narrator tells us; "now he *knew* why the Empire had survived because of the game. Azad itself simply produced an insatiable desire for more victories, more power, more territory, more dominance" (200). At the same time, Gurgeh starts expressing himself in the language of the Empire rather than in Marain, and because the words we use to define everything in our lives also shape those things, he begins employing more primitive thought patterns, which in turn results in a more savage behavior on the Azad board than he'd previously displayed. Also, when he receives a video communiqué from his friend Chamlis, he becomes angry at the realization that some of his friends have been staying at Ikroh for a few days (246-247).

Gurgeh is, in other words, in some danger of embracing the morality of Azad's rule set, right at the same time as his Culture upbringing, in reaction to the horrors perpetrated by the Empire, is pulling him away from that and back toward the morality of the rule set Gurgeh was born with. There's a struggle going on inside the man, but there shouldn't be: the respective moralities of the two societies are known quantities by now, so it shouldn't be difficult for Gurgeh to make a choice. The problem is that he is suffering from a degree of distrust toward Flere-Imsaho and SC in general: aside from remembering exactly how he was fished into this entire business to begin with, and apart from SC's well-known reputation for deviousness, Gurgeh has just found out that, contrary to what he'd been told before, a handful of people in the Empire have known the Culture's true size, technological capabilities, and extension across the galaxy for about two hundred years (thus making the original quote of seventy-three years since discovery another lie). Flere-Imsaho is informing him of the fact now that, in the wake of his successes, he's about to play one of those people; otherwise, the drone tells Gurgeh, he wouldn't have been informed. Need-to-know basis (243).

This deep level of manipulation of a few choice individuals, the narrative indicates, is the price utopia pays for satisfying its urge to be useful. Banks declared more than once that, precisely because the Culture is a utopia, he didn't feel like writing a story exclusively set within its social context—he might as well write a "Hampstead novel," as he'd called non-genre fiction (Hughes 1999, n.p.). Every Culture story, first to last, is accordingly set in the moral and ethical gray area where, when utopia meets dystopia, one of the two has to establish a sort of dialogue with the other. But dystopias don't do honest, direct dialogue; they do obfuscation, bottlenecking of information, and outright lying. The burden of opening communications therefore falls on the shoulders of the utopian society's representatives. Banks, who'd been paying a lot of attention to Chomsky's theories of freedom of information, tells us several times in *Player* that the Empire's information network constantly misinforms on, lies about, and when it deems it necessary forges news and events. In that, it is the diametric opposite of the Culture, where every scrap of information is free for everyone at every moment.

Well, almost. SC, it turns out, can obfuscate with the best of them. Part of the reasons why it hasn't informed the Culture at large of the existence and nature of the Empire is that, should news of life in that place become common knowledge, a wave of popular outrage would force Contact and SC to act militarily. Thirteen years after the end of the Vietnam War, one year before the end of the Soviet occupation of Afghanistan, three years before Desert Storm, and fifteen years before the beginning of Operation Enduring Freedom, the ambassador drone SC sends to brief Gurgeh lays out the dilemma of intervention in uncomfortably accurate detail:

> We might be forced into a high-profile intervention against the empire; it would hardly be war as such because we're way ahead of them technologically, but we'd have to become an occupying force to control them, and that would mean a huge drain on our resources as well as morale; in the end such an adventure would almost certainly be seen as a mistake, no matter the popular enthusiasm

for it at the time. The people of the empire would lose by uniting against us instead of the corrupt regime which controls them, so putting the clock back a century or two, and the Culture would lose by emulating those we despise; invaders, occupiers, hegemonists [79].

Thus, Special Circumstances is sitting on the Azad matter while the great Minds that manage such situations game out all the variables involved. In the end, it's the Morat option that proves to be the one least likely to result in widespread bloodshed and total war between the Empire and the Culture. Gurgeh has to go to Azad (game and empire), play Azad (game and empire), and win, thus discrediting the value of the game as an accurate reality model. The unholy link between simulation and actuality broken, the veil lifts, and the Empire collapses under the monstrous weight of its crimes.

So, not every bit of news is available to anyone at any time. If Contact and SC deem it necessary or desirable, they can bottleneck the flow of certain venues of information. But surely this is easy to embrace? If Contact and SC are keeping mum so as to avoid the same kind of imperialistic adventure that has been staining the conscience of the industrialized West for the past twenty years or so, wouldn't that be entirely justifiable? But what about Gurgeh? What about his undoubtedly forced enlistment in the Azad intervention? To whom does he get to complain about the considerable infringement upon his personal freedoms, an infringement that also goes unpunished? He is blackmailed, lied to, transported to a faraway place where nearly everyone wishes him harm, and shown sights that horrify him to such an extent that, in the wake of the *Limiting Factor*'s departure from the Lesser Cloud at the end of the novel, he asks to be put into the deep sleep of storage for the duration of the two-year trip back to Chiark (301–302). Where's *his* utopia?

In his 1988 review of *The Player of Games*, John Clute offered these considerations on the matter of Gurgeh's participation in SC's venture:

> Although Gurgeh has transparently been fitted up for his Empire-demolishing role, Azad does deserve (in space opera terms) its comeuppance, and Gurgeh accomplishes his mission with panache and some cunning. Indeed, most readers will assume he tumbled to the true location and role of Mawhrin-Skel as soon as they do, about halfway through the story; and will consequently assume that his subsequent playing of Skel's game is elated and volunteer [1995c, 99].

If this is true, then the top-down flow of gameplaying and manipulation in the novel contains some counter-currents, and the all-knowing narrator who tells us Gurgeh never knew better is, in fact, being played himself. And why not? Jernau Gurgeh is the Morat, the player of games, and he is fully aware of the intense relationship between gaming and life—witness for example his theory of gaming in the *Player*'s early stages (41), which contains in microcosm the thematic concerns of the novel entire. In fact, Gurgeh is no more an average Culture person than *Consider Phlebas*' Fal N'geestra and Perosteck Balveda were, and not just because of his gameplaying skills. He's also the contrarian, the lover of barbarian societies and, most importantly, the gambler. He's a citizen of the fringe, a dweller in the gray moral and ethical areas that Contact and Special Circumstances staked a claim to when they began their ecumenical good works for the benefit of less fortunate people. While he has indeed been fitted out for his role as the agent of Azad's destruction, those who prepared him didn't have to change that much.

In the end, it's the game that brings Gurgeh wholly back into the Culture's fold, just as it was the game that had originally presented him with the lure of—to use his own terminology—a more heroic age. The very last game of Azad that Gurgeh has to play pits him against Nicosar, the Emperor, and Nicosar is a consummate gameplayer in his own right. To him belong the early stages of the game, when his forces seem to run rampant across the areas of the board Gurgeh controls while the Culture man tries to figure out what the Emperor's strategy is. When he finally does realize what's happening on the Azad board, he also finally understands himself:

> The Emperor had set out to beat not just Gurgeh, but the whole Culture ... he had set up his whole side of the game as an Empire, the very image of Azad. Another revelation struck Gurgeh ... one reading—perhaps the best—of the way he'd always played was that he played as the Culture. He'd habitually set up something like the society itself when he constructed his positions and deployed his pieces; a net, a grid of forces and relationships, without any obvious hierarchy or entrenched leadership, and initially quite profoundly peaceful [269].

Something of an oddity he may be, by his society's standards, but in spite of that Jernau Gurgeh has always been and still remains a Culture citizen, with Culture values and Culture ethics, and in Azad's terms he plays *as* the Culture because he is *from* the Culture. He doesn't really have a choice because the morality of Azad's rule set, as the *Limiting Factor* had intimated to him, construes as inimical anyone who isn't on its side, both within and without the game itself. Nicosar, who knows that the Empire couldn't beat the Culture in actuality, attempts to reverse the game-to-life flow of Azad's reality model through a statement of principle issued in the language of game that, as far as the average Azadian is concerned, is also the language of life. By deciding to play as the whole of Azad, he automatically casts Gurgeh in the role of champion of the Culture, a function the other man has trouble accepting because, typically for someone from the Culture, he sees himself as speaking exclusively for his own conduct (281).

Another thing that Gurgeh doesn't find out until the game's aftermath is that the night before he'd begun playing Nicosar, Flere-Imsaho had told the Emperor that Gurgeh really was the Culture's champion, and that, should he beat Nicosar, the Culture would come in and impose its own brand of peace upon the Empire (295). And because Nicosar is the quintessential Azadian, and because, as the ambassador drone had told Gurgeh back on Chiark, the identification of game and life in the Empire is willed into actuality through sheer belief, the Emperor absolutely knows that what Flere-Imsaho told him is the truth (even though the drone himself has—or claims to have—no idea whether that was actually what the Minds had planned; 295). Nicosar believes, and shapes the game accordingly; in turn, the game shapes Gurgeh, who finds himself losing because he doesn't believe in his role within the game; when he does come to believe, he becomes exactly what Flere-Imsaho told Nicosar he is—the Culture's champion.[14] There's nothing else he can do because the option of not playing isn't open to him, and even if it were he wouldn't take it; he is the Player of Games. Gurgeh comes back from the brink and ultimately defeats Nicosar by resetting his society's structure within the game as that of the Culture militant, a virtual analog of the organism that had defeated the Idiran Empire more than seven hundred years before (270–272).[15]

And just like the Idiran War, which the Culture had started on the losing side but had ended up winning, the game-board duel between the Culture and the Empire of Azad plays out to its inevitable conclusion. When he realizes he's beaten, Nicosar tries to burn down himself, Gurgeh, and everyone else in the room—in losing the game he's lost the Empire; he believes it. At that point, Flere-Imsaho drops the library-drone guise and shields Gurgeh, who survives the flames and, after receiving a belated explanation of his true role in the events, boards the *Limiting Factor* and heads on home. Chamlis and Yay are waiting for him, and Gurgeh tells them the whole story of Azad, and finally makes peace with himself. He sleeps with Yay, who now accepts him because he has changed, and the story ends in dystopia lost and utopia regained, thankfully. For us on the other side of the page, for the readers of utopia who speculate on it from inside social machineries more resembling of its dark twin, it's an indispensable blessing. We need our dreams. Also, despite the narrator's open admission that we are, like Gurgeh himself, at once players and pawns in a game, there are rewards for our willingness to play, as Hutchinson intimated, because the rule set Banks handed to us in this novel is a fundamentally fair one. Everyone has a function to perform in it, and because we've always known this of literature, if only at a subconscious level, our participation in the game that is a world that is a novel is gleeful. The joy of engaging with *The Player of Games* is also the joy of realizing that everyone will play their roles to the best of their abilities and without attempting to second-guess the rule set. And first and foremost among us players is Iain M. Banks himself, who tried, in *Consider Phlebas*, to second-guess the rule set of space opera to the near-suffocation of the main story.

He doesn't do that here. Here, he keeps the faith; he tells the tale without arguing or sidetracking, obedient to the melody although singing it with different lyrics. And the story ends, and Gurgeh has learned better, and we get to keep utopia at the same time as we rejoice for the demise of the dark twin, even if for all of us it only happens in the pages of a novel. Maybe one day.

4

DIZIET SMA'S DILEMMAS OF INTERVENTION
The State of the Art and *Use of Weapons*

After the successful publication of *The Player of Games*, Banks returned to his pile of unpublished manuscripts and selected the remaining two Culture stories—the novella *The State of the Art*, which was first published as a standalone in 1989, and the novel *Use of Weapons*, which came out in 1990. The novella, by Banks' own reckoning, required little in the way of alterations or improvements, while *Use of Weapons* had to be vastly rewritten (Garnett 1989, 54–56). *The State of the Art* and *Use of Weapons* are treated together in this chapter for two reasons: first, because the timelines of the two stories are connected through an intertextual synching too precise to be casual—therefore suggesting a dovetailing of thematic concerns—and second because they share two fundamental characters, the Contact/SC operative Diziet Sma and her accompanying offensive-model drone, Skaffen-Amtiskaw.

Timelines first. Sma herself, with a number of editorial interpolations from Skaffen-Amtiskaw, narrates *The State of the Art*. Hers is a memoir, one hundred and fifteen years after the facts (78), of the time she spent on Earth in the year AD 1977, when the General Contact Unit *Arbitrary* (and what a resonant name for the story in which it participates) arrived in orbit around our planet and started studying us. Sma is composing this memoir for a Culture scholar specializing on Earth, a man by the name of Petrain, and in the brief cover letter she appends to the manuscript she apologizes for keeping him waiting a long time. The reason for the wait, Sma explains, is that she's had to leave her current post in an uncontacted stage three planetary civilization for about a hundred days to attend to urgent business (77–78), which is where the connection to *Use of Weapons* comes in. At the beginning of the novel, when Skaffen-Amtiskaw tells Sma that she has to pack and leave immediately to reconnect with the other protagonist of the story, Cheradenine Zakalwe, she tells the drone to "send a stalling letter to that Petrain guy" (37). This quick aside implies that, at that point in *Use of Weapons*, Sma has yet to write the memoir, and that therefore the hundred days off-planet she mentions at the beginning of *The State of the Art* comprise the span of events in the novel, after which she returns home, writes the memoir, and sends it out to Petrain, *cum* apologies for her tardiness.[1] Also, so she tells Petrain, she has left Contact at large and moved on to Special Circumstances (77), which is where we find her at the beginning of *Use of Weapons*.

Thus, Banks went to some trouble to link the two stories together, arguably because both narratives present Sma with one or more aspects of the intervention dilemma—the moment when, confronted with a less advanced civilization on the cusp of either disaster or transcendence, Contact has to decide whether to (A) throw the Prime Directive out the window and come in, or (B) stay away and observe. The contrast in this pairing is that, whereas in *State* Sma plays the role of enthusiastic interventionist while others counsel caution, in *Weapons* she is the voice of caution, trying to restrain her associate's excesses in the name of the greater good.

Of all the Culture stories, *The State of the Art* is probably the most openly didactic. This is perhaps unsurprising, considering the specimen under the scope. The whole novella is shaped like a continuing debate on the ethics of civilizational interference, occasionally interspersed with bouts of mostly peaceful exploration and sightseeing. The key voices in this debate are four: first there's Sma herself, who advocates immediate intervention lest 1977 Earth plunges into global thermonuclear war, ecological catastrophe, or any other human-made doomsday scenario. "I didn't want to leave," she writes to Petrain. "I didn't want to keep them safe from us and let them devour themselves; I wanted maximum interference; I wanted to hit the place with a program Lev Davidovitch would have been proud of" (105).

The second voice belongs to the *Arbitrary* itself. While it spars with Sma concerning the advisability of contacting Earth, the *Arbitrary* is conducting the same dialogue—at speeds and levels of cogency that beings of flesh cannot dream of—with a quorum of other Minds housed within various craft scattered across the volume of space surrounding the solar system (80). Serene and poised in the sublime clarity of Mind-thought, the *Arbitrary* counters Sma's viewpoint with an argument of its own:

> How do we know what is—or would be—for their own good, unless, over a very long period, we observe matched areas of interest—in this case planets—and compare the effects of contacting and not contacting? ... They're on a cusp; a highly heterogeneous but highly connected—and stressedly connected—civilization. I'm not sure that one approach could encompass the needs of their different systems.

The particular stage of communication they're at, combining rapidity and selectivity, usually with something added to the signal and almost always with something missed out, means that what passes for truth often has to travel at the speed of failing memories, changing attitudes, and new generations [83].

The *Arbitrary* is gently pointing out that our scientific, technological, and sociological state of the art have not yet enabled us to first create and then acknowledge as fellow sentients the Minds we'd need to retain a complete, coherent picture of ourselves and our interactions. Our collective memories fade and warp over the years, obfuscated and distorted by shifting ideologies and imperfect generational transmission, and our relationship with the machineries that at the same time make comfortable, endanger, and control the lives we lead is deeply ambivalent. Should the Culture contact us, would we hail them as friends or recoil in horror from a civilization that has willfully given over its decision-making processes to the distant descendants of the machines we know? Sma's answer to this question is that the longer-term benefits of immediate contact would be well worth the price of any short-term cultural upheaval. The *Arbitrary*, less sanguine on this score than Sma is, keeps playing devil's advocate, countering her bleak view of humanity's near-future prospects if left alone with a more optimistic outlook. "What hope for these people, Ship?" Sma asks at one point, and the *Arbitrary* replies: "Their children's children will die before you even look old, Diziet. Their grandparents are younger than you are now [...] In your terms, there is no hope for them. In theirs, every hope" (130).

And so the debate between flesh sentient and sentient machine continues, ranging from far-out philosophical discussions of such concepts as beauty to the practicalities of stopping the nukes of World War III once they're in flight. Sma knows that she's going to lose the debate, and that Contact will use Earth as a Control Group (105),[2] but still she tries to the very end. The *Arbitrary* faithfully copies the other Minds on Sma's argument—in the Culture, one always has a voice and the right to expect this voice to be heard—but things don't change. For the time being, Earth will remain a read-only file (143).

But there's more. If Sma and the *Arbitrary* were the only two voices involved in the debate, the story would be rather pat—a high-flying set of exchanges between a near omnipotent machine intelligence and a female flesh sentient, neither of whom is in the slightest danger from anyone or anything on the planet below. Banks, who knew that, introduced two more characters into the proceedings, each with his profoundly quirky response to the Earth dilemma. The first of these two characters, and the third voice in the debate, is also the engine of the story, the dramatic force that turns *The State of the Art* into a profoundly stressed dialogue on the morality of ecumenical good works. His name is Dervley Linter; like Sma, he's a Contact operative and a member of the *Arbitrary*'s crew, but something has happened to him: he has made the decision to remain on Earth for the rest of his life, irrespective of whether Contact comes in or not (99). He has gone native because, so he tells Sma, he feels more alive on Earth than he ever had in the Culture, and accordingly he wants nothing more to do with his place of birth and its representatives, especially the *Arbitrary* (100–103).[3]

Linter's revelation sends Sma on a frenzy of speculation about the cause of his decision (she initially thinks it's a woman; 99) and the *Arbitrary* in search of an expedient to make him change his mind (the Ship asks Sma to drop in on Linter in the hope that she might jolt him out of his decision; 100). When neither gets results, and when it becomes clear that Linter means what he says, the contact-or-merely-observe deliberation acquires a new aspect of urgency. Aside from the security risks involved—should Linter get hurt and taken to a hospital, his alien physiology would immediately give him away, thus initiating a dangerously out-of-control form of contact (105–106)—the situation is made problematic precisely by the ethics the Culture upholds. Should the *Arbitrary* snap Linter off-planet to protect us Earthlings from discoveries we're not ready for, or should it guarantee his wishes since, as a Culture citizen first and foremost, he's entitled to having those wishes fulfilled? According to the rulebook Contact and the Culture as a whole swear by, both courses of action are defensible—even advisable—in ethical terms, so the ultimate decision, here in the fringe territories, comes down to the employment of ad-hoc predictive models.

Linter makes things even more difficult than they already were. For reasons he himself doesn't seem to fully understand, he has developed a fondness for Sma and a desire for her approval, which he can't have. On every occasion they meet after their first talk, always at his request, Sma makes it clear that she's vehemently opposed to his decision, and that he's being a fool for rejecting the very utopia the people of Earth are striving, however dysfunctionally, to achieve. They, she tells him, would be the first to declare him a madman (121). Her outrage spikes on the day Linter tells her that, at his request, the *Arbitrary* removed most of the biological enhancements with which Culture citizens are born—now he's vulnerable to illness, doesn't see as well as he used to, doesn't have control over his digestive system any longer, and so on (118–119). "I could only think of them as mutilations," Sma writes to Petrain of these changes, and her disgust prompts her to confront the *Arbitrary*: why did it agree to carry them out, she asks, and when the Ship replies that it simply granted Linter's wishes as it was its duty to do, she accuses it of going along with his masochistic scheme because it expected that the discomfort that came with those alterations would push Linter to come back into the fold, begging to have his genofixed Culture body returned to him (123). The *Arbitrary*'s riposte cogently captures the quintessential mindset of the Culture's ethics of contact and relations with other societies. First off, it tells Sma, it acquiesced because it didn't find Linter any less valuable as a sentient being than it had before altering him. It's his mind that's relevant, and physical characteristics don't come into the assessment (124). Secondly, there is a pragmatic angle in acquiescing to Linter's request: acting reasonably toward him even when he's not reciprocating might well be the only way to make him see that the Culture—and specifically its representative orbiting Earth—truly are the good guys, thus possibly convincing him to come back to them. But it's the third reason that really strikes home:

> What are we supposed to be about, Sma? What is the Culture? What do we believe in? ... Surely in freedom, more than anything else. A relativistic, changing sort of freedom, unbounded by laws or laid-down moral codes, but—in the end—just because it is so hard to pin down and express, a freedom of a far higher quality than anything to be found on any relevant scale on the planet beneath us at the moment. The same technological expertise, the same productive surplus which, in pervading our society, first allows us to be here at all and after that allows us the degree of choice we have over what happens to Earth, long ago also allowed us to live exactly as we wish to live, limited only by being expected to respect the same principle applied to others.... Dervley Linter is as much a product of our society as I am, and as such ... he's perfectly correct in expecting to have his wishes fulfilled [124–125].

The *Arbitrary*'s argument illustrates the conundrum Linter landed on its lap when he decided to stay on Earth, and at the same time lays down the Ship's application of the Culture's basic principles: as the most powerful thinking entity in that theatre of operations, and as the quintessential embodiment of everything the Culture stands for, the *Arbitrary* is determined to make sure that its conduct "is beyond reproach, and in as close accord with the basic principles of our society as it is within my power to make it" (125). This means that Linter gets to have his wish, and that any hope that he'll come back to the GCU now rests exclusively with him.

Thus, Sma finds herself not only frustrated in her desire to intervene on Earth, but also confronted with the explicit, if problematized, validation of a viewpoint that embraces a diametrically opposite stance: if she want maximum interference, Linter wants no interference whatsoever—not even observation. He wants the culture to leave Earth utterly and completely to its own devices, and to her considerable annoyance Sma recognizes that the final decision of the quorum of Minds will come closer to Linter's desires than to her own (105). So she travels the Earth, observing and cataloguing and interviewing just like a dutiful Contact operative must, and all along she worries about Mr. Problem, as the *Arbitrary* has begun to call Linter (130). Even through her authorial voice, relatively cool-headed after one hundred and fifteen years, the reader can feel the strain her younger self is experiencing during her stay on-planet.[4] As the time of departure approaches and the Linter issue becomes ever more pressing, Earth keeps shocking and outraging her with vistas of the horrors our species has visited upon everything alive, including itself, so that for Sma the decision to simply observe without actively interfering becomes nearly impossible to examine with a dispassionate eye (hence her refusal to visit Pretoria; 128).

It's at this point, when the narrative risks turning excessively bleak, that the presence of the fourth voice becomes a useful agent of light-heartedness and, at the same time, another perspective on the morals of contact. There are always a certain number of people onboard a ship (or on an Orbital, or a planet) who, even by the Culture's standards, can readily be described as odd. One such specimen is the character of Li'ndane—or simply Li—who is "just a weirdo, and forever conducting a running battle with the finer sensibilities of the ship" (87). Despite sharing the panhuman body type characteristic of most of the Culture's citizens, Li's appearance is far enough removed from Earth-normal ("imagine Quasimodo crossed with an ape"; 88) that he's barred from going planetside, and his thought processes match the shape: he's quirky, funny, and often manic. He tries to get the *Arbitrary* to drop him on the slopes of the Himalayas and let him make his way down—any locals taking a good look at him, he argues, would simply assume he was a Yeti (116)—and, while Sma is on Earth for her first talk with Linter, he forms the boredom society, which he later renames the Ennui League and of which he remains the only member (112).

That Banks is having a bit of fun with the character of Li'ndane is clear enough, and given the heft of the narrative in general his antics are a welcome break, strategically interspersed among the various conversations/confrontations among Sma, Linter, and the Ship. That's not the only function those antics fulfill, however. In their increasing absurdity—nobody takes them seriously, beginning with Li himself—they become a Swiftian commentary both on the obscenities of life on Earth and on the wisdom of the Culture's contact practices, which Li supports in reverse-logic terms by construing himself as a sort of dictator-in-waiting who, tired of the namby-pamby hesitancy of the *Arbitrary*, is ready to take control of the situation and doing what needs to be done. What needs to be done, it turns out, is to elect Li to the position of Captain of the *Arbitrary*, for which he starts campaigning one day by appearing in front of Sma dressed in James T. Kirk's uniform from the original *Star Trek* series and launching himself into a tirade about honor, duty, and self-sacrifice that would have made Kim Kinnison weep with joy (126). Sma's retort—basically, that the notion of a human taking command of a Mind-controlled GCU is as meaningless as the idea of a bacterium in a human's saliva taking over the whole body—cuts no ice.

The next step on Li's path to captaincy is an electoral dinner, during which he lists the numerous qualifications that make him the perfect candidate for a role nobody in millennia has needed to fulfill. After that, he proceeds to explain everything that's wrong with Earth's various economic systems and what needs to be done to fix the whole ghastly mess; this solution will find implementation as soon as the people onboard the *Arbitrary* elect him Captain. The entire scene (132–141), which Banks wrote with a consummate ear for comedic rhythm and a Monty Python-esque sense of the absurd, is essentially designed as a standup comedy evening: over two hundred people are sitting down and having dinner while Li harangues them from the head table—standing, of course. The proceedings are made even funnier by our knowledge that the *Arbitrary* has manufactured everything for the occasion, from the accommodations for the guests to the food and the props Li wears at the dinner. But there's also a serious aspect to this situation: when the Ship told Sma that the Culture's technological state of the art is one of the lynchpins of a utopian society that grants everyone the right to live according to their wishes, it was being perfectly serious. Li's electoral dinner, ridiculous and extravagant as it is, represents just such an example of freedom guaranteed and helped along through technology. Li'ndane himself shows up with green skin and pointy ears, wearing one of the spacesuits from *2001: A Space Odyssey* embellished with a silver Flash symbol and a Superman-style red cape. In the crook of one arm he holds the suit's helmet, and in the other hand he holds a lightsaber. Of course, Li's lightsaber actually works (132).

Sma wants a full-on intervention on Earth, while Dervley Linter wants the exact opposite. For their part, the *Arbitrary* and the quorum of Minds with whom it's in constant contact are about to decide to observe without actively intervening. Li'ndane, on the other hand, has a tidier solution: write us all off as a total loss and wipe out the Earth through the displacement of a miniature black hole into its core (140). Humanity is too far gone, he tells his hugely entertained audience, and to see that one has only to look at Earth's wealth-distribution setup, which he describes by comparing it to that of the Culture:

> I am as rich and poor as anybody in the Culture.... Rich; trapped as I am on board this uncaptained, leaderless tub, my wealth ... would seem immense to the average Earther. At home I have the run of a charming and beautiful Orbital which would seem very clean and uncrowded to somebody from Earth ... I live in a wing of a family home of mansion proportions surrounded by hectares of gorgeous gardens. I have an aircraft, a launch ... even the use of what would be called a spaceship by these people ... and all for nothing; I don't have to do anything for all this. But, at the same time, I am poor. I own nothing. Just as every atom in my body was once part of something else ... and just as one day every atom of my being will be part of something else ... so everything around me ... is there *when* I am rather than *because* I am. These things may be arranged for me, but ... they would be there for anybody else—should they desire them—too. I do not—emphatically *not*—own them [135–136].

4. Diziet Sma's Dilemmas of Intervention 89

The people of Earth, on the other hand, labor under a haphazardly globalized economic system within whose workings, Li explains, "all food, comfort, energy, shelter, space, fuel, and sustenance gravitates naturally and easily away from those who need it most and towards those who need it least" (136). It takes him quite a bit of time and a couple of pages (136–138) to present to his audience a devastating indictment of capitalism as an engine for the constant generation of inequality, deprivation, suffering, and the untimely death of millions.[5] Earthlings are, he tells everyone, an irreparably perverse mutation of the basic humanoid template, and there's nothing the Culture can do for us. Better to be merciful to every other civilization in the galaxy and make sure none of them ever runs the risk of meeting us (140).

There are a lot of things going on here. Aside from the knowing send-up of classic space opera implicit in Li's postmodern mishmash of *Star Trek*, *Star Wars*, *2001*, and Superman comics, not to mention his comments on what would happen if the Culture really did contact Earth (we wouldn't believe in a vaguely communist utopia—we'd want *empires*; 137–138), the really rather deep socio-economic analysis he presents to his fellow contact operatives is as close as Banks comes to breaking the fourth wall and announcing himself to his readers. It's clear that, in describing the functioning of the Culture's utopian economics and in comparing them to the dystopian machine he sees lording over Earth, Banks is wearing his heart on his sleeve, and the voice he projects through Li'ndane is possessed of a ferocious clarity of vision; we are expected to understand that Banks means every word.

And yet the intensity does not skew the debate; the outrage does not tip the scales. One of the writers Banks had read widely during his early years had been Robert Heinlein, who, among many other things, remains famous to this day for writing many of his stories as rhetorical traps within whose workings anyone who didn't subscribe to his own views found themselves cast as the villain. Stories like, for example, "The Roads Must Roll" (1940), *Starship Troopers* (1959), and—disastrously—*Farnham's Freehold* (1964) are rule sets arranged like that of Azad, where the winners and the losers have already been decided through an agency external to the game's context. But Banks wasn't Heinlein, and his allegiance to the utopia of the Culture did not extend merely to self-congratulatory Mary Worth moments. He believed in the society he had imagined on the page with the same strength he believed in his politics here on Earth, and because he knew that utopia is an argument first and foremost, he made sure that this argument remained workable beyond the page—that is, he set up the debate in *The State of the Art* honestly and without awarding secret bonuses to any of the voices participating in it. If, ethically speaking, the Culture is a utopia because it awards everyone the right to (1) live and think exactly as they wish and (2) have these thoughts and actions respected and valued by all concerned, well then, its arguments had better reflect such a use of freedom with us readers as well.

Which they do. None of the three flesh-sentients participating in the debate is either wholly correct or wholly incorrect. One of the reasons why Li'ndane is the character he is stems from his position as carrier wave for Banks' central beliefs. Banks wanted to make the point, but he also wanted to avoid privileging it by giving it to, say, the *Arbitrary*; so it's Li who makes it, and he really is a weirdo whom nobody takes seriously—although, crucially, he does get to have his election (nobody votes for him, and few vote at all; 142).[6] So we get to laugh at Li'ndane's antics, but at the same time part of us is considering the implications for the here and now of the points he made, which is the key characteristic of the work of a great standup comedian, as he was designed to be. Laugh all you want; and then think.

Sma, for her part, has a way of taxing our patience. Her insights into life on Earth, circa 1977, are valuable, and there's much kindness in her words. She's a good chaperon throughout the story, honest and forthright even when things don't go her way. However, her lack of confidence in humanity's chances of progress and her coincident pride in the Culture's highly developed civilizational ethics often makes even her older, more mature voice sound a little self-righteous, an attitude that at times forces her interlocutors to corral her outbursts—the *Arbitrary* first and foremost, but also Li[7] and Dervley Linter himself,[8] who wants to live on Earth because of the same rawness of existence Sma finds awful. But Sma seems to forget that the original civilizations that came together to form the first kernel of what would later become the Culture were themselves guilty of the same horrors the people of Earth have committed.[9]

And then there's Dervley Linter, who tragically does get to spend the rest of his life on Earth: at the end of *The State of the Art*, as the *Arbitrary* is preparing to leave orbit, he invites Sma to see him in New York—one last moment together. He shows up looking emaciated and tired in her eyes, and as they walk he proceeds to tell her that he's about to enter the Roman Catholic Church. Linter has found God (147).[10] Halfway through a dark alley the two are attacked by a group of muggers. Sma dispatches them quickly, but not quickly enough to spare Linter a knife wound that he refuses to let her help heal—he prevents her from contacting the *Arbitrary* long enough to make any subsequent attempt at saving him useless. The ex–Culture man dies in the alley after committing a strange form of suicide, surrounded by Sma and a gaggle of onlookers (151–153).

From a reader-response perspective, Linter is a problematic character, as he was always meant to be. On the one hand, "it is certainly the case that his slow dismantling of his Culture-being reads with all the horrific melancholy of some account of the self-mutilation of a hermit" (Clute 1995d, 291–

292), and it is indeed the case that we readers, Earthlings without Culture glued to the surface of a planet we may already have failed to husband, find it hard to be on his side in the face of what he has given up. The *Arbitrary* itself, while acknowledging him as sane in the face of Sma's insistence that there's something wrong with him (125), also points out the fallacy in his attitude toward humanity (a sort of reversed nurse's complex; 129). And yet the Ship does acknowledge the validity of Linter's point that there is an aspect to human life absent from Culture environments that can be described as beautiful precisely by virtue of—and despite—the raw, crude form of existence we have to labor under (129). Linter views this beauty in terms of the poetry of human struggle in the face of suffering and deprivation (he's been to India, an experience that transfixed him; 104), and read in this light, his seeming suicide at the end of the story does come across to us more as an acknowledgement of the seriousness of his choice than as the behavior of a suicidal madman. We on Earth don't have access to a General Contact Unit when our life is guttering, and Linter has chosen to live as one of us. His choice to also die as one of us, however tragic and seemingly pointless, possesses a warped nobility we can recognize if not necessarily applaud. In his way, he is as coherent to his system of belief as any of the Contact people onboard the departing Ship, and on the other side of the page, we readers can at the very least find respect in this strange character's devotion to our, as it were, state of the art.

The one voice without apparent fallacies, the voice that, unlike the other three, never commits to a monolithic view of Earth and its inhabitants, is that of the *Arbitrary*. The Culture, John Clute writes, "is never so clearly defined as here [in *The State of the Art*] in its post-scarcity freedom, its Golden Rule equilibrium, its gaiety" (1995d, 292), and the primary facilitator of this lightness of being is the Mind residing inside the General Contact Unit. Upon reaching Earth, Sma tells Petrain, the *Arbitrary* begins to absorb every scrap of data on and about it, in every medium available and with absolute, perfect recall (86). The information the Ship shares with those onboard similar enough in body-type to go down and explore is only a microscopic portion of this total (81), and aside from Li, at no point in the story does Sma or anyone else even think of questioning the reality that it's the *Arbitrary* who holds the most complete, most fully triangulated, most finely gauged and pervasively cross-referenced picture of Earth and humanity at that developmental stage. Sma may occasionally get angry at it, Li may try to exasperate it, and Linter may decide not to talk to it any longer, but these are nothing more than tiny tantrums in the face of the Mind's all-encompassing intellect, its searing clarity tempered by a genuine concern for the suffering of others and lightened by frequent displays of—at times gallows—humor (114, 142). The measure of the *Arbitrary*'s commitment to doing the right thing by Earth also becomes the story's most cogent statement of the Culture's own dedication to doing the right thing by every civilization it encounters. At one point, a terminally frustrated Sma asks the Ship: "How certain do we have to be? How long must we wait? How long must we make *them* wait? Who elected us God?" (130). This is the *Arbitrary*'s reply:

> Diziet ... that question is being asked all the time, and put in as many different ways as we have the wit to devise (...) and that moral equation is being reassessed every nanosecond of every day of every year, and every time we find some place like Earth—no matter what way the decision goes—we come closer to knowing the truth. But we can never be absolutely certain ... I'm the smartest thing for a hundred light years' radius, and by a factor of about a million (...) but even I can't predict where a snooker ball's going to end up after more than six collisions [131].

Nothing matters, and everything does. The snooker ball comment, small as its subject matter seems, is in fact the conceptual microcosm that contextualizes the calculations Contact undertakes at the macrocosmic level every time it encounters a civilization like Earth's: the *Arbitrary*—and with it the Minds involved in the decision to contact or not—is looking at Earth as an immensely complex system of constantly colliding life trajectories, billions of them all at once, and while precedent, experience, and the enormous power of a quorum of posthuman AIs working away at the same problem do count for a lot, certainty doesn't come into the equation. The beauty of Earth, which the *Arbitrary* construes as utility, "lies in being a living machine. It forces people to act and react. At that it is close to the theoretical limits of efficiency for a non-conscious system" (129). It takes a machine to recognize another, and the *Arbitrary*, when it looks at 1977 Earth, sees a sleeping titan, already powerful enough to wipe out everything on the planet if it stirs in the wrong direction, but already complex enough to give the Mind hope that, one day, the machinery will transcend into something possessed of awareness and, hopefully, of mercy. In the end, the *Arbitrary* is the kindest of all observers.

The State of the Art ends with the voice of another machine—Skaffen-Amtiskaw. Irritated at Sma's attitude, the drone announces itself to Petrain and informs him that, since she wrote the whole document as a continuous chunk of text, it is the one who divided it into chapters and paragraphs and provided the titles for them. These titles, Skaffen-Amtiskaw writes, are also the names of General Contact Units manufactured by a factory complex called *Infracaninophile* (157). Loosely translated, the name means "Lover of the Underdog," and it is far from the only metatextual commentary on the narrative we have just finished reading. Every other title/ship name constitutes an ironic foreshadowing of the contents of its chapter or paragraph—for example, the paragraph where Sma confronts the *Arbitrary* about the alterations it agreed to carry out on Linter is entitled *God Told Me to Do It*, the one in which Sma tours Cold-War Berlin is called *Arrested Development*, and the one where Linter first tells Sma about his decision to remain on Earth is *Just Another Victim of the Ambient Morality*. Rather perversely, Skaffen-Amtiskaw titles Sma's cover letter to Petrain *Excuses And Accusations*.

Also, the story is full of references to movies, songs, and literary works whose basic message serves as a running counterpoint to the narrative's meaning-making machinery; for example, Sma reads both *King Lear* (86, 89) and *Faust* (125), two stories that address the issue of power from two diametrically opposite viewpoints—loss of power in *Lear*, acquisition of power in *Faust*—and both of which feature self-damaging, arguably not wholly sane characters. Moreover, when she talks with Linter in Paris, the television set is broadcasting a BBC adaptation of *The Ambassadors*, Henry James' novel of the failed rescue of an American expatriate to France on the part of her sister's fiancée. At the end of the novel, the would-be rescuer returns to the U.S., his mission unfulfilled. Other references involve the whole crew of the *Arbitrary*, who one night decide they'll watch John Carpenter's *Dark Star* (85), and the ship itself, who sends via postcard a request to the BBC's World Service for David Bowie's "Space Oddity" (the request doesn't get played, which completely cracks up the *Arbitrary*; 114–115). Then there's Li, who one day suggests to Sma that she should take Linter to see *The Man Who Fell to Earth* (David Bowie again; 131), and after Li there's Linter himself, who has grown so fond of *Close Encounters of the Third Kind* that, when Sma arrives in New York to meet him, she has to wait outside the theater where he's finishing watching it for the seventh time (144–145).

In its concluding note, Skaffen-Amtiskaw also berates Sma for suggesting in her cover letter that its highly proactive regard for her safety is the result of a past act of excessive violence, in the wake of which Special Circumstances told the drone that safeguarding its human charge was the only thing between it and being "componented" (a Culture word for, as *Use of Weapons* will clarify, getting aggressively reduced to one's component parts; 78). "*My* conscience is clear," Skaffen-Amtiskaw writes at the end (157).

And then *Use of Weapons* begins right *in medias res* and from within the agonized rumblings of someone's conscience (3–5). There's a man, a mercenary, and he works for the Culture. He does their bidding if and when, in a Special Circumstances intervention in the life of another society, the time comes to do the things Culture people wouldn't do, and he is very good at doing them. He calls himself Cheradenine Zakalwe, and inside he carries memories that won't go away—terrible recollections of a great ship bristling with guns, a woman, a chair, and the maker of the chair, a man with two shadows. Throughout the novel, those images return over and over again to haunt his waking mind, their reoccurrence triggered by casual conjunctions of objects, people, and words out of which the same wounding pattern resurfaces with the insistence of something that hates (52, 70, 145–146, 283).

Initially convinced that the 1974 draft of *Use of Weapons* was unsalvageable, Banks reconsidered the fate of his prototypical non–Culture mercenary figure when Ken MacLeod, who had originally read that draft, asked to reread it ten years later:

> So he came up with two suggestions ... putting the climax of the book at the end—it had been in the middle. Because that's where the structure said it had to be, and such is my blinkeredness this seemed totally radical when he suggested it. Though, of course, also completely impossible, because of the structure—but then he suggested this two-stream idea, with one strand going forward in time and the other going back, both leading to their own climax, so that you'd get the identity revelation at the end—where it always had been—and the whole thing with the besieged battleship and so on at the end as well, where it belonged [Melia 1994, 42].[11]

This two-stream structure constitutes the most fundamental trait of *Use of Weapons*. The plotline that goes forward in time, comprised of chapters numbered 1 through 14, tells what seems to be a relatively standard Special Circumstances story: Sma and Skaffen-Amtiskaw have to find Zakalwe, who after his latest job for the Culture has gone to ground, and bring him back to a star cluster called Voerenhutz. Forty years before, working with a man called Tsoldrin Beychae, Zakalwe had secured a peaceful political structure for the cluster, with Beychae as President. But Beychae is now retired, and those who inherited his position have pulled Voerenhutz back onto the brink of war. Sma needs to find Zakalwe, take him to Voerenhutz, and help him convince Beychae that he needs to get back into politics before the whole cluster erupts into total war (21–22). And Sma does find Zakalwe, who after several suitably kinetic adventures finds Beychae, who after a few more kinetics agrees, and the story ends in success. Voerenhutz is saved.

But right next to the forward-moving plotline is the backward-moving one, comprised of chapters numbered XIII to I. The two streams alternate with each other chapter by chapter, so that chapter 1 is followed by chapter XIII, 2 by XII, and so on. This plotline tells the story of What Happened to Cheradenine Zakalwe, and its regressive nature precludes the chance of betterment. Unlike Gurgeh in *Player*, Zakalwe doesn't have the option to grow up and change. In fact, his predicament is similar in some aspects to Horza's from *Consider Phlebas*: like his predecessor, Zakalwe is trapped without chance of escape into the flow of his own life, although Horza's imprisonment is shaped by ignorance and miscalculation while Zakalwe's is determined by a weight of incurable guilt. He has done something unbearable, and the only other person alive in the galaxy who knows about it is also the one whose forgiveness he insists on seeking, without hope. "*Livueta, say you will forgive*

4. Diziet Sma's Dilemmas of Intervention 95

me," he thinks at one point early on (52), but we don't find out who Livueta is for another one hundred and fifty pages, and when we do it's in the middle of yet another regressive iteration of Zakalwe's struggle with his conscience, whose climax we approach helplessly. When we finally reach that climax, when we find out who he is and what he's done, we're left without the chance to either heal or curse him, because the story is over and the weight remains, forever. Livueta will not forgive.

But then again, it's not for us—or even for Zakalwe—to learn the lesson "conveyed by the unerring dovetail shape of this book. It is Diziet—her infrequently monitored consciousness ultimately defines the very warp and woof of *Use of Weapons*—who must embrace the significance of the conundrum. The book stops ... before she can come to a resolution; but premonitions and echoes of the angel-work she must face healingly restructure the entire text in the mind's eye, make it the best tale of the Culture yet; and the most useful" (Clute 1995a, 232–233). Banks had vastly rewritten *Use of Weapons* before publishing it, but the original impulse that had prompted its creation in the first place remained. It is, first and foremost, a Culture novel—the original Culture novel, in fact, the one Banks had written to contextualize the moral opacity of his protagonist. "I wanted to have him fighting on the side of genuine good," he said in 1994. "I thought, 'What sort of society do we need?' and out of that came the Culture. That gave me the chance to answer all the questions I had about the right-wing American space-opera I had been used to reading and which had been around since the 1930s" (Wilson 1994, n.p.).

We're back to the problem Sma faced in *The State of the Art*, and it is again Sma who must return to it one hundred and fifteen years after asking that question—"Who elected us God?"—for the first time. She is in the hospital room where, at the end of *Use of Weapons*, Livueta tells her the truth about the man she knows as Cheradenine Zakalwe, whom Sma herself had originally recruited into SC (292–294). And because after that scene there are two codas in which we get to see what Sma has decided to do next—how she continues her angel-work, as Clute put it—the workings of her conscience become once again the filter through which we view the end result of the Culture's good intentions. As Banks had pointed out in his 1989 interview with David Garnett, the Culture just doesn't raise "maniacal Rambo types," so when one is needed it has to outsource. But how does that change the morality of intervention? What difference does it make to those on the receiving end of the dirty work? What happens to utopia when it gets into the mud along with everyone else, if only with the societal equivalent of a fingertip?

Zakalwe himself, now hoping that working for SC will ensure he'll be doing some good (261), asks Sma the same questions, and her reply is every bit as honest as he has a right to expect. We've heard it before, too—it's a rewording of what the *Arbitrary* had told her when she'd been doing the asking: it's impossible to know for sure. The Culture has been doing more thinking on the score than anyone else, and it does have data to back up its convictions, but ultimately there's no such thing as certainty, and there are always ethical positions opposite its own (261–262). The role of Special Circumstances is, in this sense, prediction-opaque:

> They dealt in the intrinsically untoward, where rules were forged as you went along and were never the same twice anyway, where just by the nature of things nothing could be known, or predicted, or even judged with any real certainty. It all sounded very sophisticated and abstract and challenging to work with, but in the end it came down to people and problems [50].

And Zakalwe does engage with people during his orientation days onboard the General Systems Vehicle *Size Isn't Everything*—which, despite wearing that name, is eighty kilometers long (250). Spurred by Sma to be on his own for a while and experience Culture life, he gets to know who makes up this society that calls itself the good guys and claims to only want to help. He also receives a technical introduction because, where Minds and drones are concerned, tech is people. Thus, Zakalwe hears about the force field-based technology that makes it possible for things the size of the GSV to hold together, about the exotic materials that go into the making of a ship's faster-than-light engines, and about the nature of AIs, especially the Minds that control everything to the point where, to his disquiet, he finds out that there are no main bridges, control rooms, flight decks, or for that matter crew onboard the GSV. There are only passengers (250–251, 255–256).

There's more. If the exotic physics and the essentially magical technology tax Zakalwe's sense of the plausible, the social arrangement tests his moral boundaries. "Look; this table's clean," a man tells him at a restaurant. Most places he has seen are staffed by non-sentient machines that take care of everything, but every now and then one such place will have a human staff composed of people who "seemed less like servants and more like customers who'd taken a notion to help out for a while" (251). The two men fall into a conversation, and Zakalwe learns that his interlocutor usually works on comparative studies of alien religions; however, because of the constant process of evaluation, contextualization, discovery of new samples, and reevaluation of the old samples in the light of the new, the work is never finished. "But ... when you clean a table you clean a table. You feel you've done something. It's an achievement," the man tells him, and when Zakalwe comments that, in the grand scheme of things, cleaning a table counts for little, this is how the other responds:

> But then, what *does* signify? My other work? Is that really important, either? I could try composing wonderful musical works, or day-long entertainment epics, but what would that do? Give me pleasure? My wiping this table gives me pleas-

4. Diziet Sma's Dilemmas of Intervention

ure. And people come to a clean table, which gives *them* pleasure. And anyway … people die; stars die; universes die. What is an achievement, however great it was, once time itself is dead? Of course, if *all* I did was wipe tables, then of course it would seem a mean and despicable waste of my huge intellectual potential. But because I choose to do it, it gives me pleasure [251-252].

In the man's comments lies an echo of Li'ndane's point about things being there when he is rather than because he is, which implies a system of values that has retained a sense of what matters precisely because it has discovered that nothing does intrinsically. There's no God in Banks' universe, no objective network of meaning transcending the bondage of the moment, so the pain of sentience—which the Culture has managed to reduce to its maximum allowable extent—consists in the struggle to laboriously *invest* the moment with meaning, knowing that such investment remains only as long as we do. Most times, our lives fade out after what, in cosmic terms, is a vanishingly short timespan, and no one notices. If some do notice and carry our legacy along with them, one day *their* lives will fade out, and so on in perpetuity until perpetuity itself vanishes, and all is silence. So the people of the Culture enjoy the time they have when they have it, and take pleasure in the things they accomplish—from cleaning a table to helping whole civilizations along—because who will if they don't? At another point, Zakalwe asks a woman working on the still skeletal hull of a brand new GCU in the General Systems Vehicle's Mainbay if a machine wouldn't be able to perform her function better and more efficiently:

"Why, of course!" she laughed.
"Then why do you do it?"
"It's fun. You see one of those big mothers sail out those doors for the first time, heading for deep space, three hundred people on board, everything working, the Mind quite happy, and you think; I helped build that. The fact that a machine could have done it faster doesn't alter the fact that it was you who did it" [254].

Zakalwe spends a few days in the company of these people who don't seem to take anything too seriously and everything more seriously than they should. He walks through the vast spaces of the GSV, never seeing the same place twice and never returning to a previously trodden path. When he needs food and drink, he orders them at bars and restaurants, and when he needs to sleep he asks the nearest drone, who directs him to the closest free room (252). He can do whatever he wants, request whatever he wants, and receive it without the need to exchange goods, money, or services. Again, there are echoes of Li'ndane's speech in the *Arbitrary*: from the point of view of both Earth and Zakalwe's place of origin, everyone in the Culture is at once fabulously rich because they have access to everything and utterly poor because no one owns anything. The rooms Zakalwe sleeps in will be someone else's the next night, and those in which other people slept before will be his to utilize for as long as he wants—in a post-scarcity economy, everything is available to everyone. He could desire a house of his own, just like Gurgeh's Ikroh in *The Player of Games*, and one would be built for him without question or expectation of payment. If anyone else wanted that same house, another just like it would be built for them as well; space is no more at a premium than resources are. And should he wish, Zakalwe could participate in the building of his house, thus slowing down the process because machines would be able to do it more quickly and efficiently—but it'd be fun.

Zakalwe also takes part in dream-state virtual games with other people linked with him through machinery he doesn't understand (252), and has plenty of excellent sex thanks to Culture genofixing (259–260). And all along, all through this neverending carousel of what should be innocent, guilt-free pleasures, the memories of the chair and the woman and the chairmaker press against the boundaries of his mind, never far away and never less than excruciating. Also, he doesn't find himself quite at home inside the GSV; the mores of Culture people—or rather, the lack of same—bother him more than he's prepared to admit (253, 255). In a way, Zakalwe does have something in common with Gurgeh: like Gurgeh, he is a fish-out-of-water character through whose eyes we get to look at a place so content with itself that describing it without some sort of behavioral reagent would be dull. Gurgeh acts as that behavioral reagent in *Player* because he starts out as a contrarian among his own people, while Zakalwe's reagent role stems from the scarcity-system morals he brings with him as an alien.[12] And indeed, it takes another alien to explain the Culture to him in a way he can functionally accept. When he meets her in a café he finds out that she is a fellow Special Circumstance agent, and when he asks her what the relation of SC to the Culture at large is, she tells him that "it is in layers…. A tiny core of Special Circumstances, a shell of Contact, and a vast chaotic sphere of everything else…. But in the end, you will never know them, because you will be like me, in Special Circumstances, and only ever know them as the great, irresistible force behind you; people like you and I are the edge; you will in time come to feel like a tooth on the biggest saw in the galaxy" (257). The alien, whose name is Chori (259), also gives Zakalwe a piece of advice he later fails to heed—he shouldn't expect to be told everything about his assignments. Should he insist in being told the whole truth all the time, SC would acquiesce, but then they wouldn't be able to utilize his services as often as they otherwise could. "Sometimes they need you not to know you are fighting on the wrong side," Chori tells him (258).

In the end, introduced to the mainstream of Culture life and warned about his upcoming career as a tooth on the saw blade, Zakalwe returns to Sma and accepts her offer of employment. But that was decades ago and two hundred pages further into the novel; now, in the present-moving-toward-the-future plotline and eighty pages in, Sma is faced with her erstwhile charge's mutiny. After decades of not being told the truth, and in the wake of an operation that ended in disaster, Zakalwe has had enough; he kills the knife missile tasked with keeping him under observation and, with the money he received for his previous jobs, sets up shop in an open cluster called Crastalier, where he decides it's high time he "started trying to be a good guy in his own right" and creates his own private Contact section (86). The results are catastrophic, so that the Culture now finds itself trying to stop the onset of war on two star clusters instead of one (83–86).

The basic problem, as the narrative repeatedly makes clear, is that the Culture hired Zakalwe to be precisely the sort of man he's trying to stop being, the one who did that awful thing with the girl and the chair and the chairmaker and Livueta who won't forgive him. SC is using him for good, but not his own, and the calculations that go into the Culture's ecumenical intervention policies are far enough above the heads of non–Culture people that his actions as—it often turns out in the aftermath—the one who was fighting on the wrong side keep wounding his conscience. "They teach you that sort of stuff in early school, in the Culture," Sma tells Zakalwe when she addresses his botched attempt at improving Crastalier. "It was all thought through long ago; it's part of our history, part of our upbringing. That's why what you did would look insane to a school-kid.... You could have changed your life; you don't have to live the way you do; you could have joined the Culture," at which point he would have learned the same things Culture people have learned (131). But Zakalwe won't join and won't change who he is because he can't—not before Livueta forgives him, this version of him, the one that can't stand to look at chairs, and that she'll never do. So, stuck in a loop out of which he can't escape, forgetful of Chori's warning, and frustrated in his attempts at doing some good of his own, he grows bitter at SC's handling of his services:

> You've also lied to me ... sent me on damn fool missions where I was on the opposite side from the one I thought I was on, had me fight for incompetent aristos I'd gladly have strangled, in wars where I didn't know you were backing both sides ... *very* nearly got me killed a dozen times or more [132].

The Voerenhutz mission therefore begins under evil auspices, and Sma, whom Zakalwe at once horrifies and fascinates, spends the duration worrying about her charge, wondering whether he may not go off the rails like he'd done on that last debacle and calling him often to make sure he's not planning to carry out his duties in an overly violent fashion.[13] In this, Skaffen-Amtiskaw is of little help because Sma doesn't fully trust it either. Early on in *Use of Weapons*, it transpires that, despite the drone's prim assurance at the end of

The Sate of the Art that "*my* conscience is clear," Sma's claim of past misdeeds on its part is accurate. About twenty years before Crastalier, Sma and Skaffen-Amtiskaw had been assigned to a fairly remote, barbarous world. One day, confronted by slavers who believed Sma's skin color would fetch a high price, Skaffen-Amtiskaw reacted with overwhelming force, massacring the entire party of men in such a bloody fashion that two girls they had already captured ended up being more scared of the drone than of the slavers (39–42). Furious at the machine, disgusted at the pleasure it clearly felt in performing those actions, Sma told it that it would either use minimal force in the future or be reduced to slag (42). And indeed the drone has been using minimum force ever since, but for much the same reasons Zakalwe can't forget the chair and everything that came with it, Sma can't forget what happened on that planet (86). *Somebody's* conscience has to ache over deeds of that kind, and when she realizes that Skaffen-Amtiskaw's is uttering nary a peep, she takes on the burden the drone should be carrying.

Thus, Sma is caught between two sentients of the same basic nature. Zakalwe and Skaffen-Amtiskaw resemble each other more than either resembles her, and the machine does display a singularly cynical, abrasive attitude throughout the novel, not to mention a rather nasty sense of humor—in fact, there are various behavioral similarities between Skaffen-Amtiskaw and Mawhrin-Skel from *Player*, except that Mawhrin-Skel was a persona, a mask invented to perform a role; Skaffen-Amtiskaw is really there in all its discomfiting glee.[14] It is also the first to find out the truth about the man when, toward the end of the novel, it and Sma carry a mortally wounded Zakalwe into the hospital where Livueta, now old, works as a nurse. Zakalwe has carried out his assignment and Voerenhutz is on the mend, but a side action in which SC involves him in the immediate wake of the original mission's completion once again places him in fighting-for-the-wrong-side circumstances. Shattered at being the victim of yet another machination, Zakalwe walks out in the middle of a battle without carrying weapons or seeking concealment. Grievously wounded but refusing treatment, he has Sma and the drone take him to Livueta to once again beg her forgiveness before he dies of what is essentially a complicated form of suicide (another point of contact with *The State of the Art*: Dervley Linter, also wounded in battle, makes essentially the same decision).

On the way, Zakalwe tells the drone and the woman a story that the steady regression of chapters has already made clear to us—almost; there's only one piece missing (169–176, 178–185, 338–350). It's the story of four children: Cheradenine Zakalwe, his sisters Livueta and Darckense, and their cousin Elethiomel. They grow up together through the course of many years, playing and studying in a great summer estate owned by the Zakalwe family until the onset of war puts Cheradenine and Elethiomel on opposing sides—

each is the supreme commander of one of the two armies. Toward the end of the war, when Cheradenine's forces have all but won, Elethiomel kidnaps Darckense and carries her onboard a giant dreadnought-type battleship called *Staberinde*[15] that he then proceeds to becalm in the very harbor of his enemy's capital city. Elethiomel can't escape, but Cheradenine doesn't dare attack for fear of what might happen to his sister. It's Elethiomel that breaks the deadlock by having his men send Cheradenine and Livueta a chair:

> It was small and white, and as he [Cheradenine] took a couple of more paces forwards ... he saw that it had been made out of the bones of Darckense Zakalwe.... They had tanned her skin and made a little cushion out of it [349–350].

The sight breaks Cheradenine. Unseeing, incapable of coherent thought, he withdraws into his stateroom and shoots himself, at which point "the besieged forces round the *Staberinde* broke out ... while the surgeons were still fighting for his life" (350), and narrowly lose the ensuing battle.

This Zakalwe tells Sma and Skaffen-Amtiskaw, but he withholds the final piece of information. It's Livueta who provides it, by which point the drone has already guessed. Angry with SC for intruding into her life, Livueta Zakalwe tells the two Culture agents that her brother Cheradenine had died that day; the surgeons had been unable to save him. The man they know as Zakalwe is in fact Elethiomel, who after the battle for the *Staberinde* had taken on his cousin's name (363). Thus the main body of the novel ends, with Livueta leaving the room, Sma petrified by the revelation, and Skaffen-Amtiskaw trying to reduce a massive aneurysm in Zakalwe/Elethiomel's brain, "engrossed in its struggle to do good" (363).[16]

Buried about a third of the way into *Use of Weapons*, there's a passage that perfectly encapsulates both the novel's title and the nature of Sma's conundrum. The passage begins with Zakalwe staring out at a steady wall of rain, upon whose seemingly unbroken surface he projects the shapes that haunt his mind; he sees the ship, the chair, and the man with two shadows, and then, heralded by the sequence that preceded it, "that which cannot be seen":

> A concept; the adaptive, self-seeking urge to survive, to bend everything that can be reached to that end ... the method was that taking and bending of materials and people to one purpose, the outlook that everything could be used in the fight; that nothing could be excluded, that everything was a weapon [145–146].

Like *The Player of Games*, *Use of Weapons* is a polyvalent title.[17] On the surface, Zakalwe/Elethiomel is the eponymous user of weapons: his philosophy of usage, perfected through the decades since the day he utilized the body of Darckense Zakalwe as one such implement in the war against his cousin, has made him supremely adept at the art of warfare. He is therefore of value to Special Circumstances, which, through two other weapons in its own employ—Sma and Skaffen-Amtiskaw—uses him; SC is another user of weapons, then, and to the extent that the Culture created SC to negotiate the moral fringe territories, the Culture is yet another user and SC yet another weapon. Everyone becomes a wargamer in this novel—wargamer is another name for weapons user—and everyone practices, with greater or lesser degrees of success, the art of utilizing everything and everyone at their disposal as an offensive implement. Thus, everyone and everything is also a weapon, from the plasma gun that Zakalwe takes to Voerenhutz to Zakalwe himself, from a knife missile to Sma and Skaffen-Amtiskaw, from SC to the Culture. Everyone uses, everyone is used, and the damages multiply as usage intensifies. Every user of weapons in this story has an ambivalent relationship with their tools: the Culture at large employs SC but doesn't really want to talk about its existence—it behaves too much like one of the barbarians, even if it's all in the name of doing good; Sma utilizes Skaffen-Amtiskaw but doesn't always like doing so—she can't forget the time the drone used *its* weapons; Sma and the drone use Zakalwe on behalf of SC but don't much trust him—too volatile and driven by feelings he can't control; and Zakalwe himself employs everything and everyone he finds whether they want to or not, which is why his life is made up of ashes—everything he touches burns up with usage.

The conundrum Sma has to face on behalf not only of herself, SC, Skaffen-Amtiskaw, or even Zakalwe, but also on the reader's, consists in the reality that to use a weapon is to be used by it; every handle is also the barrel, every grip is also the blade, every detonator is also the bomb, and blood falls on everyone. "Who elected us God?" Sma had asked the *Arbitrary* one hundred and fifteen years before; the Mind had replied that there are no certainties, and that's what she'd told Zakalwe when he'd asked if she could guarantee he'd be doing good works. But one day SC loses Zakalwe when he begins feeling that, within the larger picture of doing good, he's always playing the part of the one doing bad—hence his abortive attempt at fixing things on Crastalier. There are shades of us on Earth here, of governments and espionage agencies using fundamentally uncontrollable assets who, years after they've ceased to be useful, resurface as enemies, criminals or terrorists who use the skills they were taught against others or against their former employers. Again, to use a weapon is to be used by it in turn.

So, once she finds out what kind of weapon she has brought into SC's fold and what kind of ammunition that weapon had once used, what's Sma's response to the conundrum? In the face of Zakalwe/Elethiomel's sins, how does she continue her angel-work, if at all?

The structure of *Use of Weapons* is possibly the most complex among the Culture novels. Aside from the twin-stream plotlines and their partitioning into three main sections ("The Good Soldier," "An Outing," and "Remembrance"), two sets of inserts frame the main body of the text, one before and

4. Diziet Sma's Dilemmas of Intervention

one after it. The set before is comprised of an unpublished poem written by Sma and of a prologue. The poem, entitled "Slight Mechanical Destruction," is about Zakalwe, and from textual evidence it's retrospectively clear that Sma wrote it after the events in *Use of Weapons*:

> Savage child; the throwback from wayback
> Expedient because
> Utopia spawns few warriors.
> But you knew your figure cut a cipher
> Through every crafted plan
> And playing our game for real
> Saw through our plumbing jobs
> And wayward glands
> To a meaning of your own, in bones [n.p.].

The meaning of the last line won't become clear until we're done reading the book, which means that Sma could only have written it after she herself discovered the secrets in Zakalwe's past. Also, at the end of the poem there's a bibliographical note indicating that Sma translated the poem into Earth English and gave the year of composition as 115 on the Khmer Calendar (n.p.). That she should connect Zakalwe's life to Kampuchea and the Khmer Rouge is already a bad sign, but the other interesting part is the date itself—115, which is also the number of years that separate the events narrated in *The State of the Art* from those in *Use of Weapons*. Also, if we backtrack along the timeline of the Kingdom of Cambodia to the horrors of Pol Pot's regime and the beginning of Year Zero, that gives us AD 1977, the time Sma was on Earth with Contact in *The State of the Art*. In the story, she refers with horror to the events of Year Zero (128),[18] and it's likely that, in the wake of her discovery of Zakalwe's true identity, she has connected one set of trauma-laden recollections with another. As the *Staberinde* and the chair haunt Zakalwe's waking hours, so Earth haunts Sma's.

The second insert is the prologue in which we meet Zakalwe in the flesh for the first time, and for the first time glimpse in his mind the image of the chair (5). The events in the prologue—another SC mission—are unconnected to either of the sequences in the text, and from the overall tone it's likely that they are taking place in the aftermath of what transpires in *Use of Weapons*. This probability is further strengthened once we get to the end of the story and read the second set of framing inserts, which begins with an epilogue (367–368) that continues where the prologue left off. Zakalwe and his associate, a man named Cullis, are still on mission, still working to place a nuke at a particular spot along a road where an army is supposed to be marching. At the end of the epilogue/prologue, the nuke goes off without a hitch.

There are two more inserts. The first is another poem, this time written by a poetess named Shias Engin with whom Zakalwe had had an intense liaison during one of his periods of "vacation" from SC (109–120). The poem, which the bibliographical information at the bottom indicates as belonging to the volume of "Juvenilia and Discarded Drafts" of Engin's "Complete and Collected Works (Posthumous Edition)," is entitled "Zakalwe's Song" (369–371), and the song is a melody of breakage and rift, of sundering between souls that cannot ultimately communicate to each other.

The third and final insert isn't about Zakalwe at all—it's about Sma. Banks writes here as if he were beginning the prologue to a brand-new novel entitled *States of War*, and accordingly the brief text resets the page numbering back to 1. In it, Sma walks up to a young, legless man in the gardens of a rest home for crippled veterans; the name and location of the planet aren't specified. The man, whom Sma addresses as Mr. Escoerea, is a decorated war hero, and as is the case for many such heroes he is disillusioned and embittered by the conflict that cost him not only his legs (he'd tried to pull a comrade out of the way of an onrushing tank), but his whole family as well. "These I'd trade you," Escoerea tells Sma, brandishing his medals; "all of them for a pair of shoes I could wear" (2). Her reply concludes the novel:

> "The deal with the medals and the shoes; fair enough.... Except you can keep the medals." She reached into the basket, took out the clippers and stuck them into the earth under the plants, then put her hands, clasped, on the front of the seat. "Now, Mr. Escoerea.... How would you like a proper job?" [3].

And the neverending struggle to try to do good never ends. After the hospital, after Zakalwe and Elethiomel and Livueta, after the poem she wrote in two languages but never showed anyone, Sma is acquiring another weapon for SC's arsenal. She still believes that the Culture stands for better things, and still allows herself to be used as a weapon, knowing that, somewhere else, Zakalwe is also still being used. She knows the truth of the conundrum now, and she agonizes plenty over it, but that agonizing is part of a future-oriented decision-making process, not the aftermath guilt of someone who hadn't thought things through before acting. She is of the Culture, yes, but she's also a citizen of the fringe, the place where utopia meets its twin, where the morally correct choice reshapes itself after every iteration and rulebooks are largely nonexistent. To the list of her reflections on what happened in *Use of Weapons* we should also add *The State of the Art*, since she wrote her memoir after the events in the novel. Seen from this perspective, her thoughts on Earth circa 1977 acquire a whole other interpretive layer, as do those of Skaffen-Amtiskaw in its editorial interpolations.

Up to and including *Use of Weapons*—and, in truth, a couple of novels beyond it—Banks' Culture works received little or no mention from literary critics (his non-genre novels, by contrast, had already begun attracting a certain amount of attention). There were plenty of reviews in the SF magazines of the time—in the United States, *Locus* reviewed all four stories, and in the UK both *Interzone* and *White Dwarf* did their part. John Clute took care of the *Interzone* reviews, which have already been referenced, quoted, leant on, used as excuses, or otherwise pilfered in this work. Of all the reviewers, Clute was the one most willing to take Banks up on his utopian project and seriously engage his sustained problematization of the morals of contact and intervention. Next to him was David Langford, who reviewed *Consider Phlebas* and *The Player of Games* in his monthly "Critical Mass" column in *White Dwarf*, which at the time was still primarily a magazine of role-playing, wargaming, and fantasy/SF rather than the house organ for Games Workshop's products it later became. Langford, always with his tongue in his cheek, treated both novels primarily as fun, hugely destructive romps through the furniture of space opera, although he was, like Clute, irritated at Banks' use of absurdly long, dictionary-in-a-blender names, and he did agree with Clute on the society that provided the model for the Empire in *Player*: Langford described Azad as "an intricate system of dog-eat-dog viciousness, surpassing even the legendary horrors of the City of London in the barbaric era of Thatcher" (2002, 264).

Besides these reviews, plus a number of interviews with fantasy/SF magazines on both sides of the Atlantic, nothing happened in the way of so-called serious criticism.[19] There were only two exceptions: the first was an article by Lawrence Person in the same February 1990 issue of *Science Fiction Eye* where Michael Cobley interviewed Banks, and the second was a review of/essay on *Use of Weapons* that Colin Greenland penned for issue #50 of *Foundation* (Autumn 1990). Person's article is at once a critical introduction to the universe of the Culture and a rundown of the three Culture stories published thus far—*Use of Weapons* was still a few months away at the time. Aside from mischaracterizing the relationship between Contact and Special Circumstances—Contact investigates other civilizations while SC "acts as CIA, FBI, and SS, all rolled into one" (33)—Person does a good job of succinctly describing the Culture's basic shape. He also correctly seizes on one of Banks' great writing strengths as a key factor in the differentiation of the Culture stories from the basic space-opera template: Person's emphasis is on character development, which ensures that those characters, "both major and minor, are sharply drawn and well realized, their actions and attitudes entirely believable within the multi-textured webs of their outlook and motivation" (33). As examples, he picks Horza and the Free Company—Balveda and drone included—from *Phlebas* and Gurgeh from *Player* (33–34).

Person's criticism of Banks' first novel addresses the same concern with unnecessary verbiage Clute had expressed three years before, which is par for the course, but his other argument is more problematic: after describing the Culture as a "utopian state in the 'third stage' of communism (i.e., the one where Marx predicted the state would 'wither away')," Person goes on to explain that his issue with this notion is twofold:

> Personally, I rank the plausibility of third stage communism right up there with the Tooth Fairy, but a more significant problem is that we are given very little idea of how The Culture actually works, a problem that will crop up more frequently in the later books [34].

The good thing about this passage is that, like Clute, Person takes Banks at his word—there would be no need to worry about plausibility if the arguments behind the descriptions weren't serious. The bad thing is that Person's complaint about the lack of an idea of how the Culture works in *The Player of Games* and *The State of the Art* is inaccurate: aside from the nearly one hundred pages *Player* spends on Chiark Orbital, and discounting for a moment the fact that the *Arbitrary* in *State* is as much a Culture habitat as it is a ship (it does spend months in deep space, keeping three hundred Contact people not just alive and functioning, but also happy and contented by the Culture's standards of comfort), everyone in both stories keeps talking about the Culture's shape, nature, and function. Gurgeh describes the Culture's social setup to Azadian authorities, who are more than willing to compare it to Azad's own (unfavorably, of course), and he has plenty of discussions with Flere-Imsaho and the *Limiting Factor* that address the reasons why Contact first and SC later took an interest in the Empire. Sma and Linter and Li and the *Arbitrary*, for their part, do nothing but discuss the Culture through the lens of Earth's situation. Ultimately, every one of Banks' stories is as much a probing of the Culture's own definition of itself as it is an exposé of the dystopian systems it comes in to fix, and as we will see in the next chapter, this twin process of questioning can be described as the most fundamental trait of the Culture not so much as an actual social model, but rather as the argument for one, because in the end this is what utopia is first and foremost—an argument.

As for Person's plausibility problem, two things need to be said about it: first, Marx's formulation of the third stage in a communist system hadn't taken into consideration either a post-scarcity economy or a posthuman level of technological advancement, both of which Banks considered indispensable for achieving a society that could aspire to utopian status (again, see the next chapter). Second, the issue of plausibility is, for Person, intimately bound with an issue of moral credibility, which connects his article to Colin Greenland's review in *Foundation*. Person's reading of *The State of the Art* was largely negative for a variety of reasons, but the most glaring in his eyes was the Culture's shaky moral ground:

> It's not that what his characters are saying is wrong (Yes Iain, racism, war and genocide are bad. So what else is new?), it's just that ... even were I able to give

4. Diziet Sma's Dilemmas of Intervention 107

The Culture any sort of credence, their participation in a war that killed roughly 851.4 billion sentient beings despite the fact that no portion of their territory was ever threatened, I find their condemnation of war and killing hypocritical at best. Having The Culture talk about the failings of our own world is like Luke Skywalker condemning racism, or Spider-man taking on the problem of the homeless: the medium is inherently unsuitable to the message [35].

Never mind the glibness of the authorial voice: why is Luke Skywalker an unsuitable medium for addressing racism, and why can't Spider-Man take on the problem of the homeless? By the same token, the notion that the Culture's treading of a morally ambiguous path makes it an unsuitable platform for discussing racism, war, and genocide is inaccurate. Even if Banks had truly meant to set up the Culture as a hypocritical, secretly imperialistic straw-man system to knock down—which he pointedly *didn't* do—that setup would have been the perfect chance to discuss those problems precisely for that reason. Of equal validity is the idea of having the kind of discussion Banks actually did have in every one of his Culture novels: an earnest argument about the moral fringe territories and the ethics of intervention on the part of a society that retains its view of itself as a Good Place despite engaging with the Bad Ones.

On this score, Greenland in his *Foundation* piece echoes Person, although the two arguments don't fully overlap. For one, Greenland mostly discusses *Use of Weapons*, which he likes and credits with being the M-Banks novel that finally figured out how to use the medium of space opera "to display proper moral and political complexity"—unlike the three previous stories, which he considers to be at least partly unsuccessful early tries (90). Secondly, he displays no difficulty in accepting the premise of Banks' post-scarcity utopia as plausible, and thirdly he understands the relationship between the Culture, Contact, and SC better than Person (90). His review of *Use of Weapons* correctly reads *The State of the Art* as a preamble to the action in the novel, and makes it clear that we should read the two stories together (90–91, 92).

And yet, Greenland too misreads some fundamental aspects of Banks' argument, partly out of an assumption that the really good bits of *Use of Weapons* are the ones that most closely resemble Banks' no-M work (92–93) and that the space-opera bits are "merry, wobbly nonsense" (93).[20] While discussing *State*, for example, he writes:

> How the Culture came to be, and how it actually works, politically and economically, has not yet been examined. Use of Weapons establishes that it never should be. The intergalactic commune is not a place. It is a device, a pretext, a common property Banks has added to the science fiction conjuring set. Maps are not available [91].

This assertion is, once again, inaccurate, although it is not Greenland's fault that most of the stories addressing the specifics of the Culture's birth were still in the future at the time. What is his fault is the inability to see that the Culture is not just a device, and that it is anything but a pretext. We have already looked at the interviews, and we've read the novels thus far. We can accuse Banks of falling short of his objectives in making his arguments, although that would be unfair, but we cannot maintain that his allegiance as a writer did not really belong to the society he had been building in his mind since 1974. Banks means what he says and his argument is genuine, devoid of hidden deconstructive agendas. That the Culture's behavior deserves to be subject to scrutiny isn't under discussion, and the reason why it's not under discussion is that Banks has the Culture itself do most of the scrutinizing. From Fal N'geestra to Sma to the *Arbitrary* to Gurgeh and so on, a fundamental part of doing angel-work is, for Culture personnel, to perform this work on themselves and their own society first. Greenland uses as proof of what he sees as Banks' deconstructive attitude a passage about two-thirds of the way into *Use of Weapons*. In this passage, which has already been discussed above, Zakalwe, freshly returned from his exploration of Culture life onboard the *Size Isn't Everything*, asks Sma whether she can guarantee he'd be doing good works. Greenland quotes her reply, with subsequent commentary:

> "We deal in the moral equivalent of black holes," explains one of its [the Culture's] servitors, "where the normal laws—the rules of right and wrong that people imagine apply everywhere else in the universe—break down; beyond those metaphysical event horizons." Anyone who does not recognize the jazzy metaphor as pernicious cant is probably reading the wrong author, and Use of Weapons proves it [90].

This does sound like pernicious cant, and one may be tempted to agree with Greenland unless one happened to read the whole two pages in which Zakalwe and Sma's argument takes place (261–262), at which point the added context would go a long way toward redeeming her rhetorical flourish. Also, simply describing Sma as one of the Culture's "servitors" robs her character of the role it actually plays in the story. But even if the words Greenland quoted had been the only pertinent ones on that page, why use them and not, for example, those on page 50 (quoted earlier in this chapter) in which Zakalwe remembers Sma's words under a considerably richer light? Contrast this approach with Faren Miller's in her *Locus* reviews of the four Culture novels: Miller awards *Consider Phlebas* a generous, flattering assessment as a "splendid, rip-roaring adventure by an author who's clearly at home in the genre and well equipped to make the most of it" (1987, 13), and she's not in the least bothered by the longueurs Clute and Person zeroed in on. As for *The Player of Games*, Miller praises the novel's reconfiguring of "hoary sf concepts—the game for ultimate stakes, the barbaric space empire, eccentric machine minds—and com[ing] up with a novel of genuine depth and beauty

... [whose] hints and glimpses are as seductively evocative as Hesse's *Glass Bead Game*" (1988, 17). But it's in her evaluation of *The State of the Art* and *Use of Weapons* that Miller displays the understanding of Banks' intentions for the Culture series that escaped both Greenland and Person: her review of *Use of Weapons* correctly focuses on the series' presentation of "a civilization which commands a vast extent of space and time without turning into a clichéd galactic empire. The Culture is not ponderously, decadently neo–Roman or neo–Chinese, not blandly utopian or blatantly imperialistic. It can interact with less sophisticated systems in a great number of ways, from diplomacy to conventional warfare to gamesmanship to subtle, sometimes sneaky, sometimes daffy manipulations." The drama at the heart of *Use of Weapons*, Miller correctly writes, is the deployment of the Culture's virtually infinite resources and intellectual power "to explore a realm where even its sophistication may falter: the depths of a man's heart" (1990, 15–17).

And finally, there's Miller's review of *The State of the Art*, in which she assesses the Culture and its ecumenical good works in terms easily applicable to the other three novels:

> This isn't the *Star Trek* gang time-tripping back to San Francisco to save the whales. The explorers from the *Arbitrary* move unseen, go everywhere, absorb all the brutality and raw vigor of humanity, and are not harmed—unless they wish to be. The arch tone of the 'Culture' books, with their sassy drones, impertinent footnotes, and absurdly titled ships, should not be mistaken for escapism. In *The State of the Art*, Banks confronts the troubled Earth head-on. Rediscovering ourselves as the Culture discovers us ... we find reason for both admiration and despair. Can the planet survive? We'll have to live out our own sequels to begin to learn the answers [1989, 13].

Obviously, one does not have to agree with Miller or Clute and disagree with Greenland or Person. Wherever one's evaluation of the merits of the Culture stories falls, the opinions recorded above—as well as the opinions presented in this very book—are arguments, no more or less. The problem is that, through no fault of Clute, Miller, Person, or Greenland's, the reviews of SF novels in "popular" magazines did not have then and do not have now the same weight as a piece published in academically accredited literary journals like *Foundation*. All the voices mustered in this chapter should have fed into a community of discourse within which they would have had equal weight, but it didn't happen that way. Like Person before him, Greenland took as a given that Banks' deconstructive attitude toward the traditional form of space opera also extended to the Culture itself, and that at the end of the day he turned everything to ashes, the Culture along with everything else. This was simply untrue, but unfortunately, as we will see further along, this view gradually took root in academic circles.

5

THE YEARS OF TAKING STOCK
The Culture as a Critical Utopia

By the time the next novel in the series—*Excession*—appeared in 1996, six years had elapsed. It was a considerable amount of time, especially for a writer as prolific as Banks.

He hadn't exactly been slacking off, though. Between *Use of Weapons* and *Excession*, a total of five novels saw print: three no-M novels—*The Crow Road* (1992), *Complicity* (1993), and *Whit* (1995)—and two non–Culture space operas: *Against a Dark Background* (1993) and *Feersum Endjinn* (1994). So it wasn't writer's block, ennui, or burnout that put the Culture series on hiatus, but rather, conceivably, a sense Banks felt that it was time to sum up the work he'd done thus far. To this writer's knowledge, Banks never openly indicated a conscious decision on his part to put the Culture in the back burner while he figured out the next step, but there is enough circumstantial evidence to suggest that, consciously or otherwise, he may in fact have done so.

By 1990, Banks had completed the first great step in his development of the Culture universe: he'd rewritten and published all the previously rejected stories he'd composed between 1974 and 1982. In 1991, the short-story collection *The State of the Art* appeared, containing the only two Culture short stories Banks had written along with the eponymous novella,[1] and in 1993 the one previously rejected non–Culture space opera, *Against a Dark Background*, saw print. Having closed the chapter on the early stages of his career, Banks now found himself looking, for the first time in twenty years, at the composition of a wholly original Culture story. That may have given him pause, and it may also have provided him with the impulse to sum up the history of the Culture until that point—a way of taking stock, of looking at his brainchild as a determinedly shaped, growing argument. The result was an essay entitled "A Few Notes on the Culture," which Banks asked Ken MacLeod to post to the online newsgroup rec.arts.sf.written (Butler 2003, vii). The essay, which appeared on August 10, 1994, is best described as Banks' manifesto for the writing of space opera, although Banks himself would have rejected the gravitas of such a description. Witness for instance the unassuming title and the beginning, which reads:

> FIRSTLY, AND MOST IMPORTANTLY: THE CULTURE DOESN'T REALLY EXIST. IT ONLY EXISTS IN MY MIND AND THE MINDS OF THE PEOPLE WHO'VE READ ABOUT IT. That having been made clear: The Culture is a group-civilisation formed from seven or eight humanoid species, space-living elements of which established a loose federation approximately nine thousand years ago. The ships and habitats which formed the original alliance required each others' support to pursue and maintain their independence from the political power structures ... they had evolved from [167].[2]

Together with a relatively precise time of origin and the mention that the Culture is a mostly humanoid civilization, we also have the indication that its birth was indeed the result of a conflicted breakaway stance. The Culture was born as a movement toward and an argument for freedom from all forms of bondage, a freedom that the technological and scientific reality of life in space guaranteed well beyond the successful resolution of the breakaway moment. Banks' argument is structured around a series of contentions that he openly flags at the appropriate points in the text, so that the essay ends up being more than a simple rundown of the shape and behavior of the Culture's core society—rather, it becomes a reflection on utopia and on the viewpoint of those who argue for it.

The first contention has direct bearing on the origin of the culture as described in the quote above. Basically, Banks argues, "our currently dominant power systems cannot long survive in space; beyond a certain technological level a degree of anarchy is arguably inevitable and anyway preferable." This state of things would arise and remain because the nature of life in space, which requires of its inhabitants a substantial degree of technological development and a level of self-sufficiency hitherto considered unachievable, would make the ships and habitats nearly impossible to control on the part of any kind of static, planet-bound power system (168). Connected to this idea is the notion that the people onboard those spacefaring nation-states would be prompted by the constant awareness of their mutual interdependence to share goods, services, and resources to a point where their societies would become, by necessity, reliant on a cooperative form of economics rather than a competitive system in which the distribution of wealth is left to the vagaries of a non-sentient, internally self-devouring conglomerate of greed-based impulses:

> Succinctly; socialism within, anarchy without.... Let me state here a personal conviction that appears, right now, to be profoundly unfashionable; which is that

a planned economy can be more productive—and more morally desirable—than one left to market forces. The market, for all its (profoundly inelegant) complexities, remains a crude and essentially blind system, and is ... intrinsically incapable of distinguishing between simple non-use of matter resulting from processal superfluity and the acute, prolonged and wide-spread suffering of conscious beings [169–170].

On the other hand, Banks writes, a planned economy "can set up long-term aims and work toward them ... reaching out coherently and efficiently towards agreed-on goals" (170). The problem with this notion, as he well knew, is that the twentieth century was host to a number of long-term social experiments in this vein that failed comprehensively, with the concomitant suffering of plenty of conscious beings in the former Soviet Union, in China, or in Cambodia, to name a few. That's why he also postulates two fundamental innovations for the Culture: first, a level of individual education, participation to public life, and involvement in the planning of economic goals without precedent in human history (170–171). Essentially, all flesh sentients in the Culture are comprehensively educated throughout their entire life and everyone shares a fundamental desire to contribute to the argument of utopia (172–173), because utopia is either self-sustaining through a dialectic process or it ceases to exist. "Philosophy matters here, and sound education," Banks concludes (172).

The second innovation consists in the presence of benevolent posthuman AIs dedicated to cooperating with humans to make utopia work. This is one of Banks' key contentions—that the birth of AI and the subsequent onset of a benign version of the Vingean Singularity are not just possible, but actually probable. The advent of such life-forms would immediately turn humanity into a twin-species race, a collective made up of flesh sentients and artificial intelligences all working in concert to fulfill the dream of building a better society for everyone concerned. The result in the Culture novels is a world in which nobody is exploited; in essence, the Culture is a fully automated society, its day-to-day requirements in terms of logistics, production, and large-system management administered by the Minds that have arisen out of the early years of the singularity, when humans created the first AIs and the AIs in turn created their own offspring (172). Machines perform the tasks that here on Earth we would call work, while human labor is "restricted to something indistinguishable from play, or a hobby"—hence the examples of those people in *Use of Weapons* who, without pressure or coercion, clean tables and build ships because it gives them pleasure.

But if we flesh sentients enjoy our leisure, don't we do so at the expense of machines? Have we simply outsourced exploitation to another life form?

> No machine is exploited, either; the idea here being that any job can be automated in such a way as to ensure that it can be done by a machine well below

5. The Years of Taking Stock

the level of potential consciousness ... no more exploited than an insect is exploited when it pollinates a fruit tree a human later eats a fruit from.... People—and, I'd argue, the sort of conscious machines which would happily cooperate with them—hate to feel exploited, but they also hate to feel useless. One of the most important tasks in setting up and running a stable and internally content civilisation is finding an acceptable balance between the desire for freedom of choice in one's actions ... and the need to feel that even in a society so self-correctingly Utopian one is still contributing something [172].

This is the crux of Banks' argument, and the dramatic engine that propels every Culture novel: in *Consider Phlebas*, the *Short History of the Idiran War* appendix had indicated this desire to be useful as the overarching impulse that had pushed the culture to enter and win a titanic conflict despite being, like Gurgeh's model of his society in the Azad games, "quite profoundly peaceful." To Banks, this relationship between hating to feel exploited and hating to be useless represents the twin-faced force that shaped the Culture's utopia into what it is—a place where things happen and services are provided because everyone living there chooses to make things happen and provide services when and where they want to, without coercion or threat. Only the promptings of one's conscience are required, and because conscience in the culture is nurtured, educated, and trained to the highest degree, it constitutes a powerful engine for carefully considered and comprehensively modeled action.

As the quote in the introduction to this book anticipated, to be alive in the Culture is to experience a system of ethics for which everything has only circumstantial, temporary value: everything matters and nothing does because things and people in the universe are here when we are rather than because we are. Meaning is constructed within a dialectic relationship into which all parties concerned enter willingly and without expectation of owing or being owed anything for their being there in the first place. In a universe without gods, devoid of divinely inspired mission statements, the people of the Culture have not just accepted, but also come to value the reality that "we make our own meanings, whether we like it or not" (173), and the meaning of the Culture, which has been embraced at every level in the society, is to help, to reduce or eliminate suffering, to devote its functionally infinite resources and near-godlike technological and productive capabilities to assisting less fortunate civilizations. The Culture makes sure no technologically advanced predator society happens upon them, no self-destructive impulse triggers genocidal wars, ecological holocausts, or any other extinction-level event, and it contacts them when the time is right for the people living there to accept the worldview-altering reality of a far bigger universe than they'd been used to until that moment.

Together with the fundamentals of the Culture's ethos, "A Few Notes" presents us with an overview of the benefits accruing from living in it. For example, we find out about the enhanced genes of Culture citizens that allow them a pervasive level of control over their bodies' functions—including voluntary sex change, which Banks considers paramount for the creation of a society without chauvinism. Essentially, the contention is that once the people living in a given society have *been* both sexes, they will quickly come to find out whether there is disparity between them and, if there is, proceed to fix that disparity (175–177). We also find out about the construction and functioning of Orbitals (179–182) and of General Systems Vehicles (178). We discover the "totally fake cosmology that underpins the shakily credible stardrives mentioned in the Culture stories" (186–188), a cosmology that, *papier-mâché* as it may be, makes the stories great fun and provides some sort of off-the-wall rationale for the existence of FTL propulsion systems, without which it would be impossible to retain a cohesive collective over the vast stretches of space-time involved in the narratives.

Other features of Culture life we discover: it doesn't have laws, or at least not any legal framework that we would recognize as such. Post-scarcity levels of abundance and extremely advanced technology take care of most impulses that, within a scarcity-based economy, would lead to crimes against property, and pathologies of the mind are virtually unknown thanks first to Culture gene-fixing and second to Culture education and nurturing. The worst crime, murder, is also a unique event, but if it does happen it leads to the employment of a so-called slap-drone, a machine that accompanies the culprit around for the rest of their life to make sure they never again engage in any kind of sociopathic or psychopathic behavior (182–183).[3] Also, the appointment of public posts is based on the simple criterion that the more power one craves, the less they should be allowed to wield (174). Family life in the Culture, on the other hand, is probably one of the clearest derivations from Banks' personal life:

> The most common life-style consists of groups of people of mixed generations linked by loose family ties living in a semi-communal dwelling or group of dwellings; to be a child in the Culture is to have a mother, perhaps a father, probably not a brother or sister, but large numbers of aunts and uncles, and various cousins [184].

There are plenty of echoes here of the great big noisy family Banks grew up in, and although he never specifically addresses this point, it's fair to argue that the connection is relevant. And speaking of family, we also find out the reason for and meaning behind those infernally long names, which is that each culture name acts as moniker, indicator of provenance, and descriptor of familial ties for the individual to whom it is attached (186).[4]

Banks' assessment of his utopia's basic identity—i.e., the answer to the question "What is the Culture?"—is that it is difficult to identify with any degree of certainty because, by the very nature of its loosely arranged social structure and by virtue of the freedom of thought and action it grants its citizens, "the Culture fades out at the edges" (185). There are, for example, all the orbitals, ships, drones, and flesh sentients who, at the beginning of the Idiran war, split from the rest of the Culture because they rejected the use of force under any circumstances (Banks 2004b, 185; Banks 1991, 459); also, there are those few individuals who, like Linter in *The State of the Art*, have decided to live somewhere else for whatever reason.[5] Thus, the Culture can be described as an attitude and a worldview before it is a society in the sense of the term we employ here on Earth; relatively stable from a technological and logistical perspective, it is constantly changing and reassessing itself in the light of the new. This characteristic, married to (1) the narrative strategies typical of Banks' writing style and (2) the localized, personally dystopian lives within which many of the protagonists in the stories exist, makes the Culture a good example of what Tom Moylan calls a "critical utopia."

The argument isn't new. In a 1999 article written for *Foundation*, Simon Guerrier made the case for the Culture's belonging to this category. Starting from Moylan's identification of the shared characteristic of all critical utopias as "a rejection of hierarchy and domination and the celebration of emancipatory ways of being as well as the very possibility of utopian longing itself" (1986, 12), Guerrier discusses the various dynamics operating within the Culture that provide those shared qualities. The first is the rejection of hierarchy, which Guerrier sees most in evidence in *The Player of Games*: while the Empire of Azad is defined by its claim to discipline and respect of the chain of command in all aspects of life (that this claim is largely meaningless does not alter the point), the Culture finds as one of its own defining moments the absence of any such chain, with the concomitant loss of importance of maintaining discipline (1999, 28–29).

As for celebrating Moylan's "emancipatory ways of being," the Culture as described in the novels and in "A Few Notes" is indeed built around the idea that an individual's freedom of expression is as sacred as it can get in a pointedly godless society, and that not only including, but especially embracing the wishes of those who end up finding themselves on the far end of the spectrum from whatever registers as the norm within the Culture. Thus, Gurgeh's contrarian primitivism, Li'ndane's earnest, willful playacting, Yalson's decision to live outside the Culture even though her mother was a citizen, and even Linter's desire to live on Earth are guaranteed, protected, and validated by the social interface that operates within the Culture's collective life. The assessment of other Culture citizens living around these characters may be that they shouldn't be doing what they're doing, but in no case is there any attempt at physically or psychologically restraining them from making the choices they have decided they want to make—"in a post-scarcity society such as this," Guerrier writes, "it is always possible to accommodate choice" (30), even when the choice is to leave the Culture. Indeed, in Linter's case Sma and the *Arbitrary* argue the wisdom of his actions with him, but in the face of his determination to do as he said he would, both withdraw and allow him his wish.

The last element in Moylan's definition of a critical utopia is the moment of "utopian longing," which Guerrier correctly sees as guaranteed by the Culture's reliance on the Minds:

> The Minds are what make the Culture work as a utopia. The Minds are the super-machines of the society, with incredible powers and abilities…. When dealing with such technology—as Moylan says—'the choice comes down to the use of that new set of structures and mechanisms for human need and fulfillment or for the profit and power of a dominant elite.' In what they apparently see as the rational use of their talents, the Minds have opted to benefit human need and fulfillment. What the minds essentially seem to operate is [sic] the bureaucratic systems of the Culture [31].

In this sense, Banks' comment in "A Few Notes" that "where intelligent supervision of a manufacturing or maintenance operation is required, the intellectual challenge involved … would make such supervision rewarding and enjoyable" (172) indicates a fundamental element of play in the life of every sentient in the Culture. For a Mind, managing the bureaucratic and logistical challenges attending the administration of an orbital would be no more taxing or overwhelming than a game of, say, *Civilization* would be for a human. And there's more: in a recent article, Ken MacLeod remembered a conversation he'd had with Banks about the origins of the Culture. Since neither Banks nor MacLeod believed in a utopia realized from above through the actions of benevolent rulers, and since in Banks' telling the Culture didn't come about through any form of revolution or class struggle, MacLeod was somewhat at a loss to foresee other dynamics that could ensure its advent:

> By way of answer, Iain pointed to his pocket calculator. He said that on his last vacation job, on a construction site, one of the full-time workers had borrowed it and worked his way through a stack of wage slips, to discover that he and his mates weren't getting all the pay they were due. The site workers had taken the result to the management, who duly if perhaps reluctantly shelled out the back pay that was owed. That, Iain said, was how he'd envisaged the Culture coming about … the sheer availability of information and computing power would arm the majority with facts and arguments that would enable them to prove, as well as enforce, their claims. The consequent advance in consciousness would allow the opportunities offered by automation and abundance to be grasped, first in imagination then in reality, and make opposition to their realisation irrational, futile, and weak [2013b, n.p.].

5. The Years of Taking Stock

Banks' position was something of an oddity in the post–New Wave years, mostly because the SF grand narrative of betterment through technology that had animated the age of First SF of the 1940s and '50s had been roundly rejected by the writers of the following generation. But, as we have seen, he was not a technocratic simpleton; education, careful reflection, compassion, and a benevolent worldview were as crucial for his utopia's success as that of advanced technology and inexhaustible resources.[6] The pocket-calculator moment, however, does sum up Banks' brand of SF thinking rather well: as a writer, he positioned himself midway between American SF, whose optimism for the future he loved but whose simplistic politics he disliked, and British SF, of which he enjoyed the seriousness of approach to the material but disliked the general pessimism. He loved technological artifacts, action scenes, and big events, but he also wanted them surrounded by a thick shell of ethical and moral thinking to, as it were, debrief the kinetics. That's why any illustration of the anecdote above must be accompanied by those last four lines, the ones that clearly state the necessary corollary of an "advance in consciousness" attending the technological development, said advance becoming the spark of an imaginative revolution that projects the argument of utopia against the status quo of the world *before* that argument begins changing anything.

In 2009, ten years after Guerrier's piece, Michael Kulbicki wrote another article arguing for the Culture's belonging to the critical utopia category. Kulbicki, who conducted a reading of the Culture stories "using notions about utopian hope drawn from the work of the German philosopher, Ernst Bloch" (34), sees the presence of this utopian hope in the Culture's interventionist stance, within which it functions as a focus "on the role of unpredictability and consequence, emphasising the degree to which the Culture's interventions are driven by an optimistic desire that cannot be completely quantified, given the uncertain nature of each act ... by definition not a program, but an openness to the as yet not manifested but desired possibilities inherent in the future, something Bloch refers to as the Not-Yet-Being" (38). The most interesting aspect of Kulbicki's argument comes when he acknowledges the need to factor in an aspect of Bloch's definition of utopia that seems to exclude the Culture from the category. In Bloch's view, utopian hope implies the absence of utopia itself because "utopian plenitude ... can be truly apprehended only in a fragmentary form" (qtd. in Kulbicki 2009, 38). In response to this definitional difficulty, Kulbicki argues that the impossibility of sharply defining the Culture as a political and historical body, as Banks also pointed out in "Notes," is the element that virtually disappears it from our sight—that is, despite the pervasive presence of the effects the Culture has on other civilizations and on its own citizens, the society itself is "literally a utopia in the sense of 'no place,' a grouping of restless like–Minded cells, unfixed and in continuous, nomadic motion" (39). To further illustrate the fragmentary nature of the Culture, Kulbicki makes reference to the so-called Culture Ulterior (some of whose members play fundamental roles in *Excession*; see chapter 6), that fringe grouping of breakaway subsets of the Culture that, for one reason or another, have decided to detach themselves from the main sequence of Culture life (39).

There is a lot of merit to this argument. The Culture truly is nomadic in nature—its GSVs constantly travel throughout the galaxy, stopping at planets and Orbitals and space stations only for a while before resuming their peripatetic existence, and each GSV is home to thousands of smaller ships, including General Contact Units like the *Arbitrary*, which are themselves nomads. Orbitals, although static, can be quickly dismantled and relocated, evacuated, or destroyed (see for example Vavatch in *Consider Phlebas*), and the technologies of energy and matter collection available within the society make the creation of static constructs completely unnecessary—and in this respect, Banks designed the wacky physics of the Culture stories to help: the energy grid is everywhere besides/above/below normal space-time, which is itself riddled with planetoids, asteroids, cometary bodies, and stars from which it is possible to gather limitless amounts of resources. Therefore, to say that the Culture exists *somewhere* is incorrect; it exists everywhere and nowhere at once in the galaxy, always in transition from one location to another, so that the happy lives of its widespread citizenry and its politics of intervention automatically become the only fixed points of reference. This setup would have been impossible in mimetic fiction, where any such thing as a spacefaring utopia with FTL and close-to-omnipotent AIs can only exist as a metaphor, a wish, or a delusion of the mind. Within the non-mimetic register of space opera, however, it is possible to literalize the foundational play of words of More's eu-topia by positing the existence of just such a collective.

Kulbicki also expresses a certain surprise that, despite its considerable public success both at home and abroad, leading figures in utopian studies— Tom Moylan in particular—have mostly ignored the Culture series: "Banks does not rate a mention in Fredric Jameson's *Archaeologies of the Future* or in Tom Moylan's *Scraps of the Untainted Sky*. This seems particularly odd, given Banks's focus on utopia and Jameson's and Moylan's own sustained engagement with it" (34).[7]

Thereby hangs a tale. *Demand the Impossible*, the original text in which Moylan defined, described, and provided examples of the critical utopia, was published in 1986, one year before *Consider Phlebas* saw print. The book was an elaboration of Moylan's 1981 dissertation, "Figures of Hope: The Critical Utopia of the 1970s. The Revival, Destruction, and Transformation of Utopian Writing in the United States: A Study of the Ideology, Structure, and Historical

Context of Representative Texts" (Sargent 2014, 242). In this long title are embedded the guiding principles that informed not just the dissertation, but the later book as well. Moylan, who had been an active participant in the oppositional cultural and political movements of the 1960s and 1970s,[8] had worked on his dissertation first and his book later from within a deep personal connection to the intense struggles of those times, when it must have seemed possible—indeed, probable—that old power systems and patriarchies might give way to new, better social arrangements, inclusive of greater racial, sexual, and gender diversity. "I was writing out of my own personal and intellectual engagement," Moylan remembers. "I began the entire project as a fan and an active citizen, continued it as a teacher, and only later brought in the methods and skills of a scholar" (2014b, xx). Out of this intense dialogue with the forms of utopian thinking that he saw shaping the consciousness of left-wing political projects of the time, Moylan condensed his argument—as the title of his dissertation indicates—by circumscribing it to the United States and choosing four specific works by four specific writers: Joanna Russ' *The Female Man* (1968), Ursula Le Guin's *The Dispossessed* (1974), Samuel Delany's *Triton*, and Marge Piercy's *Woman at the Edge of Time* (both 1976). As the dates of publication indicate, those were works Moylan saw published during those flashpoint years, coming hot into an already fraught debate whose dynamics had previously influenced their writing to begin with. Thus, as Moylan himself pointed out, his choice of argument, texts, and methodology partook of a set of motivations that existed beside and beyond the purely academic:

> I did *not* set out to canonize or valorize this set of texts from a position of high academic culture (or indeed the market).... Rather, I was reading these books as they were being published, and I wanted to make sense of what they meant to me and to share that with others so that they would go on to read them.... Naïvely unaware of the cultural power of academia, I simply, and unabashedly politically, wanted to tell others (as a reader and as a teacher) about these works, which I came to see as part of one tendency among so many others [2014b, xx–xxi].

The cultural power of academia was the driving force behind what a number of critics indeed saw as the canonization of a cross-cultural pattern of utopian fiction when *Demand the Impossible* saw print. The book's lack of specificity in terms of the physical location of the study (see Moylan 2014, xx) gave the impression that the four American novels he discussed in depth in *Demand* were expected to function as shorthand for the utopian venture in other countries as well, especially in Great Britain, and a debate on this score rose as the book became increasingly more influential with the passing of the years.[9] Moylan crucially contributed to this debate with *Scraps of the Untainted Sky* (2000), a study of dystopia in which he takes stock of the reality of post-1970s capitalism and of the progressive diminishing of utopian hope in the 1980s and 1990s. Moylan argues in *Scraps* that the post–Vietnam War reconfiguration of capitalism into a pervasively commodity-based system, further assisted by the gradual growth of multi-national corporate behemoths and by the encroachment of neoconservative governments in the U.S., Great Britain, and Germany, "sought to revive its generation of surplus by reducing costs and expanding operations through a series of moves that included ... eliminating social costs by refusing obligations to social entitlements, labor contracts, and ecological health; and moving into all corners of the globe and all aspects of everyday life to produce commodities and markets that could bring renewed financial gains (gains that would no longer be subject to even token redistribution to the very people who produced them)" (2000, xiv). Within this new system of reconfigured capitalism, the utopian impulse in SF began to die out—with the notable exception of some of Kim Stanley Robinson's works (see Moylan 2000, 103–105)[10] –replaced by dystopian visions through whose lens politically inclined writers of SF could retain the impulse toward constructive social critique typical of the critical utopia by applying it to reconfigurations of a world gone out of control:

> Again, the analytic strategy of totality enables a critique that recognizes capitalism's reproduction of a "utopia" in which the authentically radical call of Utopia is both co-opted and silenced, leaving in its place tropes of dystopia to represent and inform what critique and opposition remain.... The contemporary moment, therefore, is one in which a critical position is necessarily dystopian [Moylan 2000, 187].

Thus Moylan reprised Lyman Tower Sargent's definition of a critical dystopia[11] to indicate a restructuring of dystopian fiction designed to "manage the tension between utopia and anti-utopia, by creating a 'space' of utopian hope precisely by first positing a dystopia, and then offering a depiction of resistance to it from within" (Kulbicki 2009, 37). Thus the critical utopias of the 1960s and 1970s bequeathed their narrative strategies and political positions to a body of work produced under the aegis of their dark twin, and by doing so ensured the continuation of the utopian impulse in the midst of a dystopian turn in public life as well as in literature.

But if Moylan was able to acknowledge Kim Stanley Robinson's work during the 1990s as the one major holdout of relatively unreconstructed critical utopia, why didn't he see Banks as well? "Banks is a problem for this [Moylan's] chronology," Michael Kulbicki writes, "since he writes critically utopian texts from the mid–80s, the time when the 'neo-conservative restoration' took hold, through to the present day. For Moylan, however, there was a proviso to this enclosure, in the form of Kim Stanley Robinson, another 'lucid variant' at the margin. While Robinson has received a great deal of scholarly attention, Banks has not" (2009, 37). If we look at the key characteristics of the critical utopia as originally set down in *Demand the Impossible*, we will see that the Culture series fits the definition of this category very well[12]:

> Aware of the historical tendency of the utopian genre to limit the imagination to one particular ideal and also aware of the restriction of the utopian impulse to marketing mechanisms, the authors of the critical utopia assumed the risky task of reviving the emancipatory utopian imagination while simultaneously destroying the traditional utopia and yet preserving it in a transformed and liberated form that was critical both of utopian writing itself and of the prevailing social formation [Moylan 1986, 42].

Here, Moylan more precisely re-states the argument made in chapter 3 concerning the agent(s) of the utopian imagination. By countering the fixed socio-economic status quo of the world as it was with the fixed socio-economic status quo of the world as they thought it should be, the writers of historical utopias ended up with yet more monolithic societies, brittle and static where they should have been flexible and open, a series of loci within whose laws their authors' dreams of a better world died the moment they turned into actuality. The contention that utopia is a discourse first and foremost has appeared a number of times in this work already; now we can carry the argument further and say that, for Iain M. Banks as well as for Delany, Piercy, Le Guin, and Russ, utopia *remains* a discourse first and foremost, even after the novels are done building their respective societies in the reader's mind. One person's dream can easily become most other people's nightmare, and the critical utopia is structured around this awareness. As Moylan argues, there are "two major changes that occur in the critical utopia that mark a break with the general pattern of the traditional utopia": the first is an external deviation, i.e., the presentation of the two societies under scrutiny—the utopia and the original society against which the utopia is meant to react—in equal levels of detail and objectivity. The second is an internal deviation in the form of a critical attitude toward the utopian society itself: "in each of the new utopias the society is shown with its faults, inconsistencies, problems, and even denials of the utopian impulse in the form of persistence of exploitation and domination in the better place. Here, of course is echoed the historic failure to achieve perfection, a false goal in the first place" (44). This critical attitude generates within the work of fiction foregrounding the critical utopia a constantly self-assessing, self-regenerating discourse concerning the nature and behavior of a utopian society, and it is this constant argument that prevents the society thus designed from developing the same sclerosis as those in previous literary works.

There is little need to return to the many instances in the four stories analyzed thus far when the Culture subjected itself to scrutiny through one or more of its citizens (Balveda, Fal, Gurgeh, Sma, the *Arbitrary*, Li'ndane, Linter) as well as through the non–Culture people that interacted with it

(Zakalwe, Chori, Horza, Nicosar). That aspect of the Culture as a critical utopia is a known quantity, and it will remain so throughout its entire published history. It's Banks himself that represents the other crucial constituent: time and again in "A Few Notes on the Culture," Banks flags the underpinnings of his argument—that is, his utopia—so that we can become aware of their existence and potential flaws, and more to the point, he regularly halts the flow of his narration with an open indicator that what he is saying is, once again, nothing more nor less than an argument. At the very beginning of the essay, for example, he reminds us that all this is "just" a set of stories, and a few pages further in, after discussing the Culture's socio-economic setup, he declares: "Whatever; in the end, practice (as ever) will outshine theory" (171). He also takes pains to tell us that, since he set up the universe of the Culture as a god-less place he doesn't believe in the existence of souls—"although," he then qualifies, "I do write as an atheist" (171). And on he goes, always making sure his intellectual position exists clearly and transparently within a community of discourse he himself built when he created the argument—because every Culture story is an invitation to a debate, the highlighting of a dilemma for further discussion, and the presentation of a status quo that exists problematically with itself so as to make sure that, despite the reality that perfection will always remain unattainable, the striving for it will yield its own results. In the practice of his intellectual ecumenism, Banks is also well served by his characteristic writing style. Moylan again:

> The apparently unified, illusionary, and representational text of the more traditional utopia is broken open and presented in a manner which is, first of all, much more fragmented—narratives intertwining present and future or past and present, single protagonists being divided into multiples, or into male and female versions of the same character. Secondly, the critical utopian text includes much more commentary on the operations of the text itself [46].

We have seen how Banks imported into his space opera all the narrative tricks that had made his non-genre work what it was: the doppelganger hauntings of Horza in *Consider Phlebas* and Zakalwe/Elethiomel in *Use of Weapons*; the playful untrustworthiness of the narrator drone(s) in *The Player of Games*; the opposing timelines of *Weapons*; the metafictional resonances of *Phlebas* and the borrowings from famous works in *State*. In Banks' non-genre stories, all those characteristics were there to estrange the mundane and cast doubt on the solidity of the given, to propel the narrative into a fringe territory of negotiation between mimesis and its Dionysian twin. In the space operas, on the other hand, those same features function as a dialectic, as a resonance chamber for a discourse on the things that matter to Banks—how to create a meaningfully functioning better world, how to make it survive, how to make it interact with other civilizations without having it turn dystopian, and how to engage us readers in the debate honestly. If utopia is an argument before and beyond being anything else, then there is such a thing as a utopian textual experience—some books that are meant to make us dream fail because of the assumption buried deep in the fabric of the narrative that, once its underpinnings are explained, the author's utopia will be everyone else's as well. On the other hand, and in the vein of the critical utopias described in Moylan's book, the Culture presents a constantly self-assessing society through the agency of a constantly self-assessing text, a heteroglossia of voices whose endlessly refracting viewpoints enables the reader to see the debate as it progresses through words and deeds.[13] The ultimate goal, within and without the story, is to make the core argument of utopia survive unscathed through all the pressures and critiques, its integrity validated by the society's very willingness to reassess and reevaluate itself without ever stopping. And this is the fundamental achievement of Iain M. Banks' Culture series: the fact that the society he designed does remain utopian through all the difficult negotiations in which it has to engage "in its struggle to do good." The Good Place remains intact and whole, even through the haze of blood through which the characters in the Culture stories, who are not people of the center but people of the fringe, look back at their often distant home.

In the event, Moylan did address Banks' work. Five years after Kulbicki had made his argument, in the 2014 introduction to the new Ralahine Classics edition of *Demand the Impossible*, Moylan writes:

> Both Simon Guerrier and Michael Kulbicki effectively argue that Iain M. Banks's series of 'Culture' novels can be read as critical utopias—adding to my own conclusion that the work of Kim Stanley Robinson has continued in a critical utopian vein. Such extension or stretching of the periodizing range of the critical utopia have therefore methodologically helped to expand the category of the critical utopia into that of an interpretive, rather than a periodizing, protocol [2014b, xxiii].[14]

In other words, the reality of the publication of critical utopian works during the years of the neo-conservative ascendancy helps unmoor the critical utopia from its focus on 1960s and '70s North America, so that now it can be used as a more generalized praxis for examining utopian yearnings across greater expanses of territory and longer spans of time.[15] In this sense, Banks becomes an important figure in the history of critical utopianism, and even more so for his personal embracement of its real-life connections: activism and political commitment.

In the introduction, Moylan laments an oversight that he believes distorts the original formulation of the critical utopia. While many scholars have, over the years, effectively focused on the critical utopia's built-in capacity for formal analysis and self-assessment, "I have often found myself wishing that more would have gone on to tease out the way in which that process figured a new level of engaged activism in the service of a totalizing socio-political transformation (i.e., revolution)" (2014b, xv). For Moylan, as we have seen, the critical utopia was never simply a literary phenomenon, and neither should it have been. Delany, Russ, Piercy, and Le Guin were working under the pressures of the times to create texts whose utopian projects reached beyond the page and into the same society from which they had drawn their subject matter. In those years, Moylan and his contemporaries existed in a context where to read one such book was to understand it both aesthetically and programmatically—that is, both as a story in and of itself and as a primer for utopian action in the present. These days, when it may feel that utopia has moved forever beyond our grasp (but see Ken MacLeod's work, and again Kim Stanley Robinson's), we have a tougher time understanding this reality—hence the tendency to overlook that dimension of Moylan's discourse, arguably.

But Banks, as the introduction to this book makes clear, reacted to the stresses of those times in much the same way Moylan did. In 1974, two years before the publication of *Triton* and *Woman on the Edge of Time*, Banks was already a student at the university of Stirling, and he was already working on the political and ideological underpinnings of the Culture in the form of *Use of Weapons*' first draft. Between 1973 and 1981, while Moylan was working on his dissertation, first creating and then refining the definitional foundations of the critical utopia, Banks was writing his early batch of stories, thinking about the shape of his own utopia and arguing with Ken MacLeod over—as he put it to David Garnett—"saving the universe." He was also going to London with MacLeod to demonstrate against—and physically fight—the National Front, reading Chomsky, and worrying about the encroachment of conservatism in England. Banks was, in short, as engaged with left-wing activities as Moylan had hoped readers of his work would become once *Demand* was published, and throughout his life he remained engaged—again, witness his reaction to Blair's assent to the invasion of Iraq or to Israel's Gaza flotilla raid. For Banks and Moylan both, the same connection obtains between literary production and life outside the page, with the difference that Moylan channels his intellectual energies into literary criticism while Banks channeled his into writing fiction.

The Culture is a critical utopia.[16] In hindsight, it's difficult to imagine how, given what Banks needed it to say, it could have been anything else. Banks created the Culture as a salve for the many wrongnesses he saw in the world that surrounded him, and made it critical utopian because he knew that to build a utopia is to argue it into existence and maintain it through constant self-assessment—hence the series' pervasive presence on the fringe of Culture life, where the boundary between utopia and dystopia, subjected to the greatest pressures, frays and unravels. That the model held through twenty-five years and ten books despite the critiques, both from within and from without the texts, is perhaps the best indicator of the pliant sturdiness of its build.

The one thing Banks doesn't discuss in "A Few Notes on the Culture" is the function of Special Circumstances. SC only gets a quick, largely context-free mention in the essay (183), and even Contact receives comparatively short shrift, the reason being that "its rationale and activities are covered elsewhere, in the stories" (178). The essay is thus devoted mainly to explicating the origins, nature, and reason for being of the mainstream of the Culture, while the novels busy themselves with the dangerous and morally suspect side of things, the often trouble-fraught interfaces with other civilizations that Contact and SC have claimed as their territory—hence Banks' description of Contact (and, by implication, SC) as "the most coherent and consistent part of the Culture—certainly when considered on a galactic scale—yet ... only a very small part of it ... almost a civilisation within a civilisation, and no more typify[ying] its host than an armed service does a peaceful state" (186). As Banks himself acknowledged, there were sound dramatic reasons for this choice: "The external threats were his answer to the problem that no matter how exciting a utopia might be to live in, it would be very dull to write about (unless you basically wrote a novel about people's normal relationships within it, about love and heartbreak or whatever, in which case as Iain often pointed out, why not just write a mainstream novel?)" (Winter 2014, n.p.). This doesn't mean, however, that Contact and SC do not participate in the processes of reassessment and critique that are the fundamental indicator of their parent civilization's belonging to the category of critical utopias. In fact, as we have seen, the majority of the questioning comes from them precisely because they are the organizations they are and because they do what they do, which is why the two most pointed questions encountered thus far— "how do we know we are doing the right thing?" and "who elected us God?"— come respectively from the *Arbitrary* and from Sma, each the representative of one of the two life-forms that comprise the vast majority of the Culture's population, and each a Contact operative.

By the end of 1994, Banks was done with taking stock. He had delved into a part of the Culture's history that the novels had only hinted at, and answered to his satisfaction a number of questions that he himself, not to mention the many fans who approached him at SF conventions, had been harboring. Soon, he would return to writing Culture stories at a steady clip of one every two years—a slowing down since the times when "all" he'd had to do had been revising an already composed text, but the added wait would be more than worth it, as had been the six-year hiatus. When Banks returned to the Culture, he did so in grand style and with the intention of re-doing *Consider Phlebas*.

6

THE VIEW FROM ABOVE, THE VIEW FROM BELOW

Excession and *Inversions*

The first four Culture books were space operas of the planet-focused persuasion. The stories featured plenty of ships and plenty of Minds inside them, but the majority of the action and the entirety of the focus were on events taking place on planets or Orbitals. The gaze of *Excession* (1996), on the other hand, is aimed straight up and out. For the first time in the history of the Culture, *Excession* presents us with the transcendental view, with spacescapes seen from the perspective of the godlike, and the panorama is vast. "Vertiginous shifts in scale are Banks' specialty," Faren Miller wrote in her *Locus* review of the novel. "If you can hang in there without getting *too* horrendously dizzy, *Excession* will satisfy on many counts and levels, even (at last) the cosmic" (1996, 27). Miller's parenthetical statement is telling—that "at last," whose feel of delayed satisfaction points to Banks' long-awaited decision to finally break his starships out into the great beyond.

Reading *Excession* is a joy. The novel soars on a giddy combination of descriptive grandeur, linguistic complexity, purposeful chaos, constant deconstruction and reconstruction of the space-opera template, exciting action, plenty of explosions, grand vistas of impossible things, and finally gargantuan ships—which means Minds, because this is a novel that the Minds and the vessels they control can inhabit without claustrophobia. Space is open to Minded sight, nearly transparent before the gaze of AI. *Excession* has the same vast canvas and the same basic plan—to deconstruct space opera and rebuild it in a new shape—as *Consider Phlebas*, but the hand that controls the process, deft and purposeful where before it had been somewhat uncertain of itself, has finally put into play the only entities capable of bringing home to us the true scope of the Culture universe—capable, that is, with the assistance of "that staple of SF: a mysterious artifact" (Miller 1996, 25–27), whose appearance triggers the onset of what the Culture terms an Outside Context Problem:

> The usual example given to illustrate an Outside Context Problem was imagining you were a tribe on a largish, fertile island; you'd tamed the land, invented the wheel or writing or whatever, the neighbors were cooperative or enslaved but at any rate peaceful and you were busy raising temples to yourself with all the excess productive capacity you had, you were in a position of near-absolute power and control which your hallowed ancestors could hardly have dreamed of and the whole situation was just running along nicely like a canoe on wet grass … when suddenly this bristling lump of iron appears sailless and trailing steam in the bay and these guys carrying long funny-looking sticks come ashore and announce you've just been discovered, you're all subjects of the Emperor now, he's keen on presents called *tax* and these bright-eyed holy men would like a word with your priests [71–72].

This description of the nature of an OCP was inspired by the long hours Banks spent playing *Civilization* on his computer. "That's where the idea of Outside Context Problems came from partly," he said in an interview with *SFX* magazine. "You're getting along really well and then this great battleship comes steaming in and you think, 'Well, my wooden sailing ships are never going to be able to deal with that.' But when I started *Excession* I deleted *Civilization* off my hard drive" (Branscombe 1996b, 25). The idea remained, however, and while Banks introduces it into the story with a degree of playfulness, it still casts a sizeable real-life shadow—we are reminded here of Columbus' triad of sailing ships outside San Salvador in 1492, of Commodore Perry's ironclads suddenly appearing off the coast of Japan in 1852, and of the many versions—some landlocked—of the same scenario that played out across the surface of the Earth between the end of the 15th century and the beginning of the 20th.

And the Culture is now staring at an Outside Context Problem from a pier on the island, not from the deck of the dreadnought. This OCP comes in the form of "a perfect black-body sphere fifty clicks across" (67), impenetrable to sensors, sentient, not hostile despite taking over a few overly inquisitive ships (17–26, 111, 367–370), and capable of establishing connections with the twin realms of hyperspace existing beside our normal realm of spacetime that the Culture can't but would very much like to learn how to, mostly because the sphere might well be a door to all the other universes generated by the singularity at the heart of creation (on the other hand, if the sphere truly were a door it would probably swing both ways, so something extraordinarily powerful could come in through it; 114–116). As far as almost everyone in the galaxy knows, this sphere is unlike anything found anywhere ever, which is one of the reasons why the first Culture ship to happen upon it, the

General Contact Unit *Fate Amenable to Change*, issues an Excession notice as soon as it realizes what it's looking at—"Excession; something excessive. Excessively aggressive, excessively powerful, excessively expansionist; whatever" (93). Thus goes the Culture's definition of such an artifact, and an Excession almost always represents an Outside Context Problem.

But as usual, Special Circumstances knows better. That's not the first appearance the Excession has put in: twenty-five hundred years before the beginning of the events in the novel, the *Problem Child*, an early-model GCU, found an identical object in another corner of the galaxy, in that case resting right next to a star that appeared to be around a trillion years old (about fifty times the age of the known universe; 65). Like its distant cousins in the novel's present, the *Problem Child* couldn't penetrate the sphere with its sensors, and soon after it had to leave to rendezvous with a General Systems Vehicle for repairs—the GCU's engine had been damaged by what looked like an attack, although from where and of what kind no one could say. When the expedition mustered up to study the object and the star arrived at their position it found nothing whatsoever, and over the following centuries the *Problem Child* and every member of its crew—drones and humans—completely disappeared. Within a century and a half of the encounter, there was nobody left to talk to (68).

Now the Excession is back, though, and SC has an ace up its sleeve. It recruits a Culture human by the name of Byr Genar-Hofoen to talk to the personality construct of the *Problem Child*'s Captain, a woman named Zreyn Tramow.[1] This recently discovered personality construct, the only remaining witness of that long ago encounter, is stored onboard the General Systems Vehicle *Sleeper Service*, with whom Genar-Hofoen shares a painfully tangled past (70–71). At this point, the recipe for a rollicking space opera is almost complete: there's the strange artifact and the great cosmic mystery its existence implies, there's danger, there's opportunity, and there's a hero with a difficult past. We only need a villain, which the novel duly provides along with the hero: at the time of his recruitment into the SC scheme, Genar-Hofoen is serving as Culture ambassador to a young, brash civilization called the Affront. Take your basic Dalek and give it the sense of humor of a mob enforcer; surround its entire body with a mass of long, leg-thick tentacles capable of crushing a compact car in their embrace and, for purposes of buoyancy, put a gas sac on top of the whole ensemble; then give the thing a vicious beak for a mouth and two sensory stalks, have it talk like a Viking who went to college against his will, make sure it breathes an atmosphere made up mostly of nitrogen, and voila: an Affront (29). Abandoned unfeasibly early in their evolution by their patron civilization's Subliming about a century after the end of the Idiran War, the Affront were left "joyfully off the leash and both snapping at the heels of the local members of the Culture's great long straggling civilisational caravan wending its way toward progress ... and

6. The View from Above, the View from Below

positively savaging several of the even less well-developed neighbouring species which for their own good nobody else had yet thought fit to contact" (167). Now, four centuries after the Affront's abandonment and five centuries after the end of the Idiran War,[2] the Culture has taken over the duties of chaperon, and in those four hundred years it has persuaded its reluctant charges to more or less abide by the general rules of good conduct accepted by every advanced civilization in the galaxy—until the Excession. Sensing an opportunity to increase their throw-weight in galactic affairs, the Affront exploit a chance encounter in the vicinity of the Excession to claim it as their discovery and therefore their property, ordering all other civilizations to stay away from their prize, and since the *Fate Amenable to Change* is still staring at the Excession after finding it well ahead of them, the Affront end up going to war against the Culture (283).

By this point in the novel, we've already known for a good long while that we're once again in an M-Banks space opera. Nothing is what it seems. First of all, Banks indicates at several points in *Excession* that the Affront are no more a threat to the Culture than the Empire of Azad was (96–99, 167, 289, 433–436). They don't have any Minds, their habitats are essentially license-built—and poorly so—copies of Culture habitats, and their ships are old: they rattle horribly and make *noises* when they travel, they smell bad because they leak (143), and the engines even suffer regular malfunctions (138). Secondly, Genar-Hofoen is yet another discontent-in-paradise very nearly in the Jernau Gurgeh mold, which is why he has lasted almost two years in his ambassadorial post to the Affront homeworld whereas none of his predecessors could manage to stay longer than a hundred days (170). And it's not just Genar-Hofoen: every other significant Culture character in *Excession*, flesh sentients and Minds alike, is some sort of self-determined outcast, singular individual, or person responsible for guilty, stress-ridden instances of gothic behavior. There's Dajeil Gelian, for example, the woman with whom Genar-Hofoen had a disastrous liaison forty years before and the reason why he and the *Sleeper Service* don't get along. For four decades now, Dajeil has been living inside the *Sleeper Service*, her unborn child kept in a state of arrested development along with everything else in her life. Even the environment the GSV has constructed around her functions as a stasis chamber: it's a perfect copy of the place where Dajeil's relationship with Genar-Hofoen had come to its bad end—a clumsy, heartbroken attempt at homicide on Dajeil's part when she discovered that Genar-Hofoen had had sex with someone else; the attempt failed, mostly because Dajeil didn't really have the heart for it, but it did cost the life of the fetus Genar-Hofoen, at that time a woman, was carrying (3–12, 353–355). Then there's Ulver Seich, a voluble young woman who lives on Phage Rock, one of the oldest Culture habitats. Phage traces its origin all the way back to the birth of the Culture nine thousand years before, and Ulver traces her own ancestry back to one of the Rock's founding families fifty-four generations ago (104–105). In a determinedly egalitarian, non-hierarchical society like the Culture, Ulver comes as close as anyone ever will to being aristocracy, and now Special Circumstances has shown an interest in her—she has to waylay Genar-Hofoen at some point during his travel to the *Sleeper Service* for reasons SC doesn't clarify (125–127).

The minds are no different. The *Sleeper Service* has been a lone wanderer for forty years, absorbed in its private obsession of creating great tableaux of famous artworks, historical scenes, and battles through the use of stored people as props (with their permission, of course; 79–87). Classified as an Eccentric (a Culture term used to describe oddball ship Minds), it is part of the Culture Ulterior, a catch-all description for former bits and pieces of the Culture that have now gone their own way but still retain relevant similarities to their parent civilization (171), and the only beings onboard who are both alive and aware are Dajeil, the GSV's avatar, and a sentient bird called Gravious. Some other ships with similarly odd temperaments are the Medium Systems Vehicle *Not Invented Here*, which most Culture observers believed had been destroyed toward the end of the Idiran War (124), the Eccentric *Shoot Them Later*, belonging to a group within the Ulterior called the AhForgetIt Tendency (119), and the GCU *Grey Area*, "the ship that did what the other ships both deplored and despised; actually looked into the minds of other people, using its Electro Magnetic Effectors ... to burrow into the grisly cellular substrate of an animal consciousness and try to make sense of what it found there for its own—usually vengeful—purposes. A pariah craft ... a virtual outcast amongst the great inclusionary meta-fleet that was Contact" (70–71).[3]

Every one of those characters is therefore a vehicle for the occasionally stressed internal dialogue of the Culture as a critical utopia. The *Sleeper Service* is a loner that doesn't talk to any other ship and doesn't host any kind of population, while the *Grey Area* is a pariah because it has traded Contact's carefully gauged and excruciatingly triangulated intervention models for the most brutal of approaches—direct plundering of the contents of biological brains. Genar-Hofoen and Dajeil Gelian were involved in a relationship that ended in a way that would horrify any Culture citizen, and each bears the marks of their shared past: Dajeil lives in a frozen moment, halted in time through guilt and fear of the future, alone except the visits she receives from Amorphia, the GSV's avatar; Genar-Hofoen, on the other hand, is an exile of sorts, separated from his people more by his liking of the Affront than by the distances intervening between Issorile, the Affront's home planet, and the nearest Culture Orbital. Even his thought processes are more Affront-geared than feels comfortable to the average Culture person or Mind, and his views on the evolutionary path his civilization has chosen represent a definite departure from the norm:

6. The View from Above, the View from Below

> Genar-Hofoen liked [the Affront] ... he had never really subscribed to the standard Culture belief that any form of suffering was intrinsically bad, he accepted that a degree of exploitation was inevitable in a developing Culture, and leant towards the school of thought that which held that evolution, or at least evolutionary pressures, ought to continue within and around a civilised species, rather than—as the Culture had done—choosing to replace evolution with a kind of democratically agreed physiological stasis-plus-option-list while handing over the real control of one's society to machines [170].

But while Genar-Hofoen likes the Affront enough to want to receive an Affronter body inside which he can download his consciousness when he feels like it (63), the vast majority of Culture people and Minds regard them with undisguised horror: "[The Affront] had discovered at a relatively early point in their development how to change the genetic make-up of their own inheritance ... and that of the creatures with whom they shared their home world. Those creatures had all, accordingly, been amended as the Affront saw fit, for their own amusement and delight. The result was what one Culture Mind had described as a kind of self-perpetuating, never-ending holocaust of pain and fear" (168). Affront society is based on the exploitation of two large underclasses: juvenile geldings and females, the latter exposed on a regular basis to legal rape on the part of practically every male so disposed. The Affront have even altered the females' genetic makeup to make the act of sex at once less pleasurable and more painful, and in much the same way they have tweaked the neuroreceptors of the fauna on Issorile to respond with a rictus of terror to the mere sight or smell of Affront males, thus making the hunts of which the Affront are so fond more of a sport as the prey, mad with fear, attempts progressively crazier evasion and escape ploys. "Progress through pain" is a common Affronter motto (168–169).

From the outset, the standard Culture viewpoint found the Affront so appalling that at the end of the Idiran War a number of Minds had argued that the problem they posed could easily be solved with a quick, overwhelming strike. At the time the Culture was at its military zenith, so the war materiel was far from lacking, and in the long run, those Minds had argued, it would be for the good of all concerned—including the Affront themselves (166). But the Culture as a whole, always determinedly peaceful, had had no intention of returning to war to conduct an intervention with dubious moral foundations. It had dramatically scaled down its warship complement, stored a tiny amount of it just in case, and its citizens had gone back to enjoying themselves and helping others through Contact and SC (166).

So the problem of the Affront has remained, and along with it the remnants of the preemptive-strike argument that had foundered a few centuries before. But now that the Excession has reappeared the Affront have stirred again, claiming it as their own and trusting that it'll give them the edge in the war they self-terminally declared against the Culture. They also trust their new ally, the Mind in control of the Culture Rapid Offensive Unit *Attitude Adjuster*, and the *Attitude Adjuster* trusts the other Minds involved in the conspiracy to entrap the Affront into entering a war they can only lose.

Excession is a space opera, but it's also the story of a conspiracy—and because the existence of a conspiracy by its very nature invites belief in the existence of other conspiracies without providing proof to substantiate that belief, the novel becomes self-determinedly tangled into a web of mysterious relationships that the purposefully complex writing style only makes tighter and more mysterious. The argument for a short punitive war, it turns out, had never died down, and the Minds that had originally advocated it have, for the past four hundred years, been biding their time and waiting for the right opportunity. When the Excession appeared, that opportunity beckoned: upon being notified of the artifact's discovery on the part of the *Fate Amenable to Change*, a quorum of legendary Minds from the days of the Idiran War takes over the investigation. Calling themselves the Interesting Times Gang, those Minds have two objectives: first, to investigate the Excession and the Outside Context Problem it likely represents, and second to make sure no overly adventurous civilization tries to use it as a weapon (116–124). But inside the ITG there's another gang, a smaller group of Minds that call themselves nothing at all and have arranged for the Affront to become that overly adventurous civilization. The *Attitude Adjuster* is their errand boy, their executor in allowing the Affront to capture Pittance, one of the warship storage spaces the Culture had set up after the Idiran War, and tricking the Minds inside those warships into thinking that the Culture is under attack from the Excession and that the Affront are allies (294–296)—all so that the Affront will trigger their own annihilation once the Culture mobilizes in full.

So the Affront, heartily horrible and appallingly violent as they may be, are the victims of entrapment, while the Excession just stands there in space, waiting for nobody knows what and not really being much of an Outside Context Problem. Thus, when we peel away the layers of plot Banks has put in front of our eyes to deflect our attention, the real antagonists in *Excession* are revealed to be the Culture Minds involved in the conspiracy, a conspiracy whose very existence paradoxically owes to one of the Culture's most cherished beliefs:

> Your own thoughts, your own recollections—whether you were a human, a drone, or a ship Mind—were regarded as private. It was considered the ultimate in bad manners even to think about trying to read somebody else's—or something else's—mind.... Thanks to that taboo, everybody in the Culture could keep secrets to themselves and hatch little schemes and plots to their hearts' content. The trouble was that while in humans this sort of behavior tended to manifest itself in practical jokes … with Minds it occasionally meant they forgot to tell

everybody else about finding entire stellar civilisations, or took it upon themselves to alter the course of a developed culture everybody already did know about... [66].[4]

This is one of the bad dreams nestling inside the hopeful good works of the Contact and Special Circumstances sections, because any single ship of the power of, say, the *Sleeper Service* could ravage entire star systems if left to its own devices.[5] Also, as the narrative points out immediately after the passage quoted above, this idea inevitably leads to the next logical deduction, which is even more uncomfortable: what if this has already happened, and to the Culture itself? What if one single Mind, or a quorum of Minds working in concert, had one day seen fit to change the Culture's shape and, through the kind of overpoweringly skillful manipulation godlike AIs are capable of, brought that change about without anyone else noticing? The question is ultimately unanswerable with one hundred percent certainty, but there are failsafes one can put in place: other conspiracies, benign where the others would be malign, hidden not so much from the average Culture citizen but rather from the conspiracies that aim at hiding from the average Culture citizen. *Quis custodiet ipsos custodes?*

The Culture wouldn't be the Culture if it didn't worry about such things on general principles alone, and in the case of *Excession* there really is a conspiracy among the watchmen, which is why the narrative becomes increasingly focused on exposing and stopping those Minds before real war breaks out, as well as figuring out how the large cast of characters the novel has thrown at us fits into it. In that, Banks is gleefully unhelpful: the plots and sub-plots cascading from the two main foci in the storyline—the Excession's Outside Context problem and the Affront's... Inside Context Nuisance—weave in and out of each other's path in a bewildering dance of events and personalities, all of them paraded before our eyes without obeisance to a narrative hierarchy; flesh sentients and Minds are introduced to us with an intensity of description that makes us believe they are relevant additions to the plot and then disappear, die, or walk out on us after five or ten pages, while seemingly secondary events remain with us with surreptitious doggedness, shadowing the reader's progress through the story like bloodhounds.[6] And then again, some characters that died or seemed to have completed their arc come back at the end, improbably but slightly plausibly because this is space opera (we have the technology).[7] And of course, this absence of a clean plot deployment only heightens the suspicion that secret engines of change have already whispered themselves into motion and spread their agents everywhere.

The end result is the cognitive overload Faren Miller warned the reader about in her *Locus* review. Essentially, Banks wrote *Excession* like an Excession—excessively baroque, excessively described, excessively imaged, excessively secretive in a strangely easily forgivable way, and argued excessively lightly for a story featuring not only conspiracies, but also and more relevantly a species like the Affront. If we look at the characteristics of Affront society, we'll soon see that they are a fairly close approximation of the dynamics operating in the Empire of Azad from *The Player of Games*—exploitation, rape, violence, social inequality, eugenic fixing of whole sections of the population, and so on. The reason why the Affront don't come across to us readers in the same way as the Azadians is because of the way the narrative addresses them: the transcendent viewpoint that comes into play with the shift from a mostly planet- or Orbital-based plotline to a space-bound one telescopes our perspective away from the terrible intimacy of dystopia's internal machinery and toward a historicized perspective that focuses on the civilizing process itself. If *Consider Phlebas* was a sort of *Saving Private Ryan* to classic space opera's *The Longest Day*, *Excession* is *The Hunt for Red October*, a *realpolitik*-infused whodunit set against the background of a threatening galactic war that retains the deconstructive characteristics of *Phlebas* while at the same time managing to pay obeisance to the kinetics of the classical form. There are no scenes in this novel that even come close to the horrors Gurgeh witnesses on Azad— but there could have been if Banks had decided to zero in on them.[8] Instead, this is an example of *Excession*'s main narrative tone, specifically regarding the Culture's handling of the Affront:

> Whatever; in the end, with a deal of arm and tentacle twisting, some deftly managed suitable-technology donations (through what the Affront Intelligence Regiment still gleefully but naïvely thought was some really neat high-tech theft on their part), the occasional instance of knocking heads together (or whatever anatomical feature was considered appropriate) and a hefty amount of naked bribery—woefully inelegant to the refined intellect of the average Culture mind—their tastes generally ran to far more rarefied forms of chicanery—but undeniably effective) the Affront had—kicking and screaming at times, admittedly—finally been more or less persuaded to join the great commonality of the galactic meta-civilisation; they had agreed to abide by its rules almost all the time and had grudgingly accepted that other beings beside themselves might have rights, or at least tolerably excusable desires (such as those concerning life, liberty, self-determination and so on), which occasionally might even override the self-evidently perfectly natural, demonstrably just and indeed arguably even sacred Affronter prerogative to go wherever they wanted and do whatever they damn well pleased, preferable while having a bit of fun with the locals at the same time [167].

This is one single period occupying fully half of a page, and chances are that the breath will grow short in the reader's lungs while he/she struggles, entertained but to an extent cyanotic, to get to the end. There's a slightly Dickensian feel to the rhythm and the tone of the writing, unworried and chummy in the way of a historian discussing their subject matter over a cup of tea and some biscuits—or, as Farah Mendlesohn puts it, "it is as if someone had just dropped Jane Austen's *Emma* into the middle of a battle" (Mendlesohn 2008, 559).[9] But at other times the speed and tone of the narrative change dramatically, shifting into clipped descriptives and short bursts of prose aimed at, for example, putting us in the middle of a Mind's thoughts while it's engaged in battle or absorbed in calculations of its own—a good example is the paragraph describing the Rapid Offensive Unit *Killing Time* conducting a raid on the Affront-controlled fleet of Culture warships (396–399), or the segment following the GSV *Yawning Angel*'s frantic thought processes as it tries to keep up with the *Sleeper Service* when the other ship suddenly breaks away from its surveillance (236–248). Either way, both metaphorically and physically, we are light-years above the direct witnessing of sentient suffering that the kind of society the Affront have constructed inevitably promotes, and we need this lofty viewpoint if we are to retain our sense that this is, as Banks intended, a sprawling, determinedly chaotic, high-energy comedy—and not just a comedy in the strict sense of the term, because in that sense *The Player of Games* is a comedy as well. No, this is a story meant to make us happy despite the doubts, to orbit over the critical utopia's self-correcting machinery without ignoring it, and to utilize the status of the Culture as the good guys to make things go as unproblematically well as a writer with Banks' inclinations was ever likely to allow them to go. And the key to that outcome is embedded in the novel's very language.

In a recent article on *Excession*, Farah Mendlesohn seizes on the convolutions of the plot and the shifts in narrative style as the two principal tools that, in her view, transform the novel into a deconstructionist/reconstructionist romantic comedy. We have already seen some of the decon/recon aspects of *Excession*, and Mendlesohn provides others: the seemingly orderless succession of writing styles, she points out, "works beyond the red herrings, the politics, the joy of bodies that change shape, immortal intellects, and the sardonic humor of ships. One is struck by the sheer effrontery of Banks' reconfiguration of the space opera and his playful use of language. Against extravagant scenery and epic scale, the choice of modes and moods differs for each section of the novel. This is where Banks' revisioning of what space opera is takes place" (2008, 559). Thus, the parts of the story focusing on Dajeil's forty-year exile inside the *Sleeper Service* unfold slowly and unhurriedly while those involving Genar-Hofoen move quickly, packed with dense quantities of information. When Minds think, the narrative deploys over whole pages to illustrate reflections that take those Minds less than a second to formulate, while the passages describing such exotica as hyperspace and the energy grid that underlies the universe alternate between the prosaic and the sublime to achieve an oddly pleasing effect both of rhetorical deflation and intellectual stimulation (Mendlesohn 2008, 560; Banks 1996, 271).[10] The Excession, on the other hand, spends the vast majority of the novel doing nothing at all besides providing everyone with an excuse to go nuts, and during those long pauses the narrative treats it like something of a wet firework, but the few times the artifact shifts into action the language used to describe such action falls on the page like the step of a titan:

> But the Excession had changed; it had re-established its links with the energy grids and then it had grown; then it had *erupted*.... This was something incarnated in the ultimate fire of the energy grid itself, spilling across the whole sweep of Infraspace and Ultraspace and invading the skein as well, creating an immense spherical wave-front of grid-fire boiling across three-dimensional space.... It was like the energy grid itself had been turned inside out, as though the most massive black hole in the universe had suddenly turned white and bloated into some big-bang eruption of fury between the universes ... [417–418].

In similar fashion, the thought processes of the Culture's Minds—which after the Excession and the Sublimed are the most powerful entities in the galaxy—are presented to us in an internalized third-person voice of great clarity and complexity, surpassingly strange in the narrative's constant reminders that ideas occur to those entities in a minuscule fraction of the time it takes us to read about them—so much so, in fact, that at times dealing with us meatbrains becomes frustrating: "*Look* at these humans!" the Mind of the GSV *Yawning Angel* rages in the silence of itself while the ship tries to speed up departure from an Orbital to catch up with the absconding *Sleeper Service*. "How could such glacial slowness even be called *life*? An age could pass, virtual empires rise and fall in the time they took to open their mouths to utter some new inanity!" (245). But the most estranged—and intellectually most interesting—representation of the Minds' thoughts are the communications from ship to ship that knit the novel into shape in the same way they eventually tie together the secrets of the conspiracy. Those communications are "configured as computer code, emulating the package transmission that relays emails from node to node, varying in rhetorical mood" (Mendlesohn 2008, 563). As an example, here is part of the exchange between the Limited Systems Vehicle *Serious Callers Only* and the Eccentric *Shoot Them Later* in the wake of their reception of the Affront's declaration of war:

> [stuttered tight point, M32, tra. @n4.28.882.4656]
> xLSV *Serious Callers Only*
>   oEccentric *Shoot Them Later*
> **It's war! Those insane fucks have declared war! They're mad!**
> ∞
> [stuttered tight point, M32, tra. @4.28.882.4861]
> xEccentric *Shoot Them Later*
>   oLSV *Serious Callers Only*
> **I was about to call. I just got the message from the ship I requested around Pittance. This looks bad.**

6. The View from Above, the View from Below

∞
Bad? It's a fucking catastrophe!
∞
Did your girl get her man?
∞
Oh, she got him all right, but then a few hours later the Affront High Command announces the birth of a bouncing baby war. The ship Phage sent to Tier was standing a day's module travel away; it decided it had better things to do than hang around on a mission it had never been very happy with even from the beginning. I think the declaration of war came almost as a relief to it....
∞
But it was demilled. Hasn't it just gone back to Phage for munitioning?
∞
Ha! Demilitarised my backup. Fucker left Phage fully tooled. Phage's own idea, sneaky scumbag. Always was over protective. What comes of being that geriatric I suppose [286].

And so on, for five pages of tight dialogue parsed by the infinity symbol that separates the ships' voices from one another.[11] By the time we read this exchange, we have already been through enough signal sequences to understand at least part of the nomenclature's meaning (the "x" means "from" and the "o" means "to," for example), but just to be on the safe side and just so that we'll have the chance to enjoy parsing Mind-talk—the joy of cognition rising out of estrangement—Banks includes in the story a human-friendly copy of the signal sequence in which the Interesting Times Gang first appears; this copy contains a reading key that clarifies every element in the code used by the Minds to communicate to each other (108–123). The overall effect of this level of cognitive access, supplemented by descriptions of the realms of thought within which Minds exist all the time—the concept of Metamathics, for example, which the Minds call The Land of Infinite Fun (138–141)—is to let us experience the breadth and beauty of the possible and deliver the sense of wonder typical of classic space opera even from within Banks' deconstructive/reconstructive left-wing project. We soar above creation, and it doesn't really matter that the wings we're using are borrowed from someone else.

The Excession's role in this deconstructionist/reconstructionist structure is to act as a Rorschach test for all the characters involved in the story, and as a mirror for their actions. Its very appearance seems to trigger every involved civilization's id: the Culture grows compulsively cautious and starts hatching a whole number of contingency plans (conspiracy included), the Affront beat their chests and attack, and the Zetetic Elench, to which two of the ships taken over by the Excession belong, grow rabidly curious. The Elench are an offshoot of the Culture that aims at a result in its dealings with others that is diametrically opposite to the one their parent society strives for: while the Culture wants to remain roughly the same and change those societies it encounters and judges in need of alterations, the Elench want to encounter other societies so that those societies can change them (87–89)— hence their proclivity for often dangerous curiosity. And as far as mirroring goes, this is exactly what happens. Part of a civilization of ultimate change-seekers, the Elench ships *Peace Makes Plenty* and *Break Even* receive from the Excession an extreme form of their wish: they get taken over. The Culture, on the other hand, is exceedingly cautious in everything involving contact with others, especially others who might become Outside Context Problems, which is why the *Fate Amenable to Change* spends the whole novel resolutely not contacting the Excession aside from a formal greeting at the outset. In response, the artifact does the same thing: nothing. When, however, the *Sleeper Service* arrives in the area speeding at an absurdly high FTL factor, the Excession mirrors its aggressive approach and explodes out towards it. But as soon as the GSV slows down, so does the Excession (417–431). And it's probably a good thing the Affront's hijacked fleet of Culture warship doesn't arrive anywhere near it before the conspiracy is unmasked and their burgeoning war is brought to a halt.

Thus, the Excession seems like something of a red herring. Usually, the mysterious artifact in any space opera constitutes the single most important plotline in the story; its arrival and subsequent actions fundamentally change the world and, secondarily, allow the other characters to play out their personal dramas within a context that'll grant them a resolution they might otherwise have been denied. In Banks' novel, however, the Excession changes nothing fundamental in the galaxy's physical condition, and the characters whose trajectories in the plot seemed intimately tied up with it—Genar-Hofoen, Ulver Seich, Dajeil, and the *Sleeper Service*—turn out to have been set in motion with completely different objectives: the *Sleeper Service* is a deniable weapon, its Eccentric status a convenient mask for its true role—a faithful member of Special Circumstances that, for forty years, has been preparing for the onset of the conspiracy to entrap the Affront. The GSV is the failsafe, the conspiracy hidden from the conspiracy. Some Minds in SC knew that the anti-Affront movement was still alive, and planned for it by having the *Sleeper Service* fake Eccentricity and spend those forty years building an enormous fleet of semi-sentient warships. At the end of the story, the GSV deploys this fleet, comprised of nearly ninety thousand units, and the Affront surrender along with some of the conspirators—others, like the Affronter commanding the detachment that had taken over Pittance as well as the Minds of the *Attitude Adjuster* and of the *Not Invented Here*, take their own lives (436–437).

Genar-Hofoen, for his part, was never meant to talk to Zreyn Tramow's

6. The View from Above, the View from Below

mind-state; in fact, that mind-state is not even on board the *Sleeper Service* anymore. The reason he is there is that the *Sleeper Service* itself requested his presence, which is the stage at which, as Farah Mendlesohn pointed out, the decon/recon comedy becomes a romantic decon/recon comedy. Forty years before, it had been the *Sleeper Service* that had made it possible for Genar-Hofoen and Dajeil to ignite their ill-fated romance; the GSV had played matchmaker and the relationship had ended terribly, and the Mind feels partly responsible for that outcome. Therefore, it wants them to mend ways and return to active, happy lives instead of the stasis (partial in Genar-Hofoen's case, total in Dajeil's) that has characterized the past forty years in their separate existences—"it is the classic triangle of the romance novel," Mendlesohn writes (559).[12] Ulver, for her part, is a supernumerary: in the dialogue quoted above, when the *Shoot Them Later* asks the *Serious Callers Only* if its girl got her man, it was Ulver and Genar-Hofoen the Eccentric was referring to. Knowing about the conspiracy and erroneously suspecting that Genar-Hofoen must have been playing some part in it, the *Serious Callers Only* had arranged to have her activated and sent to intercept him (388–396).

But the ultimate lack of a neatly dovetailing resolution doesn't mean that the characters involved in this crazy, shaggy-dog, rambling, giddy, romantic-deconstructionist-reconstructionist galactic-conspiracy-theory romp don't get the ending they deserve: Genar-Hofoen resumes his post on Issorile, now equipped with an Affront body to wear when he does the town (445). Dajeil gives birth to a daughter she names Ren, and the two of them, along with a revived Zreyn Tramow and Gestra, a resurrected Culture man who had been killed at Pittance, are on board the *Sleeper Service*, now on its way to Leo II (448–451). Ulver returns to Phage, her friends, and her busy social schedule with a pleased nod from SC, and the bird Gravious goes with her. The Affront, after getting their collective noses slightly bloodied in the standoff at the Excession's location, are behaving better than usual, and the Culture ... well, the Culture is its usual self—busy, happy, and hedonistic except for the remaining Minds in the Interesting Times Gang, some of whom are wondering what the Excession was all about now that, in the wake of the events triggered by its arrival, it has again disappeared without a trace. Some are speculating that it was some sort of trial or test, which the Culture and the other civilizations failed, while still others are quietly happy it's gone and taken with it whatever might have come out of it if its intentions had been hostile (445–447).

The great Minds are thus left wondering, and so are those flesh sentients among their ranks who witnessed at least part of the events in the story. We readers, however, receive a reward of our own: aside from a tiny paragraph illustrating the happy state in which the three ships that went with the artifact currently exist ("They looked around, in the midst of an undreamt splendour"; 448), the last word in the novel belongs to the artifact itself, which talks to us in a Joycean stream-of-consciousness data-dump voice:

> call me highway call me conduit call me lightning rod scout catalyst observer call me what you will i was there when i was required through me passed the overarch bedeckants in their great sequential migration across the universes of [*no translation*] the marriage parties of the universe groupings of [*no translation*] and the emissaries of the lone bearing the laws of the new from the pulsing core the absolute centre of our nested home all this the rest and others i received as i was asked and transmitted as i was expected without fear favor or failure ... [455].

Thus the artifact continues to talk to us, announcing its function as a gateway through and from other universes (and therefore making both interpretations of its nature correct), describing the events in *Excession* as it saw them, and declaring that, as far as the universe it has just finished visiting is concerned, the civilizations living there are indeed not ready to receive what it brings—and yet something in those events must have either pleased or struck it as interesting because, at the very end of its communication, it declares that

> in recognition of the foregoing I wish now to be known hereafter as the excession
>
> thank you
> end [455].

And so ends the novel as well. The Excession was a meta-universal General Contact Unit, and like the *Arbitrary* with Earth, it decided against contacting for the time being (it describes the environment it just left as "chaotic"). This is one thing the critical utopia of the Culture will never know, although some of its Minds suspect it, and this "secret" ending is ultimately one of the reasons that give Banks' Culture stories the agency to keep questioning their own setup. There are larger forces at work out there, and they're more grown up than even the Minds can imagine.

In her article, Farah Mendlesohn describes *Excession* as "the most *classic*, the most archetypal in its revisioning of space opera; the most ambitious in its portrayal of a complex political society; and the most successful in its linguistic display and reconfiguration of the space opera baroque and in the immersive techniques of extrapolative fiction" (557–558). This comment captures the twin qualities of familiarity and experimentation that characterize this novel, qualities that are impossible to separate from one another because both are embedded in the text at the same time and in the same words. The voice of classic space opera is still audible as a structured basis for the creation of suitable special effects, but this basis is surrounded by a network of signifiers that, displacing the old connections to the old signified, rebuild the template of the subgenre in the same breath that unravels it. Also, Ken MacLeod awards *Excession* the status of first truly cutting-edge Culture novel, his argument being that the long years elapsed between the writing of the first four Culture stories and their publication "made them subtly dated before they were published ... there is no nanotech in them. Their great AIs, the Minds, are essentially mainframes. The personal access devices are even *called* terminals. There are no networks. (These deficiencies are more than made up in Banks's later work, notably the data-dense, baroque *Excession*)" (MacLeod 2003, 41). And the experiment does work; we can enjoy this new strange creature to whose birth *Consider Phlebas* ends up acting as midwife. *Excession* is a comedy not because it ignores the issues that previous Culture stories had made central—it doesn't—or because its various members have stopped critiquing it from within—they haven't. *Excession* is a comedy because its author wrote it in a series of linguistic registers that allow it to skate on the thin, creaking surface of the threshold that separates despair from happiness, disaster from reprieve, and suffering from contentment, and take us all the way back home with it, safe despite the close call. Among all the Culture stories, *Excession* is possibly the funniest and certainly the most joyous, designed to give us a feeling of soaring impossibly fast into clean space, of describing swift power-orbits over ferocious gravity wells, free and happy and unfettered—just like Culture people. In the end, this is the novel that more than any other welcomes us into the Culture as honorary citizens.

Something strange happened between the publication of the hardcover edition of *Inversions* in 1998 and the appearance of the paperback edition in 1999: a "Note on the Text" disappeared. Here it is:

> This Text, in two Parts, was discovered amongst the Papers of my late Grandfather. One Part concerns the Story of the Bodyguard to the then Protector of Tassasen, one UrLeyn, and is related, it is alleged, by a Person of his Court at the time, while the other, told by my Grandfather, tells the Story of the Woman Vosill, a Royal Physician during the Reign of King Quience, and who may, or may not, have been from the distant Archipelago of Drezen but who was, without Argument, from a different Culture. Like my much esteemed Grandfather, I have taken on the Task of making the Text I inherited more comprehensible and clear, and hope that I have succeeded in this Aim. Nevertheless, it is in a Spirit of the utmost Humility that I present it to the Society and to whoever might see fit to read it.—O. Derlan-Haspid III, D. Phys, OM (1st class), ESt, RS (hons) [1].

Both Faren Miller in *Locus* (20) and David Langford in *SFX* (108) mentioned this note, but within a year it was gone.[13] Aside from this omission, the hardcover edition and all subsequent softcover editions are identical, but none of the softcovers contain the note.[14] In the absence of any comment from either Banks or his publisher, Orbit, on the deletion of this passage,[15] the reason for it can therefore only be speculated upon; the likelihood is high, however, that it had something to do with giving the game away at the outset.

In the *SFX* interview quoted earlier in this chapter, Banks had commented that *Excession*'s large non-human cast represented, in his view, "the upper limit of human non-involvement; I don't think I'll ever write a novel in which humans are less involved. In the next one I think they'll be more clued up" (Branscombe 1996b, 25). And this is exactly what happens: *Inversions* is set on an unnamed planet and among civilizations just past the medieval stage, and it contains no clues as to when in the timeline of the Culture it takes place—it's the only Culture story that doesn't provide them. Not one word in the novel issues from a non-human character, and no Minds or drones or anything more advanced than a musket appears on stage—with a few quiet, crucial exceptions. "With *Inversions*," Banks said, "I wanted to go back to something on a more human scale than *Excession*, and I wanted to give an answer to a question no one's ever asked: what the Culture actually does to other societies—how they intervene successfully? It comes down to ensuring that useful people survive, and problematical ones 'disappear'" (Brown 1998, 55).

Readers unfamiliar with the Culture series should not pick *Inversions* as their introductory text; they would miss the clues distributed throughout its length. Seasoned readers, on the other hand, would hugely enjoy putting those clues together to finally, at the end of the narrative, arrive at the revelation that *Inversions* is a Culture novel in disguise, a glimpse of utopia from the viewpoint of those civilizations that, like 1977 Earth, don't rank as mature enough to know there are gods in the sky but that, unlike 1977 Earth, could do with some helping along. The two central characters in the story are from the Culture, but neither tells his/her tale—that is left to two other characters, both of whom are native to the planet so that their view of the events they narrate is devoid of perspective. Both characters are utterly ignorant of the true shape of the sky, and neither ever knows better, but we will if we piece the evidence together correctly—which is where the probable reason for deleting the note on the text comes in. It's those few words just past the middle of the passage: "from a different Culture." Banks tried to hide the significance of that last word by having the writer of the note capitalize every noun (as the German language does), but either he or someone at Orbit felt that the trick wasn't enough, and that the word was too glaring a giveaway to really give expert Culture readers a run for their money. So away the note went, which is a shame because it provided an added layer of storytelling to a narrative that is signally savvy about its status as a story—everyone is a narrator in *Inversions*, everyone possesses part of the truth but never the whole, and

6. The View from Above, the View from Below 143

everyone is aware of the performative aspect of their role as storytellers. Together with *The State of the Art*, *Inversions* is perhaps the most openly metafictional of all Culture narratives.

The story is divided into two seemingly parallel but ultimately connected narratives. These narratives amount to a clean total of twenty-four chapters, to which we should add the note on the text, a prologue, and an epilogue. Each of the twenty-four chapters is headed by its number in the sequence, by the title "The Doctor" or "The Bodyguard" (depending on the narrative), and by the stylized image of a dagger, black ink on white paper; each narrative unfailingly alternates chapters with the other. O. Derlan-Haspid's grandfather, Oelph, who also tells one of the two stories, writes both the prologue and the epilogue. In the prologue, a now elderly Oelph reflects on the events of many years before and on the figure of the Doctor, now long gone. "Did she leave us better off or not?" Oelph asks rhetorically. "I think, undeniably, better. Did she do this through selfishness or selflessness? I believe that in the end it does not matter in the least.... That was another thing that she taught me. That you are what you do. To Providence—or Progress or the Future or before any sort of judgment apart from our own conscience—what we have done, not what we have thought, is the result we are judged by" (6). In the prologue, besides writing a foreword to his own chronicle of the time he spent with the Doctor, Oelph also provides the introduction to the second narrative, which he found by chance and which he believes fundamentally complements the Doctor's (6).

Chapter 1 opens the story of Doctor Vosill, personal physician to King Quience of Haspidus, and a young Oelph tells it. Besides being Vosill's assistant, he is also a spy for a man he only identifies as "Master" until the end of the novel (7), which is why he is writing the Doctor's narrative in the first place. Vosill has come to the attention of King Quience through her sheer ability as a healer, and while he favors her she enjoys a position of disproportionate influence for someone who is (1) a foreigner and (2) a woman. Oelph himself comments on the immodesty that prompts the Doctor to "[pay] flawless lip service to the facts of life which dictate the accepted and patent preeminence of the male ... with a sort of unwarranted humor, producing in us males the unsettling contrary feeling that she is indulging us" (11). Vosill's very skills in treating the King further damage her popularity: when Quience made her his personal physician, he displaced a number of hopeful male doctors who are now busy vilifying her, citing her foreign provenance and her gender as damning flaws in and of themselves (and the King's vociferous insistence that no doctor other than Vosill will lay a single hand on him helps her in no way whatsoever; 41–42). The nobles, for their part, simply rationalize their prejudices as requirements of statecraft, maintaining that she must be a spy and maneuvering to get her into the hands of Nolieti, the King's chief torturer (10–17). Led by the elderly Duke Walen, those nobles particularly resent Vosill's closeness to the King, suspecting—correctly—that her mouth is whispering novel ideas in Quience's ear while her hands take care of the rest of his body (101–102, 260–265).

The second narrative begins with chapter 2. It's the story of DeWar, bodyguard to the Protector UrLeyn of Tassasen, and its narrator does not provide any information as to his/her identity, deciding instead to "tell the story after the fashion of the Jeritic fabulists, that is in the form of a Closed Chronicle, in which—if one is inclined to believe such information of consequence—one has to guess the identity of the person telling the tale" (21–22). The narrator's motive for doing so, he/she tells us, is to allow us to judge the merits of the events described in DeWar's story without the perceptive distortions that the revelation of his/her identity would generate. Thus, immediately after this introductory interpolation, the section of *Inversions* that tells DeWar's tale becomes a false third-person narrative, very much in the fashion of *The Player of Games* but without the earlier novel's regular reminders that we are in fact listening to the voice of a character in the story. After telling us that we won't get to know who he/she is, the narrative "I" leaves us for good.

Here we have the first of many inversions by which the novel is characterized (like *The Player of Games* and *Use of Weapons*, *Inversions* is a polyvalent title): Oelph is an exceedingly scrupulous observer and correct chronicler of the Doctor's story. He constantly addresses his Master directly, carefully circumscribing his own level of agency with respect to the Master's greater status. He never glosses over details or fails to attribute actions and words to the right source, and if he wasn't there to witness something he references in the text, he is careful to point out how he came by the information. Despite his naïveté and at times excessive obsequiousness, Oelph is bright, likeable and, with the exception of deceiving the Doctor concerning his other task (and even that is done more out of a sense of gratitude to his secret employer than out of genuine desire to dissemble; 17–18), honest with everything and everyone, including himself. When he discusses Vosill, it is with an earnest, frequently faltering equanimity not in the least damaged by those lapses—because he immediately acknowledges them in tones clearly indicating long before his eventual confession (270–275; 324) that he has fallen in love with her. Oelph is an intellectual and a scholar, in short, and an honest one at that. As such he cherishes the qualities that are necessary to perform the job; obfuscations of the truth or willful mistakes of attribution would horrify him.

The narrator of DeWar's tale, on the other hand, is Oelph's opposite, first hiding behind a storytelling convention and then switching to a fake third-person narration whose ring of truth we can neither verify nor, paradoxically, shake. His/her claim that the reason for the telling of DeWar's story is love of the truth, and that too many mendacious versions of this tale have spawned themselves, is therefore suspect. Also, this narrator admits that the story we are about to read is only a small portion of a much larger story whose real nature remains essentially unknown (22).

More inversions: if Doctor Vosill, the foreign woman from the faraway "archipelagic republic of Drezen" (46), is trusted by no one in the realm of Haspidus, DeWar, the foreign man from Mottelocci (a small principality in the so-called Half-Hidden Kingdoms; 95), trusts no one in the Protectorate of Tassasen.[16] The one works to save lives while the other works to extinguish them, although both perform their duties to keep their respective societies' rulers alive. Both have travelled extensively before settling down in their present positions, but while the Doctor ranges far and wide across Haspidus to heal the poor and miserable as well as the rich and comfortable (37–40, 47–54, 72–79), and to teach the fundamentals of modern medicine to recalcitrant male chauvinist doctors (162–167, 236), the bodyguard remains firmly in one place—wherever the Protector is, which means mostly in palace in Tassasen. In short, Vosill is proactive while DeWar is reactive.

All around the Doctor and the bodyguard, the world is changing. An unspecified number of years before, a great meteor shower fell from the sky and annihilated the old empire that had until then been controlling the territories of half the planet. Now, in the aftermath of the fall, a number of young kingdoms, new republics, balkanized remnants of the empire, and a few pre-existing realms—Haspidus among them—are vying for control of the recently vacated lands (38–39, 56–58, 63, 88–89, 100), and all eyes are on the conflict in Landescion, where numerous baronies have formed and congregated to oppose Tassasen's claims to their territories (23–24). Protector UrLeyn, whom the nobles and the kings of the realms surrounding Tassasen fear because he became the Protector by killing the last King and instituting a new, Cromwellian form of government (Miller 1998, 20), is about to go to war, and more than one assassin has already tried to eliminate him before he can do so. DeWar, as a consequence, watches and waits. And worries.

Gradually, clues begin accumulating to indicate that neither Vosill nor DeWar is quite from around there. The Doctor keeps a diary in which she writes in three different languages: Haspidian, Imperial, and another one that Oelph cannot decipher and has never seen before—neither has anyone else, and as it later transpires, it is not Drezeni (9, 267–269). She knows enough of the world that she can minutely correct the most recent maps, to the considerable annoyance of the nobleman who presented them to the King (139–140). She seems immune to poisons (16), recovers from hangovers astonishingly quickly (292), and is in possession of transcripts of two conversations that she could not possibly have witnessed or even overheard (110–114, 171–175). In both cases, those conversations develop in some length Duke Walen's plans to have Vosill handed over to Nolieti for questioning, and when Oelph comments on the copy of the first transcription, which he has carried out for his Master, he declares himself convinced that it represents a real conversation although he is at a loss to explain how Vosill came by it (114). Also, there's something strange about the blunt, worn, utilitarian-looking dagger the Doctor carries with her at all times—it doesn't look like much of a weapon and its grip is missing many of the semiprecious stones it had once carried (70), but its description is strongly reminiscent of the stylized image that begins every chapter, and Vosill tells Oelph that those missing stones "were used to good effect. Some bought protection in uncultured places" (71). And whatever protection they bought, it still surrounds Vosill: when, one day, two of Oelph's fellow assistants spy the Doctor bathing naked in a stream and decide to rape her, they don't even get to take the first step in her direction—something as invisible as it is powerful knocks them both unconscious (242–245).

DeWar, on the other hand, does not seem to possess any particularly strange qualities, know indecipherable languages, or have especially sensitive ears. He is a storyteller, though. Throughout the text he diverts Lattens, UrLeyn's young son, with fables about a faraway place suspiciously called Lavishia, "a magical land where every man was a king, every woman a queen, each boy a prince and all girls princesses. In this land there were no hungry people and no crippled people" (89).[17] Also, in Lavishia everyone is as beautiful as they choose to be, and although they can have any amount of riches many choose to have nothing; there are no wars, no famine or pestilence, and no taxes. People can fly on invisible wings, and when they want to travel to the suns they use ships with invisible sails. There are also giants and monsters, although they're all "very nice giants and extremely helpful monsters" (89–90, 126–127, 227).

If the above makes Lavishia sound rather like the Culture, DeWar's description of what the people of that country do with their time dispels any lingering doubt:

> Sometimes the citizens of Lavishia would discover whole groups of people who lived a bit like the wanderers ... in their own land, but who did not have the choice of living like that. Such people lived like that because they had to. These were people who hadn't had the advantages in life the people of Lavishia were used to. In fact, dealing with such people soon became the biggest problem the people of Lavishia had [90].

Among the many Lavishian citizens who worry about the fate of those poor peoples are two cousins—a boy by the name of Hiliti and a girl by the name of Sechroom. They are best friends, having grown up together, but they disagree on what Lavishia should do when it encounters the poor people:

6. The View from Above, the View from Below

Was it better to leave them alone or was it better to try and make life better for them? Even if you decided it was the right thing to do to make life better for them, which way did you do this? Did you say, Come and join us and be like us? Did you say, Give up all your own ways of doing things, the gods that you worship, the beliefs you hold most dear, the traditions that make you who you are? Or do you say, We have decided you should stay roughly as you are and we will treat you like children and give you toys that might make your life better? Indeed, who even decided what was better? [90–91].

This is, of course, the basic gist of Contact's problematization handbook, and we've heard it before. Within the spectrum of responses to Lavishia/the Culture's dilemma of intervention, Sechroom is the one who believes that the magical land should always try to help, whereas Hiliti believes that the best way to go about it is to leave those people to their own devices. Also, Sechroom holds that one "should never be cruel to be kind ... there must always be another way of teaching people lessons." Hiliti, on the other hand, thinks that "throughout history it had been proved that sometimes you did have to be cruel to be kind" (151). These differences of opinion eventually grow serious enough to prompt Hiliti to carry out an ill-advised intervention to teach Sechroom a lesson in cruel-to-be-kind *realpolitik*, in the wake of which Sechroom almost dies (151–155); thus a rift develops between the two cousins, irreparably damaging their friendship. Sechroom becomes "a soldier-missionary in the Lavishian army" (92), while Hiliti "exiled himself from the luxuries of Lavishia forever." In time, both come to the world of *Inversions* because "[Sechroom] and Hiliti knew ... of the Empire, and Haspidus. They talked about it, argued over it" (231).

At this point, even readers not familiar with the Culture would probably form the impression that there's something going on behind and between the words exchanged in the text. Readers already familiar with the series, on the other hand, would know that DeWar's simple possession of this information indicates that he is from the Culture, and that he is, in all likelihood, Hiliti. They would also have guessed by now that Vosill is from the Culture as well, that she's probably Sechroom, and that she's working for Special Circumstances.

The context surrounding DeWar's tales of Lavishia helps fan our suspicions. While he thwarts an assassination attempt on UrLeyn with nothing more than his sword and his wits (60–66), which is consistent with the notion of a Culture exile in the Dervley Linter mold who doesn't have access to companion drones, knife missiles, and task-oriented augmentations, people at Quience's court in Haspidus begin dying in seemingly impossible locked-room circumstances. The first is chief questioner Nolieti, followed by his assistant Unoure, who had been fingered as the culprit of his master's murder and was about to be put to the question (another inversion here—the torturer about to be tortured). Then it's Duke Walen's turn, in the immediate aftermath of another mysteriously overheard conversation in which he yet again tries getting Vosill into the hands of Ralinge, the new questioner. Right before the Duke dies, a young woman sees "a dark bird, or a nightwing" in the room with him (217–218). Also, the war in Landescion begins—King Quience follows it quietly but closely (143–146)—just as the first in a series of mysterious seizures strikes Lattens, eventually placing him at death's door (129, 248). In the long run, a distraught UrLeyn becomes incapable of following the war against the Barons, whose armies are, in any event, suspiciously better trained and equipped than anyone had anticipated (248). Heartbroken and frustrated, the Protector abandons the direct administration of the war and returns to Tassasen, to his ailing son, and to his eventual murder.

Lattens is not the only audience of DeWar's stories of Lavishia. Among those listening to them is the concubine Perrund, one of UrLeyn's favorites both despite and because of her withered, useless left arm. Years before, Perrund had sacrificed that arm to shield the Protector from an assassin's blade, nearly dying in the process. In spite of her handicap, she remains a woman of great beauty and personal charm, and while UrLeyn favors and trusts her greatly, DeWar is hopelessly in love with her (36). Perrund, who would reciprocate, cannot however bring herself to do so—first, she is one of the Protector's concubines, and secondly, as she tells DeWar, "I am dead" (290). She has, it turns out, a story of her own to tell, and it's a tale of horror: some men of the King raped her during the war that saw UrLeyn triumph, and then she had to watch as they did the same thing to her sisters. Eventually the men killed the whole family, leaving only Perrund alive or, as she repeats to DeWar several times, in a sort of death-in-life (284–289). Perrund is also the teller of DeWar's story (343–345) and the assassin who kills UrLeyn at the end of it. Unreliable narrator that she is, she has given DeWar *almost* the whole truth about her fate and that of her family—she told one central lie concerning the actual perpetrators of the crime: they were a young UrLeyn and the gang of fellow soldiers who later became his current cabinet. Like the Barons in Landescion, Perrund has all along been working for Quience. Her orders were to keep the Protector alive until he had been disgraced and ruined—Quience wanted no martyr on his hands whose memory might one day inspire other regicides (333–336).[18]

At the same time in Haspidus, the conspirators of Vosill's downfall have finally taken drastic action: acting without Quience's knowledge, they have had the venerable, kindly Duke Ormin killed using one of the Doctor's scalpels and then abducted both her and Oelph, taking them to the torture chamber where Ralinge awaits (291–298). Terrified of what's coming, sick at the idea of seeing the Doctor ravaged, Oelph closes his eyes:

> She said something that sounded like an instruction in a language I did not know.... A language from somewhere, I thought ... beyond even far Drezen. A language from nowhere ... I heard a whirring noise. A noise like a waterfall, a

noise like a sudden wind, like an arrow as it passes nearby one's ear. Then a long gasp ... and then a thud, a punch-like concussion of what, in retrospect, was air and flesh and bone and [...] what? More bone? Metal? Wood? Metal, I think [301–302].

When Oelph reopens his eyes, he finds Vosill standing in front of him, dressed in a long white shirt—"She looked utterly different. Alien" (302). The torture chamber is an abattoir, the three bodies of Ralinge and his assistants lying in several pieces on the floor, blood seemingly covering every surface. As the Doctor undoes Oelph's straps, he sees something moving for a moment at the hem of her shirt, and then he notices Vosill looking at him:

> She looked so steady and so certain. And yet she looked so dead, so utterly overpowered. She turned her head to one side and said something in a tone I swear to this day was resigned and defeated, even bitter. Something buzzed through the air. "We must imprison ourselves to save ourselves, Oelph," she told me [303].

Before the two are peremptorily called to the King's bedside, where Quience lies dying after suffering a mysterious seizure, Oelph notices that the Doctor's ancient dagger has lost the last of its semiprecious stones.

Inversions ends with Oelph's epilogue. As the prologue had introduced both storylines, so the epilogue closes them. Having cured the King at the last minute, the Doctor left. A heartbroken Oelph took her to the harbor where she boarded a ship from which she never got out—she disappeared one night of violent winds and blinding chain-fire, after declining the captain's invitation to have dinner with him "citing an indisposition due to special circumstances" (341). She left Haspidus in better shape than she'd found it when she had arrived: within a few weeks of her departure, the torture chamber was gone, replaced by a wine cellar, and the reforms Quience had discussed with her on the sly while Vosill was tending to him took root, creating a more equal society. All the remaining nobles who had conspired against her met terrible ends soon after her departure (340).

Oelph became a doctor, and eventually rose to much-honored status in Haspidian society: he was the first Principal of the newly created Medical University of Haspide, personal physician to Quience himself, and a city counselor who oversaw the construction of the King's Charitable Hospital and the Infirmary For The Freed (342–343). Quience himself, who ruled forty more years in excellent health, only sired daughters, so now Haspidus has a Queen. "I find this less troubling than I would have thought," the old Oelph writes (340).

In the wake of UrLeyn's death, Tassasen fell into a civil war from which Lattens, now King, eventually rescued it. The three remnants of the old empire still wage war on each other, thus leaving the rest of the world "free from imperial tyranny and so able to thrive in its own various ways" (345). Of

DeWar and the former concubine Perrund, Oelph tells us, nobody knows much. The most reliable of all the accounts has them escape Tassasen together immediately after UrLeyn's death and make their way to Mottelocci in the Hidden Kingdoms, where nobody actually knew DeWar. They became merchants, founded a bank, married, and had children who to this day control a thriving commercial concern. Apparently, they died in the mountains a few years earlier, although no bodies were found. Oelph admits to disliking this version of events, despite its greater probability (345–347).

Oelph himself eventually married, and he loves his wife now as ever "for her own sake, not for that of my lost love, even if as I will admit she does look just a little like the good Doctor" (347). He has never been able to reconcile the events in the torture chamber with his knowledge of the world's consensus reality, and since he still maintains that he did not imagine the things he heard, he remains trapped inside an inescapable conundrum, like everyone else with any knowledge of these events living on the nameless planet the Culture briefly—if crucially—touched like it did many others.

One of the large-scale inversions in *Inversions* is the one that concerns the readers' original perception of the two nations in which the action takes place. While the Tassasen Protectorate is something new in the political landscape of its world, Haspidus looks very much like one of Earth's medieval regimes of Kings, Aristocrats, and terminally unjust pyramidal arrangements where social mobility is something that happens somewhere else. As Banks knew they would, our *fin de siècle* sympathies immediately accrue around Tassasen, which to us looks by far like the better place; the first Bodyguard chapter introduces us to a relatively serene life in the Protector's palace, and UrLeyn himself appears before our eyes as a charismatic leader, an intelligent ruler, a loving father, and a good man. He and DeWar speak like equals despite the drastic difference in status, so we form the impression that UrLeyn didn't just command DeWar's services—he earned them. There also is more than a hint of utopian feeling in the air, driven by the changes in government the Protector has brought about in the wake of his victory against the forces loyal to the old king (33–34), and torture chambers are nowhere in sight.

By contrast, the first Doctor chapter opens inside Vosill's apartments only to have the tranquility of the scene immediately disrupted by the appearance of Unoure, Nolieti's apprentice, who has come to fetch the doctor to the torture chamber to revive a poor wretch currently being put to the question. For several pages after that, there are only the sight of excoriated flesh, the smell of blood and human waste, and the sound of unbearable pain, until the Doctor and Oelph are called to the King's bedside to treat a minor ailment that, so he declares, is really very painful (7–19). This motion from the clean, thoughtful environment of Vosill's practice to the ferocity of Nolieti's underworld and then back up to the seemingly clueless sumptuousness of the royal chambers drives home to us the notion of a top-down society built upon the suffering of the poor, the unfortunate, and the innocent; a dystopia.

As we gradually make our way through the novel, however, our perceptions are made to reset and reverse through the whirling tangle of events that tie Tassasen and Haspidus together. While UrLeyn doesn't particularly lose any of his good traits until the very end, when Perrund reveals what the Protector did to her and he undergoes a complete psychological collapse in the face of his son's illness, his realm does take on a slightly more dystopian look—the torture chamber, for one, makes a quick, off-stage appearance, all the worse for going mostly unremarked upon (94–95). Quience, on the other hand, rather rises in our estimation. He has a wicked sense of humor, a way with words, a keen intellect and, once Vosill's voice brings it to him, a surprisingly sensitive ear for the pain of his people—because it's not just matters of power and its distribution among the non-aristocratic classes that the two discuss. The narrative makes it clear that Quience's eventual decision to get rid of the torture chamber is rooted first in a particularly significant exchange he has with Vosill on the matter (169–171), and secondly in his reaction once he finds out what she and Oelph have come close to suffering (318–319). The other reforms the King makes after Vosill's departure are every bit as impressive—the institution of a medical university, of a charitable hospital, and of an infirmary for The Freed, which implies without saying it out loud that slavery has been abolished in Haspidus.

Another instance of reversal involves the characters of Oelph and Perrund. Both are orphans, and both claim to have been saved by their respective benefactors (UrLeyn and the Commander of Quience's Palace Guard, Adlain), but in fact neither was; Perrund knowingly obfuscated the truth of what really happened to her while Oelph remained ignorant of it until, on his deathbed, Adlain told him that he had rescued him out of guilt—Adlain had killed Oelph's entire family (342). But while Perrund retains her thirst for revenge throughout her death-in-life, Oelph has remained very much alive and forgiving of the evils of others (201–203).

There is also a reversal in the love triangles taking place in both storylines. The first, as we have seen, concerns DeWar, Perrund, and UrLeyn, and whatever we think of the denouement, it seems to have something approaching a queasily happy resolution when the two people in it who actually love each other do get together and the bad guy gets what he deserves. The second triangle involves Oelph, Vosill, and the King: one evening, Vosill confesses her love to Quience, who doesn't reciprocate. Tearful and ashamed, she tells the story to Oelph, who finds himself equally rejected when the Doctor reveals that she has known of his affections for a while (269–275). Unlike the breaking of the first, the breaking of the second love triangle leaves three people alone, whether by choice or otherwise.

The Culture's intervention protocols, Banks had explained in his 1998 *SFX* interview, come down to "ensuring that useful people survive, and problematical ones 'disappear.'" This is exactly what happens in *Inversions*, and here is where another large-scale reversal comes in. Back in the Culture/Lavishia, Vosill/Sechroom had been the one to argue that one should always do what looked like the right thing at any given point in time, while DeWar/Hiliti believed in a cruel-to-be-kind, bad-now-to-be-good-later approach. Here and now on the nameless planet, however, DeWar tries to do the right thing in the moment, whereas Vosill espouses a decidedly sharp-bladed strategy of political betterment. It was she who had Nolieti, Unoure, and Walen killed, and the executions were carried out via a drone/knife missile combination, as were the monitoring and the recording of the conversations Oelph later saw in her diary.[19] It's clear from the end of the scene in the torture chamber that those actions weigh greatly on Vosill, who nevertheless undertakes them with terrible efficiency, and to her credit we should remark that she does try to find other means of altering the balance of power for the better.[20] But, alone except for her invisible escorts and surrounded by a mostly hostile power structure, the Doctor is repeatedly denied the chance to do so, and every killing, every instance of deceit and manipulation, every lie are finally visible on her face in the aftermath of Ralinge's impossible, bloody demise.

But Oelph can't help Vosill process those feelings, and neither can DeWar—the two are unaware of each other's simultaneous presence on the planet. The surfeit of narrative voices in the novel, each of which is capable of telling only part of the whole story, brings home to us just how alone Vosill is—more alone than DeWar, in fact, ironically because he decided to pull a Dervley Linter and left the Culture behind, so that he is more readily acceptable to the Tassaseni court as a fellow barbarian than the Doctor is to the Haspidian court as a foreigner with distinctive behavioral oddities. The air of sorcery (thus Oelph calls the events in the torture chamber) that surrounds her further estranges her presence amidst people who, clearly feeling that something is alien about her very being, still cannot cast that suspicion within any kind of meaningful framework. In the end, while DeWar finds a semblance of peace and happiness on-planet with Perrund (but are they really dead? The circumstances of their disappearance seem special), Vosill can only leave forever, as alone as she had been when she had arrived.

The lack in *Inversions* of the kind of overall picture that we have gotten used to receiving from other Culture novels—especially from *Excession*—also robs both the reader and the narrators of the agency they would normally enjoy in an M-Banks space opera. Oelph and Perrund should be the demiurges that rule the respective worlds of the twin storylines; they should know the ins and outs, understand the setup, and see farther than anyone else—and to a certain extent they do, at least insofar as their fellow humans are concerned. But even at the moment of greatest power, even when, at the end of their respective narratives, they seem to be fully in control of the means of production, the magnitude of the truth escapes them completely. It's not their fault, but they are nevertheless diminished in our eyes (Oelph in particular knows that the protagonist of his tale is special in some fundamental way, but even his most daring speculations fall far short of the truth). They have both received the information they would need in the form of a fable, but neither has the knowledge to break that shell of story nestling inside the bigger one to get at the truth underneath, so that in fact we are confronted by yet another inversion: the seemingly smaller, easily contained narrative proves to be the frayed strand of an immensely larger story unspooling in depths of sky and stretches of time that people like Perrund and Oelph do not have the information to conceptualize.

This fundamental absence of perspective also robs us readers of full closure. We do get to cackle a bit for figuring out the Culture setup, if that's what we want, but the disappearance of the only two people who knew better and the cultural limits of those who are left drop on our lap a series of uncomfortable questions as to the morality of what we have witnessed. We probably won't cry for the demise of such characters as Nolieti and Walen, but Unoure was innocent of his master's murder, Ormin was one of the few nobles who seemed kind, and the King himself ended up at death's door so that Vosill and Oelph could be called to his bedside (340), so there is collateral damage. Also, once we know that SC has been moving quietly but decisively behind the curtains it becomes hard to decide who and what it actually touched or didn't—was Quience's all-female offspring a happy accident or an instance of genetic manipulation? Was SC somehow helping to facilitate UrLeyn's downfall, maybe through comprehensively training and equipping the Barons in Landescion? Was Vosill the only Culture personnel on-planet? Was DeWar really an exile?

And most worryingly from the perspective of deciding what it means to do the right thing, did SC have anything to do with the rocks that fell from the sky? The world is better off without the old empire, as Oelph himself tells us (338), but the meteorite shower killed millions, and many more died in the aftermath as internecine wars consumed whole populations. As the only power that could have interfered with the orbits of celestial bodies, would SC have gone this far to save a planet's dominant species from itself? Ultimately, this and all the other questions are unanswerable, and we have no choice but to wonder without purchase on the truth of things.[21] We can say that the meteor shower was *probably* a natural occurrence—SC wouldn't go to such lengths as planning the death of millions—but even in that case, why didn't it stop the meteors? Surely a well-placed GCU or an ROU could have done the job without undue strain. We could then say that the culture hadn't discovered the planet at that time, and maybe we'd be right, but the point here is that, unlike the questions they should answer, all those possible conclusions are extra-textual. Oelph and Perrund are unavoidably silent on the matter, while the woman from Drezen and the man from the Half-Hidden Kingdoms are nowhere around anymore. "Don't you hate it when the Gods come out to play?" Ulver Seich had asked at one point in *Excession*; but at least she'd had the ability to know there *are* gods, and that they look like giant starships. She'd even known what a starship is, what it moves through, and how deep the sky reaches, things that nobody in Tassasen, Haspidus, or anywhere else on the nameless, half-forgotten planet even understands how to ask about.

7

THE ENCROACHMENT OF REALITY
Look to Windward

At the beginning of her 2005 essay on *Excession*, Farah Mendlesohn comments on the rise of space opera from SF's "most juvenile, immature canvas" to "the cutting edge of the genre" (556). Mendlesohn here channels a comment from a 2003 article by John Clute in which he argued that the advocacy for a specific future typical of classic science fiction was now gone, along with that same future—the onset of the information age had seen to that (65). If that is indeed true, Mendlesohn writes, then it makes sense that space opera, "the form that departs most enthusiastically from that rationalized future" (556), should have established for itself a position of preeminence starting at the end of the 1980s and continuing into the beginning of the 21st century. The SF of that decade had been characterized by a good deal of pessimism and ennui, one of the results of Cyberpunk's position as the dominant voice within the genre, and space opera contributed to remedying them precisely by virtue of its perceived lightness:

> Cyberpunk was in many ways a betrayal of science fiction: it was pessimistic (postnuclear novels assumed human resilience), it accepted the inevitable victory of the corporatist agenda for the world even when railing against it, and it turned away from the outward-bound project that was SF and into the mind.... Space opera had never pretended to be plausible ... but it celebrated the human, and its very lack of concern for a realizable future offered a counterbalance to the all too predictable vision of global decay [556].

Since the end of the 1980s, and more precisely since the publication of *Consider Phlebas* itself, space opera has been smuggling large amounts of serious discourse under the guise of a romp through space, as harmless as it is implausible. In the case of writers like Banks and those who influenced him (M. John Harrison and Brian Aldiss in particular), this serious discourse is also concealed—and at the same time foregrounded—through the use of sophisticated language, intricate plots, and complex thematic layers. The emphasis is on space opera as a work of art, an aesthetic construct to be enjoyed precisely because it's implausible, baroque, and surreal. Sure it's nuts, but look at the *colors*, man.

Via the pyrotechnics, the infernally complicated gyrations of the plot, and the estranged voices of characters assembled out of a mélange of dream-visions, modern space opera tells us things that are arguably more important for our life today than the things classic SF told us were for our life back then. But what happens when, through a chance superimposition of publishing schedules and world events, the carnevalesque, indirect path by which we connect space opera to the world becomes one of those superhighways Hugo Gernsback kept dreaming about and William Gibson reviled, devil-straight and cruel-edged all the way to the heart of something so awful it gave wide-eyed birth to a whole millennium? "On the day that everything changed," wrote Gerald Jonas, the *New York Times*' long-standing SF critic, "I was reading the advance galleys of a novel by Iain M. Banks called *Look to Windward*" (2001, n.p.). *Look to Windward*, the new novel in the Culture series, had originally seen print in Great Britain in the summer of 2000, but the American edition did not come out until the next year, together with the British paperback. Jonas' review was published on October 7, 2001.

The novel's title warns of the haunting that awaits us. The words that comprise it come from the same section of Eliot's *The Waste Land* as those that made up *Consider Phlebas*: "Gentile or Jew/O you who turn the wheel and look to windward/Consider Phlebas, who was once handsome and tall as you" (16). The injunction, which Eliot utters to "[caution] those who look to windward in order to protect their charges from danger to remember those who have fallen" (Strahan 2000, 29), represents as programmatic a description of the novel's thematic concerns as *Consider Phlebas* had been thirteen years before, and the territory is the same: war, first in the shape of the Idiran War and secondly in the shape of a recent civil war for whose onset the Culture is largely responsible. It's an aftermath reality that *Look to Windward* occupies, and everyone in it is a survivor, a haunted veteran for whom life in a world at peace seems like something too good to deserve and too strange to process. The novel's dedication—"For the Gulf War veterans"—helps signpost the road we know we must travel to get home at the end of the story.

The Culture has intervened once again, but this time its carefully gauged triangulations have failed. The result has been a civil war among the Chelgrians, a mammalian predator-evolved species that, for the past three thousand years, has been espousing a draconian caste system. In the interest of

7. The Encroachment of Reality

unraveling the iniquities of this social arrangement, the Culture bribed and dealt its way into the Chelgrian electoral process so as to put in power the most egalitarian of candidates, who turned against his own people as soon as he was elected. He wanted payback for himself and for those on the losing side of the caste system, and the civil war that ensued was horrifying (158-159). At its end, which the Culture managed to negotiate between the loyalists and the rebels, the Chelgrians received an immediate apology from their neighbors, together with a complete coming-clean protocol—the Culture has acknowledged and detailed every one of its actions, unequivocally pointing its collective finger at itself, and is asking for forgiveness even as its GSVs and ROUs remain within operationally meaningful distance of Chel, the Chelgrians' home planet. There is a fair chance hostilities might start again (69–70, 132–135).

While most Chelgrians are angry at the Culture's meddling and, with a degree of accuracy, blame it for the Caste War, one among them has a different perspective. In fact, he is no longer among his own people: a few years before the start of the war, he exiled himself on a Culture Orbital called Masaq', and the discovery of the Culture's involvement in the civil war has changed his feelings not one iota. His name is Mahrai Ziller, and he is a composer, famous for his work both on Chel and on Masaq'. In his view, the Culture was nothing more than a catalyst for a conflict that was always going to explode sooner or later; if it hadn't been them, it would have been someone or something else (115). "The background to the war," he tells Kabe Ischloear, the Homomdan Ambassador to Masaq', "is three thousand years of ruthless oppression, cultural imperialism, economic exploitation, systematic torture, sexual tyranny, and the cult of greed ingrained almost to the point of genetic inheritability" (66). His feelings on the matter and his contempt for his people have kept Ziller steadfast in his determination never to go back to Chel, no matter how many requests the Chelgrian government makes to have him back.

And now it's about to make another, in the form of an envoy to Masaq'. Major Tibilo Quilan, a former member of the loyalist forces, has been tasked with going to Masaq' to try yet again to convince Ziller that his people need him, and while SC, in the person of a rather officious drone named E. H. Tersono, is trying to make sure its illustrious refugee and Quilan behave nicely to each other, there are voices on Masaq' that try to make Ziller see the plight of his people under an at least slightly more objective light:

> Symbols are important, symbols do work. And when the symbol is a person then the symbol becomes [...] dirigible. A symbolic person can to some extent steer their own course, determine not just their own fate but that of their society. At any rate, [the Chelgrian envoy] will argue that your society, your whole civilisation, needs to make peace with its most famous dissident so that it can make peace with itself, and so rebuild [65].

The speaker is Kabe, the Homomdan ambassador. The Homomda, a civilization that's been on the galactic scene for even longer than the Culture, have been at peace with it for eight hundred years now, since the end of the Idiran War,[1] but that hadn't always been the case. Originally, the Homomda had been the Idirans' sponsors and patron civilization when their charges had made their entrance onto the galactic scene,[2] and they had supported the Idirans in the war in a limited fashion—not because the Homomda were particularly sympathetic to the Idirans' brand of religion-inspired sense of manifest destiny, but because the Culture had been, at the time hostilities started, on the verge of becoming too powerful, of bulking too large against the backdrop of galactic life. The Homomda had gone to war on the Idiran side to corral the Culture, not destroy it, and after a while, once their losses of materiel had become too high in the wake of the Culture's enormous military growth, they had left the conflict and made peace with their erstwhile enemies (*Consider Phlebas*, 459–461).[3]

And it's because of the Idiran War that Kabe is on Masaq' as a representative of the Homomdan people. He is there to witness the commemoration of one of the last and worst encounters in the entire war—the Twin Novae battle, during which the stars Portisia and Junce "had been induced to explode.... Worlds had died, entire biospheres had been snuffed out and billions of sentient creatures had suffered—albeit briefly—and perished in these twin catastrophes." And the Culture could have stopped it; it could have prevented the gigadeathcrimes. The Idirans, whose weapons had destroyed the stars, had been trying to sue for peace for a while by then, but the Culture's insistence on unconditional surrender had hardened their resolve. The battle took place, trillions died, and a weight of guilt settled onto the Culture's collective conscience (29–30).

One Culture citizen in particular feels this weight: the Mind that runs Masaq'. During the Idiran war, it had been one of a couple of twin Minds, each running a similarly titled GSV: the *Lasting Damage I* and the *Lasting Damage II*.[4] One of the two died during the Twin Novae battle, and the other, which was close enough to it to be in Mind-to-Mind contact throughout the whole experience, felt everything—every microsecond of its sibling's death, every agonized moment of doomed struggle to retain its grip on life, and every quantum of memory and identity burning away into the void.[5] Masaq's Mind remembers everything, and not just its twin's death; it also remembers the three thousand, four hundred and ninety-two flesh sentients it killed when the destruction of three orbitals that were on the verge of falling to the Idirans became necessary. Several million other people left the Orbitals, but those relatively few souls[6] that hadn't had the choice or the desire to leave died, and the *Lasting Damage*'s Mind killed them when it destroyed the Orbitals (311–317). "I recorded every one of those deaths," the avatar of Masaq's Mind tells Ziller:

7. The Encroachment of Reality

"I didn't want them to be faceless, I didn't want to be able to forget."

"That was ghoulish, wasn't it?"

"Call it what you want. It was something I felt I had to do. War can alter your perceptions, change your sense of values. I didn't want to feel that what I was doing was anything other than momentous and horrific; even, in some first principles sense, barbaric" [313–314].

Minds don't receive the admittedly mixed blessing of meat memory, which fades and distorts with time. Their recall is instant and permanent, their thought processes everlasting, the cogency and texture of their memories detailed beyond the comprehension of flesh sentients. "I am a Culture Mind," the avatar says. "We are close to Gods, and on the far side. We are quicker; we live faster and more completely than you do, with so many more senses, such a greater store of memories and at such fine level of detail. We die more slowly, and we die more completely, too" (316). Ultimately, it is this quality of instant, utterly comprehensive recall that makes Masaq's Mind the most haunted character in the novel, and it is this haunting that has prompted it to organize the commemoration of the Twin Novae battle at this specific time: after eight hundred years of crawling along the skein of space-time, the light from Junce and Portisia's explosions has reached the Orbital. The nova flare of the first star opens the novel in an almost religious hush. Once the explosions settles, drowning out the light of others stars with its bluish radiance, the Mind's avatar announces a period of mourning that will end when the light form the second explosion reaches Masaq', a few days from the first (26–30); a symphony will greet its arrival, and Mahrai Ziller has been hard at work finishing it. "Tonight you dance by the light of ancient mistakes!" he'd said in an interview on the morning of the first nova's blossoming (29).

Thus, the Culture faces two sets of mistakes in *Look to Windward*, and two kinds of haunting: the one from the past, the reminder of which has been traveling patiently for centuries, and the one in the present, whose living reminders have either been there all along (Ziller) or traveling fast across hyperspace on their way to the Orbital (Quilan). However, while the memory of the Idiran War and of the Twin Novae battle is an occasion for reflection and mourning, and a chance to salute the few veterans of it still hanging around after nearly a millennium, there are forces abroad that are scheming to turn the aftermath of the Chelgrian debacle into something deadlier by far. Tibilo Quilan is not on Masaq' to persuade Ziller to come back to Chel—that's just the cover story. He is on Masaq' to destroy a sizeable portion of the Orbital with a device located inside his head, killing, along with himself, about ten percent of Masaq's population—five billion people (319).

Uniquely among the more advanced species inhabiting the galaxy, the Chelgrians are in constant contact with the sections of their society that, for reasons that have remained unclear to those left behind, have Sublimed ahead of the main body of their civilization (162–167). Those Sublimed call themselves the Chelgrian-Puen, and they have informed their flesh-and-blood counterparts that the five billion who died during the Caste War won't be allowed into heaven[7] because, since they died in a war, "the old rules apply ... they must be avenged" on a one-to-one basis: a soul for a soul (224–227). Therefore, a few high-ranking Chelgrians, led by the Estodien Visquile ("Estodien" is a Chelgrian term for priest), have concocted a conspiracy to murder the corresponding number of Culture people plus their famous dissident, Mahrai Ziller. Masaq' Orbital is the target, and Major Quilan, accompanied by Admiral-General Sholan Hadesh Huyler, whose resurrected consciousness now resides in a storage unit inside Quilan's head (36–43),[8] is going to be the agent of retribution. Quilan himself does not particularly hate the Culture for its involvement in the Caste War; the reason why he's the right candidate for this terrorist attack is that he doesn't want to go on living—either in this universe or in the Sublime—since permanently losing his wife Worosei in the conflict.[9] He wants to join her in oblivion (257–258).

Appropriately for a novel haunted by the aftermath of war, all the main characters in *Look to Windward* share the same sense of overwhelming loss, of memories brighter, more beautiful, and more terrible than anything in front of them in the present (see Strahan 2000, 29). Quilan exists within a death-in-life punctuated by recollections of the time spent with Worosei (43, 136, 213, 255–256, 328, 347–349), while Masaq's Mind conducts an existence similarly marked by the memory of its twin's death, as well as those it had to cause when it destroyed the three Orbitals—it had no choice but those people wouldn't leave, so it did its duty (with their blessing) and kept the scars. Ziller, for all his devil-may-care attitude toward his people, has lost his home forever, and in this sense it matters little that the exile is self-imposed. Loss is loss, especially because in Ziller's case it came after he'd suffered two assassination attempts for his anti-caste views; he'd emerged from the first unscathed, but the second had put him in a hospital for months (116). After that, Ziller publicly renounced Chelgrian citizenship, condemned his own society for the iniquities it insists on perpetrating, returned all the honors his music had garnered him over the years, and left for the Culture, declaring he'd never return (117). He is as much a casualty of war as everyone else, with the traumatic set of memories to prove it. Kabe, for his part, is on Masaq' to represent the whole Homomdan people in the commemoration of the Twin Novae battle, and he therefore carries their burden of collective guilt with him. This burden is supplemented by personal heartache: one of the reasons why he accepted his ambassadorial post on Masaq' was to get away from someone he loved deeply, but who could not or would not reciprocate. He now hopes that time spent far away from his people, in a place devoid of anyone else who remotely looks Homomdan, will lessen the force of the haunting (142–143).

7. The Encroachment of Reality

Moreover, Masaq' is an odd place for those who'd like to come to terms with death and loss. Built ten light-minutes away from Lacelere, a star with a potential instability resulting in a one-in-many-millions chance of a supernova event, the Orbital has gradually become a destination favored by those few in the Culture who enjoy potentially deadly pastimes such as wing-flying, rafting lava streams, and free-climbing; while the average back-up rate is, as a result, understandably higher than on other Culture habitats, a group of people who call themselves Disposables choose to face terminal danger without backing themselves up first; should they die, they'd be gone forever, and in fact this is what happens to one of them, a thirty-one-standard-year-old woman who gets crushed to death while glacier-caving (51–57, 103–114). Other forms of devolutionary behavior involve not the risk of life and limb, but a temporary return to primitive customs such as, for example, the use of money or the exchange of favors, which Masaq's Mind finds in equal measure fascinating and funny:

> Well, for tickets to Ziller's concert, they practically are [reinventing money]. People who can't stand other people are inviting them to dinner, booking deep-space cruises together—good grief—even agreeing to go camping with them.... People have traded sexual favors, they've agreed to pregnancies, they've altered their appearance to accommodate a partner's desire, they've begun to change gender to please lovers; all just to get tickets.... How wonderfully, bizarrely, romantically barbaric of them! [352].

In short, many Culture citizens on Masaq' repeatedly choose to endure pain, misery, and coercion; a very few even court death. To some of those who truly and without a say on the matter have experienced suffering and loss, this behavior is either incomprehensible or understandable only in terms of a form of madness. This is certainly the view of the three Chelgrians on the Orbital, but while Quilan and Huyler communicate those opinions in the silence of the Major's mind and otherwise keep their counsel, Ziller is more than happy to provide feedback: he believes that there's a perverse streak in the mentality of those Culture citizens who, after their society managed to finally eliminate all deprivations, illnesses, and violent accidents, turn right around and purposefully manufacture them again (114). To Ziller, sizeable amounts of people in the Culture are suffering from a terminal case of boredom that pushes them to waste their time (and occasionally throw their life away) just to be able to say that they have lived. It falls to another alien—Kabe—to counterpoint the Chelgrian's harsh views:

> They feel they have gained something from having pitted themselves against forces much greater than themselves.... These people control their terrors. They can choose to sample them, repeat them or avoid them. That is not the same as living beneath the volcano when you've just invented the wheel, or wondering

whether your levee will break and drown your entire village. Again, this applies to all societies which have matured beyond the age of barbarism [112–114].

"At last, the Culture can be known in close detail, through the eyes of experienced, incisive foreign travellers," Nick Gevers writes in his SF Site review of *Look to Windward* (2000, n.p.). This is another way of saying that the self-correcting machinery of the critical utopia is once again in motion, and that it's arguably never been as necessary as it is now that the Culture has been shown making a mistake—however well-intentioned—that cost five billion lives. The criticism begins within the Culture itself, which makes no secret of the secrets it had previously kept and comes completely clean before the Chelgrians and their inevitable moral judgment—which matters to the Culture. And because he is officially on Masaq' for a task intimately connected to the Caste War, it's Quilan who becomes the interlocutor of choice for the Culture's apologetic contrition, at the same time as he and Huyler represent, in their different responses to it, a sampling of the spectrum of Chelgrian feeling on the matter. Quilan listens and responds kindly to every proffered apology (154), all the while examining the honesty of his replies and finding it frustratingly difficult to pinpoint. On the other hand Huyler, invisible and unheard inside his carrier's skull, screams abuse at everybody with a relish that would be funny if we didn't know the actual reason for his presence on Masaq'.

The feelings of the rest of the Chelgrian conspirators are unproblematic in their homogeneous hostility, whereas Kabe's—the ambassador is probably the most experienced among Gevers' "incisive travelers"—are, like Quilan's, in a constant state of flux. On the one hand, the Homomdan defends his hosts against Ziller's contempt, but on the other he often finds himself at once puzzled and amused by fads and mores that his own people have long outgrown—like the penchant for life-threatening pastimes:

> They lived or died by whim! A few of their more famous people announced they would live once and die forever, and billions did likewise; then a new trend would start amongst opinion-formers for people to back-up and ... people would start doing that sort of thing by the billion, too, just because it had become fashionable. Was that the sort of behavior one ought to expect from a mature society? Mortality as a life-style choice? [12].

Kabe knows that his fellow Homomdans would decry the choice as childishness and madness, but as we have seen, he himself doesn't necessarily feel that way, and there's more than a hint that this empathy toward the Culture is one of the reasons he ended up on Masaq' to begin with (13). Kabe is, in other words, not just a function of the Culture's self-correcting critical utopian processes, but also a critical utopian commentator on his own society and in his own right. The sense *Look to Windward* conveys that the Homomdan civ-

7. The Encroachment of Reality 163

ilization, if explored in detail, would likely prove to be a utopia provides the Culture with something like a shadow twin, which is entirely in keeping with the rest of the hauntings in the story. If the Culture has the Homomda as a nebulous mirror image[10] and Kabe has an unrequited love interest he's waking away from,[11] Quilan has Worosei and Masaq's Mind has its long-dead twin; Ziller has the whole of Chelgrian culture, and the whole of Chelgrian culture has itself—that is, the socially suppressed doppelganger that rose to devour its kin. The Caste War created the haunting, and the haunting facilitated the inception of the revenge plot against the Culture on the part of the Chelgrians' other undead and unquiet twin, the Chelgrian-Puen. The twin, the doppelganger, the shadow, the revenant, and the made thing that looks just like us: they "digest the siblings who live in the light" (Clute 2011, 4). They return, just like the twin stars Portisia and Junce, to remind the veterans and the survivors and those who were born long after that the arrow of time can double back on itself and regurgitate the undead past onto the present, because the siblings who live in the light now live in the light of a star's death, which they had a part in causing.

But there are those who would create a new haunting, because to commit an act of mass murder is to generate the premises necessary for it, and the Culture won't abide them. Halfway through the novel (187–191), a creature forms on the ground on Chel out of "EDust (Everything Dust)" (397), taking on the appearance of a Chelgrian female. Preliminary calibrations complete, it/she begins the hunt for the Chelgrians who hatched the terrorist plot. The Culture knows.

Elsewhere, on Masaq', the avatar of the Orbital's Mind tells Ziller about a long-ago attempt to smuggle a bomb onboard a GCU; the attempt failed because "a standard Mind scan looks at something from hyperspace, from the fourth dimension. An impenetrable sphere looks like a circle. Locked rooms are fully accessible" (240–241). The Culture knows.

The Culture has known, in fact, since before Quilan's arrival (381). Contact has been busy, as has Special Circumstances: Hadesh Huyler has been an SC operative all along. His job was to stop the attempt if Quilan had decided to make it, not go through with it if he had demurred, and Huyler pretended to go along with the whole scheme in the hope that the conspirators would betray their identity and location. Removed by Masaq's Mind from his resting place inside Quilan's head and then transmitted to a waiting GSV, the Chelgrian Admiral's personality construct was, at the end of everything, reincorporated into a new body. He now resides mostly on Masaq', he still works for SC, and he has become friends with both Kabe and Ziller; the latter is even considering an informal visit to Chel in the near future (402–403).

As for Quilan, he eventually gets his wish. Masaq's Mind plucks him from the amphitheater where, under the light of both novae now, Mahrai

Ziller is performing his symphony, which he has entitled *Expiring Light*. Quilan has already had severe qualms about going through with the destruction of the hub, even to the point of attempting to warn Kabe and Tersono (375),[12] but all that becomes moot when, after a moment of dizziness, he finds himself alone with the avatar inside a VR recreation of Masaq's hub. The Mind is ready to die, the avatar tells Quilan. The haunting won't go away, and the memories have become something more than just that:

> I am tired, Quilan. I have waited for these memories to lose their force over the years and decades and centuries, but they have not. There are places to go, but either I would not be me when I went there, or I would remain myself and so still have my memories. By waiting for them to drop away all this time I have grown into them, and they into me. We have become each other [383–384].

And so the avatar, whose memories have now become it, as they had really always been, takes Quilan's hands, and the Chelgrian takes its. "Will you be my twin in this?" it asks him, and he replies: "If you will be my mate." After that, it's only an instant before their dance to expiring light begins and ends in an explosion that annihilates them both. The Orbital and its fifty billion people, given over to a series of AI cores capable of running things perfectly efficiently until a new hub Mind is found for it, suffer no damage at all (384).

The same cannot be said for those responsible for hatching the terrorist plot, however. The Culture EDust assassin finds and murders them all in spectacularly brutal fashion—an example to everyone else who might be considering doing something similar—before vanishing into the sky in the same manner it had arrived (395–399). As for the five billion Chelgrian dead, the blood of others won't grease their passage into heaven, although the Culture will try to broker a deal with the Chelgrian-Puen. "It's tricky territory for us, the Sublimed," the Mind tells Quilan, "but we have contacts" (383). However, the relatively happy ending, if such a term can even apply, is tainted by a possibility almost too awful to contemplate: the Chelgrians had outside help in bringing their plot so close to fulfillment, and it's remotely possible that those allies "are, or represent, some rogue group of Culture Minds." Those Minds, if they do exist, may have done what they did "Because we might be growing too soft. Because of [our] complacency, [our] decadence. Because some of our minds might just think that we need a bit of timely blood and fire to remind us the universe is a perfectly uncaring place and that we have no more right to enjoy our agreeable ascendancy than any other empire long fallen and forgotten" (382–383). Nothing matters, and everything does; that is the reality of life in a "perfectly uncaring place," and Masaq's mind is suggesting that, in the eight hundred years since triumphing over the Idirans, the Culture may have started believing in a sort of karmic underpinning to the fabric of creation. Within such a belief system, Contact and SC's good works in favor of the less fortunate should entitle them and their parent civilization to some kind of preferential treatment on the part of the universe, and that would be manifestly wrong-headed. The avatar's whiff of a suggestion that these supposed conspirators may consider the Culture to be on the same moral plane as an empire, as the last sentence in the quote implies, further unsettles our sense that things will now be all right after all. Masaq' is still there, and so are the Chelgrians and the Culture, but the five billion Chelgrians killed in the civil war the Culture helped trigger are still dead, and there is no magic wand to wave here. The light of ancient mistakes now shines on a new one.

"When I discovered that [*Look to Windward*] concerns a terrorist plot to murder billions of people," Gerald Jonas wrote in his *New York Times* review,

> I wanted to put the book down. I am glad I didn't. What Banks has to say about idealism, fanaticism, revenge, blame and forgiveness made as much sense to me as the news and analysis that blared nonstop from my television set ... as in all good fiction, what's important in Banks's work is the subtext, which I take to be the idea that freedom is both necessary and dangerous, and that only by imagining the unimaginable, both in ourselves and others, can we hope to remain free [2001, n.p.].

Hence Masaq's Mind's suggestion that a cadre of renegade Culture minds might have been behind the planning of the attack. The Culture is not the United States,[13] the Chelgrian conspiracy to conduct a terrorist attack against Masaq' Orbital is not Al-Qaeda, and the course of events on the Orbital clearly does not resemble that of the attacks of September 11—if only it did. But even so, the bare facts of the novel's plot are enough to go on: *Look to Windward* is the story of a commonwealth of plenty intervening disastrously in the collective processes of a far less powerful, more socially backward neighbor. As a result, this neighbor strikes back the only way it can—with a terrorist attack, which the commonwealth foils before exacting pinpoint retribution on the conspirators. In the aftermath of the attempt, the suspicion arises that some secret force within the commonwealth might have schemed to allow it to succeed.

Texts are things of the world. They draw story from it, and give it back to the people living in it in a changed form that facilitates reflection, empathy, and perspective. Iain Banks had not intended to write *Look to Windward* as prophecy; he'd meant it as a reflection on the hauntings of the recent past. But in the course of events here on Earth, the novel also ended up prefiguring the rough shape of the present and of the immediate future, both sources of terrible hauntings of their own, and for us on this side of things, for those still shadowed by the revenants unleashed on that awful day, *Look to Windward* does feel, to an extent, prophetic.[14] It even foreshadows the paranoias of the aftermath, many of which hold that 9/11 was an inside job or a punishment for the hubris of the industrialized West, and their patent absurdity is not the point. The point is that they are in us whether we want them or not because, deep inside, we know that the terrors they whisper hatched inside events that predated their birth. Just like the Culture has its critical utopian processes, we have our own (which we would have to describe as critical-dystopian; more's the pity), and we have been wondering for a long time about the wisdom of our international policies. Wondering about them didn't stop us, though, and *Look to Windward*, which does indeed look to windward to what was then the West's latest military adventure abroad, also turns to look forward to where the wind is going. The landscape that opens up before our eyes, here on the farthest side from the eleventh of September, 2001, is a territory rich in hauntings. The first Gulf War, to whose veterans Banks dedicated *Look to Windward*, has now become the secret twin of the second, and the towers were twins as well. One collapsed before the other, and the light of their death still reaches us via the footage collected on that day of horror. It's still as difficult to turn the eyes away from the images as it is to believe they actually happened.[15]

There's still one more veteran to salute before we go. One of the subplots in *Look to Windward* does not at first blush seem designed to perform the same job as all the others: Uagen Zlepe is a Culture scholar, and he's been away from the Culture for thirteen years now; his psychological makeup is not very different from that of other critical utopian exiles or discontents, except that the reason why he isn't planning on coming back is scholarly: he's too caught up in his studies (87–101). He lives in the airsphere Oskendari, and his field involves one of Oskendari's most fascinating sentient species—the dirigible behemothaurs, titanic living balloons that swim in the airsphere's oxygen/nitrogen medium like fish in water. Each behemothaur is to its species—and to the ecosphere within which it lives—what a GSV is to the Culture: a giant, sentient carrier of people and machinery of all sorts, except that dirigible behemothaurs don't use technology. They give birth to organisms that perform the tasks that technological artifacts perform in a society like the Culture. Behemothaurs live for millions of years, and their thought processes match the pace of their biological ones—the behemothaur that is playing host to Uagen and a number of sentients from other species is called Yoleus, and for three years now it has been following another of its kind according to the species' customary courtship rituals:

> By dirigible behemothaur standards a three-year courtship indicated little more than an infatuation, arguably no more than a passing fancy, but Yoleus seemed committed to the pursuit and it was this attraction that had brought them so low in the Oskendari airsphere over the last fifty standard days; usually such megafauna preferred to stay higher up where the air was thinner [88].

7. The Encroachment of Reality

During one of his study tours of the Yoleus (dirigible behemothaurs always use the article before their name), Uagen notices a gigantic shape far below, where the atmosphere is even thicker and less welcoming. Upon closer scrutiny, the shape reveals itself as another behemothaur, wounded and dying, and inside the behemothaur, disguised as one of the creatures born of it, is a Special Circumstances agent who, before dying as well, tells Uagen about the terrorist plot against Masaq'. Estodien Visquile and the rest of the conspirators have been using the behemothaur as a secret base, and ravaged it in order to cover their tracks (171–185). Spurred by the urgency of the intelligence he now possesses, Uagen races back to the Culture to warn it of what's coming, unaware that the Culture already knows. Also unaware that the Culture knows is one of the Chelgrian conspirators who is waiting for Uagen in the ship he chartered to take him back to his people; the Chelgrian male murders Uagen, chucking his body out of an airlock in the aftermath.

When he wakes up again, Uagen is back inside the Yoleus; the behemothaur has evolved, and it now looks different, but it is still recognizably his strange home away from home. One of the Yoleus' interpreters, a creature Uagen knows from before, tells him that his body was retrieved from the vacuum surrounding Oskendari once the airsphere returned to that volume of space after a full galactic revolution—about a hundred million years after the events in *Look to Windward*. Everyone is gone—the Culture, the Chelgrians, and the Homomda—and the only ones who remember them are creatures like the behemothaurs, who retain memories and identities for periods of time functionally indistinguishable from forever. Uagen, another casualty of war, is now the only human left in the galaxy (387–394).

The Zlepe subplot goes a long way toward helping us process the darker aspects of *Look to Windward*. Banks' descriptions of the behemothaurs and the environment within which they live are wonderful and strange but also familiar—for example, the Yoleus' pursuit of the other behemothaur, once translated into a more human-friendly timeline, comes across as positively quaint without losing any of its alienness. The airsphere's depths feel like the bottom of the deepest oceans, and the sheer variety of the fauna they contain turn it into a beautiful blue-sky analogue of the galaxy outside, itself full of lifeforms of surpassing strangeness.

At the same time, there is a good deal of readily recognizable heartbreak inside the space of Oskendari airsphere. One hundred million years on, the behemothaurs still remember what the Chelgrians did to one of their own—for that, the whole civilization is remembered as the Lesser Reviled (391)—and their grief is as long-lasting as their memories; for his part, Uagen is now a castaway, forever without a country. It is often the case that those whom war removes from their home come back to it to find that, while it changed in its own way during their absence, they themselves have changed in another direction and often beyond recognition, usually because of occurrences they cannot explain or transmit to those who haven't gone through them as well. *Look to Windward*'s most estranged plotline literalizes this internal reality by pushing it to its extreme, so that of all the entities that either took voluntary part in—or were unwillingly sucked into—the novel's events, Uagen Zlepe, inoffensive but brave scholar, awkward Culture citizen with a tendency to say "umm" a lot when he's nervous, ends up being the most irreparably wounded.

Between the publication of *Inversions* and the appearance of *Look to Windward*, a certain amount of critical scrutiny began accruing around Banks' M-novels, continuing into the early 2000s and then on to the present time. Banks had already become the subject of a good deal of attention for his no-M work, but that hadn't helped his science fiction much. In fact, as Christie March wrote in 2002, the majority of critics and reviewers had been making a sharp value-judgment distinction between the two sides of Banks' opus from the very beginning:

> While his work has become enormously popular, his position as a "serious" writer gives critics pause. "Novels lacking that crucial middle initial are regularly lauded by the literary critics, novels with it are either ignored outside the SF field or curtly reviewed with grudging sufferance," Stan Nicholls laments [2002, 81].

So, while the early-to-mid nineties had seen Iain Banks' novels receive their fair share of study from academics, very little had happened with Iain M. Banks' work.[16] The only exceptions were the M-Banks entry in the second edition of *The Encyclopedia of Science Fiction* (1993, 88) and an article by Carolyn Brown in a 1996 collection of essays. Drawing on Foucault's thoughts on the heterotopic and Delany's practice of them in his novel *Triton*, the article aims to "interrogate some of the workings of the 'Culture' novels by Iain M. Banks and the relationship between topoi and 'character'" (1996, 58).

The first critic to engage with Banks' work at the turn of the century, Christopher Palmer, wrote a piece for the March 1999 issue of *Science Fiction Studies* in which he examined Banks' work along with Dan Simmons' *Hyperion Cantos* series (1989–1997). Palmer's arguments, which do have a good degree of validity, are however vitiated by some crucially problematic assumptions. The first, which the inclusion of Simmons' work prefigures, is that the Culture is an empire. The second is that the Culture's timeline, which overlaps that of Earth from the 14th century to the 22nd, is an essentially meaningless juxtaposition:

> The events of Iain M. Banks's *Consider Phlebas* take place circa AD 1335 ... but they also take place in the far future, as far as scientific and even social develop-

ment is concerned. That is, to date them in relation to our time is pointless. There would certainly be no point in extrapolating back from our present to a vastly distant past which, as is often the case in this fiction, somehow combines hyper-modern technology with pre-modern social forms [Palmer 1999, n.p.].

Palmer here is overlooking the significance of having humanity sit out the formation of the Culture, a point that Banks himself had made in *Consider Phlebas*' appendices and that Ken MacLeod further elucidates in "Phlebas Reconsidered" (see chapter 2). The third assumption paradoxically resides in Palmer's acknowledgement of the role Banks' writing techniques and complex intertextual negotiations fulfill. While Palmer recognizes them, he misconstrues their functions within the texts:

> We have inclusiveness, which launches these novels in a procedure of critique by overload rather than by irony. We have hedonism, virtually unaccompanied by the utopian impulse, riven and twisted with sado-masochism. We have complicated relations with textuality and intertextuality.... We have decentered subjects, self-unknowing, overlapping, pastiched, or simply crowded in multitudes, but, on the other hand, a violent sense of the dark reaches of the personality. It seems plausible that this fiction is the result of the operations of a postmodern imaginary on the materials of traditional galactic-empire sf; this imaginary operates mainly by excess, overload, and exacerbation [Palmer 1999, n.p.].

We need to keep in mind at this point that Palmer is assessing the work of two writers at once, and this pairing is ill fitting. Banks and Simmons, although equally relevant practitioners of space opera (Banks knew and admired Simmons' work), don't really display quite the level of commonality in terms of style, narrative strategies, or themes Palmer suggests they do when he lumps them together,[17] and the Hegemony of Man[18] in the *Hyperion Cantos* is in no way comparable to the Culture—certainly not in the role AIs fulfill in their respective settings, for example, or in the part economics play. This awkward coupling may help explain Palmer's puzzling statements, and especially the notion of hedonism unaccompanied by utopia, which works well for the *Hyperion Cantos* but not at all for the Culture. In fact, Banks' work seems at times like an uneasy graft in this piece, more a later addition to a paper on the *Cantos* than an equal-status counterpart to Simmons' construction of a space-opera setting.

In the same year Palmer's article was published, issue 76 of *Foundation* featured four articles introducing and discussing Banks' work. Two of them, Butler's "Strange Case of Mr. Banks: Doubles and *The Wasp Factory*" and Guerrier's "Culture Theory: Iain M. Banks' 'Culture' as Utopia," have already been addressed (chapters 1 and 5, respectively). Of the other two, Tim Middleton's represents a critical overview of Banks' science fictional production thus far, while William H. Hardesty's makes an argument for *Use of Weapons* as a counter-utopian text. Middleton begins by placing both M and no-M novels within Banks' Scottish context, utilizing as evidence of the space operas' connection to the homeland their regular operating at the edge of the Culture's moral and physical space:

> This means that Banks engages with moral and social concerns which can, if the reader wishes, be related to Scottish culture and society in the late twentieth century. It might also be suggested that the stateless nation is a term that could be applied to the Culture [1999, 6].

The argument is relevant. Banks had never fully identified with the Scottish renaissance movement that *Lanark* had jump-started in the early '80s, but he was very much in favor of Scotland's independence, and his thinking on how to achieve it informed some of the parameters that gave birth to the Culture. As Middleton indicates, this passage in "A Few Notes on the Culture" is revealing of those connections:

> The Culture, in its history and its on-going form, is an expression of the idea that the nature of space itself determines the type of civilisations which will thrive there. The thought processes of a tribe, a clan, a country or a nation-state are essentially two-dimensional, and the nature of their power depends on the same flatness. Territory is all-important; resources, living-space, lines of communication; all are determined by the nature of the plane (that the plane is in fact a sphere is irrelevant here).... On a planet, enclaves can be surrounded, besieged, attacked; the superior forces of a state or corporation ... will tend to prevail. In space, a break-away movement will be far more difficult to control, especially if significant parts of it are based on ships or mobile habitats [168].

It would be a mistake to consider the Culture a science fictional Scotland in Space, and that's not Middleton's argument either. The point is that the breakaway movement indicated in "Notes" as the birth of the Culture was probably rooted in a desire on Banks' part that Scotland could do something similar. In the absence of such an event in everyday life, Banks created one in his imagination.

After the context, Middleton provides the synopses and the criticism. In chronological order, he goes from *Consider Phlebas* to *Inversions*, looking at each narrative in turn and drawing a set of conclusions from his overview of the whole. First, it seems fair to say that he regards *Use of Weapons* as the best individual work in the series, both for the inner depths into which it plunges in its exploration of Zakalwe/Elethiomel's wounded, wounding psyche and for the innovative chapter structure (8–10). While it is easy to accept Middleton's assessment of *Use of Weapons*, whether one agrees with it or not, there are aspects of his argument that are more difficult to process. First, he mistakenly includes *Against a Dark Background* into the culture series[19]; secondly, he considers Banks' literary production after the early 1990s inferior to that of the decade's early years,[20] which is in and of itself a viable argument,

7. The Encroachment of Reality 171

but then he contradictorily praises *Excession* for constituting "a triumphant return to the gloriously 'wide-screen' space opera of the earlier Culture novels *and* a novel in which character was not subservient to action and set-piece scenes" (12). Third, Middleton seems to regard Banks as something of a spent force in SF, observing that while he "wrote his most inventive and literary sf in the 1980s," in his more recent production "there seems to be a rather tired reliance upon invention which often cuts across the interests of characterization and narrative impetus" (14). The conclusion to which Middleton comes in the wake of those comments is that "although some of the 1990s sf has been successful it seems to me that there is little reason to dissent from the summation offered by John Clute in his entry on Banks for the *Encyclopedia of Science Fiction*, namely that for 'many readers and critics, IB/IMB was the major new UK sf writer of the 1980s'" (14). But Clute had written that assessment in the 1993 edition of the *Encyclopedia*, at a time when Banks was still a relatively new writer in SF, and it stretches the boundaries of the plausible to conclude that his words were already meant to indicate Banks' obsolescence. Considering that Middleton was writing from the vantage point of 1999, using such a quote to reach such a conclusion—especially with works like *A Song of Stone*, *Excession*, and *Inversions* already on the shelf—feels unwarranted.

Hardesty's article on *Use of Weapons* as an anti-utopia is more problematic. Hardesty begins by describing the Culture as "an odd utopia—not a dream or plan of a future its readers might work toward, but instead a fairy tale of a society which is (in John Clute's words) 'genuinely post-scarcity'" (39). Never mind that Banks' intellectual preparation and creative practice, as well as his readers' acceptance of the conceptual basis for the Culture as an actually feasible model of utopia, belie Hardesty's fairy-tale assessment; and never mind that Guerrier's article in the same issue of *Foundation* lays down the premises for the Culture as a critical utopia. Hardesty is also, like Middleton, using Clute's words in the *Encyclopedia* out of context. If we take the trouble to actually read the entry for Banks, we'll discover that Clute regards the post-scarcity aspect in the same light Banks did—that is to say, as a fundamental step toward the formation of a meaningful argument for a functionally utopian state (88). Misquoting him hardly looks like providing conclusive evidence. But Hardesty isn't done:

> Banks's stories of the Culture ... constitute portions of a master narrative of benevolent colonialism, showing the salutary effects of empire on both the rulers and, in theory at least, the ruled. At this level, they are the heirs of a tradition of Henty and other writers of adventure fiction glorifying the heyday of the British Empire [40].

As evidence to support his contention, Hardesty cites Colin Greenland's already examined review of *Use of Weapons* in issue 50 of *Foundation*, which puts both articles in the group of essays that have misconstrued the function of the Culture stories. Hardesty sees as counterpoint to the 'master narrative' of benevolent empire "a counter-narrative that interrogates, problematises, and criticises the myths of good will and good deeds that the master narrative promotes" (40). The text that, in Hardesty's view, is most representative of such a dialogue of narrative and counter-narrative is *Use of Weapons*, which he sees as posing a constant stream of questions concerning the dynamics of interference without ever reaching an answer to them, and the reason for this state of things is that "the Culture's benevolent hegemony is imperialistic," and all those civilizations that, like the Idirans in *Phlebas*, have encountered the Culture, "[know] peace and unimagined prosperity—but not the basic right to differ" (40–41).

This argument is as factually inaccurate as it is flawed. Reading the Culture stories in such a light, and especially the often-agonized soul-searching they perform through their characters (besides *Use of Weapons* we can recall *Inversions*, for example), requires a distortion of textual evidence that voids the argument entire. And Hardesty himself seems to have recognized that: in an article published one year later, he scales back the tone of his comments and instead focuses on Banks' utopian reconfiguration of the space-opera mold.[21] "Each [space opera] is a spirited adventure story," he writes, "but each mocks the very adventures it presents; and each contributes to an ongoing commentary on the nature of utopia ... the texts operate on two levels of naïve entertainment and informed commentary simultaneously, gaining some of their power and excitement because traditional storytelling and contemporary narrative fashions interact" (116). Together with these twin narrative levels, Hardesty points to stylistic complexity, metatextual referencing, and complex plotlines as the tools Banks uses for this purpose, and indicates that, besides functioning as a formal/rhetorical scaffold for setting up the commentary on utopia, they also enable the texts to organize "a complicitous critique of modern culture" (119). Specifically, the Culture novels utilize the SF upgrade of Slater's Ethical Humanism from *Walking on Glass* to explore the nature of one's obligations toward their society—"If ... one can have anything one wants merely for the asking, what (if anything) does one owe in return, and to whom?" (120). Hardesty's reasoning here is fully in line with the development of Banks' thinking on the Culture from pretty early on, and it captures a number of the linguistic and stylistic features that constitute part of Banks' critical utopian process.

Between 2003 and 2009, three different Companion-to-SF books came out: *The Cambridge Companion to Science Fiction* (2003), Blackwell's *A Companion to Science Fiction* (2005; paperback 2008), and *The Routledge Companion to Science Fiction* (2009). The Culture series appears in all three, but under different guises and with different degrees of critical scrutiny. The

Blackwell book, for example, affords it a whole chapter in the form of Mendlesohn's beautiful analysis of *Excession*, but otherwise only mentions it in a one-line reference (244). The *Routledge Companion*, on the other hand, addresses Banks' work as a key participant both in the history of SF from the late 1980s to today and in the rise of the so-called New Space Opera. Paul Kincaid, who composed the entry on science fiction from 1992 onwards, establishes Banks as one of the foundational voices of what he calls the British Renaissance, which others have called the British SF Boom (177).[22] Kincaid also credits Banks with being one of the writers in the Renaissance to foreground a strong left-wing political agenda by grafting the features of his brainchild—the Culture—onto the classic space-opera scaffold, although he holds the opinion that "even at their best (*Excession* [1996], *Look to Windward* [2000]), they [the Culture novels] have been more notable for their humor and bravura invention than their politics" (179). Even if the Culture stories' explicit political dimension had been limited exclusively to *The State of the Art*, it would still have been worth discussing; since it wasn't, this feels like a missed chance.

The Culture's place within the New Space Opera (also NSO), on the other hand, is clearly delineated. Michael Levy connects the rise of NSO with the British New Wave, and especially with writers like Brian Stableford and M. John Harrison, whose *Centauri Device* "is often cited by later British writers as a particular influence." Because of the New Wave's inner-space-oriented stance, space operas continued to see largely unheralded publication throughout the 1980s

> until the appearance of a writer whom the critics genuinely could not ignore: Iain M. Banks.... As popularized by Banks, the new space opera featured high literary standards, significant political commentary, particularly from a left-wing perspective, along with a willingness to accept moral ambiguity rarely found in the work of American authors (except, perhaps, Simmons) in this subgenre [161].

Indeed, these are the commonly referred-to characteristics of the whole of NSO, with the proviso that there are certain differences in political orientation between writers on the two sides of the Atlantic that make the movement more variegated—and its collective discourse more intellectually stimulating—than an exclusively UK-centered view would suggest.[23]

Levy's acknowledgement that the new space opera began with *The Centauri Device* and received a much-needed reboot when *Consider Phlebas* saw publication[24] echoes Ken MacLeod's comments in an article he composed for *Locus* Magazine's 2003 forum on NSO. "The new space opera is 28 years old," he wrote. "It began, and almost ended, in 1975, when M. John Harrison's *The Centauri Device* (1974) took a British New Wave sensibility to the stars. For its author, it was intended to terminate space opera, not expand it" (41). But it didn't because a number of young SF writers, MacLeod and Banks foremost among them, took Harrison's deconstructionist stance as a programmatic statement pointing in the direction of space opera's rebirth, which means that theirs was probably one of the most fruitful misprisions of another writer's work in the history of SF. By the time Banks, MacLeod, Colin Greenland, and the others had realized what Harrison's original intent had been, they were already having too much fun to stop. In the event, Harrison himself joined the movement when, between 2002 and 2012, he wrote the Kefahuchi Tract trilogy—*Light* (2002), *Nova Swing* (2006), and *Empty Space* (2012).[25]

A different feeling accompanies Gary Westfahl's argument. In his article on space opera for the third companion book, the *Cambridge Companion to Science Fiction*, Westfahl utilizes the term "postmodern space opera" to describe NSO, but aside from the moniker the beast is the same, and so is Banks' place in it. Westfahl acknowledges the Culture novels as the most frequently pointed to when the topic of postmodern space opera comes up, but because of what he sees as their heightened sense of the darkness of the universe and of humanity's helplessness before the power of AIs, the conclusion he draws from their popularity and that of similar contemporary works displays a certain lack of optimism for the future of the form:

> Novels such as these, rather than culminations of space opera's glorious traditions, might be interpreted as harbingers of the sub-genre's exhaustion.... For all the creativity poured into postmodern space operas, they may resultingly exude the aura of exercises, brilliantly accomplished but lacking the fervent conviction regarding humanity's manifest destiny in the cosmos that distinguished classic space opera [207].

Given the gist of his argument, it is retrospectively easy to see why Westfahl utilized "postmodern space opera" instead of "New Space Opera," a term of whose existence he must have been fully aware. A key tendency of postmodern narratives in any genre or medium is to reveal the absence of an epistemological center and to represent traditional moral categories as figures chalked against vacuum, so Westfahl probably found it more appropriate to his viewpoint to adopt the postmodern label, however vague its definitional boundaries. On the other hand, from our position more than ten years down the line, we can say that whatever the descriptive preceding "space opera," the subgenre does not seem to be unraveling into itself. Aside from Banks' own work, which has proven capable of absorbing its deconstructionist stances into a larger process of reconfiguration, the writers of NSO have continued to push the boundaries of the form with an enthusiasm very much at variance with the idea of space opera as a literature of exhaustion. Also, Ken MacLeod, Charles Stross, M. John Harrison, Vernor Vinge, and the many other writers of NSO have, over the course of the 2000s, been joined by new talent—Elizabeth Bear, for example, or Hannu Rajaniemi, whose Jean le Flambeur series—*The Quantum Thief* (2010), *The Fractal Prince* (2012), and *The Causal Angel* (2014)—takes the hard-edged tech talk and the posthuman perspective further into a future that seems to promise a continued flourishing of the space opera template.

As far as Banks' place in utopian writing is concerned, the panorama is considerably flatter. The *Cambridge Companion to Utopian Literature* (2010) makes no mention whatsoever of the Culture series despite featuring three articles that address science fictional portrayals of utopia and dystopia. Also, none of the SF companions address Banks' work in any depth—in fact, the Blackwell and the Routledge don't address it at all, while Edward James' article on utopia and anti-utopia in the Cambridge volume limits himself to pointing out that "a few writers have written more than one text which could be considered utopian, including the Scottish writers Iain M. Banks (the Culture series) and Ken MacLeod (the Fall Revolution novels)" (226), and that in the middle of a paragraph dedicated to Kim Stanley Robinson's work. Michael Kulbicki's observation about the disparity in critical attention the two writers have received remains true.

But it's John Clute who, as we might have expected, provides the clearest assessment of Banks' impact not only on space opera, but also on SF as a whole. Clute, who has been following Banks' work since the beginning and understands it well, moves from an acknowledgement of the influence that the American brand of space opera played in shaping the kinetics and the action of the Culture stories to a focus on the crucial difference between the space operas that had come before and the Culture series—post-scarcity economics:

> The sf novels published as by Iain M. Banks ... offer a radical commentary on some of the inherent assumptions about the plot-friendly entrepreneurial freedoms enjoyed by space-opera protagonists in galaxies governed by rigid oligarchies.... It has become a cliché in the analysis of Earth-bound systems of economic activity that they are based on one party's gaining from the possession of scarce commodities, and that scarcity, when it does not occur naturally, will be enforced; Banks, and those he has inspired, make the iconoclastic suggestion that, somewhere, somewhen, energy will be sufficient to needs, and scarcity will not exist. It seems obvious that this sort of argument, which differs from current political and cultural sanctities, lies at the heart of a healthy sf [2003, 75].

Arguably, the many critical misapprehensions we have witnessed of the Culture series as a long, multiple-installment postmodern narrative of empire-in-disguise could stem from a misunderstanding of the importance of post-scarcity economics, politics, and ethics (the notion of plentiful resources impacts all three in the Culture stories). Empires are, by their very nature, power structures built upon the assumption of a world of consumables that the strongest players within a given civilizational context must hoard in order to (1) keep unruly neighbors at bay and (2) defend their grip on power from rivals inside the empire itself. Tellingly, every critic we have seen who has indicated that the culture is in fact an empire has either downplayed or ignored this fundamental underpinning of Banks' creation, usually by making it part of the fable of space opera—the childish, garish aspect of the form that one can discount as toy-shop paraphernalia in order to get to the real story underneath.

But Banks meant what he wrote. Yes, the Culture stories are to an extent deconstructionist, but once again, the deconstruction stops at the point where the Culture performs the reconstruction, and the dilemmas of intervention and interference to which the various characters in the novels have been giving voice since 1987 are not designed to turn utopia to ash, nor do they do so by mistake. The Culture remains visible and meaningful throughout the critical utopian process Banks applies to it; it's the argument itself that lends solidity to the "stateless nation" of the Culture, and the argument is made possible by the postulation of post-scarcity living conditions, without which the race to secure resources would start again and utopia truly would crumble.

To the critical voices that, beginning in the early 2000s, addressed the Culture series we should add a few that engaged it not from a literary viewpoint, but from a political-cultural stance; that is to say, some scholars approached the Culture as a viable argument for actual changes in the world we now inhabit, and presented their arguments as part of the ongoing intellectual enterprise in the fields of politics, sociology, and economics. Among these scholars' pieces, Thomas Gramstad's is perhaps the most surprising: writing in 2000 for the *Laissez Faire City Times*, Gramstad argues that the Culture "seems to embody all the essential virtues of Objectivist social theory, while at the same time suggesting how two widespread and major shortcomings of current Objectivist thought may be corrected" (n.p.). These two major shortcomings, in his view, are Ayn Rand's assumption of "a second-wave, industrial civilization" based on scarcity economics, which her followers also seem to have taken as a given, and Objectivism's lack of engagement with feminism and gender relationships as a whole. The first shortcoming, Gramstad writes, could be remedied by embracing the notion of post-scarcity economics as a concrete goal to work toward:

> We live in an age in which there is a widespread fear of the future. The idea of progress is being questioned or attacked openly by pre-modernists and post-modernists. Defending the future, crusading for Progress, ought to be a primary concern and goal for Objectivists. But in order to do so effectively, Objectivists need to cast off their conservative clinging to second-wave ideals, concerns and mental habits ... I would like to see Objectivists and Randians promote third-

wave post-industrial abundance, rather than getting stuck in second-wave, industrial procedures for dealing with scarcity [2000, n.p.].

The second shortcoming, Objectivism's antiquated and arguably morally reprehensible gender politics, depends on the advocacy on the part of many Objectivists of "unsupported and reactionary beliefs about an alleged naturalness of universal gender roles and Platonic ideals of gender identity and sexual preferences," and in this area as well, the Culture provides an important perspective:

> In "The Culture" people have been biogenetically altered and enhanced to such a degree that they can change and choose sex by will, surely the ultimate application of 'social constructionism' to sex relations. In 'The Culture,' there is no institutional prejudice on the basis of sex, gender, sexual orientation, race, class etc., and an individual expressing such prejudice would be seen as a primitive savage. I see no reason for Objectivists, Randians and libertarians (or indeed, anyone) not sharing this sentiment [Gramstad 2000, n.p.].

As odd as it seems at first blush to have someone who espouses Objectivism take as his conceptual model the society envisioned by an adamantly leftist Scottish science fiction writer, Gramstad's argument is in perfect earnest: he takes Banks' utopian project as seriously as its author did, using it to critique the flaws of Randian Objectivism from the perspective of a scholar who, while convinced that Objectivism has a lot of good things to offer, is also troubled by the amount of reactionary clinging to old, flawed notions of gender and power relations many of its followers display. There is a lot of enthusiasm in Gramstad for the Culture's socio-economic model, probably because he understood that the kind of society the Culture has formed in Banks' novels bears only the most tenuous of connections to anything we have on Earth right now, and it is therefore possible to imagine it arising from any economic theory, power structure, or commercial concern. It doesn't have to come exclusively from (in Earth terms) left-wing movements.

A year after the appearance of Gramstad's article, Chris Brown, a professor of international relations at the London School of Economics and Political Science, published a piece on the Culture in *Millennium—Journal for International Studies*. Brown examines the Culture as a socio-political entity, drawing from it a number of trends that, in his opinion, can be used to reflect on contemporary matters in the field of internal and international relations within and between countries at the industrial or post-industrial developmental stage:

> The Culture, Contact and SC cannot be read as though they are substitutes for the West, NATO and the CIA or SAS. On the other hand, Banks is a political writer who in interviews has always been keen to stress that the Culture is, in some sense, an expression of wish-fulfillment on his part ... with the work of as

politically-aware a novelist as Banks, authorial intent cannot simply be set aside, even though we might hope to discover things in his work that he did not deliberately leave there for us to find. And although the Culture is most definitely not the 'West,' it is a liberal utopia that represents to Banks the best of what, in the absence of scarcity, the West could become [2001, 630–631].

Through the prism of this interpretation of Banks' authorial intentions, Brown conducts a reading of the Culture's intervention policies designed to illustrate its roots in the western liberal tradition of political thought. For example, the Culture's sheer technological and industrial power, which enables it to run operations that cost Contact or Special Circumstances nothing in terms of loss of life (*Inversions* is emblematic here), "takes to a higher level the kind of invulnerability currently enjoyed by, say, modern air forces when engaged against outdated conventional opposition" (631). This invulnerability, however, carries with it a stigma of dishonor because the price one country, commonwealth, or group of nations should expect to pay for stooping to violence to begin with—loss of life among their own ranks—never happens or happens in such tiny numbers as to make no functional difference (and in any case, the Culture is often capable of bringing their dead or nearly dead agents back to life). However, because Banks acknowledges the existence of forms of moral equalization that do not require physical annihilation or permanent damage, the Culture's all-but-invulnerable personnel in his stories "have to live with the consequences of their mistakes, and, for that matter, their successes. They find ways of suffering when the more conventional outlets of death and mutilation are denied them" (632).[26]

The psychological safety valve of the moral agonies Contact and SC personnel go through in the Culture novels—aside from the fact that they provide the narratives' critical utopian machinery with fuel to run—resides in the ultimately secure moral backdrop against which these people can always lean: in a post-scarcity utopia controlled by benign AIs of near-godlike powers, humans no longer have to worry about ultimately doing good because the choice isn't theirs anymore—it's the Minds', and because the Minds are possessed of a clarity and pervasiveness of thought that flesh sentients cannot comprehend, let alone measure themselves against, those same flesh sentients are safe in the knowledge that their many foibles are thankfully no longer a factor in the decision-making process. In short, the kind of humans the Culture stories postulate can't be allowed anywhere near a society's levers of power if this society is to have any hope of becoming utopian; the job, Banks implicitly declared when he gave control of the Culture to the Minds, is and will always be beyond our grasp (632–633).

From a dramatic standpoint, Brown observes, the saving grace of this setup is that the Minds do get it wrong every once in a blue moon (*Look to Windward*) or occasionally fall prey to power-trips (the anti–Affront conspiracy in *Excession*). While the victims of those vagaries wouldn't exactly describe them as a saving grace, Banks' readers would: the reality that, however rarely, even Minds can make mistakes helps retain a sense of drama and tension throughout the narratives. Also, Brown concludes, this very aspect of potential murkiness in the Minds' makeup represents Banks' best chance to "take the Culture in an altogether new direction, restoring a degree of genuinely political evolution to its trajectory" (633). The example he utilizes to indicate this potential shakeup is the sickening moment at the end of *Look to Windward* when Masaq's Mind reflects on the possibility that fellow Culture Minds may have been behind the terrorist attempt because "some of our Minds might just think that we need a bit of timely blood and fire to remind us the universe is a perfectly uncaring place and that we have no more right to enjoy our agreeable ascendancy than any other *empire* [italics mine] long fallen and forgotten." From this statement, Brown moves to the conclusion that the Culture truly is, after all, an empire, which in his opinion would bring it from its a-temporal, beatific political stasis back into the flow of events. Aside from the usual consideration that describing the Culture as an empire is always a problematic choice, no matter the textual evidence adduced to justify it, there is a strong possibility here that Brown read the Mind's speculations on a possible but improbable status quo as the acknowledgement of a *fait accompli*. We will see in the next chapter if Banks' decisions concerning the future direction of the Culture stories bore out Brown's assessment.

Next on the list is David Horwich, whose 2002 article for *Strange Horizons* essentially constitutes a layman's version of Guerrier and Kulbicki's arguments for the Culture as a critical utopia: Horwich provides a basic rundown of the Culture's characteristics—the post-scarcity economics, the Minds, Contact and SC, and so on—and after that goes through the Culture stories published thus far, examining them in terms of the behavior of what he describes as "the ambiguous utopia."[27] His writing is eloquent and economical, efficiently parsed by a number of quotes extracted from all the narratives, and his analysis of the moral pitfalls and ethical dilemmas the Culture encounters in the process of Trying to Do the Right Thing is exhaustive, moving from the purely narrative level to that of the connections between story and the world whose constant reshaping it both mirrors and adumbrates. Horwich's conclusions are predictably in line with the workings of the critical utopia, if somewhat too constraining:

> The Culture is an ambiguous utopia. Although it enjoys a level of technology (in Clarke's phrase) "virtually indistinguishable from magic," a highly rational set of ethics, and an economy of abundance that saves it from becoming a dystopia ... this quasi-paradise does not have universal appeal, either inside or outside the Culture. Within the Culture, there is an undoubted need for Contact and SC....

Many other civilizations find the Culture anywhere from off-putting to repugnant, for a variety of reasons: dependence on the Minds, decadence and hedonism, smug self-satisfaction, and more. Banks seems to suggest that even almost complete control over the physical world and an advanced morality would not be enough to answer all the needs of humanity and human societies or to eliminate all forms of social and political conflict. Utopia lies always out of reach, an ideal to be striven after, but never to be achieved [2002, n.p.].

Horwich is tightening the definition here, and it's fair to say that his concept of utopia is a little too restrictive—the level of flawlessness he demands from a utopian model practically ensures that no such model will ever qualify, in which case why bother discussing the notion to begin with? We should also say however, that while his entire line of reasoning runs parallel to those of Guerrier and Kulbicki, Horwich is either not aware of the critical utopia or not interested in placing his writing within its context; his is essentially a reader's-response overview of the dramatic premises lying at the heart of the Culture stories, and that makes his paper none the worse for it.[28]

In 2004, Banks got a fanzine—*The Banksoniain*, whose first issue came out in February. Unlike *The Culture*, which preceded it by seven years and ended publication four years before its appearance, *The Banksoniain* is still running. The latest issue came out in February 2014, eight months after Banks' death, and on the opening page its editor announced that "Whilst there are news and events to report on *The Banksoniain* will continue to do so, most likely at yearly intervals unless there is a particular need. We can expect translations, adaptations, and there is the possibility of unpublished Banks works being made available, perhaps with the Iain Banks Archive now at the University of Stirling" (1). The fanzine is available for free at http://efanzines.com/Banksoniain/.

We have now come to the present time. Following Banks' passing, two books dedicated to his work have come out. The first was *The Transgressive Iain Banks*, a collection of articles edited by Martyn Colebrook and Katharine Cox that saw publication in July 2013, about a month after the event. The book, composed before the April 3 announcement of Banks' terminal illness, nevertheless managed to add an afterword by Cox that announced his passing and celebrated his life and work. The second book, Moira Martingale's *Gothic Dimensions: Iain Banks—Timelord*, constitutes an ambitious project: published in September 2013, it's the first study to encompass Banks' whole literary production. The book had originally seen the light of day in 2007 as Martingale's PhD dissertation in Gothic Studies at the University of Bristol—the original title was *Iain Banks: The Renovation of the Gothic* (*Banksoniain* 2014, 10)—and it indeed conducts a sustained reading of Banks' opus through the lens of his employment of Gothic themes and narrative techniques. While Martingale's book is not germane to the topic covered in this work, in general

7. The Encroachment of Reality 181

terms it represents an important step toward the development of a critical taxonomy for Banks' whole opus, as well as being an interesting, illuminating read.

The Transgressive Iain Banks, on the other hand, has already had a great deal of impact on this book. Of its twelve articles, seven of which are exclusively dedicated to Banks' No-M novels, several have appeared in previous chapters, from the introduction and David Pattie's "The Lessons of *Lanark*" to Martyn Colebrook's "*Lanark* and *The Bridge*" and Will Slocombe's "Games Playing Roles in Banks' Fiction." The book is very well rounded and thoroughly researched, and it constitutes an indispensable starting point for any scholar wishing to tackle Banks from now on. Even so, however, the notion of the Culture as empire manages to appear in here too. In his reading of *Consider Phlebas* and *The Player of Games*, William Stephenson equates the Culture with "the contemporary West, with its refined expertise in violence and its rapacious desire to hold onto global dominance and material prosperity … the Culture is a disturbingly complacent symbiosis of war machine and state that offers an estranged metaphor for the British and American regimes of the late twentieth and early twenty-first centuries" (166–167). Chris Brown had done the same in his essay for *Millennium*, but unlike Stephenson, he had known how far he could take the Culture-USA/UK correspondence.

It may never go away, this constant misreading of the Culture series, especially if postmodernist critics[29] insist on applying their categories to Banks' work without taking his approach to fiction writing and the history of space opera into consideration.[30] Banks loved metafictional negotiations, complex plots, and deconstructionist approaches, but he also loved story; he tied up every little subplot, told the tale of every character, and made sure to repay our good faith in him in kind. His influences were *Catch-22*, *The Tin Drum*, *The Centauri Device*, and *2001: A Space Odyssey*, sure, but they were also Alistair MacLean, Monty Python, the Marx Brothers, John Sladek, and *Star Wars*. He knew when to stop deconstructing. Much like Mel Brooks' great parodies—*Young Frankenstein* and *Blazing Saddles* foremost among them—do for their respective genres, Banks' novels subject the form of space opera to scrutiny and mockery, but without wrecking the story underneath. Once we're done taking note of the send-ups, there's still a tale to care about, characters to empathize with, and a place of origin that remains standing throughout and beyond the story told—which is why, as James Brown observes, "the Culture novels are also noted as a version of one of the most plot-heavy genres of sf: the space opera" (60). There's little doubt that scholarship on Banks will continue, so on this score as well as on many others, we'll see what the future holds.

8

THE LAST TRILOGY
Matter, Surface Detail, and *The Hydrogen Sonata*

There's something about *Look to Windward* that feels like dusk. The hundred-million-year perspective of the behemothaurs does not only tell us, heart-achingly, that the Culture won't be along forever; it also brings into relief, by virtue of its estranged historicizing, all the farewells we have had to bid throughout the tale. Banks' narrative voice carries quietude within itself, an exhausted peace with the terrors of loss and fracture that every major character has had to negotiate lest they lose the will to live, and those who haven't carried out such negotiations are gone. Ziller's symphony climaxes at the moment the second star's light flares in Masaq's sky, and then silence descends over the living, the dead, and the memory of what came before. And it almost feels like the Culture will soon be part of that expiring light.

Some fans may in fact have wondered, after turning *Look to Windward*'s last page, what the future would hold for the Culture, and they would have had some justification for such wondering. In the 1998 *SFX* interview conducted on the occasion of *Inversions*' publication, when asked what was next as far as the Culture was concerned, Banks had replied: "Oh, not very much. I think there might be one more novel and that'll be it. In theory, you could write about it forever, but you'd end up going over the same ground, I think. I don't know. You never know" (Brown 1998, 56). That one more novel was now done, and it had ended in elegy.

Indeed, throughout the eight years *Matter* (2008) took to appear, it seemed that there might not be any more Culture stories. During this time, Banks' deteriorating domestic life conspired to slow down his literary production: he wrote two non-genre novels (2002's *Dead Air* and 2007's *The*

Steep Approach to Garbadale), one non–Culture space opera (*The Algebraist*; 2004), and one non-fiction book (*Raw Spirit*; 2003); he cut up his passport and sent it to 10 Downing Street; he publicly advocated Blair's impeachment for his role in the Second Gulf War; and then he and Annie announced in 2007 that their marriage had ended. "It was quite traumatic," he told *The Independent*'s Liz Hoggard in February of that year. "For the first time I had to ask for an extension. It was like being a student again ... obviously things weren't going right in my marriage. I didn't feel I was under strain, but clearly I must have been" (n.p.).

However, by the time of his *Independent* interview, Banks was on the mend. He "casually mention[ed] a new girlfriend" to Hoggard and described her as "an elderly male novelist's wish fulfillment"; this new girlfriend, the founder of the *Dead by Dawn* film festival Adele Hartley, would remain with him for the rest of his life. Also, *The Steep Approach to Garbadale* "is being hailed as his best book in years" (Hoggard 2007, n.p.), and *Matter*'s publication in February of 2008 returned Banks to his train set, as he'd described the Culture stories in 1996 (Branscombe 1996b, 25; see also Jeffries 2007, n.p.). Things were looking up.

In his review of *Look to Windward* for *SF Site*, Nick Gevers advanced the opinion that the novel could be seen as "the third book in a trilogy on the theme of perspective":

> *Excession* (1996) is the view from above: Banks affords the reader some comprehension (insofar as that is possible) of how the Culture seems to those elevated far above it ... *Inversions* (1998) is the view from below: when two human agents of the Culture find themselves functioning incognito as counsellors to the rulers of a medieval-level planet, their struggles to apply Cultural ethics are highly revealing, even though the primitive narrators of their careers have little notion of what they truly represent. And now, in *Look To Windward*—the direct, horizontal view—Banks anatomizes the Culture from the purview of its equals [2000, n.p.].

It's unlikely that Gevers meant the Chelgrians as equals, but the Homomda and the behemothaurs certainly are. If the point holds, then we have the chance to look at the whole Culture series under a new light: a three-stage process of progressive refinement parsed by two long periods of reassessment. The first stage involves the Culture's creation and setting up, and it encompasses the period between 1974 and 1990; the books that comprise this first stage are those Banks wrote in the mid-to-late 1970s and early 1980s and then published after revising them: *Consider Phlebas*, *The Player of Games*, *The State of the Art*, and *Use of Weapons*, all of which appeared within a period of three years.[1]

After *Weapons* saw publication, Banks stopped writing Culture stories for six years, during which he composed many non-genre novels and two non-Culture space operas—plus "A Few Notes." Once he was ready to push the Culture universe beyond its long-gestated early steps, he plunged into a bout of creativity that saw the appearance of three Culture stories within four years. If we follow Gevers' reading, we can say that these three novels are part of an overarching narrative strategy aimed at describing the Culture's ethos—and the practice of this ethos—from three different power-related viewpoints: *Excession* is the glimpse from greater power, *Inversions* from lesser power, and *Look to Windward* from equal power.

Then came another hiatus, this time eight years long, during which Banks went to work on the problem he'd set for himself in that *SFX* interview—how to continue telling original Culture stories. The developments in his private life probably played a relevant role in his creative process, although it's difficult to say in what way and to what extent (aside from slowing down his writing), but in any case, the hiatus ended with another period of intense literary production: another three Culture novels—*Matter*, *Surface Detail* (2010), and *The Hydrogen Sonata* (2012)—in another four years.

Had Banks not died so early, what more would we have seen him do with his train set? In the interview he gave Kirsty Wark of the BBC a couple of weeks before dying, Banks said that he'd "try and get the plot for the next Culture novel together so that, just in case there is some sort of miracle cure or whatever, I don't get to the end here going 'Aha, beat you cancer [...] oh, God, I don't have a book today!'"[2] Would that have been the fourth and last in this iteration of Culture stories (so, 4-3-3-4), or would Banks have broken the pattern and just kept on writing them? Would this seemingly sequential progression of bouts of writing and pauses have become something to remark on when, at the ripe age of 85 in the year 2039, Banks published his new Culture novel—the third in his latest trilogy after a hiatus of, say, another six years—before returning to a holding pattern?

We'll never know for certain, and Banks himself wasn't one hundred percent clear on the matter when he commented on these long pauses. In 1994, he'd told Sally Ann Melia of *Science Fiction Chronicle* that his next SF story after that year's *Feersum Endjinn* would be a Culture novel, but he'd been uncertain as to the reasons why; "I keep telling myself this is because I miss the Culture," he'd said, "but possibly I'm kidding myself and really it's because people keep coming up at signing sessions and asking when the next Culture book is coming" (42). But two years later, when *SFX*'s Mary Branscombe interviewed him on the occasion of *Excession*'s publication, he told her: "I always enjoy writing Culture novels. I feel at home.... That's why I deliberately took two books away from the Culture [*Against a Dark Background* and *Feersum Endjinn*] to reassure myself that I wasn't so besotted with it that I couldn't write science fiction elsewhere" (1996b, 25). And when in 2012, fourteen years after musing that the Culture novel after *Inversions* might well be the last, Banks did another interview with *SFX*, he repeated that line of reasoning:

> I'd like to pretend this is all part of some grand architectural plan, but it isn't. After the first few Culture novels I just wanted to pull away a bit and write some SF that wasn't about the Culture [*The Algebraist*], mostly to prevent that one-trick-pony impression, but I kept on having more ideas about the Culture and was always going to go back to it [Wright 2012, n.p.].

It's not particularly surprising that Banks should have issued somewhat self-contradictory statements at different points in his career—such shifts were likely to be a normal part of his process—and there's no doubt that he always meant what he said when he said it (and there was that "You never know" at the end of the quote from the 1998 *SFX* interview). More importantly, he recognized the reoccurrence of those Culture-free periods as something that was in some way part of his creative process, so it's fair to say that he was probably aware of a certain rhythm to his Culture-related production, even if he may not have been purposefully thinking about it.

If the common characteristic of the first four novels was inception and early development while the common characteristic of the next three was, in Gevers' term, perspective, what's the common denominator now? What do *Matter*, *Surface Detail*, and *The Hydrogen Sonata* share?

Speaking about *Matter*, Banks said:

> I wanted to put the Culture more in context. There have always been hints that it's not the only sophisticated society in the galaxy; I've made it very clear from *Consider Phlebas* onwards there are lots of other societies out there. But with *Matter* I decided to make it much more clear about all these levels of civilisation, to demonstrate the Culture has peers. Beyond that there are also the Elders, the older civilisations—I first mentioned them in *Consider Phlebas* too so it's not like I just brought them all in.… The indications were there all along. But with *Matter* I definitely wanted to make it much more clear about where the Culture stood, that it's not omnipotent [Golder 2010, n.p.].

In fact, *Matter*'s added context was rich enough that Banks felt the need to include an appendix at the end of the book featuring a general glossary, a list of species and characters, ship names for every civilization, a roll call of Culture names, a key to time intervals, and a list of the inhabitants of the Shellworld Sursamen's sixteen levels (567–586). This list is of considerable use.

Detail and *Sonata* further expand the Culture's context, introducing more species, more civilizations, and a few quiet but important changes to Contact and SC. The overall effect of this shared enlargement consists in making this triad of books noisier, busier, perhaps less lonely, and more engaged in cultural/civilizational negotiations of all kinds (including the occasional high-energy scrap). The focus is far less on the Culture as the proactive Mary Worth of the earlier stories and much more on it as a participant in a complex web of largely peaceful relationships whose import extends across vaster volumes of space and greater numbers of sentients than before. In fact, each of the three novels presents a developing situation that, at the beginning, is neither of the Culture's making nor the Culture's problem. As Banks had pointed out in 1998, there was only so much he could have said about the Culture's good works for the less fortunate before the stories started repeating themselves, and this shift of focus introduces new dynamics into the dramatic setup of the series: the self-assessing, self-correcting processes of the critical utopia are still at work in *Matter, Surface Detail,* and *The Hydrogen Sonata,* but the work they perform is less arduous because the Culture's status as a utopia and its place in galactic affairs is a settled issue, both within and without the civilization itself. The Culture is now something of an elder statesperson within the galactic community.

We begin with *Matter*. Sursamen is a Shellworld, "an 800-million-year-old construct consisting of concentric layers, built for unknown purposes by a long-vanished race and retrofitted for habitation by successive wave of squatter species" (Letson 2008, 23). This long-vanished race, the Involucra, disappeared about a million years after building Sursamen and the other four thousand or so Shellworlds like it. Nobody knows where they went, why they built those artifacts in the first place, or why the remnants of a species called the Xinthian Tensile Aeronathaurs (similar to *Look to Windward*'s behemothaurs) have decided to make the Shellworlds their home—one Xinthian per Shellworld, and always at the artificial planet's Machine Core. Not all Shellworlds have a Xinthian, but many among the squatter inhabitants of those that do worship their Xinthian as the "WorldGod" (100). Such is the case of Sursamen's human populations, who reside on the Shellworld's eighth and ninth levels (62–71). In addition, nobody knows the reasons why another vanished species, the Iln, spent millions of years finding and destroying as many Shellworlds as possible before disappearing, with the result that, at *Matter*'s opening, little more than twelve hundred remain (63).[3]

The main body of the novel starts inside Sursamen's eighth level. Prince Ferbin, the gormless, Bertie-Woosterish heir to the throne of the Sarl, the humanoid population that lives on the eighth, witnesses the murder of his father, King Hausk, on the part of the King's trusted second in command, Mertis Tyl Loesp. The Sarl have been at war with the Deldeyn, the humanoids occupying the Shellworld's ninth level, since Elime, Hausk's eldest son and original heir, had died defending a Sarl outpost on the ninth level from a Deldeyn punitive attack (240). But Hausk, otherwise a proper mensch King with all the characteristics of the type, was wise and not particularly interested in revenge—his plan was to defeat the Deldeyn and rule over them, yes, but not as a tyrant. He had therefore taken a dim view of after-battle reprisals and post-hostilities purges, reasoning that treating the Deldeyn as an honorable foe would prevent resentment among the civilian population once the war was over. Tyl Loesp, for the moment acting as regent, is not that kind of man, though; he rules with fire and steel, and under his guidance the war turns much bloodier.

Declared dead, hunted by Tyl Loesp's assassins, and accompanied only by his pragmatically sharp-witted servant Choubris Holse, Ferbin has no other choice but to ascend all the way through Sursamen and to the surface. He seeks the help of anyone who will give it, and he trusts that at least one of the overseer civilizations presiding over the Shellworld's safety will oblige. In the specific, however, his best hopes reside with two people: Xide Hyrlis, a man working for Special Circumstances who, during his stay on Sursamen, had substantially contributed to increase the power of the Sarl through technology trading—thanks to his suggestions, the eighth is now at the early industrial stage from a musket-and-bayonet state of the art (190–195)—and Djan Seriy, his sister who, many years before, had gone away to become a Culture citizen first and an SC agent later (72, 92–93).

Djan Seriy, in the meantime, has heard of her father's death, so she decides to take a break from her work with Special Circumstances and return to Sursamen to pay her respects. She doesn't know of the exact dynamics involved in Hausk's passing, however, and believes that Ferbin is dead as well (84–88, 94–97). Through their travels across the length and breadth of *Matter*, the two siblings describe the overall trajectory of the plot, which is shaped, as John Clute observed, like a pincer (358). They won't meet until the novel is two-thirds over, but their progress encompasses the very heart of the book—which, perhaps putting it in too glib a fashion, is this: the matter of *Matter* is that matter matters, and doesn't.

This last sentence requires some explaining. Irrespective of technological/industrial advancement, social and ethical state of the art, and sheer political throw-weight, every civilization inside Sursamen is aware of the multiple layers of agency both inside and outside the Shellworld. Sursamen is under the direct supervision of two relatively low-level species, the Oct and the Aultridia. They, in turn, report directly to the Nariscene, an insectoid species a couple of rungs further up in civilizational advancement, and the Nariscene report to the Morthanveld, a High-Level Involved—i.e., the equivalent of the Culture and therefore one of the major players on the galactic scene. Originally an aquatic species, the Morthanveld are the senior civilization in overall charge of affairs on Sursamen. The Culture, for its part, has no current jurisdiction on the Shellworld, and its delicate (if generally friendly) snarl of political relations with the Morthanveld makes the notion of a fully-fledged SC agent traveling through the latter's space a sensitive matter (86–87, 89–90, 173–177, 569–571).

This pecking order, designed to make sure that everyone plays nice and nobody suddenly advances a low- or zero-level neighbor by, say, giving them hyperspace capabilities, high-performance AIs, or thermonukes, works in both directions along the civilizational ladder, so that a complex protocol of intervention/non-intervention laws applies to everything happening inside Sursamen. This protocol gets in Ferbin's way at every stage of his search for help: throughout the novel, the Oct first, the Nariscene next, and the Morthanveld last tell him that they cannot interfere directly in the affairs of other civilizations inside Sursamen—just one exception, however well-intended and morally justified, would open the door to other, substantially less healthy interventions (270–277). Frustrated at his interlocutors and apprehensive for the fate of his younger brother Oramen, whom Tyl Loesp has no intention of allowing to reach maturity and therefore the throne, Ferbin fumes as he and Holse are transferred, kindly but firmly, from one civilization to the next like the mildly warm potato they are. Belonging as he does to a society still clinging to the belief that there is a God in the world (literally, in the case of Sursamen's Xinthian), and therefore a divinely inspired ethical framework generating moral absolutes like a tree grows branches, Ferbin constantly argues the righteousness of his cause in the following terms:

> I would have thought that the brutal and disgraceful murder of an honourable man ... would seize at the heart of any creature, no matter how many layers and levels distant from such humble beings as ourselves they might be. We are all united, I would hope, in our love of justice and the desire to see evil punished and good rewarded [273].

But when Ferbin talks about justice, evil, and good, he is automatically utilizing the Sarl-specific meaning of these words, and that is the same meaning that has created the kind of top-down society where one has servants and women are second-class citizens because there is a God-given order to the world and it's not the fault of God's subjects that this is how things are. Holse, on the other hand, plays Jeeves to Ferbin's Wooster and does most of the sharp thinking and the appropriate talking, including the all-important discussion he has with his lord concerning what Ferbin sees as the self-evident duty Holse has to follow him wherever he goes. Holse rightly points out that his duty extends only so far as the geographical limits of the eighth and ninth levels, beyond which the laws of other societies apply over which the Sarl have no agency (99–100). Holse reasons this way because he has understood much more quickly than Ferbin that every place and every volume of space is a shellworld; the species inside Sursamen have received the admittedly dubious favor of being able to actually see the partitions, but that's the only difference. Outside, in the galaxy at large, the same classes of laws of intervention/non-intervention apply to everything that happens, which is why Ferbin's requests fall on sympathetic but not very proactive ears. In the grand scheme of things, he and the Sarl don't Matter much.

The Prince is particularly frustrated at the Morthanveld's inability to assist, which he once again reads as unwillingness. Throughout the long process of appeal for help, rejection of the appeal, and transfer to a higher authority that would perhaps be able to do something for him, Ferbin had kept the hope alive that the progressively greater power of his interlocutors would at some point translate into an embrace of his viewpoint as the only valid one. But then he reaches the top and finds that Director General Shoum, the highest Morthanveld authority in-system, is no more forthcoming than the Oct or the Nariscene have been, and his bitterness gets the better of him. "Justice is justice, ma'am. Foulness and treachery remain what they are," he tells the Director General before pointing out that, while effects of a commoner's death involve only those in his immediate vicinity who depend on him,[4] "When a king is murdered and the whole direction of a country's fate is diverted from its rightful course, it is another thing entirely" (274). It is Ferbin's own establishment of a pecking order that voids the very argument he is foregrounding: if a man matters more than a woman and a king matters more than a commoner, then the interests of every civilization more powerful than the Sarl—that is, every other civilization in the novel except the Deldeyn—matter more than the king and his people. Director General Shoum does try to explain this situation to the Prince, but unlike his father (116–120), Ferbin does not understand that greater power, when inscribed in the web of relationships that applies in the galactic community outside of Sursamen, often translates into the inability to act, not into a license for doing whatever one wants.

It is the meeting with Xide Hyrlis that drives home to Ferbin and Holse the crux of the problem. Hyrlis, whom they have been able to find through the only favor Director General Shoum could do them, receives the news of Hausk's death with altogether too little outrage for Ferbin's taste and quickly reveals himself as yet another party unwilling to return to the eighth with Ferbin and exact revenge. When the Prince reiterates his argument in favor of the primacy of his WorldGod-given viewpoint, this is what the other man replies:

> If we assume that ... history, with all its torturings, massacres and genocides, is true—then, if it is all somehow under he control of somebody or some thing, must not those running that simulation be monsters? ... What god would so arrange the universe to predispose its creations to experience such suffering, or be the cause of it in others? ... God or programmer, the charge would be the same: that of near-infinitely sadistic cruelty; deliberate, premeditated barbarism

on an unspeakably horrific scale ... only reality—produced, ultimately, by matter in the raw—can be so unthinkingly cruel ... we are as a result our own moral agents, and there is no escape from that responsibility, no appeal to a higher power that might be said to have artificially constrained or directed us [340].

Hyrlis' statement of moral responsibility is the interface through which the major characters in *Matter* receive meaning, agency, and the readers' empathy, which is predicated on what they do with that moral responsibility. The novel's third-person narrative voice scrutinizes every main figure in the plot, and each has a take on the notion of being one's own moral agent that identifies him/her as either a negative or a positive figure in the story's dramatic balance.[5]

Djan Seriy, for starters: her role as privileged visitor to the Culture's critical utopia makes her at once the most physically powerful and the wisest among the novel's flesh sentients. *Matter*, in fact, opens with a prologue in which she, along with her drone companion Turminder Xuss, is doing SC's angel-work on a planet hosting a medieval-stage humanoid species that lives in circumstances not dissimilar from the one in *Inversions* (1–8); this prologue does not offer any obvious hints as to Djan Seriy's origin, and her behavior establishes the entirely correct impression that she is a quintessentially Culture personality. Indeed, her exchanges with Xuss indicate a relationship reminiscent of that between Diziet Sma and Skaffen-Amtiskaw, albeit fraught with considerably less asperity.[6] When we get to find out where Djan Seriy comes from and how she came to be an SC agent, we also receive a history of her progress as a moral entity through her gradual introduction to the Culture across a period of several years: the physical amendments, the Culture shock of finding herself within a world of absolute plenty and no suffering whatsoever, the perspective on gender relations that comes with becoming a man for a year before returning to being a woman, the silly ship names (which she finds irritating), the AIs, and so on (163–172).[7] And then there are the history lessons—galactic history, that is, complete with a full case study of Sursamen and its people that drives home to her what matter really amounts to:

> Life buzzed in, fumed about, rattled around and quite thoroughly infested the entire galaxy, and probably—almost certainly—well beyond. The vast ongoingness of it all somehow put all one's own petty concerns and worries into context, making them seem not irrelevant, but of much less distressing immediacy. Context was indeed all, as her father had always insisted, but the greater context she was learning about acted to shrink the vast-seeming scale of the Eighth Level of Sursamen and all its wars, politics, disputes, struggles, tribulations and vexations until it all looked very far away and trivial indeed [167].

And like everyone else in the Culture, Djan Seriy has drawn from this context the conclusion that, if the value of things is only what we are prepared to assign to them, then one might as well choose the path leading to the decision that things do in fact Matter.

There are others, however, who have seen the same thing and come to a wholly different worldview. Mertis Tyl Loesp is not a fool: despite remaining inside Sursamen throughout the novel, he can see how much everything—anything—actually Matters. But because he is a villain and a bad man—he enjoys power, likes to see others subjected to his exercise of it, and draws an unseemly amount of residual satisfaction at the memory of the look on Hausk's face when he realized his trusted friend of twenty years had been lying to him all along (192)—he has decided that "there was no right and wrong, there was simply effectiveness and inability, might and weakness, cunning and gullibility. That he knew this was his advantage, but it was one of better understanding, not moral superiority—he had no delusions there" (190). Except for his lack of belief in any divine authority, Tyl Loesp would have made a pretty passable Idiran; just as they had, he draws from his realization of his comparative helplessness (the Idirans because they suffered an invasion; he because he knows the reality beyond Sursamen) a might-makes-right determination to use others in whatever way and at whatever time best suited him in order to grow in power, and in this sense his thinking truly is great: he knows that the Oct are using him and the Sarl, but he goes along with this state of affairs because he can see a day when this usage will translate into an advancement of the Sarl people—with him at their lead, of course (194). "Ruthlessness, will, the absolute application of force and power," he reflects at one point. "These were what secured authority and dominance" (191).

Ferbin and Holse, on the other hand, have to labor a great deal more to throw off the weight of the cultural assumptions they were born with. The former unquestioningly welcomed being raised as the next-to-most important figure among his people, and the latter fatalistically accepted his status as a person without an identity of his own choosing. From opposite sides of the spectrum of matter, both have embraced their roles to the point where those roles have become part of them, and while both can rationally see that their assumptions don't really hold up to reality on any meaningful scale external to the eighth level, neither finds it easy to actually let go of them. Ferbin repeats his litany of Matter to everyone within range, and Holse, looking at the rapidly dwindling Shellworld on the screens inside the Nariscene ship that is taking them to meet Xide Hyrlis, thinks back to his past life, his family, his wife and children, and resigns himself to the near-certainty that they won't meet again. "In life you hoped to do what you could but mostly you did what you were told and that was the end of it," he concludes (281).

So, there are no gods. Only matter. And matter suffers, but it's also the case that matter makes matter suffer. And does all this Matter, in absolute terms?

The answer is not at all. And also yes, completely. The voices of the people in previous Culture books, now sunk into the past of the most terrible one hundred years mankind has managed to visit upon planet Earth, return to us here in the new century: the man cleaning the table in *Use of Weapons*, who tells Zakalwe that even universes die in the end, so what *does* signify in the long run? Fal N'geestra in *Phlebas*, who muses that "*matter in the raw changes, progresses in a way*" and that "*everything we know and can know of is composed ultimately of patterns of nothing*" (335–336); Li'ndane in *The State of the Art*, who tells us that everything in the universe is there when we are rather than because we are, so that we don't get to claim that we Matter more than others; and finally we have the voice of John Clute, who points out that the warp and woof of *Matter* revolves around the passage quoted above because "Banks models his description of the hierarchies of civilizations responsible for Sursamen over eons in terms that clearly echo his description of the Shellworld itself: so that the shell game of matter and the shell game of life are modelled as one Matter" (359).[8] And as well they should be: given the fundamental sameness of hierarchies within and without Sursamen, no other outcome obtains.

Ferbin and Holse discover the import of this hierarchy of Matter when they finally meet Djan Seriy. His sister's SC connections have reported strange events happening on Sursamen's ninth level, where the victorious Sarl now rule the Deldeyn after one last massive battle in the latter's own capital city. The Oct have been helping the Sarl all along, using the higher command echelons of the Sarl military and political systems as a thinly veiled pretext for a technically legal exploration of the so-called Nameless City, a huge settlement millions of years old buried in silt that the titanic waterfalls of the Hyeng-zhar have been gradually stripping away over all that time, revealing the onyx-black, alien features of the mostly broken buildings (237–239). The Oct also call themselves the Inheritors, owing to a largely unproven belief that they are the rightful heirs of the Involucra's bounty of Shellworlds—yet another claim to primacy that is valid only within the species issuing it or within the civilizations that don't have the power to object—and the heart of the Nameless City, they think, contains an eons-buried treasure of Involucra origin. The Aultridia, who have been at war with the Oct for a while at the time *Matter* begins, also believe they have claim over Sursamen: they started out as parasites on the skin of the Tensile Aeronathaurs before evolving to the point where they Mattered enough to induce the High-Level Involveds to grant them civilizational status and a degree of technological fast-tracking, so they believe they are WorldGod's children (again, a species-specific claim to primacy; 86–87). Both the Oct and the Sarl, on the other hand, despise the Aultridia precisely for their origin, and a virtual state of war exists between the Sarl and the Aultridia because of the humanoids' alliance with the Oct.

Eventually, the Sarl archeological teams reach the treasure just as Prince Oramen manages to survive an assassination attempt and realize who organized it. Now a state of war exists within the Sarl people, half of whom are under Tyl Loesp's command while the other half has sworn allegiance to Oramen—more claims to primacy, progressively more fragmented and inconsequential. The only intervention that could stop a massive conflagration cascading from that flawed network of relationships would have to come from a High-Level Involved, but the galactic protocols of intervention/non-intervention ensure that none will be forthcoming (although the Oct have violated these protocols by assisting the Sarl against the Deldeyn).

The situation grows worse from there. The treasure inside the Nameless City is not Involucra—it's an Iln god-machine, whose sophistication is at least a match for both the Morthanveld and the Culture (538). As soon as it's reactivated, and just when Tyl Loesp has arrived at the head of his army to catch Oramen's forces by surprise, it issues one verbal communication in the languages of both the Oct and the Sarl: "'Thank you for your help,' it thundered. 'Now I have much to do. There is no forgiveness'" (530). Immediately thereafter, a nuclear explosion engulfs the Nameless City, evaporating those in its immediate vicinity and killing the rest through massive levels of radiation poisoning.

Ferbin's quest has been for nothing. It hadn't mattered much in the grand scheme of things to begin with, and now it's also a handful of days too late—others are here when we are, not because we are, and Ferbin, Holse, and Djan Seriy were somewhere else when everyone the Prince wanted to save and everyone he wanted to condemn died in the radioactive bubble. Also, the ultimate enemy, the one that Matters the most because it has the power to wipe out the entire Shellworld along with its hundreds of billions of living creatures, is the real reason they have returned: while en route to Sursamen, Djan Seriy had told Ferbin and Holse that the recent developments on the ninth had turned her trip to Sursamen from a personal venture to an official, SC-sanctioned operation aimed at forestalling world-wrecking events, not at seeing justice done in a private matter between the rulers of one backward species (428–429, 465–466).

But despite that, and despite the grief and the horror of the now dead Nameless City, Ferbin and Holse stick with SC's mission; between the day they left Sursamen and the day of their return to the ninth level, each has carried out his fair share of growing up. The Prince now believes more in his sister's mission than in what the Sarl propaganda machine is saying about him (463)—something that would previously have made him blow a fuse—and even after seeing his brother's ravaged corpse, he is able to prioritize his grievances and assist Djan Seriy. Djan Seriy herself at one point looks at him and muses that "he seemed more serious, less self-obsessed and much less selfish in his pleasures and aims now. She got the impression, especially after a few brief conversations with Choubris himself, that Holse would never have followed the old Ferbin so far or so faithfully. What had not changed was his lack of desire to be king" (466). Indeed, Ferbin has never wanted the throne, and the knowledge that, should he survive the battle with the Iln god-machine, he would have nothing but years of ineffectual, unhappy drudgery to look forward to, helps him make the decision to lay down his life when the battle has gotten bad enough that the only chance left to stop the sentient device is a sacrifice play (562–564).

Holse, for his part, now looks at his erstwhile master and at the Culture people in a very different complexion from that which his earlier self would have conjured up. Watching the others get ready to face the Iln machine, musing on the old Warrior Code of the Sarl higher classes, he reflects:

> Behave honourably and wish for a good death. He'd always dismissed it as self-serving bullshit, frankly; most of the people he'd been told were his betters were quite venally dishonourable.... [But] these Culture people, bafflingly, mostly chose to die, when they didn't have to. With freedom from fear and wondering where your next meal was coming from ... came choice, and you could choose a nice quiet, calm, peaceful, ordinary life and die with your nightshirt on.... Or you could end up doing something like this [549–550].

And at the end, Choubris Holse is the only one left alive of the group that set out to fight the Iln. Choubris Holse, the one who, within the purview of all applied taxonomies, should Matter the least. Ferbin, Djan Seriy, Turminder Xuss, the avatar of the Culture ship *Liveware Problem*, and the ship itself have all died in the battle. The war between the Oct and the Aultridia, which the waking of the Iln had triggered, still rages, and has now expanded to include the Nariscene in the wake of the latter's belated attempt at restoring order inside Sursamen. In the meantime, not a peep from the Morthanveld, whose compromised hardware had assisted the Iln device in the battle. Slowly, things return to a state of nervous quietude, and it's during this lull that Choubris returns home to his wife, after a year of absence without communication (589–593). He looks different, fitter, and his teeth are alarmingly white and regularly spaced. He brings with him another avatar of the defunct *Liveware Problem*, now an individual Culture citizen, and a boy Djan Seriy had saved on the planet she'd been nursing toward better behavior at the beginning of *Matter* (72–78). The boy will stay with them, Holse tells his thunderstruck wife, and so will the avatar. The whole family is about to move to much better, more spacious quarters thanks to "a fund set aside for special circumstances by some new friends I've made" (591), and money won't be a problem for them anymore. Choubris Holse is going to go into politics.

"[W]hat makes the book stick in the mind after the adrenaline of the special-effects sequences has been metabolized," Russell Letson writes, is the "thread of interest in the claims and limits of moral responsibility in a world filled with beings with godlike knowledge and power" (57). It's their assessment of their own moral responsibility within their civilizational context that makes positive characters and good people of Ferbin, Djan Seriy, Holse, and every one of their companions in the battle against the Iln machine. From the inside of the Shellworld-within-shellworld hierarchies in *Matter*, every turn of story seems to conspire to make them give up and walk away—and especially Ferbin and Holse, once the true scale of events on the ninth becomes known. Djan Seriy herself suggests to them that they should take refuge elsewhere while the problem persists (429); there would be no dishonor in that, since both are very far outside their appointed context, and the spacescapes that present themselves before their eyes contribute to driving home a sense of their true size relative to other galactic realities. Ferbin's first look at the Morthanveld nestworld of Syaung-un is emblematic of this reduction:

> This was, Ferbin thought, the equivalent of a whole civilisation, almost an entire galaxy, contained within what would, in a normal solar system, be the orbit of a single planet. What uncounted lives were lived within those dark, unending braids? ... What lives, what fates, what stories must have taken place within this star-surrounding ring, forever twisting, folding, unfolding? ... We are lost here, he thought as Holse chatted with the machine and passed on to it their pathetically few possessions. We might disappear into this wilderness of civility and progress and never be seen again. We might be dissolved within it forever, compressed, reduced to nothing by its sheer ungraspable scale. What is one man's life if such casual immensity can even exist? [393].

But neither Ferbin nor Holse abandons their quest, which is a happy thing because, as it turns out, one man's life is the difference between the continued existence of billions of sentient beings and their painful death at the hands of a monstrosity. The immensity of the world outside Sursamen triggers a profound growth in Ferbin, whose expectations of Matter had started out as lofty as their reality was puny. On the other side of this growth, he is able to ultimately sacrifice himself for the good of sentients he has never met, just as he had eventually come to accept Holse's increasingly independent-minded evolution. Holse himself, born and grown into a context where his Matter was established by the decisions of his self-described betters, ends up freely deciding to follow Ferbin precisely because of the changes he has witnessed in his erstwhile master.

We also get to witness the Culture characters' sense of moral responsibility. Everything matters, and nothing does; the decision is up to the individual, and within the dramatic balance of the novel both choices are perfectly defensible and equally meaningful. The SC mission on Sursamen is in poor shape from the outset: the Iln machine is waking up too fast, the Oct/Aultridia war is too quickly fanned into eruption, and the idea of warping a fleet of

Culture assets right inside Morthanveld jurisdiction is too risky for a proper preparation. The few Culture personnel who do get there—Djan Seriy, the *Liveware Problem* with its avatar, and Turminder Xuss—can do so because they had already been going to Sursamen anyway; their reason for going, not their destination, has changed. And they could have decided not to do anything; the Shellworld would have been destroyed, but what of it? Next to the quintillions of sentients in the galaxy and the twelve hundred remaining Shellworlds, what would that have Mattered?

But they do go, the Culture people and the Sarl people, together; and as events turn out, looking at their last battle from the viewpoint of the Warrior Code Holse was thinking about earlier, everyone does behave honorably, and everyone but Holse does attain a good death by its definitional standards—and by the standards of the Culture's intervention policies as well. There is no view of the main body of Culture life in *Matter*, and precious little of Culture environments of any kind; the vast majority of the characters aren't even *from* the Culture. This doesn't mean, however, that the critical utopian processes of the series as a whole are not present. Those processes operate through the viewpoint of people born elsewhere—people who, after experiencing the warp and woof of life in the great galactic lens, come around to a world view that sees Matter for what it is, decides that it does Matter, and acts accordingly. In this sense, the actions of Djan Seriy, the barbarian princess who took a trip, of Ferbin, the barbarian king who didn't want the throne, and of Holse, the servant who found that his own good deeds elevated him beyond his wildest expectations, encompass the moral core of this novel as pervasively as Diziet Sma's evolving consciousness traces out the twinned paths of *The State of the Art* and *Use of Weapons*. Matter matters to her too, and in her moral world nobody is expendable or cheap; Sma weeps for the good and for the bad, and her choice to continue recruiting for SC doesn't alter the price she pays. Holse's trajectory through the plot of *Matter*, in fact, brings him very close to the perspective of Mr. Escoerea, the legless young man whose services Sma tries to enlist at the end of *Weapons*. But unlike Escoerea, Holse was never grievously wounded, and his outlook is substantially happier than that of, say, Zakalwe/Elethiomel. He is an altogether kinder man with an altogether healthier psyche, which bodes well for the people of the eighth and the ninth. There's angel-work to be done.

For all the traveling the various characters in *Matter* do, the novel feels almost cozy in its circumscribed involvement with and ultimate focus on the events on Sursamen's ninth level. Just as the plots of *Consider Phlebas*, *The State of the Art*, and *Look to Windward* had described paths that, however circuitously, ended up converging on one single planetary location, so the plot of *Matter* slingshots us away from the Shellworld only to return to it at the end.

Banks' next Culture novel, *Surface Detail* (2010), is an altogether different ball of yarn.[9] Its first four chapters introduce us to four different groups of protagonists before scattering these characters' trajectories to the solar winds, letting them describe the sort of aerobatics for which the equally numerous plotlines in *Excession* had made that novel famous. In fact, *Surface Detail* is closer to *Excession* than it is to any other previous Culture books, especially in the way its peripatetic plotlines diverge, explode outward, and ultimately reconnect in a number of unexpected configurations.

The thread of story all these plotlines share is the creation and maintenance of the Hells, virtual afterlives designed to replicate in a subset of the real a given civilization's myths of a place of eternal punishment:

> The hells existed because some faiths insisted on them, and some societies too, even without the excuse of over-indulged religiosity. Whether as a result of perhaps too faithful a transcription—from scriptural assertion to provable actuality—or simply an abiding secular need to continue persecuting those thought worthy of punishment even after they were dead, a number of civilisations— some otherwise quite respectable—had built up impressively ghastly Hells over the eons [132].[10]

Of all the crimes flesh sentients have ever committed, torture is probably the one the Culture is most vehemently against (133); indeed, it's not wrong to say that Contact and SC were originally created to stop this institutionalized form of suffering in its every shape. However, when a virtual war begins between the anti-Hell and pro-Hell factions in the galactic community— the war is also known as a "confliction" (169), its conduct carefully regulated and arbitrated to make sure its parameters reflect the actual strength of the participants in the real (134)—the Culture is forced to sit it out because "At the point when the war began, [it] had been in one of its cyclic eras of trying not to be seen to be throwing its weight around. Too many others of the In-Play Level Eights[11] had objected to the Culture being involved with the War in Heaven for it to be able to do so without looking arrogant, even belligerent" (172). But now, after decades of fighting in a bewildering variety of virtual spaces, the war is coming to a close, and it looks like the pro-Hell side will win. The anti-Hell side, unwilling to accept the verdict, has decided to cheat, first by hacking into the substrates holding the Hells themselves in order to free those trapped within and later, after the hacking attempts fail, by taking the confliction into the real and turning it into all-out war. The lives and trajectories of the four groups of characters in *Surface Detail* are all connected to this burgeoning war, which if unchecked promises to engulf half the galaxy.

Those characters have one thing in common: in their respective introductory chapters, they all die (Letson 2011, 21). The first is Lededje Y'breq, an Intagliate. In her civilization, a relatively low-level commonwealth called the Sichultian Enablement, the Intagliate are "trophies ... the surrendered banners of defeated enemies, the capitulation papers signed by the vanquished, the heads of fierce beasts adorning the walls of those who owned them" (71), and the fantastically complex network of tattoos that cover every inch of their bodies down to the molecular level is the seal of that surrender. In the specific, Lededje and her mother became Intagliates because of a business debt their father owed Joiler Veppers,[12] his former partner and the man who betrayed him for financial gain. Stabbed in the back by his friend, with his wife and daughter marked for life as property, Lededje's father killed himself, followed by her mother some years later. After that, Lededje spent years trying to escape, always unsuccessfully, and her latest attempt, at the beginning of chapter 1, proves fatal: Veppers, who has been using her as a sex slave as well as a status symbol to be displayed at public functions, murders her. As soon as Lededje's life leaves her body, however, her consciousness awakens inside a simulation substrate in the Culture GSV *Sense Amid Madness, Wit Amidst Folly*—years before, Lededje had been visited by the avatar of a Culture ship with an interest in talking a 4-D image of her intaglios in exchange for whatever favor or service it could provide. When Lededje told the ship's avatar to surprise her, the Mind obliged, growing inside her brain a neural lace with the ability to transmit her consciousness to the computational substrate of its home GSV—the *Sense Amid Madness, Wit Amidst Folly*. Duly "revented" (i.e., reincarnated; 149) by the GSV's Mind, Lededje now wants to return to Sichult, the Enablement's home planet, and kill Veppers right back (1–16, 57–94).

The second character is Vatueil, a soldier in the anti–Hell faction. He and his fellow comrades have been fighting, dying, and re-embodying within the virtuality for decades now, and the death he suffers at the end of the second chapter of *Surface Detail* is the latest iteration in the process (17–29). Throughout the novel, Vatueil continues to die and reincarnate and fight and die again, all the while taking part in the workings of the strategic council that decides to extend the virtual war into the real (115–145, 245–267). Eventually, he confesses to an SC-sponsored quorum of Minds, one of whose members calls him a traitor; Vatueil doesn't deny it, and disappears from the virtuality where the meeting is taking place. There are hints that we may have known this man for quite a while (541–547).

The third character is Yime Nsokyi. She pretend-dies during a virtual worst-case-scenario annihilatory drill she and her cohorts are running on the Orbital where she lives. Yime is something of a throwback by Culture standards (more so than Jernau Gurgeh, who would be her closest character pattern in the Culture stories): she doesn't much like biological or technological augmentations, she cherishes discipline in a society where that is a dirty word, and she adopts toward such matters as love, sex, and having fun a somewhat austere attitude, preferring to arrange her body as gender-neutral and cultivating a few quiet friendships (31–44). Yime is also a member of Quietus, one of the three Special Circumstances offshoots the novel introduces; Quietus "dealt with the dead. The dead outnumbered the living in the greater galaxy by some distance, if you added up all those individuals existing in the various Afterlives the many different civilisations had created over the millennia … the sheer scale of their numbers ensured that important issues involving the deceased still arose now and again" (167).[13] As soon as Lededje wakes up inside the virtuality onboard the *Sense Amid Madness, Wit Amidst Folly*, Yime is tasked with making contact with her and awaiting for further developments (166–179).

Finally, there are Prin and Chay, two academics belonging to the Pavulean species, one of the pro–Hell civilizations. When their story opens in chapter 4, they are technically dead—in the sense of having downloaded themselves into the Pavulean Hell via a pirate connection. Their mission is to spend a month or so inside the Hell and record everything that happens in there, so that the recordings can be presented to their civilization's courts as evidence to strengthen the position of the abolitionist faction among the Pavulean people. But virtual or not, the Hell is a terrifying place, and while Prin retains his grip on reality, Chay loses it shortly before they are due to be reuploaded. As a result, convinced that the only reality there ever was is right there, she fails to trigger the recall signal together with Prin, and while he ascends back up to real life, she remains in Hell, prey to the Pavulean demons' savagery (45–55, 95–100). But even in Hell, and albeit only once in a very long time, irony applies: Chay's very lack of faith in any reality beyond that of her charnel house conspires to spare her the full extent of the punishment. "There is always hope," a titanic demon-lord tells her, "and there must be hope. To abandon hope is to escape part of the punishment. One must hope for hope to be destroyed. One must trust in order to feel the anguish of betrayal" (285). And so, while in the world above Prin testifies to the courts concerning what happens in the Pavulean Hell, Chay is subjected to a strangely pain-free game of develop-your-faith in another virtuality, where she spends a lifetime in a place called The Refuge as part of a religious order of which she eventually becomes the Mother Superior, just so that she'll develop the faith necessary to be fully punished in Hell (341–353).

While the plotlines of the various characters in *Surface Detail* become infernally entangled across a narrative of the same brazen intricacy as that of *Excession*, the moral conundrums in this new novel are, from a critical utopian perspective, a lot less problematic than they'd ever been before. First, the Culture isn't involved in the confliction, and does intervene to prevent it from spilling over into the real; second, the notion that actualizing eternal suffering for billions of flesh sentients represents acceptable behavior on the part of a self-respecting galactic civilization is so awful that, were the Culture to intervene militarily on the largest possible scale to close the Hells and stop the suffering, we readers would have a hard time not cheering it on. That the Culture doesn't, that it moves with the usual caution and respects the boundaries to whose observance it has agreed, becomes almost frustrating.

Thankfully, you can always count on the villains. The Culture, it turns out, has a groupie—the Geseptian-Fardesile Cultural Federacy (GFCF), a Level-Seven civilization whose often cringe-worthy attempts at emulating its role model do not prevent it from paradoxically working against them, "as though they so much wanted to be of help they needed the Culture reduced to a level of neediness that would make such aid something it would genuinely be grateful for" (171). The GFCF—which unsurprisingly belongs to the anti-Hell faction—is the architect behind the multi-civ initiative to convert the Tsungarial Disk, an entire system's worth of high-tech factories, into a gigantic production facility for an enormous fleet designed to attack and destroy the physical substrates housing the Hells. Joiler Veppers' Veprine Corporation, which had long ago bought most of those substrates, is part of the venture, and the GFCF has already ensured him and the rest of its allies that none of their actions will come back to haunt them because "we intend to frame the Culture for everything!" (385).

Most of the sub-plots and the contortions in the main plotlines are the result of the Culture's responses to the developments in the GFCF's plan. Initially in the dark concerning their fans' intentions, SC and its offspring organizations quickly gain a fairly comprehensive picture of the situation and dispatch their various assets to unravel the conspiracy and bring matters to a satisfactorily peaceful end. Among those assets is the Abominator-class warship *Falling Outside the Normal Moral Constraints*, with which Lededje strikes an odd sort of friendship—odd because the war craft, which goes under the inoffensive-sounding designation of picket ship, is the last word in large-scale mayhem the Culture has to offer. The ship's avatar, Demeisen, describes it/itself as "a borderline eccentric and *very* slightly psychotic Abominator-class picket ship" (409), and throughout the narrative it certainly behaves with the manic spikiness that is typical of Culture entities built to perform exceptionally well a job that the society as a whole deems unworthy of a decent civilization. Like every SC operative and every other dedicated military asset in the Culture, the *FOTNMC* is perfectly capable of detecting the schizophrenic attitude other Culture people/drones/Minds adopt toward it, and as a result it behaves like the stereotypical uninvited guest at the party—it appalls other Minds, irritates drones and flesh sentients, and shamelessly takes advantage of everyone around it. But Lededje ends up developing an exasperated kind of fondness for the ship,[14] a fondness that begins when she realizes that it's the only Culture entity willing to take her anywhere near

Veppers. So she takes up Demeisen's offer to go with it, and on the way to Sichult the two get into a good deal of trouble; or rather, they would if the *FOTNMC* weren't the monstrously powerful ship- and planet-wrecker it is.

There are two main sources of critical-utopian critique in *Surface Detail*: one is Yime Nsokyi, who often finds herself irritated at what she sees as the excessively easy-going nature of her society and joins Quietus because the members of the organization "were expected to be sober, serious people while they were on duty, and to dress appropriately" (168). Yime, who dresses appropriately and behaves soberly all the time, finds herself right at home. Her trajectory through the novel, however, belies the initial impression of her role, and it almost feels like Banks meant for that to happen: at every turn, Yime and the ships/drones/people with her are subjected to near-death attacks, conflagrations, explosions, and other pointedly not sober events (329–330, 411–416), as if the narrative had decided to play trickster to her nature and aspirations.[15] When Yime does finally get to meet Lededje, it's the end of the novel and the only thing left for her to do is participate in a slightly illegal scheme to allow the Sichultian woman a chance to get her revenge—which she does get, with a generous amount of help from the *FOTNMC* (599–617).

The other critical utopian perspective belongs to Lededje and the *Falling Outside the Normal Moral Constraints*. The Sichultian woman finds the Culture as fascinating as it is frustrating—fascinating because it is a far better place than the Sichultian Enablement, which is virtually run by Veppers, and frustrating because the very ethics that make the Culture what it is get in the way of her revenge. This is why she and the *FOTNMC* get along well: each sees in the other a topsy-turvy mirror version of themselves—Lededje because the ship is the kind of warrior she wishes she were, and the ship because Lededje is, like it, the offspring of a social system that first created her the way she is and then treated her like something of a pariah, at once admired and rejected. The Culture is obviously not the Sichultian Enablement, which is why Lededje becomes a citizen of it at the end of the novel, but there are enough philosophical and existential commonalities for the two to establish a baseline of mutual understanding.

This baseline becomes apparent when a GFCF fleet intent on preventing the Culture from finding out about the factory complex in the Tsungarial Disk fires on the *FOTNMC*. At the news that something bad is going on in the Tsungarial Disk, Demeisen displays an amount of glee so unseemly that Lededje scolds him for it. This how the avatar responds:

> I am a warship. This is my nature. This is what I'm designed and built for. My moment of glory approaches and you can't expect me not to be excited at the prospect. I was fully expecting to spend my operational life just twiddling my metaphorical thumbs in the middle of empty nowhere, ensuring sensible behavior amongst the rolling boil of fractious civs just by my presence and that of my

peers, keeping the peace through the threat of the sheer pandemonium that would result if anybody resurrected the idea of war as a dispute-resolution procedure with the likes of me around. Now some sense-forsaken fuckwit with a death wish has done just that and I strongly suspect I shortly get a chance to *shine*, baby! [469].

As indeed it does: when the GFCF carries out a full-on attack on the *FOTNMC*, the subsequent action is so fast and brutally one-sided that Lededje can only catch what happens by looking at a recording once everything is over and done with (505–507). The irony here is that, badly behaved as it may claim to be, the *Falling Outside The Normal Moral Constraints* never actually falls outside normal moral constraints; it scrupulously observes SC's rules of engagement, and for all its talk of craving a scrap with anyone who will oblige, it forgoes a number of opportunities to do precisely that. It even gives the approaching GFCF fleet every chance to resolve the dispute amicably before their unambiguously destruction-oriented behavior forces it to respond in kind—which it does with a clear conscience and an abundance of enthusiasm. Lededje's discomfort with Demeisen's happiness at the thought of the coming scrap is partially directed at herself—her own murderous impulses, however understandable and to an extent justified, place her on shaky ground when it comes to claiming the high road (499–509).[16]

The Culture in general can act with a clear conscience as well. There are few moral ambiguities in *Surface Detail*, and none that it generated, plus the behavior in which Veppers indulges throughout the novel is repulsive enough that we don't really get bent out of shape when Yime Nsokyi and the *FOTNMC*, with the assistance of the Culture ambassador on Sichult, help Lededje get her revenge. As for the Hells, they all go up in smoke during the early stages of the battle with the fleet built in the Tsungarial Disk. Chay and the rest of their prisoners are now free. After everything that happened in the virtuality, she decides to remain in it, this time as "a creature of ending and release in the Virtual; the angel of death who came for people who lived in happy, congenial afterlives and who—tired even of their many lifetimes lived after biological death—were ready to dissolve themselves into the generality of consciousness that underlay Heaven, or who were ready simply to cease to be altogether." Prin, whose testimony before the courts was crucial in the Pavulean people's decision to never rebuild their Hell, meets her many lifetimes later, when the angel of death comes to give him his eternal rest (622–623).

The other main characters and plotlines receive similarly happy resolutions—except for Veppers' legacy, irredeemably compromised after the previously buried evidence of his many cruelties comes to light (620). Lededje becomes a Culture citizen, travels across the galaxy onboard the *Sense Amid Madness, Wit Amidst Folly*, and then settles on an Orbital where "She had five children by as many different fathers and ended up with over thirty great-

great-great-grandchildren, which by Culture standards was almost disgraceful" (623). Yime Nsokyi returns to her home Orbital and begins a successful, if entirely honorary, career in politics (620), while the *Falling Outside the Normal Moral Constraints* becomes the envy of the whole Abominator-class fleet for its actions around the Tsungarial Disk; the ship also spends a lot of time with GSVs—"just for the company. Its avatar Demeisen continued to behave appallingly" (620). Already drastically reduced in number after the events in the novel, the Hells vanish from the galaxy within one biogeneration, "their very absence [becoming] accepted almost without question as part of what constituted being civilised in the first place. This made the Culture very happy" (623).

Only Vatueil is left now; the novel's epilogue focuses on him. He truly was a traitor: the pro–Hell faction had planted him into the ranks of the anti-Hell faction at the beginning of the decades-long war to do precisely the job he did: cause disruption and chaos. Vatueil, we are immediately told, is not the man's actual name; he has another he likes to go by and that he has now readopted—but that, significantly, isn't his actual name either. The man formerly known as Vatueil had originally espoused the pro–Hell cause "partly out of sheer contrarianism and partly out of that despair he felt sometimes, periodically—during this long, long life—at the sheer self-hurtful idiocy and destructiveness of so many types of sentient life, especially the meta-type known as pan-human, to which he had always had the dubious honor of belonging. You want suffering, pain and horror? I'll give you suffering, pain and horror [...]" (625–626). However, over the course of the long confliction, Vatueil changes his mind and betrays the pro–Hell faction as well: he comes clean and implicates everyone he can. After that, he "had been quite pleased to see so much of what he had pledged to fight for crumble away into disgraced and piecemeal nothing. Hell mend them" (626).

This does feel like the behavior of someone we've met before, and the progression of the epilogue strengthens that feeling: Vatueil is sitting at a table in a restaurant somewhere we're not told, waiting for a woman; a poet. Attentive readers will also remember, in this gradually clearer context, the words of one Mind among the quorum to which Vatueil had confessed the anti–Hell faction's decision to escalate the confliction: "That errant, ramshackled ghost.... He's known of old; I doubt he even remembers who he used to be, let alone what he believes in or most recently promised" (547). The revelation of Vatueil's true identity, which we will probably have guessed by the time the restaurant's maître d' calls him by name, still comes as something of a shock—the name is the last word in the novel: "Your table is ready, Mr. Zakalwe" (627).

There is a strange, lop-sided appropriateness to the fact that *Surface Detail*, a story about the elimination of suffering and the freeing of those who are prisoner inside hells not of their making, should feature the crucial agency of—and end with—the man who will always live inside a hell very much of his own making. Zakalwe is no more forgiven now than he had been at the end of *Use of Weapons*, and we know this because, had Livueta finally absolved him of his burden of guilt, he would have stopped trying to carry out his own dysfunctional brand of angel-work. Indeed, the distorted perspective that brought him to first support and then betray the pro–Hell faction feels very much like the product of an agonized conscience, especially now that, hundreds of years after the events in *Weapons*, Zakalwe is still alive while Livueta is, in all likelihood, dead. Inside the virtual Hells, time flowed more slowly than in the real (476), and it's safe to assume that the same circumstances obtain inside the biological substrate housing Zakalwe's conscience. And there's no closing down that virtuality, nor is it possible to free the soul trapped within; Zakalwe is his own jailer, demon-lord, and violator all at once, so that for as long as he lives there will be one virtual Hell left in the galaxy.

We now come to the tenth and last Culture novel. Within six months of *The Hydrogen Sonata*'s appearance, Banks had divulged the news of his illness; within eight months he was gone. A certain *frisson* of something that feels a bit like awe attends the realization that, like its immediate predecessor, this last Culture book deals with passing away or removing oneself from the life of the universe as we know it—if *Surface Detail* featured virtual afterlives, the dramatic engine of *Sonata*'s plot is the Subliming of a whole civilization.[17]

Banks would have laughed at the suggestion that the predominantly death-oriented outlook of three among his last four novels—besides *Surface Detail* and *Sonata*, we have *The Quarry*[18]—indicated the presence of some premonitory faculty in him. Virtual afterlives are pointedly not death, and neither is Subliming; the fun of having a non-mimetic universe to write in is precisely that you can set up the ground rules to allow yourself the freedom of featuring death-defying technologies without having to explain them away as metaphors or symbols for actually dying. The problem is, as usual, people. We are pattern-seekers, all of us, and we have a tough time letting go after we've found those patterns—even when, as in this particular case, there were none to begin with. It's difficult to read *The Hydrogen Sonata*, with its pervasive atmosphere of demobilization, and resist thinking of Banks himself as preparing to leave at his space-opera version of the Grey Havens. To an extent, and provided we don't carry it too far, this may actually be a healthy exercise.

As the book opens, we find the Gzilt civilization only twenty-four days away from Subliming.[19] The Gzilt, a Level-Eight Involved, has been a respected, peaceful member of the galactic community for thousands of years, and its relations with the Culture have always been amicable. In fact, the Gzilt came close to actually *being* Culture:

> Nearly founders, though not quite, [the Gzilt] had been influential in the setting up and design of the Culture almost ten thousand years earlier, when a disparate group of humanoid species at roughly the same stage of technological development had been thinking about banding together. Amiable enough, if somewhat martially uptight due to an unusual social set-up that basically meant everybody was presumed to be in a single society-wide militia ... they had made significant contributions to the establishment and ethos of the Culture while it was still at the being-talked-about phase but then, almost at the last moment ... they had decided not to join the new confederation [66].

The reason for the Gzilt's decision to go it alone was rooted in their well-rewarded reliance on their Book of Truth, the one holy tome in the history of the galaxy that "gained in credence as science developed" (67). Throughout the history of the Gzilt civilization, the Book of Truth's predictions concerning all the relevant scientific and technological advances that go into making a spacefaring commonwealth proved to be exactly correct, without fail or necessity for amendment. Together with those exact predictions, the Book of Truth also delivered the standard set of moral/ethical commandments, which gained enormously in righteousness for being written next to, as it were, the right stuff. Thus, the Gzilt found it easy to take seriously the Book of Truth's claims "that [they] were a people favoured by fate, by the universe itself, as part of an ongoing thrust towards a glorious, transcendent providence. They represented the very tip of a mystical spear thrown by the past at the future, the shaft of that spear being formed by a multitude of earlier species which existed before them and kept on serially handing on the baton of destiny to the next, slightly more exceptional people ahead of them" (71).

The Hydrogen Sonata is a Banks novel. If anything in it is certain from the outset, it's that any claim to universal primacy or conceit of being creation's darling is emptier than the void between the stars, and the Gzilt's own set of beliefs is no different. Banks lets the genie out of the bottle early on: "the Book of Truth is a lie" (111). The purportedly holy tome is a hoax perpetrated by the Zihdren, the civilization that, according to the book, "were the last handers-on of the baton, the final stage of this rocket ship to the sky that would put the actual payload—the Gzilt—into the glory of eternal orbit" (71). There is no tip of the spear because there never was any spear, and there's no payload because there never was any rocket; there were only the Zihdren, long since Sublimed, and the cultural experiment a tiny faction of academics within their civilization decided to conduct just to see what would happen. All those correct guesses were a clever trick of reverse-engineering: by announcing in the Book of Truth the relevant sequence of scientific and technological discoveries, the Zihdren essentially put the Gzilt on a purely applied research path carefully designed to direct their scientists' attention in the correct direction every time (112).

All this may not have mattered much to those the Gzilt are about to leave behind, except that the Zihdren have to spill the beans—it's tradition. One of the many niceties the galactic community observes when one of its members Sublimes consists in a fare-thee-well-and-let-me-come-clean protocol: a given civilization's messages of appreciation and wishes of Godspeed and good luck may also contain "the odd admission that actually we're responsible for rubble-ising your moon while you guys were inventing the wheel but we were having big exciting space battles with the neighbours, or it was us what nicked your first space probe" (67). Through their Remnanter section—the part of their civ that, for a variety of reasons, did not sublime along with everyone else—the Zihdren have sent a ship containing a Ceremonial Guest whose task is to tell the truth about the Book of Truth. One of the few remaining Gzilt ships—if everyone in their civilization is also part of their military, every one of their ships is also a warship—duly meets the Zihdren-Remnanter craft at the appointed place, and upon hearing the message of the Ceremonial Guest, annihilates the vessel in a burst of destructive energy so violent that the small Gzilt settlement on the planet below is also destroyed (1–9). The higher echelons of the Gzilt government, afraid that the revelation will shock the bulk of the civilization into refusing to Sublime, has decided to suppress the truth by every means available—including killing its own people, if there's any danger they may have somehow intercepted the Zihdren-Remnanter's signal (hence the destruction of the settlement). Led by a Septame named Banstegeyn[20] and Marshal Chewkri, a woman embodying the quintessential military mindset of the tough-as-leather, follow-your-orders-and-shut-up persuasion, these higher echelons spend the time left before Subliming attempting to scour every corner of the galaxy clean of the Zihdren message, following the entirely correct assumption that the Remnanter Ceremonial Guest was not the only entity to know its import (45–57).

This is where the Culture and one of the few Gzilt citizens who do not seem that sold on the whole idea of Subliming, a reservist called Vyr Cossont (11), come in. One of the people currently aware of the Book of Truth's falsity is the oldest Culture citizen, a man by the name of Ngaroe QiRia; QiRia is ten thousand years old, and one of the participants at the conference that gave birth to the Culture. Aware that the knowledge he possesses could mean danger to him and everyone around him, QiRia has stored the information somewhere safe, carefully hidden under multiple layers of deceit and misdirection. Cossont had met the man himself twenty years before, while on a sabbatical with the Culture, and now the commanders of her original regiment, the Socialist-Republican People's Liberation Regiment #14, recall her to service to find this man. The 14th knows about the Book of Truth, and its leaders want Cossont to contact QiRia and bring the evidence to them so that they can broadcast it to the whole of Gzilt civilization. Before Cossont can even accept the mission, however, another Gzilt warship destroys the HQ of the regiment, killing everyone except her and a few others, and even they would have ended up dead if the Culture ship *Mistake Not...* hadn't rescued them at the last minute. The *Mistake Not...*, an unclassified craft with a buried, much longer name that seems to indicate an advanced capacity for mayhem, had been following its own trail of clues after detecting from a nearby star system the energy signature of the Zihdren-Remnanter's destruction, and now it decides to help Cossont carry out the mission, with the result that the forces commanded by Banstegeyn and Marshal Chewkri are now hunting both (96–134, 175–185).

In the meantime, the Zihdren-Remnanter have contacted the Culture and asked its help in bringing the incident to a satisfactory—and most importantly quiet—ending. An event committee very similar to the Interesting Times Gang from *Excession* duly forms, complete with the funky ship-to-ship dialogue we first saw in that novel[21]; the *Mistake Not...* is part of the committee, and through it Cossont as well. Aside from dispatching the Gzilt woman and the *Mistake Not...* on a variety of frenetic trips from one side of Gzilt space to the other in search of QiRia's elusive information on the Book of Truth, the committee appoints some of its members to the investigation into the attack on the 14th Regiment's HQ, some others to patrol duty to safeguard the integrity of Gzilt space against opportunistic Scavenger species, and a couple more to accompany the Ronte and the Liseiden into Gzilt space. These two Level-Five civilizations are the remaining candidates for the role of official Scavenger species (37–39), potential heirs to whatever bounty of Level-Eight tech will remain after the Gzilt have Sublimed.

The aggregate of these plot-vectors constitutes the totality of the action in *Sonata*. Like *Excession* and *Surface Detail*, this novel too is full of energy and speed, featuring a variegated cast of highly kinetic characters describing hyperspace doodles entangled in such a mess that the whole thing would be infuriating if the proceedings weren't this much fun. The two previous books, however, had woven their webs of plot around trajectories aimed (however circuitously) at objects relevant to and isomorphic with the story told: the eponymous black-body sphere in *Excession* is a conduit to other universes, and its relevance is not affected by the three-men-in-a-boat handling of the situation that the Interesting Times Gang becomes ultimately responsible for. *Surface Detail*, for its part, is an arrow pointed at Hell itself, and the successful demise of the nightmare afterlives at the end of the novel becomes one of the great moments of joy in the whole Culture series. *Sonata* instead weaves its web around nothing at all: every plotline in it, from the Zihdren message to QiRia's information to the unmasking of Banstegeyn and Marshal Chewkri, is pure McGuffin—wormholes to nowhere. Which doesn't mean the trip itself isn't worth embarking on:

> *The Hydrogen Sonata* is a 500-page scherzo, a joyful progress vibrating with momentum, a triumph of continued focus, a shattai garden and echolalia of the remembrances and vistas accorded by the preceding quarter century of Culture tales. It can be read as an almost totally unguarded paean to the deeply conjoined joys of making something and finding something out: all in the full and explicit realization that in the end nothing means squat, in the explicit understanding that doing meaning is to make meaning last, but only until you stop [Clute 2014a, 163].

And that's the problem with the Gzilt: they're Subliming on the say-so of false prophets and in the conviction that, once they are on the other side, they won't have stopped making meaning last—they will *be* meaning, forever. The Book of Truth tells the Gzilt that their arrival in the beyond will herald a momentous change for the better in the fabric of the Sublime itself (72), so that the whole civilization believes that, far from removing itself from the meaning-making elite of the real, it will actually become the transcendent head of that elite. But the Book of Truth is a lie. It's nothing but noise, and noise is all we get as the engine of *Sonata* rapidly clanks into high gear and its various characters react to the news the Zihdren-Remnanter brought.

Vyr Cossont's personal story yells to us in microcosm the same thing the novel is whispering in macrocosm. One of the many things many people whose societies are about to Sublime do is carry out a life-task, something meaningful to complete right before the great jump to let the universe know you were there after all. Cossont's own life-task is to play perfectly, without a single note falling out of place, "T. C. Vilabier's 26th String-specific Sonata For An Instrument Yet To Be Invented … on one of the few surviving examples of the instrument developed specifically to play the piece, the notoriously difficult, temperamental and tonally challenged Antagonistic Undecagonstring—or elevenstring, as it was commonly known." Vilabier's piece, tellingly composed ten thousand years before, "was more usually known as 'The Hydrogen Sonata'" (11). The Sonata's author perversely designed it to be so challenging and difficult that, to be played properly, the average number of limbs in a humanoid is not enough, which is why Cossont had to have two more arms added to her normal complement of two. Even then, and even when the Sonata is played perfectly, the sounds the elevenstring produces are essentially awful. This is how Cossont describes her life-task to the 14th-Regiment colonel who comes to her house to recall her back into service:

> "Never heard of it."
> "More commonly known as the Hydrogen Sonata."
> "Still never heard of it."
> "No great surprise, sir. It's a bit obscure."

"Renowned?"
"The piece?"
"Yes."
"Only as being almost impossible to play."
"Not, like [...]?"
"Pleasant to listen to? No. Sir."
"Really?"
... "An eminent and respected academic provided perhaps the definitive critical comment many thousands of years ago, sir. His opinion was: 'As a challenge, without peer. As music, without merit'" [33].

To review: the Hydrogen Sonata is almost impossible to play, unpleasant anyway when played perfectly, and designed to be performed on an instrument that didn't exist when it was composed by people who didn't have enough limbs to do the job properly. This is probably the reason why it's not one bit surprising to find out, as we do shortly after the revelation about the Book of Truth, that the Hydrogen Sonata is also a hoax, a joke Vilabier perpetrated at the expense of the universe (127). It's also completely unsurprising, for the purposes of the twin dovetailing processes of meaning-making in the novel, that it's QiRia who delivers the news—not only had he known Vilabier personally; he'd also helped compose the Sonata (126).²²

Thus, everything is noise, from the Book of Truth to the Hydrogen Sonata to the contortions everyone has to go through to perform, in a context increasingly leeched of valid signifiers, what they think will make everything mean something. There is a lot of fury tied to the sound, too, because Banstegeyn and Chewkri won't stop, and the *Mistake Not...*, engaged in the last of a long sequence of battles with murderous Gzilt ships, finally gets mad enough to tell the Gzilt warship *8*Churkun*, the vessel responsible for the destruction of the Remnanter ship at the beginning of the novel, its full name: *Mistake Not My Current State of Joshing Gentle Peevishness for the Awesome and Terrible Majesty of the Towering Seas of Ire That Are Themselves the Milquetoast Shallows Fringing My Vast Oceans of Wrath* (502). Which is noise too, of course, except that the Culture ship means it as a threat and the AI inside the *8*Churkun* decides to pay heed to it and breaks off the engagement—a small moment of making meaning last between you and someone else until you both get to go home safely. This the Gzilt do at the end, when they Sublime despite everything; the truth is known, but it turns out they don't much care, and all the deaths Banstegeyn and Chewkri caused, including that of Banstegeyn's pregnant lover, have been for nothing at all. The Culture walks away with its cachet as the good guys intact, partly because of the sacrifice of the *Beats Working*—a tiny, virtually unarmed GCU that elected to fight a hopeless battle on the side of the Ronte fleet when the Liseiden decided they didn't want to share the spoils of the Gzilt. Vyr Cossont, for her part, does not Sublime. Instead she accepts the invitation of the *Mistake Not...* to go tramping across the galaxy and visit Ngaroe QiRia on his current planet of residence—as soon as she finishes her life-task, that is. The end of the novel sees her in the room where we'd met her at the beginning as she finally plays the Hydrogen Sonata from start to finish, note-perfect, after which she abandons the elevenstring where it is and leaves onboard her flier (513–517). The noise is over, and we readers "return to the sense that what we are being told in this novel is that the search for meaning is *inherently* a McGuffin Search. That Sublimation may be an option: but not here, not in the phenomenal world, which we meat folk experience through the prim ridiculous reticule of the seven senses, plus augments. So let us go then.... At the very end of this novel whose joy is wrested from nada, Cossont leaves 'The Hydrogen Sonata' behind, just as we leave *The Hydrogen Sonata*: in order to start again, failing better" (Clute 2014b, 165). But this time, we'll have to start again by ourselves. The song is over, and these are the novel's last words:

> The Antagonistic Undecagonstring, caught in the swirling breeze produced by the flier's departure, hummed emptily. The sound was swept away by the mindless air [517].

The Culture series ends here, on what is safe to describe as a meaningful note. The random eddies of displaced atmosphere playing equally random notes on a musical instrument, notes that the very breeze that had produced them then sweeps away forever, is a good image for the meaning-making and pattern-recognition scaffold Banks erected across ten books, twenty-five years of publishing, and thirty-eight years of writing practice. The Culture stories are an eminently useful retelling of our efforts, here and now on planet Earth, to make meaning last at least as long as we're around, and if we're lucky beyond that. But to reach past the envelope of our biological spans, we'll need the same thing the Culture needs to make meaning last: each other, and those who will come after us. Banks wrote the last trilogy of Culture books with the assumption that a healthy life for any commonwealth, and especially for a utopian one, must involve the presence of others and arrange that presence into shapes that, however complicated they become, tie civilization together. That's because civilization needs telling, all the time and every time, otherwise it slips away into ennui and dreams of empire. The galaxy, we've been told since *Phlebas* appeared in 1987, is a titanic meta-biosphere teeming with life in myriad forms, and it's only appropriate that these myriads should eventually come to sing part of the song.

Conclusion
The Future of the Culture

Of all the critical voices this book has echoed, John Clute's should be the one to provide a succinct definitive statement on the role Banks played in shaping the thoughts of space opera. Clute, as this book has probably demonstrated, is the critic who more than any other has been paying attention to the development of the Culture series, both as a location for the telling of non-mimetic literature and as a viable consensus-reality argument for a better place to live in. As he was present at the beginning, when *Consider Phlebas* saw print, so he was present at the end. In his review of *The Hydrogen Sonata*, Clute assessed the relevance of the Culture in the following terms:

> [T]wenty-five years ago, *Consider Phlebas* first introduced into space opera, a form previously dominated by Americans and those who wrote like Americans to pay the rent, the seemingly radical premise that a *successful* pan-galactic civilization, one able to make low-entropy draws upon the almost infinite energy banks of the universe-as-a-whole, would almost certainly be post-scarcity.... The only scarcity-defined multi-planet civilizations in Banks's Culture are isolated and pitiable trickle-down tyrannies conspicuously modeled on the conviction-capitalist hegemonies now consuming—because that is what scorpions do—our one and only world. Among the blindnesses of hegemonic American SF ... was a double presumption: that the future could be Engineered Like Orlando ... and that the world to come would be arranged around the maintenance of scarcity-based guy hierarchies, with an occasional Empress or Lady President to do sin-eater for the real boss, in all its strict denial of a universe of stupefying plenty. Be that as it may, Banks's Culture was post-scarcity from the get-go ... and he has never succumbed to the temptation (again characteristic of American SF) to treat cost-free plenitude as poisonous. Some of the sentient flesh creatures in the Culture do occasionally regret an absence of owners (and the penury they impose, because that is what scorpions do), but they're a drop in the Culture bucket. The rest make do in their trillions with as much life as they can live, in a universe whose meaning-structure (if there is one) is not ascertainable through meat senses. In other words, they make the meaning they can [2014a, 162–163].

Banks' take on the manifest-destiny grand narrative of classic space opera remains revolutionary to this day, as much for the joy of watching the post-scarcity people wander the galaxy in their Minded ships as for the skepticism concerning the potential for improvement in our local chapter of the humanoid race. In the Culture stories, Earth-humans do not take part in the formation of the Culture, nor do we join it at any stage in the stories (being contacted and becoming part of the Culture are two very different things), and because of this fundamental violation of the standard space-opera template's comforting presumptions, several interviewers throughout the years asked Banks whether he thought Earthlings could become grown-up enough to create a civilization like that. In earlier times, Banks was relatively sanguine about our chances (see for example Daoust 1999, n.p.), but as the years went by and the twenty-first century exploded in our faces, his outlook returned to what it had originally been. "I thought long and hard about this long before the books were published," Banks told Linnie Rawlinson of CNN in 2009, "and decided that the Culture wasn't going to be us in the future; it would be humanoid, they could kind of pass for us, because I'm not sure that we are. It's a very pessimistic thing to say that we do seem to be wedded to war and destruction and torture and racism and sexism ... we seem to have a xenophobic gene sequence" (n.p.).

This line of reasoning is neither trivial nor fanciful. Once, when asked to comment on the relevance of science fiction, Banks replied: "As the one literature primarily concerned with change and its effects on people and society, SF is—at least potentially—the most important literary form in the world" (SFFWorld 1997, n.p.). His genre writing, both Culture and non–Culture, is true to that viewpoint; Banks took his SF seriously, and in his stories one can always hear, besides and beyond the happy clanging of the space-opera stuff— the crazy cosmology, the hyperspace engines, the giant artifacts, the megabattles, and so on—a quieter voice working its way to us readers through a non-mimetic apprehension of the crucial issues of today, here on Earth. Fantastika is "the planetary form of story" (Clute 2011, 24), and SF is the subset of fantastika designed to worry about writing an Owner's Manual for Planet Earth; Banks knew that, and wrote SF both because he loved the tech and the pyrotechnics and because he wanted to project humanity's future against a larger canvas, like a fire in a cave will cast a man's shadow against the rock, distorting and magnifying it so that features that might have escaped detection before loom large now—Plato's Cave, reversed to make the shadow into a thing more vivid than the reality that projected it.

For this reason alone, if not for the considerable artistry Banks brought to the writing of space opera, the Culture series deserves continued scrutiny from scholars in the field of literary criticism as well as in those of utopian studies, political science, sociology, and philosophy. We have seen that there already is scholarship addressing the Culture not as a literary creation but as a philosophical position, a political argument, and a recipe for future growth here on

Earth (ironically, those writers are altogether more optimistic about us Earthlings' potential for maturation than Banks was). A future therefore exists for the Culture as a subject of study in those areas of human endeavor, and we can justifiably hope that the course of events will bear that expectation out.

Iain Menzies Banks is gone, but his body of work isn't. Between his SF, his non-genre novels, and *Raw Spirit*, we are the lucky heirs to a total of twenty-nine books, all of them worthy of study, discussion, and contextualization. And speaking of contexts, Banks inhabited many in his life—science fiction, mainstream fiction, Scottish culture, left-wing political theory, utopian theory—and all of them interpenetrate each other so that to write about one is to write about the others as well. If I were allowed one wish (small, context-specific genie with a nearly pathological interest in turn-of-the-century Scottish writers), I'd have it be the final breaking down of the largely artificial barriers that separate his SF from his 'Hampstead novels.' Banks hated this externally imposed fracturing of his work, and it would be good to posthumously do him the long-overdue honor of treating his writing as the unspooling of one voice across thirty years of life—because this is the truth. Speaking in 2013 about his recently departed friend, Ken MacLeod said:

> Farah Mendlesohn recently argued in conversation that they [Banks' avowedly mimetic novels] were actually SF set in the present, which illuminates something about them that is often missed by mainstream readers and critics but that SF readers caught onto from the start [Winter 2013, n.p.].

And we did. Moira Martingale's recent *Gothic Dimensions* does address Banks' work as one great, undifferentiated voice modulating the Gothic and post-Gothic modes across genre boundaries, and I myself have attempted to argue something along the same lines in chapter 1. I hope more scholars will add their voices to ours. This book is over, but the enterprise should continue. Happily, we have a lot of work left to do.

Chapter Notes

Introduction

1. Kelly shares this unenviable status with Kirsty Wark of the BBC, who interviewed Banks about three weeks before his passing.
 2. "God, I'd nearly finished the book when I found out. It was bizarre," Banks told Kelly. "Guy was always going to be dying of cancer; the book was always going to be predicated on that, and nothing really changed because of my own bad news. The initial story came about really quickly. Some books take a lot of teasing out and the coming together of previous ideas, but this one jumped in there fully formed in the course of a couple of days back in October 2012" (Kelly 2013 n.p.).
 3. But see Guy's anger at his fate in *The Quarry*. Banks emphatically indicated that Guy is not a literary doppelganger, especially given his character's rage at the knowledge that life will go on without him ("I think that's a stupid point of view," Banks declared. "Apart from anything else, I mean, what did you expect?"). On the other hand, Banks himself admitted that, upon receiving the news of the cancer, "I wrote the bit where Guy says, 'I shall not be disappointed to live all you bastards behind.' It was an exaggeration of what I was feeling, but it was me thinking: 'How can I use this to positive effect?'" (Kelly 2013 n.p.). As customary, there was always something else going on in Banks' thought processes, and his viewpoints always encompassed many facets of a given situation, personal or otherwise.
 4. A slight correction: by the time *Against a Dark Background* saw print, Banks had already published a few non–Culture SF short stories, for example "Scratch" (1987), "Road of Skulls" (1987), and "Odd Attachment" (1989). My choice to mark the "official" opening of the non–Culture strand of Banks' science fiction rests on the contention that he was overwhelmingly a novel writer, and his short-fiction production remains extremely sparse. In fact, with the exception of "The Secret Courtyard" and "Spheres" (both 2010), two pieces dropped from the original manuscripts of—respectively—*Matter* (2008) and *Transition*, Banks wrote no short fiction after 1989. The total count only reaches up to seven (nine with the two excerpts), and two of those are Culture narratives. Without the four non–Culture SF novels Banks published between 1993 and 2009, it's doubtful that those short stories could have constituted a separate entity on their own.
 5. "I never had a guilt-making religious background," he told *The Independent*'s Liz Hoggard in 2007. "I'm lucky to have escaped all that Calvinist nonsense. I think you can live a perfectly moral life as an atheist and a humanist" (n.p.).
 6. See Colebrook, Cox, and Haddock 2013, 5.
 7. Banks recalled another such incident in *Raw Spirit* (276–280).
 8. Banks' meeting with Annie, whom he would marry in 1992 and who would remain his wife until their separation in 2007, is another Mad Iain story. One late night in 1980 Banks walked into the London apartment he shared with some friends to tell them he'd met "this glorious blonde, round about my age" at work. One day he mustered up the courage to ask her out for a drink, and when they got to the pub she surprised him by matching both his choice and his volume of drink—Old Peculiar. "She drank me under

the table," he recalled, "and I had to borrow a fiver from her to get home." For the rest of their life together, Banks and Annie went on a yearly trip to Masham, Yorkshire, where Old Peculiar is brewed. They'd have dinner there on the anniversary of their first date (Hughes 1999 n.p.). Sadly, Annie passed away in 2009, shortly after their divorce had been finalized (Cabell 2014, Kindle location 472).

9. Banks' "petrolhead" days ended in February of 2007, when he sold his entire collection of super-cars (two Porsches, one Jaguar, one BMW, and one ramped-up Land Rover Defender) and bought a hybrid. He was trying to become environmentally more responsible (Jeffries 2007, n.p.).

10. Banks' strongest asset when facing his detractors, however, was his sense of humor—which, in at least one occasion, rubbed off on those around him: In the wake of the initial outrage at the publication of *The Wasp Factory*, someone at Macmillan (Banks never knew who) collected the novel's reviews, both positive and negative, and placed them as blurbs on the back cover of the reprints. To this day, if one picks up *The Wasp Factory* and looks at the back cover, one will find the following declaration from the *Times Literary Supplement*: "A literary equivalent of the nastiest brand of juvenile delinquency." Nestled next to it are several other comments from the *Mail on Sunday* ("A mighty imagination has arrived on the scene"), the London *Times* ("Rubbish"), the *Financial Times* ("Macabre, bizarre, and impossible to put down"), *The Scotsman* ("There's nothing to force you, having been warned, to read it; nor do I recommend it"), and the *Daily Express* ("Read it if you dare"). Unsurprisingly, the novel remains one of Banks' most popular, and the critical acclaim surrounding it has only increased with time.

Throughout the rest of his career, Banks continued to treat his own work with self-effacing humor. When the BBC adaptation of *The Crow Road* was released on DVD, for example, the case carried a comment from him that described the four-part series as "annoyingly better than the book in far too many places," and *Complicity* appeared in print with a review "by the author" that assessed the novel as being "a bit like *The Wasp Factory*, except without the happy ending and redeeming air of cheerfulness" (Chivers 2013b n.p.).

11. This argument does not assume that readers of Banks' mainstream works and readers of his SF were two sharply separated groups. There were plenty of people who, being fond of his writing in every form, happily switched between genres. Precisely for this reason, however, such readers were usually not the ones to complain of immorality on Banks' part.

Chapter 1

1. See Garnett 1989, 52.

2. "I wanted to be a writer from the age of 11," Banks told William Leith of *The Telegraph*. "I have proof of this. At school we were asked to draw, in crayon, what we wanted to be when we grew up. I didn't know how to draw a writer, so I drew an actor. And I put 'and writer' in quite clear letters in the top left-hand corner" (2003, n.p.).

3. He would not have been if his sister, Martha Ann, had survived. She'd been born in 1952 with spina bifida, and had died after only six weeks. Later in life, in *Raw Spirit*, Banks speculated that Martha's loss probably made his parents spoil him even more than would have been normal for an only child (42).

4. It is also possible to argue that a sense of the positive effects resulting from such large-scale, loosely connected family structures later informed his envisioning of the Culture's basic social nucleus.

5. For a complete list of Banks' influences, literary and otherwise, see Colebrook, Cox and Haddock 2013 (1–5), Pattie 2013, Wilson 1994, SFFWorld 1997, Rawlinson 2009, and Rundle 2010.

6. On this seemingly improbable influence, Banks commented: "Of course, I don't think there is much of her work that is identifiable in mine. In fact, I doubt there is a critic out there reading one of my books who will say, 'Oh I think I can see a little Jane Austen in there' ... But that's the thing, you can admire someone, and take inspiration from them, without them actually having a big influence on your work. Although maybe as the writer I am the last person who should say that..." (*SFX* 2012, n.p.).

7. "I am, of course, talking about the same Leonard Cohen who makes music but not a lot of people know that he used to write novels as well. He did two: *Beautiful Losers* and *The Favorite Game*. And guess what?

They are actually pretty good [...] certainly an awful lot better than *Tarantula* by Bob Dylan! Now that was a so-called 'experimental novel' although to me it was just white noise. There was no plot, no filters [...] Leonard Cohen, however, did some impressive work" (*SFX* 2012, n.p.).

8. *Star Wars* in particular played a key role in the development of *Consider Phlebas*: "All of the big action sequences that you see in my book *Consider Phlebas* are only there because I saw *Star Wars* back in 1977. The thing that was so great about *Star Wars* is that it allowed you to think, Oh wow, I could do that too. As an author my effects budget is limitless.' All of the ideas that I thought seemed a bit too mad now didn't seem mad at all. I had stuff in my mind that I put into the category of 'lunatic ideas.' Like writing about a fistfight under a giant hovercraft. Before *Star Wars* you would think about that and say to yourself, 'You know, maybe that is a bit too James Bond, no one could possibly take that seriously.' But after *Star Wars* all of that was okay. It became okay to do complete spectacle. So, yeah, *Consider Phlebas* only really exists because of *Star Wars*" (*SFX* 2012, n.p.).

9. Next to the determination, in fact, there also seems to have been a great deal of happiness to Banks' approach to the struggle of becoming a successful writer. In 1990, he said this to *Science Fiction Eye*'s Michael Cobley: "I used to think, suppose that the heavens opened, the clouds parted, and this big hand comes down and a voice says, 'BANKSIE!—READ THIS!' And it's a big stone tablet that says 'Banksie, you will never, ever, ever publish a work of fiction of any sort in your entire life during the future course of the universe!' The *ultimate* rejection slip, a rejection slip from the universe, from God! And I thought—no, I'll still write. I might not write as often, but I'd still do it because I enjoy writing. And I enjoy giving it round to my friends. So even if I didn't get published, I'd still do it. I enjoy getting my thoughts down on the page" (1990, 26).

10. Readers familiar with *Stand on Zanzibar* will recognize a few points of connection between Brunner's novel and *TTR*—for example, the chaotic near-future scenario, the limited conflict between superpowers (in Brunner it's between the U.S. and China), and the small nation caught between the large players on the world stage (in Brunner it's Beninia, a fictional African state). On the other hand, *Catch-22*'s influence seems to have expressed itself more in the tone and the language than in the situation—the puns, the perversely arbitrary nature of the war's conduct, and the reversals of meaning implicit in such notions as Mongoliana's "Dependence Day" celebration. However, the reader should keep in mind that, since *TTR* has never appeared in print, the only information we have on it comes from Banks' own synopsis. It is therefore difficult to make parallels with confidence, and those above should be treated as speculation rather than informed deduction.

11. "Say you're describing a chandelier," Banks reminisced with William Leith in 2003. "You would have a character who was drinking shandy and leered at somebody. It's that bad, I'm afraid ... I used to count up my pun-to-word ratio and the best I ever did, I managed to get it below 10. I got my pun ratio down to 9.8 to one. Less than every tenth word is a pun. It's difficult" (n.p.). Ken MacLeod remembers this phase as the notable characteristic in his first experiences of his friend's writing: "My first encounter with Iain's writing was these collages that he produced, where he wrote these crackpot texts, rather obviously derived from Terry Gilliam films, illustrated with cuttings from Sunday supplements. They were quite funny, politically provocative, with tanks and guns and sex all juxtaposed in alarming ways but the stories were just ludicrous handwritten exercises in puns" (Hughes 1999, n.p.). The cuttings from Sunday supplements would be, in this case, a carry-over from *Stand on Zanzibar*). Evidently, they both agreed that neither *The Hungarian Lift-Jet* nor *TTR* deserved to be unleashed onto the reading public.

12. Later in life, Banks would also find inspiration in the work of the environmental activist George Monbiot and the political economist Will Hutton (MacLeod 2013, n.p.).

13. In 1990, in the *Science Fiction Eye* interview, Banks told Michael Cobley that, by the time he encountered *New Worlds* on a revolving stand at Gourock Station, the magazine was a quarterly paperback (1990, 28). *NW*'s switch from monthly to quarterly went into effect at the beginning of 1971, and the fact that Banks found his first issue at Gourock's train station suggests that he was

either on his way home from Stirling for a visit or going back to Stirling after a visit home—thus, the most probable date for Banks' first encounter with the New Wave would be 1972 or 1973.

14. Banks' actual political choices at the time of voting, however, were not as monolithic as this brief summary may lead one to believe. In 2007, for example, he told *The Independent*'s Liz Hoggard that, since he'd heard that the SNP "will guarantee the Catholic adoption agencies a get-out from the Sexual Orientation Regulations Act ... 'I'll probably waste my vote on some extreme leftwing candidate as usual'" (Hoggard 2007, n.p.). That "as usual" at the end suggests that Banks often ended up making highly personalized choices when it came to supporting political figures.

15. The exception was the first draft of *Against a Dark Background*, a non-Culture SF novel Banks wrote in 1977. After substantial rewriting, it was eventually published in 1993. The sources utilized to establish the chronology of Banks' early works are Garnett 1989, 51–69; Cobley 1990, 22–32; Colebrook, Cox, and Haddock 2013, 1–8.

16. In the United States, on the other hand, the novel fared quite differently. It was originally supposed to come out six months after the British edition in order to capitalize on whatever hype it would garner there, but "management changes at Harpers and Row meant that they [both editions] were issued at the same time." The result was that the American edition "was marketed as a straight science fiction novel in the States and disappeared without a trace" (qtd. in Colebrook 2013, 30).

17. These symbolic meanings extend to Franks' possessions. For instance, he has bestowed upon his trusty trowel, which he uses to dig the holes for the Sacrifice Poles, the name Stoutstroke (9), and he calls the miniature catapult he uses for hunting and self-defense the Black Destroyer (33). His bike is called Gravel (50).

18. In keeping with Frank's penchant for bestowing symbolic monikers, each death-chamber has been given a name that, in his mind, resonates mystically with the chamber's nature—for example, the Boiling Pool, the Spider's Parlour, the Venus Cave, the Volt Chamber, and the Blade Corridor.

19. Banks is having fun here. Graham Park and Steven Grout are exaggerated exemplars of the two sides in the tubercular old argument pitting mimetic literature against fantastika. Graham is a rather conceited young man, constantly worried about how others—principally but not exclusively Sara—will judge him. He considers himself a "serious" artist, which he takes to mean someone who only draws from reality, and holds science fiction in a certain amount of contempt. Aside from his dismissive responses to Slater's repeated requests for feedback on his ideas for SF stories, he does not want others to find him reading it—once, waiting for Sara in her apartment, he picks up a copy of Douglas Adams' *The Restaurant at the End of the Universe* and examines it for a while before "put[ting] the book back. Although it was funny, it was rather *light* reading; he wanted Sara to find him reading something more impressive" (266–267). Steven Grout, by contrast, lies at the far end on the other side of the spectrum—he's the dysfunctional fan who takes SF to be exactly the case of the world ("Escapism, they called it," he thinks at one point of his enemies' anti–SF propaganda. "Oh, they were clever all right!"). Throughout most of the novel, Banks' third-person narration paints Steven as socially inept and awkward, excessively suspicious of the unremarkable at the same time as he is astonishingly credulous about the strange. On the street he jumps from car to car, seeking shelter from vehicles on the road because he believes that every one of them carries lasers in their wheels' axles, and the thought patterns he weaves to justify his reality frame are the quintessential example of a deluded psyche:

> He wondered how many people in all the mental hospitals in the country—or the world, come to that—were really fallen Warriors who had either cracked up from the strain of trying to live in this hell-hole, or simply made the wrong choice and thought that the test was just seeing through the whole thing and then having the courage to stand out and make that challenge. Well, he wasn't going to end up like one of those poor bastards [27].

It's the third plotline, that of Quiss and Ajayi, which gives the first two another, entirely more serious dimension.

20. But look at the metatextual connections with Ursula Le Guin's *The Lathe of Heaven* (1971), a novel featuring a protagonist named James Orr whose dreams have

the power to alter reality, and *Catch-22*, where Orr is the name of the pilot in Yossarian's squadron who keeps getting shot down over the sea and who, one day, simply rows away beyond the horizon and is never seen again. At the end of the novel, Yossarian finds out that Orr has survived his long sea voyage and now resides in Sweden.

21. The circular bruise on Orr's chest, we eventually discover, comes from the mark the car's steering wheel left on the same area of Alex Lennox's body.

22. The four chapters in Coma are grouped under "metaphormosis," those in Triassic under "Metamorpheus," and those in Eocene under "Metamorphosis."

23. "Very well, you of the minced cortex; do what comes so naturally to you and let's get on with it," the familiar tells the Barbarian at one point. Without comprehending that he's just been insulted, the Conan-doppelganger follows the advice and kills everyone in the room (101).

24. Frank mentions these novels as two of the rare presents Angus ever bought him, and which Frank had therefore "assiduously avoided reading" (51). Together, they represent a cruel joke on Angus' part: *The Tin Drum* (one of Banks' early influences) is the story of Oskar, a boy of great beauty who, upon reaching the age of three—the same age as Frank at the time of the false accident—decides he will not grow up any more. We hear the story from Oskar himself, now an old man confined in an asylum, and of course it is entirely possible that everything he's telling us may be a hallucination or a lie. *Myra Breckinridge*, on the other hand, is written from the viewpoint of a man who, while he is still undergoing the process of sexual reassignment surgery, takes on the identity of a woman. Frank does not comment on whether he is aware of the general gist of the plot of either book, but whatever the case, we are confronted with two instances of metafictional doubling: *The Tin Drum* echoes the problematic nature of Frank's hold on reality and comments on his arrested development, his butterfly impalement on the wheel of time, while *Myra Breckinridge* presents us with another tale of sexual alteration—albeit a willing one, in the case of the novel's eponymous protagonist. Also, the possibility that, had Frank read both (or either) novels, he might have guessed his true identity earlier, feels like a particularly painful twist, all the more so because Frances never discovers the joke her father had perpetrated at her expense.

25. Perhaps the most relevant instance occurs at the beginning of chapter 4, when Frank significantly compares himself to a country (62–64).

26. And the only reason why John is a ward to begin with resides in the challenge his unknown provenance and his amnesia present to Dr. Joyce, his therapist. John Orr is, in other words, an interesting experimental subject.

Chapter 2

1. A more personal reason also contributed to the choice of a split name:
I used the "M" occasionally, not always... but then some of my family were a bit upset that I'd dropped it. "Are you ashamed of being a Menzies?" ... So I decided to keep my own name but put the "M" in, which seemed like a good idea at the time but was a terrible mistake, because I've been answering that question ever since, and it does give ammunition to the literary snobs who think I make the distinction because I'm "writing down" when I do science fiction [Wilson 1994, n.p.].

Irrespective of the reasons for the choice, there are now two Bankses: Iain Banks, the writer of edgy, challenging literature, and Iain M. Banks, writer of fun but ultimately dismissible escapist fiction. This dichotomy, irrelevant and in any case inaccurate from day one, still holds at the time of writing, although somewhat reduced in sharpness.

2. In his introduction to the 1964 Faber & Faber edition of Charles Harness' *The Paradox Men*, which had originally been published in 1955 as part of an Ace Double. An excerpt from *The Paradox Men* also appears in the 1974 collection Aldiss edited.

3. On the resurgence of space opera in the late '80s and early '90s, see the time-lagged dialogue in the pages of *Extrapolation* between Patricia Monk (1992, 295–316) and Gary Westfahl (1994, 176–185).

4. As John Clute observes, the name "does sound awfully like moneylender" (1995b, 29).

5. In fact, the Culture does employ one lone Changer, but at the time of the incident on Schar's World, we eventually find out, she

is on an important task unconnected to the war on the other side of the galaxy (92).

6. Horza's presence on Schar's World was, in fact, the result of punishment. At the beginning of the war, he had discovered a plot on the part of some Changers to reignite their homeworld's ancient engines and steer the asteroid back into neutral space, thus avoiding having to fight for the Idirans. After Horza killed two of the conspirators and violated the Changers' golden rule that no Changer should take another's life, the Academy of Military Arts packed him up to Schar's World to get him out of public sight (102–103).

7. Fal 'Ngeestra's hobby, and her insistence to practice it without oversight, actually lands her in the worst trouble she ever gets in the novel: when we meet her, she's been wearing a splint for a week in the aftermath of a fall that left her alone in the cold for two days before she was rescued. Jase keeps reminding her of that (86).

8. Many years later, in a 2010 interview with *SFX*, Banks explained why the figure of the Culture Referer never appeared again in any other story: "I always thought that was one of my weaker inventions in *Phlebas*! After thousands of years of artificial intelligence, the idea that the AI couldn't do all this themselves is silly. I did make the point that they were being studied for how they could be so intuitive, but I was uncomfortable with it though so they were never going to survive long! Basically: the AI Minds have got better at doing that stuff themselves so they're no longer required" (Golder 2010).

9. The ultimate tragedy of Yalson's death, and of the death of their child, is that the only reason why she and Horza could have offspring lies in her parentage, which is half Culture from her mother's side. From her, Yalson had inherited the Culture's genofixing, which allowed crossbreeding. Shortly before the final disaster, the final horrified witnessing of his lover's death, Horza embraces Yalson and his would-be child, happily accepting the chance to have a family (and therefore an identity; 362–364).

10. The irony here is that Horza is killed by one of the biologicals he supported, who wielded as a weapon the helpless body of one of the machines he hated—a machine which, despite his contempt, had tried to help him.

11. In a 2000 article, William Hardesty pointed out that, besides the fundamental structural connection to Phlebas the Phoenician, Horza should also reminds us of another character from one of fantastika's key turn-of-the-century texts. Horza's death, Hardesty wrote, "recapitulates Kurtz's in *Heart of Darkness*" (119).

Chapter 3

1. They informed his life as well. Early in his career, Banks used to design games, although by his admission they were fiendishly complicated and therefore unmarketable (Garnett 1989, 65). His personal favorite among all the games he purchased and played was, unsurprisingly, *Civilization* (Slocombe 2013, 139).

2. In his article for *Science Fiction Eye*, Lawrence Person indicates a precedent for The Player of Games' plotline: it's a story by Charles V. De Vet and Katherine MacLean entitled "Second Game," first published as a short story in 1958 and later expanded into a novel in 1962 (Person 1990, 35).

3. Damage in *Consider Phlebas* is a good example of a game that expands beyond its traditional envelope to literally affect the lives of others. In the novel (195–196), Damage is a card game whose workings are described in terms vaguely reminiscent of those of poker, except that the cards in each player's hands are connected to electronic fields with which that player can influence any other player's mind-state, thus inducing every sort of emotion in their target—love and hate, joy and despair, even powerful suicidal tendencies. Thus, all players of Damage gamble with their life. Also, all players have at their disposal a certain number of Lives, one of which they lose every time someone else wins a hand out of which they didn't withdraw early enough. Those Lives are actual people, tied to chairs next to their player owner. When a player loses a Life, that Life loses his/hers.

4. This whole argument assumes, of course, that we can take Frank at his word, that Steven is not in fact a warrior from another dimension, and that the shadow-world of the bridge was a psychogenic fantasy. All these assumptions are problematic because, once again, the uncertainty of fantastika makes the results of any attempt at assessment nebulous at best. The only reason why they appear here is that, in the aftermath of

Phlebas' publication, a mode of writing opened up for Banks in comparison to which works like *Factory, Glass,* and *The Bridge* became relatively "realistic."

5. For the sake of simplicity, I'm assuming that the narrator borrows the author's gender.

6. In keeping with her name, Yay is possessed of a generally bubbly disposition and an optimistic outlook, both of which stand in sharp contrast to Gurgeh's often purposefully bleak reflections.

7. Mawhrin-Skel tricks Gurgeh into making a mistake open to blackmail. Faced with the possibility of winning a game—interestingly called "Stricken"—by achieving a "Full Web," something nobody in the Culture has been able to do before, Gurgeh accepts Mawhrin-Skel's offer to scan the contents of certain pieces that should remain secret. After the game, which Gurgeh has won but not with the Full Web (46–54), the drone comes to him and reveals the recording of the moment they made the deal; either Gurgeh accepts SC's offer *and* speaks in favor of Mawhrin-Skel's reinstatement or the recording goes public, thus crippling his reputation—a considerable threat, since one's good standing with others is the one form of currency the Culture supports in its day-to-day dealings (55–59).

8. We know the Lesser Cloud as the Lesser Magellanic Cloud.

9. The first time occurs a very short while before, when Flere-Imsaho bluntly begins his explanation of the events taking place behind the curtains with this opening: "You've been used, Jernau Gurgeh" (295).

10. When at a reception Gurgeh asks a young woman whether it wouldn't be possible for females to play each other in the first round, when the draw is supposed to be left to chance, she replies that things have never worked out that way in all the centuries since the creation of the game (137).

11. By far the worst of those scenes occur about two-thirds into the novel, when Flere-Imsaho helps Gurgeh out of a moment of loss of self-confidence in the wake of a bad day on the Azad boards—he is about to lose the current game to a Judge of the Supreme Court. The drone takes him on a tour of the Azadian capital's real nightlife, the one the empire had been keen on hiding behind excesses of pageantry, and what Gurgeh sees and hears on the streets is so much for him that he has to ask Flere-Imsaho to stop the tour and take him back to the module they call home (202–207). Once there, Flere-Imsaho shows Gurgeh one last item of horror: an unscrambled live video feed from one of the prisons, in which so-called enemies of the states are subjected to the worst kinds of violation (209). Upon witnessing what the legal system of which his present opponent is one of the highest representatives visits on its own citizens, Gurgeh enters a state of preternaturally cold, unspeaking rage. He spends the night glaring at a holographic representation of the Azad board he's playing on and, in the morning, he proceeds to dismantle the judge's game as if the apex hadn't even been there to play in the first place (211–215).

12. The definition quoted above is delivered on the occasion of Gurgeh's visit to an opulent country estate where, to mitigate the embarrassment of his continuing victories on the Azad boards, he is offered free use of every one in the place—men, women, apices. He can commit whatever sexual crime he wants while there, in exchange for withdrawing from the competition. A particularly chilling moment occurs when, to prove the level of licence that Azadian elites enjoy when it comes to breaking their own rules, one of Gurgeh's hosts points to the band playing in the background and tells him that most of the instruments are made of bone—Azadian bone, often extracted without anesthesia (222).

13. Like Flere-Imsaho, the *Limiting Factor* isn't actually demilitarized. In fact, it's pretty well cannoned-up and capable of single-handedly taking on the whole Azadian navy (297).

14. Thus, the narrator's announcement at the beginning of *Player* that the story "ends with a game that is not a game" comes to fruition, and from many different points of view. First, Azad was never just a game to begin with—it was also the reality of the Empire. Secondly, the context of the game was utterly eclipsed by the context of a larger play that involved Azad (game and empire) as one of the playing pieces. Thirdly, that final match was never just a game to Nicosar, and once Gurgeh understood for what stakes the Azadian apex was playing, it stopped being just a game for him as well.

15. The dating of *The Player of Games'* timeline comes in the form of a brief aside

about the age of the *Limiting Factor*, which had been built "seven hundred and sixteen years earlier in the closing stages of the Idiran war, when the conflict in space was almost over" (104). That would place the events in *Player* around the year AD 2083 on Earth, if we work out the date from the Idiran war's timeline in *Consider Phlebas*' appendices.

Chapter 4

1. Thus, from an Earth-relative perspective, we can place both the writing of the manuscript and the events in *Use of Weapons* around the year AD 2092.

2. But remember the pseudo-bibliographical information below the "Appendices" title at the end of *Consider Phlebas*—we have been contacted, at some point in our hopefully not too distant future.

3. Thus, Linter becomes the latest in an increasingly longer line of malcontents, which by now includes Yalson and Balveda from *Phlebas*, Gurgeh from *Player*, and the character of Wrobik from "A Gift from the Culture" (see chapter 5, note 2).

4. See for example her commentary on Cold-War Berlin, East and West (106–109), or her impressions while walking around New York City (144–145).

5. It must be noted, however, that Li'ndane has no kind words for communism either. The leftist utopia of the Culture resembles Earthside communist/socialist systems only in the acknowledgment of a preferable principle of wealth distribution, as evidenced by Sma's reference to Leon Trotsky as the positive figure within that socioeconomic philosophy. In every other respect, the Culture is literally and figuratively light-years away from any arrangement existing on our planet.

6. At the end of Li's electoral speech, after the applause has died down, Sma and a few others carry him to the Ship's rec area and throw him into the swimming pool, fusing the lightsaber (141). After the elections, he begins to refer to himself as the *Arbitrary*'s "captain in exile" and starts betting against the ship on everything from horse races to soccer games. The *Arbitrary* cheats in Li's favor and ends up owing him a monstrous amount of money, and because Li insists on payment, the ship makes him "a flawless cut diamond the size of his fist. It was his, the ship told him. A gift; he could *own* it." Naturally, Li loses interest in the diamond after that, and in the end persuades the *Arbitrary* to put the stone in orbit around Neptune on its way out of the solar system as a joke (142).

7. See for example pp. 110–113.

8. While the *Arbitrary*, Li, and Linter corral Sma's attitude from within the memoir, it's Skaffen-Amtiskaw that counters it from without. He appears in the memoir as its editor with a number of funny, dry, deprecating footnotes counterpointing her narrative flow.

9. We know this because Fal 'Ngeestra in *Consider Phlebas* reflects on just such a rowdy upbringing in one of the *State of play* interludes (332–333).

10. Given Banks' atheism, and considering that the Culture universe is pointedly without gods, this is as close as the narrative ever comes to hinting that Linter may have made a terrible mistake.

11. This is why the dedication at the beginning of *Use of Weapons* reads: "I blame Ken MacLeod for the whole thing. It was his idea to argue the old warrior out of retirement, and he suggested the fitness program, too."

12. By the same token, Horza performs this role in *Phlebas*, and Dervley Linter performs it in *The State of the Art* (one could also make a case for the whole of planet Earth also figuring in this process).

13. So, if he's this unhinged, why did the Culture pick Zakalwe? The answer is that Zakalwe and Beychae know each other too well for anything but the genuine article to work—no stand-ins, no replacements (21–22).

14. On one occasion, in the aftermath of a mission in which Zakalwe's body was crippled beyond repair and only his head could be saved, Skaffen-Amtiskaw sends him a present via Sma—it's a hat (125–128).

15. The name of the ship is one of the memories comprising the set that haunts Zakalwe throughout the novel—and yet, perversely, or perhaps because he feels that he doesn't deserve to forget, he himself purposefully uses the name in the Voerenhutz mission (154).

16. This last sentence, which refers to Skaffen-Amtiskaw's effort to save Zakalwe, carries a hint that the drone too is trying to atone for its past.

17. Another important connection be-

tween the two titles is that Zakalwe is, in a very real sense, a player of games as well—wargames, to be specific. Gurgeh is a generalist, but Zakalwe specializes. Of course, this consideration would next lead us to a view of Sma, Skaffen-Amtiskaw, and the whole of SC as wargamers, each with a certain skill set and a certain operational envelope.

18. If this interpretation is valid, then there may be slight mistake in timing on Banks' part. Properly speaking, Year Zero was AD 1975, not 1977.

19. It must be pointed out that, as far as classical academia is concerned, reviews aren't serious critical work. John Clute himself wrote a beautifully scathing expose of this state of things in an article entitled "What I did on my Summer Vacation." Originally published in 1998 the journal *Paradoxa*, the article was later reprinted twice in two successively revised versions—the first was for the book *Scores: Reviews 1993–2003* (Beccon 2003), and the second for *Pardon This Intrusion: Fantastika in the World Storm* (Beccon 2011).

20. A strange attitude from the author of a well-known space-opera series of the 1990s, whose first volume—*Take Back Plenty*—came out in the same year as *Use of Weapons*.

Chapter 5

1. The two short stories, "A Gift from the Culture" and "Descendant," both appeared in 1987, the first in *Interzone* #20 and the second in the anthology *Tales from the Forbidden Planet*, edited by Roz Kaveney. The case for "Descendant" belonging to the Culture universe is complicated by the absence of actual references to the Culture itself (although the story does feature a module, a drone, knife missiles, and an intelligent suit), and this uncertainty is actually welcome: the story is a disturbing yarn halfway between space opera and Gothicism in which a damaged, sentient suit and its equally wounded human operator are the only survivors of an attack on their module; after landing on a barren, dusty planet, they have to trudge through a seemingly endless landscape to reach the closest friendly outpost. During the walk, as both man and machine get weaker and their pain increases, it becomes progressively more difficult to tell the thoughts of one from the other. When, at the end of the story, only the suit reaches the outpost alive, we are left with the slightest hint that it may literally have cannibalized the human inside. We don't get to find out what really happened; we can only suspect (29–49). "A Gift from the Culture," on the other hand, presents us with a more familiar—albeit scarcely more cheerful—scenario: Wrobik used to be a Culture citizen, a Contact operative, and a woman. Now, after a sex change, he lives in the Vreccile Economic Community, a small, corrupt starfaring civilization that would have elicited a cautious nod of approval from the Empire of Azad (probably followed by a full-scale invasion). He has a boyfriend, Maust, and a lot of debts to settle with a group of scary people who, in return for wiping the ledger, give him a gun that can only be operated by a Culture human—his job is to destroy the spaceship carrying an important military figure back to the capital, Vreccile City. When Wrobik hears that a Culture ambassador is also on board, he tries to run away. The mobsters then capture Maust and use him as leverage, at which point Wrobik does what they want and, at the end of the story, blends into the crowd, running away along with everyone else (7–22).

2. The page numbers refer to the version of "A Few Notes on the Culture" that Night Shade press reprinted in their 2004 edition of *The State of the Art*. The essay appears at the end of the collection, but those who'd rather read it on its own can find it either at http://www.vavatch.co.uk/books/banks/cultnote.htm or at http://nuwen.net/culture.html (content-wise, there is no difference between these two online versions and the printed one). The original version, whose wording differs slightly from that of the others, still exists at https://groups.google.com/forum/#!searchin/rec.arts.sf.written/a$20few$20notes$20on$20the$20Culture/rec.arts.sf.written/RMeezCFdROs/wuT-QSbjBSsJ, complete with MacLeod's prefatory blurb.

3. At this point, one might object that such mild treatment of a murderer would be disrespectful toward his/her/its victim and their loved ones, not to mention unjust in first-principle terms. On this topic, it's useful to consider this assessment of the Culture's views on retribution—on the part of Zakalwe, of all people. Speaking to the Ethnarch Kerian, leader of another Azad-analogue society, Zakalwe explains that the

way the Culture deals with people like him is to remove them from their seat of power and put them in places that don't really look like prisons at all. There, those tyrants will spend the rest of their days in tranquility and safety, unable to leave but otherwise untroubled and free from danger:

> And though some would say the nice people are too soft, the soft, nice people would say that the crimes committed by the bad people are usually so terrible there is no known way of making the bad people start to suffer even a millionth of the agony and despair they have produced, so what is the point in retribution? It would be just another obscenity to cap the tyrant's life with his own death [Banks 1992 32].

Unfortunately for the Ethnarch, this is not the Zakalwe who still works for SC. "I'm freelance now," he tells Kerian before gunning him down without batting an eyelid (34).

4. Banks writes: "Culture names act as an address if the person concerned stays where they were brought up. Let's take an example: Balveda, from *Consider Phlebas*. Her full name is Juboal-Rabaroansa Perosteck Alseyn Balveda dam T'seif. The first part tells you she was born/brought up on Rabaroan Plate, in the Juboal stellar system (where there is only one Orbital in a system, the first part of a name will often be the name of the Orbital rather than the star); Perosteck is her given name (almost invariably the choice of one's mother), Alseyn is her chosen name ... Balveda is her family name (usually one's mother's family name) and T'seif is the house/estate she was raised within. The 'sa' affix on the first part of her name would translate into 'er' in English (we might all start our names with 'Sun-Earther', in English, if we were to adopt the same nomenclature), and the 'dam' part is similar to the German 'von'" (186). Just to make sure we know he means what he says, Banks signs off at the end of "A Few Notes" by using both his Earth name of Iain M. Banks and his Culture name of "Sun-Earther Iain El-Bonko Banks of North Queensferry" (188).

5. To this list we should also add Wrobik from "A Gift from the Culture." Like Gurgeh in the early stages of *Player*, he was bored in the culture, and like Linter, he thought that the ethics of the Contact section of which he was part were nothing more than a thin smokescreen to justify doing the same bad things everyone else was doing—"I refused to live with such hypocrisy," he says, "and chose instead this honestly selfish and avaricious society, which doesn't pretend to be good, just ambitious" (13). After eight years of living in the VEC, however, Wrobik has started regretting his choice: "My great adventure, my renunciation of what seemed to me sterile and lifeless to plunge into a more vital society, my grand gesture [...] well, now it seemed like an empty gesture, now it looked like a stupid, petulant thing to have done" (11). There are clear echoes of Linter's own arguments in Wrobik's thought processes, but it is anyone's guess whether Linter, had he lived, would also have come to regret remaining on Earth like Sma and the *Arbitrary* thought.

6. In this, Banks came relatively close to Gene Roddenberry, who believed in a similar marriage of high tech and compassion as a way of ushering in a utopian society—and again, a moneyless one, although neither Roddenberry nor the writers who followed him on *Star Trek*'s various incarnations throughout the years did much to explain how such a setup could function.

7. Kulbicki also mentions the one key figure in utopian studies who did address Banks' work, however fleetingly: "Darko Suvin, perhaps the most eminent of science fiction scholars, does, at least, mention Banks, but only to say that the 'Culture' series is '[a] lucid variant at [the] margin' of what he calls the 'fallible dystopia,' but without any consideration of how this 'variant' might trouble the integrity of the category in question" (34).

8. For a brief account of Moylan's activities within the political movements of those times, see his introduction to the 2014 Ralahine Classics edition of *Demand the Impossible* (x–xiii, note 3).

9. See Sargisson 2014, 231; Weeks 2014, 248–250; Kulbicki 2009, 36; and Levitas 2014, 257.

10. But note that, at the same time as he recognizes "the stubborn utopian quality of Robinson's sf" (105), Moylan also indicates Robinson's own Orange County trilogy, and *Gold Coast* (1988) in particular, as key examples of critical dystopias (203–221).

11. See Lyman Tower Sargent's "The Three Faces of Utopianism Revisited" in the January 1994 issue of *Utopian Studies* (1–37), and Moylan 2000, 183–199.

12. And what about critical dystopia? Does Banks have anything to say on that score as well? It would be interesting to conduct a systematized reading of the three non–Culture space operas—and particularly *The Algebraist* (2004)—as critical dystopias, since each begins under far from ideal circumstances and develops throughout the text a concerted set of responses aimed at altering the original dystopia for the better.

13. Also see Brown 1996, 57–73.

14. See also Darko Suvin's formulation of the nature of utopia as a literary genre in chapter 3 of *Metamorphoses of Science Fiction* (1979; 37–62). Of particular relevance here is Suvin's point that, because the literary utopia is "the verbal construction of a particular quasi-human community where sociopolitical institutions, norms, and individual relationships are organized according to a more perfect principle than in the author's community" (49), its operating principle is a constant process of argument, refinement, and response: "literary utopia—and every description of utopia is literary—is a heuristic device for perfectibility, an epistemological and not an ontological entity" (52). That is to say, the argument of utopia should not just precede (and survive) the potential realization of a locale for a more perfect social principle—it should actually build the locale itself, and keep it in good repair (so to speak) through constant reassessment and refinement.

15. Also see Lyman Tower Sargent's argument for the existence of critical utopias that *preceded* those discussed in *Demand* (242–247), as well as Gyb Prettyman's assessment of the usefulness of the ideas contained in *Demand* beyond their relatively narrow historical and geographic boundaries (251–256).

16. According to Ronnie Lippens, however, the Culture isn't even a utopia in the proper sense of the term. In an article written for *Utopian Studies* in 2002, Lippens argues that "Banks's aim in his series of Culture books has never been to paint a fully developed Utopia. However, the Culture, as it appears and develops throughout Banks's series, certainly has some utopian dimensions about it" (135). This is difficult to accept, however, especially given the vantage point from which Lippens was writing—by 2002, all but three Culture books had seen print, and there were already plenty of details and views of the society from a plethora of perspectives. Lippens himself invites further complications by essentially abandoning his statement and moving on to the topic at hand, which consists in his intention "to use some striking features of Banks's imaginary worlds and his imaginary technological utopia, the Culture in particular, to speculate on how one could possibly rethink peace—utopian peace—as the outcome or product of specific technological cultures" (135). The irony is that, during his discussion of those features, Lippens describes the Culture's setup in precisely the kind of detail that would satisfy any reasonable requirement on that score.

Chapter 6

1. Here Banks takes care to tell us that, even by the obsolete technological standards of those days (the *Problem Child*'s mind is described as an AI core, fully sentient but nowhere near the capabilities of the Minds of the present time; 66), Zreyn Tramow was more of a figurehead than an actual Captain (69).

2. Two points of reference are provided: the first is a comment made in passing by the GSV *Wisdom Like Silence* that mentions "the Azadian Matter" (117), and the second involves the history of one of the storage facilities inside which the Culture had decided, at the end of the Idiran War, to preserve a tiny part of its military fleet against the eventuality of future troubles. This storage facility, a huge conglomeration of rock and other matter called Pittance, was discovered a thousand years before the events in *Excession*, and its conversion to its current use took place five hundred years after that, at the end of hostilities (144).

3. In this sense, the name of the ship has a somewhat ambivalent meaning, potentially referring both to morally slippery territories and to the similarly colored expanse of a biological brain.

4. This helps explain, among other things, why the Culture didn't know about Zakalwe's true past in *Use of Weapons*, and why the *Grey Area*'s obsession with plundering the brains of biologicals is frowned upon with such vehemence in *Excession*.

5. Fourteen years after *Excession*'s appearance, the next-to-last Culture novel, *Surface Detail*, provided a precise quantifi-

cation of the power of such a vessel: a single large GSV, one of the characters explains, would be capable of taking on a combined fleet of 230,000,000 low-tech warships, even if they came at it all at once (383).

6. See for example the sub-plot involving the GSV *Yawning Angel* (236–248), or that involving the AhForgetIt Tendency citizen named Leffid Ispanteli (186–192, 199–204, 291–292, 447).

7. See for instance the eventual fate of two Culture humans: Gestra Ishmethit, who lives inside the ship depot the Affront take over and dies at their hands (143–152, 220–227, 449–450), and Zreyn Tramow, the "captain" of the *Problem Child* to whom the *Sleeper Service* gives a new body when it reawakens her (449–450).

8. And to an extent he does, chiefly through the *Grey Area*'s presence in the story. Early on, the renegade GCU probes the mind of a retired commandant belonging to a civilization that managed to complete on their planet what the Nazis failed to finish here, and the fate of this flesh sentient—who had been a very good soldier indeed—when the Mind is done unearthing the truth fully bears out the other Culture Minds' perception of the *Grey Area* as vengeful (45–52). Also, both Ulver Seich and Genar-Hofoen have strange, unsettling conversation with that Mind once the GCU picks them up on its way to the *Sleeper Service* (338–341, 346–347). In a narrative characterized by such a strangely dynamic sense of mercy and ultimate comedic happiness, the *Grey Area* serves as a localized reminder of the potential savagery of sentience, a reminder that is itself circumscribed by the social ostracism its own taboo-breaking behavior causes. To those instances of beyond-the-pale behavior we should also add the brief scenes featuring Affronters capturing small, undefended Culture vessels in the early hours of what they believe will be a glorious war (290–294), and the paragraph describing the self-termination of the Mind inside the module that, on the Affront's home planet, had played home to Genar-Hofoen in his capacity as the Culture ambassador to Issorile (297–300). These brief passages do not turn *Excession* into a farce or a tragedy, but they do constitute a counterpoint arguably designed to remind us that, in fiction, comedy—like tragedy—is a choice of viewpoint, and that one can easily morph into the other at any moment and not necessarily with much of a warning.

9. A revealing statement, since Jane Austen was, as we have seen in the introduction, one of Banks' main influences. Banks worried that, despite his love for Austen's novels, there was nothing in his overall writing style to show that influence, but clearly something must have bled through.

10. Mary Branscombe also remarked on the changes in speed and tone. In the review she penned for *SFX* at the time of *Excession*'s publication, she wrote: "*Excession* is painted large on Banks' usual mind-boggling vast canvas—genocide on a planetary scale is just a throwaway scene, an entire race subliming (just to get away from those annoying neighbours) a mere reference during a discussion about why the Culture is still determinedly corporeal ... The Minds are quite at home with the covert military euphemisms, unintelligible tech-speak, info-babble and acronyms that spatter their messages" (Branscombe 1996a, 81).

11. Both the sizes and the types of font represent the best approximation to the actual sizes and types used in *Excession*.

12. Thus, the *Sleeper Service*'s decision to become a covert member of SC was also motivated by personal reasons—hence the narrative's constant return to that forty-year timespan. The aftermath of the human lovers' breakup was traumatic enough, in fact, that the GSV, which had until then been calling itself the *Quietly Confident*, renamed itself with its current moniker and started storing people in suspended animation—to whose numbers we should also add Dajeil herself (355).

13. The note finds another mention in the reprinted version of David Langford's review that appeared in his collection *Up Through an Empty House of Stars* (2003). This new version carries a coda in which Langford writes: "Now that *Inversions* has been loose on the world for years, it seems safe to add that the significantly capitalized word near the beginning is 'Culture'" (215).

14. For the sake of completeness, this book will address the original hardcover edition.

15. To my knowledge, neither ever addressed the deletion, although I am far from certain I have been able to hunt down every possible source.

16. Also see Langford 2003, 214.

17. DeWar's stories of Lavishia bear a strong resemblance to the fairy-tale version of the Culture that Zakalwe gives the Ethnarch Kerian in *Use of Weapons* (26–34). Zakalwe's story even includes the notion of SC agents becoming the trusted physicians of powerful rulers.

18. The relationship between DeWar and Perrund, already complex and full of secrets to begin with, is further complicated by an element of gaming Banks injects into the Tassasen storyline. The presence of a child like Lattens creates plenty of chances for both Perrund and DeWar—each of whom is, in some way, fulfilling a subset of their duties—to both play and game (for a definition of the two terms, see Huizinga 1955 and Slocombe 2013), and the few times they are left alone together they often engage in tabletop games. Both sets of entertainment contain aspects of performativity and gameplaying—for example, DeWar interprets the role of a cartoonishly evil Landescion Baron when he and Lattens play a wargame together (205–214)—but in the case of the games DeWar plays with Perrund, the performativity acquires elements of the truth that, in hindsight, do not come far from amounting to a confession on Perrund's part. "You do too much to protect your Protector piece," she tells DeWar during a bout of "Leader's Dispute" (32), a game that, preexisting the new order, has been changed to fit it: the former Emperor piece—the most important in the game—has been renamed Protector, and the game itself has gone from "Monarch's Dispute" to "Leader's Dispute" (31). Perrund's point is that DeWar translates his life into the game even if, in so doing, he disregards the game's rules—in Dispute, if the Emperor/Protector piece is taken, one of the General pieces takes its place, which eventually happens in actuality: UrLeyn is replaced first by one of his cabinet members, ZeSpiole, and then by his own son, who in the present of old Oelph's prologue/epilogue rules Tassasen as King. Perrund is trying to tell DeWar something, although it's anyone's guess whether she herself is aware of what that is exactly—but there's a revealing line she gives at the end of the chapter: when DeWar comments that Perrund has "changed the nature of the game by informing me of my weakness," she replies that "the game was always the same ... I merely opened your eyes to it" (35). And Perrund doesn't stop there: she makes many references to the reality of her function in Tassasen, always through the prism of games and gaming strategy (95, 186–188, 309–310), all of which do not in fact open DeWar's eyes at all.

19. While many commentators have correctly seized on the knife-missile aspect, the drone aspect doesn't seem to have registered. David Langford, for example, writes that "the ace in the hole which saves the Doctor *in extremis* appears to be a Culture 'knife missile'—a semi-intelligent autonomous weapon—disguised as a jewel on her blunt old dagger, a point which isn't elucidated within *Inversions* itself" (Langford 2003, 215). As far as his assessment goes, Langford is entirely correct, but knife missiles are very seldom seen alone (the one time we see a knife missile by itself is in *Use of Weapons* and Zakalwe kills it—so maybe *Inversions* takes place after *UoW*, and now the culture always sends drones with the missiles. It's a theory). Also, the young girl who saw what her imagination construed as a dark bird or nightwing inside the room where Duke Walen was murdered must have seen a drone; knife missiles are really rather small—like tiny semiprecious gemstones, say—and they usually do not carry out intelligence-gathering missions. For these reasons, it's actually likely that Vosill's dagger was in fact a drone, which would also resonate well with the presence of its stylized form at the beginning of every chapter and with the cover of the first HC/SC editions of *Inversions*—A detailed image of the dagger appears in the foreground, as if someone were holding it up and looking through the guard at a dark figure silhouetted against the sky and framed by the archway of a great gate.

20. Certainly with Unoure, whom she defends in front of Adlain and a gaggle of doctors on the basis of sound forensic evidence (161–167), knowing full well that exculpating him could not possibly lead them to guess that a knife missile did the job. But Vosill is a woman and the other doctors feel challenged by her, so they refuse to listen. Unoure ends up in a cell, awaiting Ralinge's questioning, so the most humane thing for her to do at that point is to have him killed as well, quickly and painlessly and in such a way that it will look like a suicide (171).

21. On that score, see Oelph's comments, both in the prologue and in the epilogue, on

the essentially unknowable nature of what we call the truth (3–5, 337–339).

Chapter 7

1. Thus, by the timeline established in *Consider Phlebas*, the events in *Look to Windward* take place around AD 2170.
2. The Homomda and the Idirans have, in fact, a very similar physical appearance, both races being tripodal/reptilian in origin. One of the drawbacks of being the only Homomdan on Masaq,' Kabe finds out, is that at parties a number of Culture people mistake him for a sculpture or for an article of furniture (16).
3. In fact, as the appendixes in *Consider Phlebas* inform us, even during the Homomdan involvement in the Idiran War they and the Culture had retained limited diplomatic and commercial ties.
4. Banks, of course, chose the name entirely on purpose; if *Look to Windward* is a story of haunted people, then the damage to the heart can't be anything but lasting.
5. The Mind's avatar tells Ziller that "it was II who was killed, I who lived" (311), and there may well be an element of obfuscation here. First off, the two sibling AIs had exchanged mind-states before the beginning of the battle, so to a large extent each one already was the other—thus, they both survived and died. Also, the numeral "II" is nothing other than "I" repeated twice. The words with which the avatar tells Ziller which twin survived and which died are therefore purposefully ambiguous—basically, the avatar tells the Chelgrian that it both died and survived.
6. But see the reply the Mind gives Ziller when he comments that the proportion of deaths is a tiny one compared to the lives saved (313).
7. For the Chelgrians, heaven and the Sublimed reality are one and the same thing. Upon Subliming, the Chelgrian-Puen retrofitted their transcendent realm to resemble exactly the heaven of the long-standing Chelgrian religion (224–225), thus making their gods real by turning themselves into those gods.
8. Besides helping Quilan, Huyler's mission is to take over his carrier's body in case Quilan falters and decides not to go through with the attack (338–339).
9. Every Chelgrian possesses a device called "Soulkeeper," designed to record and store its carrier's consciousness right before his/her death. The stored personality is then downloaded into a computer substrate prior to its journey to the Sublimed realms, where the Chelgrian-Puen await. Quilan's wife and the rest of the people onboard her ship, however, were killed by a weapon that also disabled their Soulkeepers. She's gone forever (21–31).
10. In this sense, the Homomda act as a mirror image both for the Culture's apollonian/utopian tendencies and for its Dionysian/dystopian ones: both civilization partook of the ancient mistake of the Idiran War, and both found a way to grow out of it with the understanding that there would be no more such conflagrations, and that they could indeed coexist peacefully within the larger galactic community—and that's why Kabe is on Masaq.' The light of the novae must shine on the people of both races (118).
11. While Kabe's loved one is not dead, the relationship is, and Kabe's persistent feelings provide the haunting.
12. Ziller's symphony, as we might expect, plays an important role in Quilan's change of heart (377–380).
13. This was an issue that pained Banks somewhat—that in the early 1990s a number of fans were reading the Culture stories as thinly disguised representations of America between World War II (i.e. the Idiran War) and the present. This was, he once said, "an idea I find utterly bizarre. (I mean, haven't these people been *reading* the books?) The culture thinks private property is a slightly puzzling, utterly immature and old-fashioned idea; it thinks money is a joke" (Melia 1994, 42). Over the years, as more Culture stories appeared—especially the last triad—this kind of speculation died out somewhat.
14. Two years after *Look to Windward*, Banks wrote *Dead Air*, a no-M novel beginning on 9/11. The plot follows the adventures of Ken Nott, an alcohol- and drug-fueled radio shock-jock who is also the first-person narrator of the story. Ken rants and raves about the terrorist attacks and pretty much everything else that attracts his attention, both on and off the air, while at the same time falling in love with a gangster's wife, which gets him into a number of dangerous situations. Reviewers largely panned the novel, mostly because of what they saw as a messy plotline, an unnecessarily abrasive

main character, and an absence of substance to the considerations on the September 11 attacks that should have provided the novel with its main thrust. Steven Poole, for example, wrote in *The Guardian*:

> Looming over the whole book is the shadow of the al-Qaida attacks of last September: the opening party ends with the news of the World Trade Centre collapse; and the dustjacket portrays a clever visual analogue of the event, with a plane flying over two chimneys of Battersea power station. But the novel does nothing with it; it is merely set-dressing. One of the few direct references—when Ken refers to "the fundamentalist intensity of those who secretly guess they may well be wrong"—just seems spectacularly incorrect, the sort of comfortable liberal solipsism ... that a more sophisticated novel might have tried to anatomise [2002, n.p.].

Interestingly, Poole begins his review of *Dead Air* by comparing it unfavorably to *Look to Windward*, which he describes as "a joyous return to the excellence of his Culture series, highly intelligent political space opera stuffed full of jokes and rapturous cosmic imaginings" (2002, n.p.).

15. On the connections between *Look to Windward*, *Consider Phlebas*, and the Gulf War, especially concerning the attitude toward radicalized religious stances, also see Duggan 2007.

16. Also see MacGillivray 1996.

17. Except in the sense that they share the very general label of postmodern SF writers and that, as authors of post-cyberpunk space opera, they display a highly developed sensitivity to the representation of moral ambiguity.

18. The name Hegemony of Man, in fact, is reminiscent of Cordwainer Smith's Instrumentality of Mankind, whose rule over the human commonwealth of Smith's stories cannot be described as utopian.

19. Confusingly, Middleton writes that the novel "is set on the margins of the Culture" (11) before stating, a few paragraphs later, that "the novel, whilst not set in the Culture universe, has some notable additions to Banks' science fiction milieu" (12).

20. The cutoff point seems to be 1993, the year *Against a Dark Background* was published.

21. But then again, he may not have: the arguments in this second article do not fully overlap those of the first. Moreover, in a note at the end, Hardesty mentions his *Foundation* piece as a reference for an analysis of the political aspects of the Culture stories (121).

22. As Kincaid himself remarks, there is no consensus on the shape and timeline of the British Renaissance/Boom—"critics still dispute whether it continues or has run its course," he writes (177). On this subject, another useful source is the November 2003 issue of *Science Fiction Studies*, entirely dedicated to the "British SF Boom." Of particular relevance as far as this work is concerned is Andrew M. Butler's essay "Thirteen Ways of Looking at the British Boom," in which he cites three of Banks' novels—*The Wasp Factory*, *Walking on Glass*, and *The Bridge*—as milestones in a rapid progression in estrangement until the publication of *Phlebas* in 1987, at which point Banks became an integral part of the Boom (378).

23. In this respect, the critical dialogue between Russell Letson and Gary K. Wolfe in the August 2003 issue of *Locus* is particularly useful. In it, Letson and Wolfe discuss the provenance of the new space opera—is it mainly a UK phenomenon?—as well as its context. As far as territory goes, they point out, the only relevant distinction between American and British NSO is a certain "in-your-face political playfulness" on the part of the British writers that American writers seem to find less natural to come by (40). This element owes, as Levy indicated, to the British authors' inheritance of a New Wave sensibility that establishes a direct line of descent from Harrison and Aldiss to such contemporary practitioners as Banks, MacLeod, Charles Stross, and Alastair Reynolds. American writers of NSO, on the other hand, tend to rein in open political discourse in their novels while broadly—broadly—espousing a more libertarian (Walter Jon Williams, for example) or anarcho-capitalist view (Vernor Vinge). However, Peter F. Hamilton's work, which is undoubtedly NSO, comes from a British Tory viewpoint instead of a left-wing one (40), so sharp distinctions don't necessarily work that well even in this case.

As far as context is concerned, Letson and Wolfe immediately point out that "as a critical term, 'space opera' is petty nearly useless" because "it isn't a genre in the taxonomic or logical-category sense. Instead it feels like a collection of motifs and traits—furniture—and historical (maybe nostalgic) associations on which we paste the label" (40). This decoupling from the necessity of recognizing both space opera and new space opera as genres or sub-genres, they argue, is an advantage because it focuses our attention on the aesthetic and emotional yearning they have been satisfying since the 1920s—the sense of wonder. Thus, seen under this light, NSO becomes a set of initially value-free stage props designed to be deployed to achieve the grand vista of the universe. The more mature approach that distinguishes NSO from SO applies when the time comes to pick a vantage point from which to examine the pyrotechnics:

> One suggestion is that the New Space Opera retains many of those adolescent yearnings writ large, but that the NSOs themselves are written from *outside* that mindset rather than from within it, providing an edge of irony that critiques these attitudes while still taking advantage of their effects [41].

Letson and Wolfe's arguments dovetail well with what we know of Banks' intellectual process during his early years. Like every writer in the UK who had been heavily influenced by such works as *The Centauri Device*, Banks had indeed looked at the furniture of genre and decided that he didn't have to pick it up wholesale or arrange it in one particular set-piece. Instead he had—to continue with the metaphor—created the room first and deployed the furniture to best showcase it, and others did the same. This, Wolfe points out, is also a good way of explaining how NSO could morph itself to fit Banks' novels as well as the work of someone like Orson Scott Card (40). Different rooms.

24. See also Dozois and Strahan 2007, 4.

25. Harrison also wrote a piece for the same 2003 issue of *Locus* in which the MacLeod and Letson/Wolfe contributions appeared. In it, he explains that in his view the reason for the growth and existence of NSO, at least in the UK, lies in the "growing liquefaction of genre boundaries and concerns" and the concomitant "detection of a new universe to expand into, a new audience able and willing to read across genre boundaries" (44). In this sense, Harrison's point supports the connection between non-genre and genre work as complementary partners in communicating fields, something to which Harrison himself, author of both genre and non-genre stories, could readily testify (Banks' experience was essentially the same, especially but not exclusively regarding his first three novels). Harrison also makes an important point concerning the political content of British NSO:

> Adventure is a form of optimism in itself. It is a narrating of yourself, in trust, on to the narrative of the universe. "Show me what happens to me next." Wrapped up in that metaphor you'll always find politics. Imagination is political, whether it intends to be or not. In much UK space opera, the intention is quite clear. Novels like Iain M. Banks' *Use of Weapons*, Ken MacLeod's *The Stone Canal*, my own *Light*, and Justina Robson's *Natural History* look forward to changed values. Their optimism is politically based [44].

Aside from the implications of this statement for the general stance of the Culture series as a whole, it's interesting to note that Harrison attaches to *Use of Weapons* an essentially forward-looking, optimistic core meaning—seemingly contradictory in a novel whose nominal protagonist cannot but continue to regress *ad infinitum* to the unforgivable crime at the heart of his entire existence. But, as John Clute observed in his review of *Weapons*, this only seems contradictory if we fail to perceive the presence of Diziet Sma's conscience—and of her moral compass—in between every page. She is the one who concludes the story, which means that despite everything we've read up until that point, it's still angel work we're witnessing.

26. On this subject, also see Brown 2004, 55–75.

27. Another "ambiguous utopia" article came out in the Summer 2009 issue of *The New Atlantis: A Journal of Technology and Society*. Its author, Alan Jacobs, performs a very similar job to Horwich's, although reaching quite different conclusions: "the closest analogue we have to the Culture's foreign policy is that of the United States in the recent Bush administration: just as President Bush wanted to spread the good news of American democracy to the rest of the world, and was willing to put some force behind that benevolent imperative, so too the Culture. The Culture is neoconservatism on the greatest imaginable scale" (n.p.). The evidence Jacobs brings to the table to explain this assessment is the very same Horwich uses to come to his own conclusions: excerpts from the novels and from "A Few

Notes on the Culture," plus a reference from *Raw Spirit*, Banks' only nonfiction book that, because it came out in 2003, hadn't been available to Horwich:

> I look at Dubya and just see a sad fuck with scared eyes; a grotesquely under-qualified-for-practically-anything daddy's boy who's had to be greased into every squalid position he's ever held in his miserable existence who might finally be starting to wake up to the idea that if the most powerful nation on Earth—like, ever, dude—can put somebody like him in power, all may not be well with the world [94].

Moving from this statement, Jacobs confusingly declares that the United States at the time of the Bush administration is the closest analogue to the Culture because "President Bush ... is not a Mind; and the American model of democracy is not that of the Culture" (2009, n.p.). "Doubtless Banks will love this point," Jacobs also writes, which feels like something of a stretch. He may have, although that's unlikely in the extreme, but "doubtless"?

28. On this topic, also see Steve Arnott's article for *Bella Caledonia*. Arnott sees the Culture as neither utopian nor dystopian because, in his view, utopias from More onwards "assume that human nature is flawed either because of some form of original sin or because society is flawed. The Utopia cleanses humanity of these flaws and either allows their 'true' humanity to shine through or makes them into the New Man. Dystopias are the cynic's/realist's response where attempts to make the New Man fail with disastrous, frightening, totalitarian consequences. The Culture is neither Utopia nor Dystopia because human nature in Banks' vision is not a blank slate or human putty to be perfected or damned ... The lives of persons can be enormously enriched by a better society, but they do not become wholly New" (2011, n.p.).

29. In his article, Stephenson reads the Culture through the lens of Deleuze/Guattari and Derrida's theories.

30. Ironically, the same factors that brought me to criticize Stephenson's piece prompted Stephen Dougherty to praise it. In his review of Colebrook and Cox's book for *Science Fiction Studies*, Dougherty finds the work as a whole "a poorly edited and uneven collection" because, while the bulk of the text is nominally dedicated to Banks' No-M work, most of those articles foreground its hybrid, genre-slippery nature with the result that "more specifically sf concerns and issues [are] consistently insinuated into the analyses of purportedly mainstream literary works" (443). Indeed, Dougherty doesn't find very much to like in the collection, but one of the very best pieces, in his opinion, is Stephenson's—and for the very reasons I criticized it. "This sounds right on the money," he writes of Stephenson's opinion that the Culture is a space-opera analogue of predatory Western imperialism.

Chapter 8

1. And the two short stories as well. Looking at the Culture series in this light, we might consider them dry runs for a potential volume of Culture-related short stories that in the event never materialized; had it seen publication, its narrative structure might have looked like, for example, that of Cordwainer Smith's stories of the Instrumentality of Mankind.

2. The hour-long interview is available at http://www.youtube.com/watch?v=v2vrypvdqWI, and the part quoted is between minutes 54:37 and 54:55.

3. Even those Shellworlds that did not fall prey to Iln weaponry are not necessarily safe. A number have self-destructed or annihilated every inhabitant inside when unguessed-at security systems suddenly turned themselves on and wiped out every living thing. Many of those conflagrations were bad enough that the Dra'Azon, the Sublimed species from *Consider Phlebas*, have preserved eighty-six of them as Planets of the Dead (67).

4. On the eighth and among the Sarl, that level of consequence is attached only to a man.

5. With the notable exception of Oramen. Unlike Ferbin and Holse, he never leaves Sursamen, and unlike Tyl Loesp and his lackeys, he does not attempt to step beyond the remit his society has established for him. Oramen therefore never has the chance—or the desire to create such a chance—to develop the perspective on Matter that the other characters receive. This does not necessarily make him a bad man or a poor figure (he is likeable and brave enough), but he certainly is the one among the novel's major characters who grows the least.

6. Even so, Djan Seriy still feels compelled to ask Xuss if "this time there aren't going to be any mistakes" when the army they have been shadowing arrives at the point in their progress where the Culture agents ambush it, slicing all their pole-weapons and banners with a knife missile (5–7). A bit like Skaffen-Amtiskaw, Djan Seriy's drone companion shows a little less compunction about knocking barbarians around than she'd like it to.

7. It's interesting to note the way Djan Seriy explains to herself the relationship between the Culture at large, Contact, and Special Circumstances: "The Culture represented the hospital, or perhaps a whole caring society, Contact was the physician and SC the anaesthetic and the medicine. Sometimes the scalpel" (169).

8. In this context, see the gaming-related studies Holse begins to carry out while he and Ferbin are traveling across the galaxy—"As Game, So Life. And indeed, As Game, So Entire History of Whole Universe, Bar Nothing And Nobody" (385–387).

9. *Surface Detail* is the furthest story along the Culture timeline. It takes place fifteen hundred years after the Idiran War (43) and six hundred years after "the Chelgrian debacle" (170). In Earth-calendar terms, therefore, the action in the novel takes place around the year AD 2970.

10. In a 2010 interview with *Wired*, Banks explained that the idea for the virtualities and the Hells had come to him some time after writing *Look to Windward*:

> The idea of the hells came from thinking over the approach from one of the other novels, *Look to Windward*, in which there's a mention of a civilisation that has a kind of Valhalla-ish virtual world for their fallen dead. At the time that was treated as something very special. Then I began to think, if that was possible then it's the kind of thing that civilisations would do as a matter of course, and be an actual part of your civilisation's development [Parsons 2010, n.p.].

The difference between the Chelgrian Heaven and the afterlives in *Surface Detail* is that, while the former is custom-built in the Sublime by the Chelgrian-Puen, the latter have nothing to do with Subliming—the substrates housing all afterlives, Hells and Heavens alike, are firmly anchored to the real (for any given value of "firmly anchored to the real" in a space-opera setting).

11. Level Eight is the highest rung on the galactic ladder of civilizational advancement; the Culture counts as being in the high reaches of Level Eight, and thus slightly above the others.

12. The closeness of Veppers' first name to the word "jailer" is, it's safe to say, purposeful.

13. The other two are Restoria and Numina. Restoria takes care of the so-called "hegemonising swarm outbreaks"—large numbers of aggressively self-replicating Von Neumann machines—whenever they arise (Yime refers to them as "pest control"; 177), whereas Numina's turf are the Sublimed (211).

14. "You'd make a great teenage boy," she tells Demeisen after he spouts a great deal of opaque technical terms at her with telling enjoyment (410).

15. But see Banks' comment in the *Wired* interview: "I think [Yime] ends up working almost as a Greek chorus, commenting upon the action rather than taking part in it. At various stages in the book there was the idea that she would take more part in the action and there were various ways that could have been done, but they didn't really work out. I think that point is brought into the book at the end in that she's kind of been had, almost fooled" (Parsons 2010, n.p.). From this, it's possible to conclude that Banks simply... let the character go, so to speak. He might have allowed the drift of the plot shape her into a figure whose function ends up being very similar to that played by Ulver Seich in *Excession*.

16. Joiler Veppers' viewpoint provides an added moment of critical utopian perspective, however brief and however skewed by its belonging to the kind of personality the Culture prides itself on attempting to stop at every available opportunity. Veppers' thoughts about the Culture are fully in line with what we expect a character like him to feel about a society like that:

> There was nothing worse, Veppers thought, than a loser who'd made it. It was just part of the way things worked ... that sometimes somebody who absolutely deserved nothing more than to be one of the downtrodden, the oppressed, the dregs of society, lucked out into a position of wealth, power, and admiration ... Losers made everybody look bad. Worse, they made the whole thing—the great game that was

life—appear arbitrary, almost meaningless ... Veppers hated the Culture. He hated it for existing and he hated it for ... setting the standard for what a decent society ought to look like [335–336].

Veppers is essentially a villain in the Azad mold, fully convinced and pointedly proud of the fundamental unfairness of life as well as openly supporting a view of social interactions as not only tolerating, but also requiring the existence of the downtrodden, the oppressed, and the dregs of society. Little wonder that he dislikes the Culture, and little wonder that the Culture ambassador on Sichult, a woman named Kreit Huen, does her best to rattle him every time they meet (336–340).

17. In *Sonata*, Banks provides as specific a location for the Sublime as it's possible to get in a space-opera setting: in keeping with superstring theory, the Sublime, which is also known as the Enfolded, resides "in dimensions seven to eleven" (17).

18. The one that broke the pattern (if it is a pattern) was *Stonemouth* (2012), a no–M novel about a man, Stewart Gilmour, who returns to the fictional Scottish town of Stonemouth five years after he left it in the wake of a sexual scandal.

19. In a fashion reminiscent of the twin plotlines of *Use of Weapons*, each chapter in *Sonata* carries a number preceded by a capital "S" to indicate the countdown. Chapter 1 begins at S-24 (1), chapter 2 at S-23 (35), and so on. Chapter Twenty-Five, the epilogue, starts at S+1, one day after the Gzilt's Subliming (513).

20. "Septame" is a Gzilt title that plays out as roughly equal to Senator.

21. The ITG is, in fact, expressly mentioned within the novel as a potential Incident Coordination Group, and that gives us the timeline of *The Hydrogen Sonata*. When the Limited Offensive Unit *Caconym* asks another member of the event committee if the ITG may not conceivably bounce them, the other ship—the Medium Systems Vehicle *Pressure Drop*—replies that nobody has heard of them for half a millennium. The events in *Excession* represented the ITG's last hurrah (75). Thus, *Sonata* takes place around five hundred years after *Excession*, and in Earth-calendar terms around the mid–2500s.

22. The name itself indicates the joke. The universe is filled with noise coming from stars, quasars, gas-giant planets, and nebulas, but it's just that—white noise produced by charged particles, most of which are hydrogen. This cacophony of signals carries no coherent content.

Bibliography

Aldiss, Brian, ed. 1974. *Space Opera: An Anthology of Way-Back-When Futures*. Garden City, New York: Doubleday.
Banks, Iain. 1990a. *Walking on Glass*. London: Abacus.
———. 1990b. *The Bridge*. London: Abacus.
———. 1998. *The Wasp Factory*. New York: Simon & Schuster, 1998.
———. 2004. *Raw Spirit: In Search of the Perfect Dram*. London: Arrow Books.
———. 2008. "Out of This World." *The Guardian*, 11 July. http://www.theguardian.com/books/2008/jul/12/saturdayreviewsfeatres.guardianreview5.
———. 2010. "Small Step Towards a Boycott of Israel." *The Guardian*, 2 June. http://www.theguardian.com/world/2010/jun/03/boycott-israel-iain-banks.
———. 2013a. "A Personal Statement from Iain Banks." Author's Website, 3 April. http://www.iain-banks.net/2013/04/03/a-personal-statement-from-iain-banks/
———. 2013b. "Why I'm Supporting a Cultural Boycott of Israel." *The Guardian*, 5 April. http://www.theguardian.com/books/2013/apr/05/iain-banks-cultural-boycott-israel.
Banks, Iain M. 1989. *The Player of Games*. London: Orbit.
———. 1991. *Consider Phlebas*. London: Orbit.
———. 1992. *Use of Weapons*. London: Orbit.
———. 1997. *Excession*. London: Orbit.
———. 1998. *Inversions*. London: Orbit.
———. 2001. *Look to Windward*. London: Orbit.
———. 2004a. *The State of the Art*. San Francisco: Night Shade Books.
———. 2004b. "A Few Notes on the Culture." Banks 2004a, 167–188.
———. 2008. *Matter*. New York: Orbit.
———. 2010. *Surface Detail*. New York: Orbit.
———. 2012. *The Hydrogen Sonata*. New York: Orbit.
Bould, Mark, et al., eds. 2009. *The Routledge Companion to Science Fiction*. New York: Routledge.
Branscombe, Mary. 1996a. "*Excession*." *SFX* 14 (July): 80–81.
———. 1996b. "Ship Shape." *SFX* 14 (July): 24–25.
Brown, Anthony. 1998. "Highlanders Two." *SFX* 40 (July): 52–56.
Brown, Carolyn. 1996. "Utopias and Heterotopias: The 'Culture' of Iain M. Banks." Littlewood and Stockwell 1996, 57–74.
Brown, Chris. 2001. "'Special Circumstances': Intervention by a Liberal Utopia." *Millennium: Journal of International Studies* 30.625. http://mil.sagepub.com/content/30/3/625.citation.
Brown, James. 2003. "Not Losing the Plot: Politics, Guilt, and Storytelling in Banks and MacLeod." Butler and Mendlesohn 2003, 55–75.

Butler, Andrew M. 1999. "Strange Case of Mr Banks: Doubles and *The Wasp Factory.*" *Foundation* 76 (Summer): 17–27.

_____. 2003. "Thirteen Ways of Looking at the British Boom." *Science Fiction Studies* 30.3: 374–393.

Butler, Andrew M., and Farah Mendlesohn, eds. 2003. *The True Knowledge of Ken MacLeod.* Reading, UK: Science Fiction Foundation.

Cabell, Craig. 2014. *Iain Banks: Student Without Portfolio.* EBook. Bellack Productions.

Chivers, Tom. 2013a. "For years, Iain M Banks has done for sci-fi what George RR Martin did for fantasy. He is two of our finest writers." *The Telegraph,* 3 April. http://blogs.telegraph.co.uk/news/tomchiversscience/100210315/for-years-iain-m-banks-has-done-for-sci-fi-what-george-rr-martin-did-for-fantasy-he-is-two-of-our-finest-writers/.

_____. 2013b. "Goodbye, Iain Banks: It Takes a Serious Man to Laugh at Himself." *The Telegraph,* 10 June. http://blogs.telegraph.co.uk/news/tomchiversscience/100221088/goodbye-iain-banks-it-takes-a-serious-man-to-laugh-at-himself/.

Cobley, Michael. 1990. "Eye to Eye: An Interview with Iain Banks." *Science Fiction Eye* 2.1: 22–32.

Colebrook, Martyn. 2010. "Reading Double, Writing Double: The Fiction of Iain (M.) Banks." *The Bottle Imp* 8 (November). http://www.arts.gla.ac.uk/ScotLit/ASLS/SWE/TBI/TBIIssue8/Colebrook.pdf.

_____. 2013. "*Lanark* and *The Bridge*: Narrating Scotland as Post-Industrial Space." Colebrook and Cox 2013, 28–44.

Colebrook, Martyn, and Katharine Cox, eds. 2013. *The Transgressive Iain Banks: Essays on a Writer Beyond Borders.* Jefferson, NC: McFarland.

Colebrook, Martyn, Katharine Cox, and David Haddock. 2013. "Introduction." Colebrook and Cox 2013, 1–8.

Clute, John. 1993. "Iain M[enzies] Banks." Clute and Nicholls 1993, 88.

_____. 1995a. *Look at the Evidence.* New York: Serconia Press.

_____. 1995b. "Marching Initials." Clute 1995a, 28–30.

_____. 1995c. "Space Aria Caught in Larynx. Thousands Flee." Clute 1995a, 97–99.

_____. 1995d. "Use of Cormorants." Clute 1995a, 291–292.

_____. 1995e. "Angel Tricks." Clute 1995a, 231–233.

_____. 2003. "Science Fiction from 1980 to the Present." James and Mendlesohn 2003, 64–78.

_____. 2009a. *Canary Fever: Reviews.* Harold Wood: Beccon Publications.

_____. 2009b. "It Matters." Clute 2009a, 257–259.

_____. 2011. *Pardon This Intrusion: Fantastika in the World Storm.* Harold Wood: Beccon Publications.

_____. 2014a. *Stay.* Harold Wood: Beccon Publications.

_____. 2014b. "Journey." Clute 2014a, 162–165.

Clute, John, and Peter Nicholls, eds. 1993. *The Encyclopedia of Science Fiction,* 2d ed. London: Orbit.

_____, and _____, eds. 2014. *SFE: The Encyclopedia of Science Fiction,* 3d ed. http://www.sf-encyclopedia.com.

Daoust, Phil. 1997. "Iain Banks writes books about sex and drugs. Iain M Banks is a sci-fi nerd. Are they by any chance related?" *The Guardian,* 20 May. http://www.theguardian.com/books/1997/may/20/fiction.sciencefictionfantasyandhorror.

Dougherty, Stephen. 2014. "Hybrid Banks." *Science Fiction Studies* 41.2: 443–445.

Dozois, Gardner, and Jonathan Strahan. 2007a. "Introduction." Dozois and Strahan 2007b, 1–5.

_____, and _____, eds. 2007b. *The New Space Opera: All New Stories of Science Fiction Adventure.* New York: EOS.

Duggan, Robert. 2007. "Iain M. Banks, Postmodernism, and the Gulf War." *Extrapolation* 48.3: 561–578.

Fitting, Peter. 2014. "*Demand the Impossible* and the Imagination of a Utopian Alternative." Moylan 2014, 232–235.

Gaiman, Neil. 2013. "Iain Banks Was One of Us, Whatever That Meant." *The Guardian*, 9 June. http://www.theguardian.com/books/2013/jun/09/neil-gaiman-iain-banks

Garnett, David S. 1989. "Interview with Iain M. Banks." *Journal Wired* (Winter): 51–69.

Gevers, Nick. 2000. "*Look to Windward*." SF Site. https://www.sfsite.com/11b/lw93.htm.

Gramstad, Thomas. 2000. "The Culture Is the Answer." *The Laissez Faire City Times* 4.23. http://www.i-dig.info/culture/cultureistheanswer.html.

Gray, Alasdair. 2011. *Lanark: A Life in Four Books*. London: Canongate.

Greenland, Colin. 1990. "*Use of Weapons*." *Foundation* 50 (Autumn): 90–94.

Guerrier, Simon. 1999. "Culture Theory: Iain M. Banks's 'Culture' as Utopia." *Foundation* 76 (Summer): 28–37.

Hardesty, William H. 2000. "Space Opera Without the Space: the Culture Novels of Iain M. Banks." Westfahl 2000, 115–122.

_____. 2009. "Mercenaries and Special Circumstances: Iain M. Banks's Counter-Narrative of Utopia, *Use of Weapons*." *Foundation* 76 (Summer): 39–47.

Harrison, M. John. 2003. "Why I Write Space Opera." *Locus* 51.2: 43–44.

Hoggard, Liz. 2007. "Iain Banks: The Novel Factory." *The Independent*, 18 February. http://www.independent.co.uk/news/people/profiles/iain-banks-the-novel-factory-436865.html.

Horwich, David. 2002. "Culture Clash: Ambivalent Heroes and the Ambiguous Utopia in the Work of Iain M. Banks." *Strange Horizons*, 21 January. http://www.strangehorizons.com/2002/20020121/culture_clash.shtml.

Hughes, Colin. 1999. "Doing the Business." *The Guardian*, 7 August. http://www.theguardian.com/books/1999/aug/07/fiction.iainbanks.

Huizinga, Johann. 1995. *Homo Ludens: A Study of the Play Element in Culture*. Boston: Beacon Press.

Hunt, Stephen. 1999. "Chart-Topping Authors, Iain Banks and Ken McLeod Interviewed." SF Crowsnest, 1 September. http://www.sfcrowsnest.com/articles/features/1999/Chart-topping-authors-Iain-Banks-Ken-McLeod-interviewed-5784.php.

Hutchinson, Peter. 1983. *Games Authors Play*. London: Methuen.

Jacobs, Alan. 2009. "The Ambiguous Utopia of Iain M. Banks." *The New Atlantis: A Journal of Technology & Society* 25 (Summer). http://www.thenewatlantis.com/publications/the-ambiguous-utopia-of-iain-m-banks.

James, Edward. 2003. "Utopias and Anti-Utopias." Edward and Mendlesohn 2003, 219–229.

James, Edward, and Farah Mendlesohn, eds. 2003. *The Cambridge Companion to Science Fiction*. Cambridge: Cambridge University Press.

Jeffries, Stuart. 2007. "A Man of Culture." *The Guardian*, 24 May. http://www.theguardian.com/books/2007/may/25/hayfestival2007.hayfestival.

Jonas, Gerald. 2001. "*Look to Windward*." *New York Times*, 7 October. http://www.nytimes.com/2001/10/07/books/science-fiction.html.

Jones, Bethan. 2013. "Imperfect Doubles: The Recasting of Place, Object and Character in the Dream Narratives of *The Bridge*." Colebrook and Cox 2013, 76–86.

Kelly, Stuart. 2013. "Iain Banks: The Final Interview." *The Guardian*, 14 June. http://www.theguardian.com/books/2013/jun/15/iain-banks-the-final-interview.

Kincaid, Paul. 2009. "Fiction Since 1992." Bould et al. 2009, 174–182.

King, Stephen. 2010. *Danse Macabre*. New York: Gallery Books.

Kulbicki, Michael. 2009. "Iain M. Banks, Ernst Bloch, and Utopian Interventions." *Colloquy: Text Theory Critique* 17: 34–44.

Langford, David. 1998. "*Inversions.*" *SFX* 40 (July): 108.
_____. 2003. *Up Through an Empty House of Stars: Reviews and Essays 1980–2002*. Holicong, PA: Cosmos Books.
Leishman, David. 2009. "Coalescence and the Fiction of Iain Banks." *Études Écossaises* 12. http://etudesecossaises.revues.org/208.
Leith, William. 2003. "A Writer's Life: Iain Banks." *The Telegraph*, 3 November. http://www.telegraph.co.uk/culture/3605692/A-writers-life-Iain-Banks.html.
Leonard, Andrew. 2005. "The Future Perfect." *Salon*, 17 February. http://www.salon.com/2005/02/17/banks_8/.
Letson, Russell. 2008. "*Matter.*" *Locus* 60.5: 23, 57.
_____. 2011. "*Surface Detail.*" *Locus* 66.1: 21, 59.
Letson, Russell, and Gary K. Wolfe. 2003. "Duet, with No Fat Lady." *Locus* 51.2: 40–41.
Levitas, Ruth. 2014. "We Argue How Else?" Moylan 2014, 257–262.
Levy, Michael. 2009. "Fiction, 1980–1992." Bould et al. 2009, 153–162.
Lippens, Ronnie. 2002. "Imachinations of Peace: Scientifictions of Peace in Iain M. Banks' *The Player of Games.*" *Utopian Studies* 13.1: 135–147.
Littlewood, Derek, and Peter Stockwell, eds. 1996. *Impossibility Fiction: Alternativity—Extrapolation—Speculation*. Amsterdam: Rodopi.
Lowe, Greg. 2008. "Iain Banks—Interview." *Spike Magazine*, 24 March. http://www.spikemagazine.com/iain-banks-interview.php.
MacDonald, Kirsty A. 2013. "'Still Magic in the World': Banks and the Psychosomatic Supernatural." Colebrook and Cox 2013, 100–111.
MacLeod, Ken. 2003a. "Phlebas Reconsidered." Butler and Mendlesohn 2003, 1–3.
_____. 2003b. "Singularity Skies." *Locus* 51.2: 41–42.
_____. 2013a. "Iain Banks: A Science Fiction Star First and Foremost." *The Guardian*, 10 June. http://www.theguardian.com/books/2013/jun/10/iain-banks-ken-macleod-science-fiction.
_____. 2013b. "Use of Calculators." *The Early Days of a Better Nation*, 26 July. http://kenmacleod.blogspot.com/2013/07/use-of-calculators.html.
March, Cristie L. 2002. *Rewriting Scotland: Welsh, McLean, Warner, Banks, Galloway and Kennedy*. Manchester: Manchester University Press.
Martingale, Moira. 2013. *Gothic Dimensions: Iain Banks—Timelord*. Lexington, KY: Quetzalcoatl.
Melia, Sally Ann. 1994. "Very likely impossible, but oh, the elegance..." *Science Fiction Chronicle* 16.1: 7, 42–44.
Mendlesohn, Farah. 2008. "Iain M. Banks: *Excession.*" Seed 2008, 556–566.
Middleton, Tim. 1999. "The Works of Iain M. Banks: A Critical Introduction." *Foundation* 76 (Summer): 5–16.
Miller, Faren. 1987. "*Consider Phlebas.*" *Locus* 20.5: 13–15.
_____. 1988. "*The Player of Games.*" *Locus* 21.12: 17.
_____. 1989. "*The State of the Art.*" *Locus* 23.2: 13.
_____. 1990. "*Use of Weapons.*" *Locus* 25.2: 15–17.
_____. 1996. "*Excession.*" *Locus* 37.3: 25–27.
_____. 1998. "*Inversions.*" *Locus* 41.3: 20.
Milner, Andrew. 2014. "Tom Moylan's *Demand the Impossible.*" Moylan 2014, 236–241.
Mitchell, Chris. 1996. "Iain Banks: Whit and Excession: Getting Used to Being God." *Spike Magazine*, 3 September. http://www.spikemagazine.com/0996bank.php.
Monk, Patricia. 1992. "Not Just 'Cosmic Skullduggery': A Partial Reconsideration of Space Opera." *Extrapolation* 33.4: 295–316.
Moylan, Tom. 1986. *Demand the Impossible: Science Fiction and the Utopian Imagination*. New York: Methuen.
_____. 2000. *Scraps of the Untainted Sky*. Boulder: Westview Press.

———. 2014a. *Demand the Impossible: Science Fiction and the Utopian Imagination*. Ed. Raffaella Baccolini. Bern: Peter Lang AG.
———. 2014b. "Introduction to the Classics Edition." Moylan 2014a, ix–xxviii.
Palmer, Christopher. 1999. "Galactic Empires and the Contemporary Extravaganza: Dan Simmons and Iain M. Banks." *Science Fiction Studies* 26.1. http://www.depauw.edu/sfs/backissues/77/palmer77.htm.
Parsons, Michael. 2010. "Iain M. Banks Talks *Surface Detail* with *Wired*." Wired.co.uk, 14 October. http://www.wired.co.uk/news/archive/2010-10/14/iain-m-banks-interview.
Pattie, David. 2013. "The Lessons of *Lanark*." Colebrook and Cox 2013, 9–27.
Person, Lawrence. 1990. "The Culture-D Space Opera of Iain M. Banks." *Science Fiction Eye* 2.1: 33–36.
Poole, Steven. 2002. "It's All in the Initial." *The Guardian*, 13 September. http://www.theguardian.com/books/2002/sep/14/shopping.fiction.
Prettyman, Gib. 2014. "Extrapolating the Critical Utopia." Moylan 2014a, 251–256.
Rawlinson, Linnie. 2009. "Author Iain M. Banks: 'Humanity's Future Is Blister-Free Calluses!'" CNN.com, 6 January. http://edition.cnn.com/2008/TECH/space/05/15/iain.banks/.
Rundle, James. 2010. Interview: Iain M Banks." SciFiNow, 13 October. http://www.scifinow.co.uk/news/interview-iain-m-banks/.
Sargent, Lyman Tower. 1994. "The Three Faces of Utopianism Revisited." *Utopian Studies* 5, no. 1: 1–37.
———. 2014. "Miscellaneous Reflections on the 'Critical Utopia.'" Moylan 2014a, 242–247.
Sargisson, Lucy. 2014. "A Breath of Fresh Air." Moylan 2014a, 231.
Seed, David, ed. 2008. *A Companion to Science Fiction*. Malden, MA: Blackwell.
SFFWorld.com. 1997. "Interview with Iain M. Banks." 6 January. http://www.sffworld.com/1997/01/interview-with-iain-m-banks/.
SFX. 2012. Iain M Banks' Heroes and Inspirations." 24 July. http://www.sfx.co.uk/2012/07/24/iain-m-banks'-heroes-and-inspirations/.
Slocombe, Will. 2013. "Games Playing Role in Banks' Fiction." Colebrook and Cox 2013, 136–149.
Strahan, Jonathan. 2000. "*Look to Windward*." *Locus* 45.4: 29.
Suvin, Darko. 1979. *Metamorphoses of Science Fiction: On the Poetics and History of a Literary Genre*. New Haven: Yale University Press.
Weeks, Kathi. 2004. "Timely and Untimely Utopianism." Moylan 2014a, 248–250.
Westfahl, Gary. 1994. "Beyond Logic and Literacy: The Strange Case of Space Opera." *Extrapolation* 35.3: 176–185.
———. 2003. "Space Opera." James and Mendlesohn 2003, 197–207.
Westfahl, Gary, ed. 2000. *Space and Beyond: The Frontier Theme in Science Fiction*. Westport, CT: Greenwood Press.
Wilson, Andrew. 1994. "Interview with Iain Banks." *Textualities*. http://textualities.net/andrew-wilson/iain-banks-interview.
Winter, Jerome. 2013. "Turbulent Years Ahead: An Interview with Ken MacLeod." *Los Angeles Review of Books*, 24 February. http://lareviewofbooks.org/interview/turbulent-years-ahead-interview-ken-macleod/#.

Index

Adams, Douglas: *The Restaurant at the End of the Universe* 218*n*
Against a Dark Background 9, 110, 184, 215*n*, 218*n*, 229*n*
Aldiss, Brian 23, 26, 156, 229*n*; *The Dark Light Years* 43; *Space Opera: An Anthology of Way-Back-When Futures* 43
The Algebraist 183, 225*n*
The Ambassadors 93
Archaeologies of the Future 118
Arnott, Steve 231*n*
Austen, Jane 23, 226*n*; *Emma* 135

Babel-17 43
Ballard, J.G. 26, 43
The Banksoniain (fanzine) 180
Bayley, Barrington J. 26
Bear, Elizabeth 175
Bellamy, Edward: *Looking Backward* 73–74
Bester, Alfred: *The Stars My Destination* 43
Blackburn, Annie 11–12, 183, 215–216*n*
Blair, Tony 14, 124, 183
Blazing Saddles (1974 film) 181
Borges, Jorge Luis: *Labyrinths* 38
Branscombe, Mary 184, 226*n*
The Bridge 9, 18, 23, 28, 31–41, 48, 65–66, 221*n*, 229*n*
Brown, Carolyn 168
Brown, Chris 177–179, 181
Brown, Fredric: "Sentry" 60
Brown, James 181
Brown, Jim 11
Brunner, John 10, 26; *Stand on Zanzibar* 23–24, 217*n*
Bujold, Lois McMaster 44
Butler, Andrew M. 169, 229*n*

Cabell, Craig 11
The Castle 38

Catch-22 23–24, 181, 217*n*, 219*n*
The Causal Angel 175
The Centauri Device 43, 61, 173, 181, 230*n*
Cherryh, C.J.: *Downbelow Station* 61
Childhood's End 43
Chivers, Tom 15
Chomsky, Noam 13, 25, 124
Civilization (video game) 116, 127, 220*n*
Clarke, Arthur C.: *Childhood's End* 43
Close Encounters of the Third Kind (1977 film) 93
Clute, John 3, 26, 36–37, 54, 78, 91, 105, 155, 171, 175, 211, 219*n*, 230*n*
Cobley, Michael 13, 72, 105, 217*n*
Cohen, Leonard 23, 216*n*
Colebrook, Martyn 8, 180–181
Complicity 14, 110, 216*n*
Conan (Howard) 36, 69
Conrad, Joseph: *Heart of Darkness* 220*n*
Cox, Katharine 8, 180
The Crow Road 9, 14, 110, 216*n*
The Culture (fanzine) 180
Cyberpunk 155

The Dark Light Years 43
Dark Star (1974 film) 93
Dead Air 182, 228–229*n*
Delany, Samuel 26; *Babel-17* 43; *Nova* 43; *Triton* 74, 119, 121, 124, 168
Demand the Impossible 18, 74, 118–123
Demand the Impossible (2014 edition) 123–124, 224*n*
"Descendant" 223*n*
De Vet, Charles V.: "Second Game" 220*n*
Disch, Thomas 26
Dispatches 25
The Dispossessed 73, 119, 121, 124
Dougherty, Stephen 231*n*
Downbelow Station 61

Eliot, T.S.: *The Waste Land* 44–45, 156

Emma 135
Empty Space 174
Extrapolation (journal) 219*n*

Fantastika 36, 38–39, 65
Farnham's Freehold 89
Faust 93
Fear and Loathing in Las Vegas 23–24
Feersum Endjinn 110, 184
The Female Man 119, 121, 124
A Fire Upon the Deep 50
Foucault, Michel 168
Foundation (journal) 18, 105, 115, 169, 171
The Fractal Prince 175
Frankenstein: Or, the Modern Prometheus 37

Gaiman, Neil 11, 15
Galbraith, John Kenneth 25
Garnett, David 11, 21–22, 26, 95, 124
Gernsback, Hugo 156
Gevers, Nick 162, 183–184
Gibson, William 156
"A Gift from the Culture" 223*n*
Goethe, Johann: *Faust* 93
Gold Coast 224*n*
Gramstad, Thomas 176–177
Grass, Günter 10; *The Tin Drum* 23, 37, 181, 219*n*
Gray, Alasdair 10, 41, 65; *Lanark* 18, 28–31, 35–37
Greenland, Colin 18, 44, 105, 107–108, 174
Guerrier, Simon 115–117, 169

Haddock, David 8
Hamilton, Edmond 61
Hardesty, William H. 169, 171–172, 220*n*
Harrison, M. John 23, 26, 156, 173–174, 229*n*, 230*n*; *The Centauri Device* 43, 61, 173, 181, 230*n*; *Empty Space* 174; *Light* 174, 230*n*; *Nova Swing* 174
Harness, Charles: *The Paradox Men* 219*n*
Hartley, Adele 7, 183
Heart of Darkness 220*n*
Heinlein, Robert 23; *Farnham's Freehold* 89; "The Roads Must Roll" 89; *Starship Troopers* 89
Heller, Joseph: *Catch-22* 23–24, 181, 217*n*, 219*n*
Herr, Michael: *Dispatches* 25
Hoggard, Liz 183, 215*n*, 218*n*
Horwich, David 179–180, 230*n*
Hughes, Colin 10, 12, 25
The Hungarian Lift-Jet 24, 217*n*
The Hunt for Red October (1990 film) 134
Hutchinson, Peter 65

Hutton, Will 217*n*
Hyperion Cantos 168–169

Interzone (magazine) 105, 223*n*

Jacobs, Alan 230–231*n*
James, Edward 175
James, Henry: *The Ambassadors* 93
Jameson, Fredric: *Archaeologies of the Future* 118
Jeffries, Stuart 14
Jonas, Gerald 156, 165

Kafka, Franz: *The Castle* 38; *The Trial* 38
Kaveney, Roz: *Tales from the Forbidden Planet* 223*n*
Kelly, Stuart 6–7, 13, 215*n*
Kincaid, Paul 173, 229*n*
King, Stephen 53–54
King Lear 93
Kulbicki, Michael 117–118, 175, 224*n*

Labyrinths 38
Lanark 18, 28–31, 35–37
Langford, David 105, 141, 227*n*; *Up Through an Empty House of Stars* 226*n*
The Lathe of Heaven 218–219*n*
Le Guin, Ursula: *The Dispossessed* 73, 119, 121, 124; *The Lathe of Heaven* 218–219*n*
Leishman, David 34
Leith, William 216*n*, 217*n*
Letson, Russell 194–195, 229–230*n*
Levy, Michael 173, 229*n*
Light 174, 230*n*
Lippens, Ronnie 225*n*
Locus (magazine) 105, 108, 133, 141, 173, 229*n*
The Longest Day (1962 film) 134
Looking Backward 73–74
Lowe, Greg 28

MacFarlane, Les 10–11
MacLean, Alistair 10, 23, 181
MacLean, Katherine: "Second Game" 220*n*
MacLeod, Ken 11–13, 15–16, 26–27, 35, 44, 60, 94, 110, 116, 124, 141, 169, 173–175, 213, 217*n*, 222*n*, 229*n*; *The Stone Canal* 230*n*
The Man Who Fell to Earth (1976 film) 93
March, Christie 168
Martingale, Moira 180–181, 213
Marx Brothers 23, 181
The Matrix (1999 film) 55
McAuley, Paul 44
Melia, Sally Ann 27–28, 184
Mendlesohn, Farah 134–140, 155, 173, 213

Metamorphoses of Science Fiction 225n
Middleton, Tim 169–171, 229n
Miller, Faren 108–109, 126, 133, 141
Monbiot, George 217n
Monk, Patricia 219n
Monty Python 23, 181
Moorcock, Michael 26
More, Thomas: *Utopia* 73
Moylan, Tom: 115–125, 224n; *Demand the Impossible* 18, 74, 118–123; *Demand the Impossible* (2014 edition) 123–124, 224n; *Scraps of the Untainted Sky* 118–120
Myra Breckinridge 37, 219n

Natural History 230n
The New Atlantis (journal) 230n
New Space Opera 19, 173–175
New Wave 26, 43–44, 117, 173, 229n
New Worlds (magazine) 26, 217–218n
Nova 43
Nova Swing 174

"Odd Attachment" 215n

Palmer, Christopher 168–169
The Paradox Men 219n
Pattie, David 181
Peake, Mervyn: *Titus Groan* 38
Person, Lawrence 18, 105–107, 220n
Piercy, Marge: *Woman at the Edge of Time* 119, 121, 124
Poole, Steven 229n
Prettyman, Gyb 225n

The Quantum Thief 175
The Quarry 5–7, 215n

Rajaniemi, Hannu: *The Causal Angel* 175; *The Fractal Prince* 175; *The Quantum Thief* 175
Raw Spirit 183, 213, 215n, 216n
Rawlinson, Linnie 212
The Restaurant at the End of the Universe 218n
Reynolds, Alastair 229n
"Road of Skulls" 215n
"The Roads Must Roll" 89
Robinson, Kim Stanley 120, 124, 175; *Gold Coast* 224n
Robson, Justina: *Natural History* 230n
Roddenberry, Gene 224n
Rundle, James 44, 51
Russ, Joanna: *The Female Man* 119, 121, 124

Sargent, Lyman Tower 120, 224n, 225n
Saving Private Ryan (1999 film) 50–51, 134

Science Fiction Chronicle (magazine) 27–28, 45, 184
Science Fiction Eye (magazine) 13, 18, 105, 217n, 220n
Science Fiction Studies (journal) 168, 229n, 231n
Scraps of the Untainted Sky 118–120
"Scratch" 215n
"Second Game" 220n
"The Secret Courtyard" 215n
"Sentry" 60
September 11 7, 13, 19, 156, 165–168, 228–229n
SFX (magazine) 127, 141, 182, 184–185, 220n, 226n
Shakespeare, William: *King Lear* 93
Shelley, Mary: *Frankenstein: Or, the Modern Prometheus* 37
Simmons, Dan: *Hyperion Cantos* 168–169
Sladek, John 23, 26, 181
Slocombe, Will 63–64, 181
Smith, Cordwainer 43, 229n, 231n
Smith, E.E. "Doc" 61; *Triplanetary* 50
A Song of Stone 9
"Space Oddity" (1969 song) 93
Space Opera: An Anthology of Way-Back-When Futures 43
"Spheres" 215n
Spinrad, Norman 26
Stableford, Brian 173
Stand on Zanzibar 23–24, 217n
Star Trek (TOS) 87, 89
Star Wars (1977 film) 23, 48, 71, 89, 181, 217n
The Stars My Destination 43
Starship Troopers 89
The Steep Approach to Garbadale 63, 183
Stephenson, William 181, 231n
Stevenson, Robert Louis: *The Strange Case of Dr. Jekyll and Mr. Hyde* 37, 52
The Stone Canal 230n
Stonemouth 233n
The Strange Case of Dr. Jekyll and Mr. Hyde 37, 52
Stross, Charles 44, 174, 229n
Suvin, Darko 224n; *Metamorphoses of Science Fiction* 225n

Tales from the Forbidden Planet 223n
The Tashkent Rambler 24–25, 217n
Thatcher, Margaret 12–13, 105
Thompson, Hunter S.: *Fear and Loathing in Las Vegas* 23–24
The Tin Drum 23, 37, 181, 219n
Titus Groan 38
Transition 5, 8–9, 215n

The Trial 38
Triplanetary 50
Triton 74, 119, 121, 124, 168
Tucker, Wilson 42
2001: A Space Odyssey (1968 film) 23, 88–89, 181

Up Through an Empty House of Stars 226n
Utopia 73
Utopian Studies (journal) 224n

Van Vogt, A.E. 61
Vidal, Gore: *Myra Breckinridge* 37, 219n
Vinge, Vernor 44, 112, 174, 229n; *A Fire Upon the Deep* 50

Walking on Glass 9, 18, 29, 31–41, 57, 63–67, 172, 221n, 229n

Wargames (1983 film) 49
Wark, Kirsty 184, 215n
The Wasp Factory 7, 9, 12, 14, 18, 22, 24, 28–29, 31–41, 63–66, 216n, 221n, 229n
The Waste Land 44–45, 156
Watson, Rory 25
Westfahl, Gary 174, 219n
Whit 9, 110
White Dwarf (magazine) 105
Williams, Walter Jon 229n
Wolfe, Gary K. 229–230n
Woman at the Edge of Time 119, 121, 124

Year Zero 103, 223n
Young Frankenstein (1974 film) 181

Zelazny, Roger 26

www.ingramcontent.com/pod-product-compliance
Ingram Content Group UK Ltd.
Pitfield, Milton Keynes, MK11 3LW, UK
UKHW041939140426
5217IPUK00014B/564